TAKE ME HOME

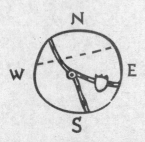

TAKE ME
Home

A Novel

MELANIE SWEENEY

G. P. Putnam's Sons

NEW YORK

PUTNAM
— EST. 1838 —
G. P. PUTNAM'S SONS
Publishers Since 1838
An imprint of Penguin Random House LLC
penguinrandomhouse.com

Library of Congress Cataloging-in-Publication Data

Names: Sweeney, Melanie, author.
Title: Take me home: a novel / Melanie Sweeney.
Description: New York: G. P. Putnam's Sons, 2024.
Identifiers: LCCN 2024007480 (print) |
LCCN 2024007481 (ebook) |
ISBN 9780593716090 (trade paperback) |
ISBN 9780593716106 (ebook)
Subjects: LCGFT: Romance fiction. | Novels.
Classification: LCC PS3619.W442628 T35 2024 (print) |
LCC PS3619.W442628 (ebook) |
DDC 813/.6—dc23/eng/20240216
LC record available at https://lccn.loc.gov/2024007480
LC ebook record available at
https://lccn.loc.gov/2024007481

Printed in the United States of America
1st Printing

Book design by Shannon Nicole Plunkett

For Mom and Josh

TAKE ME HOME

« CHAPTER »

One

When Hazel zipped into the parking lot of the Living Room Café, the old clunker with its faded indie-rock bumper stickers and duct-taped license plate frame wasn't there. Which meant, more importantly, the owner of the car wasn't there. A Christmas miracle. With only two hours to finish and submit the final paper of her first semester of graduate school, the last thing Hazel needed standing—or sitting—in her way was Ash Campbell.

She'd hustled to the café directly from proctoring her advisor's Intro to Psychology final, her last chore as Dr. Sheffield's favorite errand girl. Hustled even though she knew that more than likely Ash had already swooped in and taken her study spot. He had an infuriatingly reliable 5:05 arrival time. But she'd hoped anyway. She *needed* this.

And, damn it, by sheer willpower and a few questionable rolling stops (and apparently some favor from the cosmos because her clock now read 5:07), she'd beat him here. Finally, a small mercy. Hazel marched into the café, head held high, already pulling her laptop from her messenger bag and angling for the back corner.

Except—

She checked out the front window again. No, his car still wasn't in the lot. And yet, there he sat across the café in *her* chair, monopolizing the only working outlet in the place. Ash's eyes, dark as black coffee, lifted to hers just as a chilly December gust blew the door shut and knocked her forward. She dropped her laptop back into her bag.

"You're here," she accused.

"Rough day?" He gestured vaguely at her with his coffee mug before grinning into a sip.

Yeah, she was wearing an ugly plaid shirt from the back of her closet because she hadn't done laundry in two weeks, her hair was falling from the hasty bun she'd jammed a pencil through when her hair tie broke, and she was practically vibrating from the three coffees she'd already downed this afternoon. So what?

"You missed a button," he said.

She refused to give him the satisfaction of checking her shirt. "I have to finish a paper."

Ash leaned back into the velvety green wingback chair, one ankle propped over the other leg in indulgent leisure. It was a comfortable chair, big enough to sit cross-legged while she worked. But fancy, too. A seat of power, as though every word Hazel wrote while sitting in it deserved to be leather-bound and embossed. If ever she needed that power, she needed it right now.

He looked pointedly at all the unoccupied seats between them, but she didn't follow his gaze. None of the other tables had outlets. None of the other chairs had the green one's magic. They'd had this argument a hundred times. With a huff, she crossed the threshold to the front counter.

"Isn't the semester over?" Ash asked across the café.

"Not for two more hours."

He *tsk*ed. "Cutting it pretty close."

"Shut up."

He laughed as she yanked out a stool.

"I put your Swiss Miss abomination on the menu." He nodded at the sign above the counter. In his aggressive, spiky handwriting, the newest addition read, *Baby's First Coffee.*

One time she'd mixed a hot chocolate packet into her coffee.

"It's basically a mocha," she snapped.

"The tiny marshmallows really elevate things, too."

"I don't have time for this."

The kitchen door swung open, and Cami emerged, her natural curls swept back with her usual sunshine-yellow head wrap. She gave Hazel a bright, "Hey, hon," over a shallow crate of mugs before she began restocking the open shelves with them, the tattoos on her sculpted brown arms flexing.

At the Living Room, the default was a *for here* cup. Mostly thrift-store finds, the mugs were mismatched in size and style. All the tables and chairs were, too, salvaged and given their second (or third or fourth) home. With all its eclectic art, warm lamps, plants, and cozy nooks, it was *homey.* Not like any home Hazel had ever lived in, but still. It would have been a perfect student coffeehouse, except it was too far from campus to cross most undergrads' radar. Plus, the one espresso machine was in constant disrepair, limiting the menu to drip coffee, teas, sandwiches, chips, and, if you came early enough, the muffin of the day. Several other places offered triple-shot lattes and a dozen types of baked goods until two a.m., like the surrounding bars.

She'd found the café back around midterms on the heels of a breakdown in her tiny apartment, the first cracks beginning to show from the unrelenting demands of her psychology PhD program. When she'd walked into the Living Room, its ambience had soothed her low-grade panic with the comforting smells of coffee, soil, and the old paperbacks crammed into shelves. The smooth, tactile velvet of that big chair. Cami had selected a mug for her that said *I Like Big Books and I Cannot Lie* and remarked, "I've been needing someone for this one." It buoyed her. Hazel had worked here, from that green chair, ever since.

Or tried to.

"Coffee?" Cami asked, pulling Hazel's hard glare from the current occupant of the chair. Wordlessly, Cami connected the dots. "Yeah, sorry, hon. He got here ten minutes ago. Give me your cord."

Ten minutes? She hadn't stood a chance.

Hazel tossed the end of her laptop cord over the counter for Cami to plug in on her side. Her computer was so old, the battery wouldn't last fifteen minutes without a power source, which was why, unlike some people, she didn't have a million other seats to choose from.

"He lives upstairs. Why can't he work up there?" Never mind that in a couple of hours Ash would also step behind the counter for the late shift.

"I need the noise," he said, like there wasn't an entire coffeehouse and old Frank with his crossword between them.

She twisted in her seat. "Play music."

"I need voices. Talking." He was fully engrossed in his laptop screen. It wasn't even plugged in. A new spark of anger ignited in her chest.

"Turn on the TV then. Or a podcast."

"Too distracting."

"It's not like anyone's here right now."

Ash cast a wounded expression toward Frank, who was either ignoring them or didn't have his hearing aid turned up. "He's here. You're here."

"Hey, *I* am not your ambient noise. I'm here to work. Which would be easier for me to do in *that* chair with *that* outlet."

He smirked at his screen. "Keep talking. This is really working for me."

With a growl, Hazel spun back around on her stool, fixing Cami with a wide-eyed expression that said, *See what I have to put up with?*

Cami raised an equally loaded eyebrow. "I'm not sure if this is a nerd thing, a white people thing, or a straight thing, but it's the strangest flirting I've ever witnessed."

"You," Hazel said, flinging open her laptop, "are dead to me."

But as soon as Cami turned away to pour her coffee, Hazel gave Ash an involuntary once-over. And fine, she could forgive Cami for hoping there was something more to their bickering. Ash was a passably attractive guy who, under different circumstances, might have held her interest. She didn't *need* to look at him to know this. She didn't need to sample the triple chocolate ice cream in the northside campus dining hall to know she liked it, either, but she did that pretty regularly, too.

Anyway, good looks only went so far. They certainly didn't offset his total inflexibility on the issue of the chair and, thus, the threat he posed to her academic career. Nor how much pleasure he derived from being the constant wrench thrown into her gears. Nor their *history*, which was a whole other thing.

Any appeal really boiled down to the fact that he had nice hair and dressed well. Probably an old girlfriend deserved the credit for that because Ash hadn't always worn understated floral ties and nerdy-chic gray cardigans that stretched across his shoulders. And his hair hadn't always been so artfully mussed.

Nope, this new look was a big-time glow-up from the moody, apathetic teenager she'd met at Lockett Prairie High School, who'd shaved his head and wore nothing but obscure band T-shirts, jeans, and a faded pair of black high-top Chucks that were held together by duct tape. And a scowl, couldn't forget that. He had been basically the human embodiment of the old, bumper-stickered-to-hell car he still drove.

Hazel didn't trust his reinvention. It was too slick, too *whimsical*. He still had those dark, overly thick eyebrows and the scar cutting through the wing of one of them. The full, pouty mouth—the better to brood with. He still had the distracting habit of drumming his fingers, cracking his knuckles, incessantly clicking pens. He may have fooled everyone else with his new, charming, easygoing persona, his polished appearance, but Hazel still felt the same *friction* around him. She knew the real Ash under the costume, and she wasn't interested. Nope. Not at all.

Cami *thunk*ed a mug of coffee down on the counter, snapping Hazel back around on the stool. The bold, black brushstroke lettering on the mug said *Wifey*.

"Cute."

She laughed and fetched the little pitcher of creamer. "Honey, this is *my* café. My hot takes come with the coffee."

Hazel clicked open her seminar paper. She couldn't afford to even *think* of Ash right now. She was down to—*shit*—an hour and forty-nine minutes.

Pointedly, Hazel hefted the enormous stack of articles and notes out of her bag and dropped them with a loud clap onto the counter. Her dramatics immediately bit her in the ass, however, when an ivory invitation fell from the stack. It slid across the counter and over the edge. Hazel's stomach fell right along with it. Casting a suspicious side-eye, Cami picked it up.

Hazel didn't have time for this, either, for its hand-lettered calligraphy or monogrammed sticker. When she'd opened it in her apartment building's mail room a month ago, Hazel had been distracted, hadn't braced herself at all. And then there it was, an honest-to-God, formal invitation. She'd shoved it into her bag and, not as successfully, out of her mind.

"Whose wedding?" Cami asked, a note of pity confirming whatever dour thing Hazel's face was doing.

"My dad's."

Cami leaned in. "Are y'all not close or something?"

"No," she said too quickly. She tried to soften it, adding, "No, nothing like that," because Cami was already mustering protective cool aunt energy on her behalf, imagining some parental hurt Hazel truly hadn't suffered. Her parents were *fine*. But the wedding was a *tomorrow* problem, not a *today* problem. She plucked the envelope from Cami's hand and tucked it back into her bag.

Then came Ash's perfectly ill-timed, chiding voice across the café. "Thought you had to finish a paper."

"Shut up. You don't exist."

She was already scanning through her notes, mentally sweeping everything else off the counter to focus only on what mattered, so she heard his echo of her words—"Ah, right. I don't exist"—but didn't fully register until a minute later that it had been oddly mirthless, almost . . .

Nope, no more distractions. She was at the finish line. After this, everything she'd put off could come for her, but not before she shut the door on this long, grueling semester.

A HALF HOUR LATER, TINNY RINGING PULLED HAZEL FROM HER ESSAY, followed by a voice. "This is Ash."

She un-Quasimodoed herself, straightening her spine and rolling her neck. Her eyes were slow to refocus past the short distance of her screen. Her coffee had gone cold, but Cami was by the door, flirting with a UPS delivery woman, so she reached over the counter to refill her mug herself.

"Ah, shit. Really? Five hundred?" Ash rose from the green chair, squeezing the back of his neck. He met Hazel's gaze then turned away and drummed his fingers on the table. "Four days?

I was supposed to go home tomorrow." *Tap, tap, tap, tap, tap.* "No, I get it. Just crappy timing. Go ahead and do the repairs."

Hazel supposed this explained why his car wasn't out front.

He ended his call and hastily packed up his belongings. The evening crowd had filled in around them while Hazel was lost in her paper, and he had to weave his way to the front. As he stalked past her to the door, he grunted, "All yours," as if she'd orchestrated his personal crisis just to lure him out of the chair. Through the big front windows, she tracked his path to the door that led up to his loft.

Hazel surveyed her sprawl—laptop, a stack of articles, highlighters, pens, paper clips, two separate legal pads of notes, a worn APA manual, coffee. She'd practically moved in here, and she was so close to being done. Maybe she'd just finish her paper and then relocate to the chair.

While she debated this, the UPS woman left, and Cami sidled casually back behind the counter, some thought brewing behind her narrowed eyes.

"What?" Hazel asked, wary.

Cami's gaze darted pointedly to Hazel's bag, and she knew instantly what she was referencing: the invitation. "Lockett Prairie," Cami mused. "Small world."

Unease pricked Hazel's skin. She sensed where Cami was going with this. Best to get ahead of it. "I'm not leaving for a few more days."

Guilt flared. She'd put her father off for weeks about her travel plans.

She switched tacks. "If you're thinking I should give Ash Campbell a ride across Texas, you haven't been paying attention. We'd kill each other before we reached the hill country."

Cami's look suggested killing each other wasn't the only way it might go, but she raised her palms. "Okay."

They didn't even know if he needed a ride.

Plus, it was an eight-hour drive. He'd probably eat corn nuts or beef jerky or something that would make her gag the whole way.

"We have a bad history *specifically* with being in cars together," she said.

Cami, who was already turning to welcome a customer, laughed. "I said okay."

But Hazel's mind supplied one final defense, just in case: *That party freshman year.* The first and *last* time they'd acknowledged each other in undergrad. She knew he'd let the last four years harden around that night, preserving it like amber, just like she had, because when she'd found her new favorite study spot two months ago and returned the next day to discover Ash already seated in the wingback, claiming it was *his* regular spot, he'd set his jaw and said entirely too smugly, "There are, like, *twenty thousand* other places to study." Throwing back her own words from that night.

Hazel's laptop screen dimmed, reminding her of her paper. Even when he wasn't here, Ash was still a distraction. She rubbed her tired eyes, retraced her mental steps, and got back to work.

HAZEL WAS UPLOADING HER ESSAY TO THE ONLINE SUBMISSION PORtal when Ash returned at five minutes to seven. He'd changed into black jeans and a gray Henley for his evening shift behind the counter—his barista uniform, though there wasn't officially an employee uniform. He refilled her mug, complete with her usual shot of creamer and two sugars, without asking and said, "So, I was right."

"Shush. I'm almost done." She hesitated over the submit button, though there was little she could do at this point to improve her paper. Clicking it, she let out a long sigh, and brought her mug to her lips.

He was waiting.

She humored him. "You were right about what?"

He nodded behind her at the chair. "You only want it when you can't have it."

"I was just already settled in over here."

"Sure," he said before rounding the counter with a turkey and Swiss sandwich and a carafe of decaf. And then he morphed into the kind, gentle café barista he was with everyone else, squeezing Frank's shoulder. The old man blinked up at him, coming out of his crossword daze, and took his dinner with a grateful smile.

Frank tucked his napkin into his collar so it hung like a bib and bowed his head in private prayer. He looked like a father at the head of the empty table. Though he rarely seemed approachable, engrossed in his word puzzles, he came *here* to do them. He chose that big farm table for a reason. She'd never wondered about it before, but now, her heart squeezed for him. Did he have no family or friends? Didn't he ever want a hot meal, especially on a chilly night like this?

More often than not, Hazel also ate a sandwich for lunch or dinner, but that was merely a convenience because she was already here studying. It wasn't really eating alone when eating wasn't the main thing you were doing.

"You want one, too?" Ash returned, distractedly thumbing his phone.

"No," she said. Swear to God, if her stomach growled . . .

"Got a date tonight or something?"

"What?"

"Do you have a date later?" He enunciated every word slowly, eyes still glued to his phone. "You usually eat around now."

This was the weirdest part of their dynamic. When he was on the clock, it was like the whole chair feud and that party freshman year and their tense orbiting of each other the last semester of high school didn't exist. He served her attentively, knew her usual orders like he did everyone else's. Sometimes, he even stripped back a few layers of snark and attempted to make normal conversation. If she was feeling particularly starved for human interaction, she let it play out.

Though maybe this wasn't one of those times. He didn't look up from his phone.

Hazel chewed her lip and contemplated heading back to her apartment. After her scramble to finish her paper, a restless, buzzy exhaustion had set in. Just last year, she'd have thrown on a short dress and boots and gone to sweat it out at the Fox with her roommate and all the other students drinking and grinding away their stress. But she'd already learned her lesson about going to undergrad bars.

Anyway, dancing wasn't in the cards. Stress had cinched her shoulders up to her ears, and her back and butt protested all the sitting she'd done in the last week to knock out her final projects. She arched to stretch out some of the tension and mused, through a pitiful groan, every vertebra popping, "I think Frank needs a pet."

Ash's gaze lifted to hers then dipped. He stopped scrolling.

Her cheeks heated. Casually tugging her shirt hem back down, she pushed on. "I'm serious. A cat maybe. Or an older dog."

"Because . . ."

"He's obviously lonely. Why else would he come here every day? For your company?"

He flashed her a quick, winning smile and dropped it just as quickly. "Why do *you* come here every day?"

"This is the only place I can get any work done."

"I've been here for three years. You had other places before now."

"That was in undergrad."

He waited for her to explain, but when she tried to put into words how working with Dr. Sheffield had overtaken her life, she felt pathetic.

His phone dinged. He muttered, tapped out a message, sighed, and stuck it back in his pocket. Then, placing both forearms on the counter, he leaned in, giving her his full attention.

And Ash's full attention was . . . a lot. Somewhere between studious and serial killer-y. She couldn't look right at him, opting instead to wonder at the marvel of his hair, which she suspected would hold a curl if she twirled it around her finger. She could smell his fresh, citrusy laundry detergent under all the plants and coffee beans.

"Can't work at home?" he asked.

"You're one to talk."

"I've already said I don't like the quiet. What's your excuse?"

Between her wannabe rockstar neighbor and the train that rattled her windows several times a day, her apartment could serve as an enhanced interrogation site for all the noise she had to put up with. It was all she could afford on her graduate stipend now that her old roommate, Sylvia, had moved to Houston. Ash would probably understand the constraints of thrifty living, considering his own place, his old car, but he at least *looked* put together. He projected a self-possessed ease that was foreign to her, seemed to genuinely enjoy his job here at the café. And if the floor plans she sometimes glimpsed on his laptop were any indication, despite his slacker ways in high school, he'd apparently managed to stick with architecture, which was a challenging five-year program. Whereas for Hazel, school, once straightforward and simple, felt more like a fun house maze lately. In her rawest moments, she questioned whether she was cut out for a PhD at all.

Not that she would admit any of that to Ash. She decided to treat his question—why did she come here every day—like it was just another of the small, inconsequential ways they needled each other and dismissed it with an eye roll. Her indifference was helped by his phone dinging yet again. He frowned at the screen.

"More bad news?" she asked.

"Eavesdrop much?"

"You took a call in a public place."

He slid his phone onto the counter in front of her. It was open to a popular forum for alumni and current students. He'd asked for a ride to or near Lockett Prairie for the holidays. The responses ranged from **Where?** to the observation that he should have asked before most students left town. The comment he pointed at said, **Who the hell wants to go to Lockett Prairie for anything?**

Hazel could relate to that one.

"I posted on Craigslist, too."

She snorted. "Hoping to get murdered for Christmas?"

He gave her a tight smile and pulled his phone back. "Don't really have any other options."

If Cami were still here, she'd be telepathically nudging Hazel from the kitchen.

"You could rent a car. Or take a bus?"

"Nah, I'm strapped. I still have to buy most of my Christmas gifts, and with my dad—" He stopped himself, cleared his throat. "Not your problem. I'll figure something out." He didn't meet her eyes when he said this. Then he disappeared without another word into the kitchen.

Not her problem. He'd said it himself.

But watching Ash experience frustration didn't bring her the pleasure she might have thought. He'd looked so downcast. Also, there was a compulsive little part of her that desperately wanted to solve problems for people, to make things perfect, to *please*. Even apparently, *confusingly*, to please Ash Campbell. And that part was already weighing what it would take to give him a ride.

No matter how she turned it over, it would surely be a shit show for them both. And the timing didn't work. He'd said on the phone he'd planned to leave tomorrow, whereas Hazel could conceivably delay her departure for six more days, just soon enough to arrive the night before her father's Christmas Eve wedding. She needed those days to figuratively sage her life and plan for a smoother spring semester.

And anyway, contorting herself to accommodate everyone else this fall had only earned her extra stress. She needed to strengthen her backbone, not bend it again, even if that made her feel selfish.

Besides, *this* wasn't her problem.

When Ash returned from the kitchen, he busied himself wiping tables and tidying the café. The late evening crowd filtered in, and other than drumming his fingers over his phone in his pocket, clearly itching to check his leads, he didn't rush anyone through their usual small talk. She negotiated with the pushy voice inside of her—if he asked about her plans at all, she'd be honest, see if he was desperate enough to angle for a ride.

But he didn't bring it up again, and finally, despite a gnawing, unresolved feeling, she left.

LATER THAT NIGHT, NETFLIX ASKED IN ITS JUDGY WAY IF SHE WAS STILL watching, alone, in her sad apartment. She'd intended to eat a well-balanced meal, wash her hair after way too many days of dry shampoo, and tackle the mountain of dirty clothes overfilling the hamper, but here she was again with a microwave burrito, rewatching *Schitt's Creek*. She didn't need Netflix's sass about it.

As she clicked *Yes*, Hazel received two text messages.

The first was a picture of a massive ice cream sundae. Sylvia's accompanying message said, Congrats on finishing your first semester, smarty! Dave thinks it's a stretch for me to eat a sundae for your accomplishment, but I say teamwork makes the dream work! Hope you already had yours.

The second text came so soon after, Hazel didn't flip her phone over right away, assuming it was some other shot of Sylvia's boyfriend eating one of his weird, organic yogurts in protest, like all the other times they'd indulged in their post-finals ritual the last few years. But curiosity won out.

And her regret was instant. The text was from her father. If you're coming tomorrow, you'll want to leave in the AM. Expecting a big PM storm. Otherwise, best to wait a day.

Tomorrow? Hazel groaned. She'd put off giving him her arrival date because she knew it would seem like she wanted to spend the least possible amount of time there. And yeah, that was *true*, but she hadn't wanted to voice it, to endure his long, disappointed silence or, worse, lie about some obligation keeping her at school. But now, because she'd put off that uncomfortable conversation, he had apparently decided for her, expected her to wake up early the very next morning, without *one day* to decompress after finals, and drive across the state. She'd for sure be using the excuse of that storm to push it back, but still.

She tossed her phone into the blankets with another long groan.

But soon enough, her frustration faded. It was almost a relief to have it decided, to not have to tiptoe her way through the minefield of proposing a last-minute arrival. A relief, too, that her father was so unaware of her reluctance to come. If she was going to spend a week with his new family and watch him get married and experience the whole ordeal of Christmas, the last thing she wanted to add to the mix was unnecessary baggage. It was going to be awkward enough as it was.

Nope, his utter obliviousness meant at least she could smile and get through it, then get back to planning her fresh start next semester, when she would learn to assert herself, to solve her own problems, to say *no*. After this one last yes.

<< CHAPTER >>

Two

The Student Center wasn't *entirely* vacant. A custodian buffed the wide hallway floor. A lone student played something mournful on the piano. But even at the early hour, it didn't bode well that Ash could hear the squeak of his shoes on the linoleum all the way to the rideshare board. Everyone had left town already.

The cork map of the state, where people needing rides or offering them pinned their contact information, had probably last been used in earnest at the turn of the century. Ash had often wondered who still thought this a relevant system in a world with social media and a feature in the university's transportation app for this exact same purpose. But after exhausting all those options himself and coming up with nothing more concrete than a moving truck driver's sketchy response on Craigslist—Might could swing through to grab ya, if you're not too pansy assed to get your hands dirty—he'd prayed to find a note on this board anywhere in the vicinity of Midland, the closest major city to home.

He'd even ventured onto a dating app last night—had to update it first, it had been so long—with the aim of pivoting a potential hookup into borrowing someone's car but realized there was no non-creepy way to word such a message. If this didn't pan out, his last resort was the bus, like Hazel had suggested, but the eight-hour drive would balloon to thirteen, and he'd have to buy a second ticket for the one oversize, delicate gift he already had, and there were no side-by-side seats available for four days. Then he'd still need a ride for the final twenty miles west to Lockett Prairie . . . Et fucking cetera.

Only three cities had notes—Dallas, Houston, and El Paso. The two nearest Dallas weren't folded up in a feeble attempt at privacy like the others. Both were asking for rides, not offering them.

El Paso was at least in the right direction, and he could probably get dropped off early—it was less than an hour straight north from I-10 to Lockett Prairie. He unpinned the pink paper. His heart leapt at the loopy writing: *Have car. Need gas money to El Paso. Leaving on 12/18. Text, don't call.*

Today was the eighteenth. *Finally*, a break. Ash texted immediately. Then he pulled one of the extra thumbtacks from the cork map and pinned the flyer he'd made—yep, he had gone full Luddite at this point—papering over most of West Texas. He tacked another to the community bulletin board nearby. The flyer wasn't clever or particularly eye-catching, but the board had been recently cleared, so it couldn't be missed, assuming anyone actually walked by. In all caps, he'd written, *NEED A RIDE TO LOCKETT PRAIRIE ASAP. WILL PAY $$$$$.* The excessive dollar signs were an uncomfortable promise, but he'd figure that out later.

His phone rang—not a response to his text, but an incoming video call from his oldest sister. He debated not answering. But Maggie never called without texting first. And she'd planned to fly home with her family yesterday, which meant a call from her could be about their dad. Ice trickled down his spine. His thoughts went straight to the worst possible scenarios, which had been on mental speed dial since Thanksgiving.

Yet again, he kicked himself for not going home in November when his car was still running. He'd worked through Thanksgiving at his various jobs to negotiate time off at Christmas. But if he'd gone home, he would have been there for his father's accident, could have helped, could have verified his mother's cheery reports that it was just a freak fall and not a relapse of his MS, rather than what Ash *did* do—pace, google, and bite his fingernails down to the bloody quicks. If he couldn't get to Lockett Prairie now because of his shit car, that trade-off would have been for nothing.

Ash accepted Maggie's call, bracing himself for the surroundings of a hospital room on her end. He couldn't make out the shifting shapes on the screen, nor the muffled scraping sound like something was sliding across her mouthpiece.

"Maggie?"

The shapes gave way to a ceiling fan. Footfalls retreated, then a little voice called, "Mama, Mama, Mama."

His niece. And he recognized that fan. It was the one in his parents' living room. "Maggie?" He winced as his voice echoed in the empty Student Center hallway.

Soon, his sister's face peered at him upside down, confusion and impatience pinching her eyebrows together. She picked her phone up and her face righted, but the terse expression remained. "Why are you FaceTiming me?"

"You called me. Or Cosette did, I guess."

Her expression softened. "She was playing with my phone. Where are you?"

He turned his shoulders to block the closed campus bookstore behind him. Even though Cosette had called by accident, he couldn't quite shake the worry that Maggie's name on his screen had triggered. "Everything okay there? How's Dad?"

She frowned at his evasion. "Dad? He's—" A smaller voice

cried out from somewhere on her end, and Maggie twisted from the phone to ask someone to grab Isabel, her younger daughter, before she climbed out of her high chair. "I'm sorry, what? Are you coming in time for dinner? Cosette has been asking nonstop when Uncle *Ash* is going to be here."

He smiled at her emphatic pronunciation of his name. Last summer, at his niece's fourth birthday party, Cosette had been patently unable to form the *sh* sound and kept calling him Uncle Ass. To both Maggie's and Ash's annoyance, their three younger sisters hadn't helped matters by laughing hysterically and then coaching her to repeat the mispronunciation. By the end of the party, even Ash's own mother had begun to slip up.

Damn it. This sucked. He didn't want to disappoint them, didn't want to tell them that, barring a miracle, he wouldn't be coming home today at all. "Dad, though?" he pressed, unable to stop himself.

"Didn't Mom tell you his last appointment was good?"

"Mom doesn't want anyone to worry. But since you're there, in person . . ."

"I mean, he's currently giving my toddler handfuls of chocolate chips with her breakfast," she said, projecting her scolding voice.

"Maggie, be honest. Is he—"

"It's chaos here." She was on the move now, looking off camera. "Just get here soon, okay? I could use the extra hands. Nick's work trip got extended."

"Nick's not with you?" Her husband was a climate journalist who traveled frequently.

"And June didn't get her ticket until the last minute—surprise, surprise—so she's on a red-eye in two days."

That his middle sister had put off something so important was indeed no surprise, but it tightened his jaw another notch.

He should have reminded June weeks ago, even offered to help her if money was tight, which he assumed it was. But he'd already dipped into his savings to help the twins last month, and although his savings existed for just this purpose—taking up slack—he had hoped not to dip in again so soon. Especially since other, bigger expenses were on the horizon, no matter what his mother claimed. His stupid car helped absolutely nothing.

Maggie scolded Cosette not to pull on the Christmas tree, not to touch the heater, to stop playing with Grandpa's walker. Then, as Maggie stooped to physically remove her, Ash caught a glimpse—his first—of the walker. He swallowed thickly.

"Dinner then?" she repeated, turning back to the camera.

"Yes," he said, with more certainty than he felt. "I'll be there."

ASH WAS SECURING ANOTHER OF HIS FLYERS TO THE MAGNETIC BOARD just inside the café entrance when Hazel jogged in, a chunky red scarf wrapped excessively around her throat and up over her nose for the five-second trek from her car. She breezed past him then doubled back, peeking over his shoulder to read the flyer. He could feel her at his back and straightened involuntarily at the near contact, wanting, absurdly, to lean back into the warmth of her, to have her hook that defiant chin of hers into the dip of his shoulder.

"Asher, no," she said, her voice muffled by the scarf.

Ah, the name thing again. It had been a couple weeks since she'd pulled that one out. He knew she knew his name, that this was just payback for never giving her the chair, but as juvenile a tactic as it was, it worked. Her pretending not to know his name made him unconsciously flex, as if by making himself physically bigger, she'd have to *see* him. He hated to but gave her exactly the reaction she was looking for, correcting, *"Ash."*

Unwrapping her scarf, she marched off to claim the green chair with her bag, then came back to the board. "You're going to end up with some wacko serial killer. Like . . . the Merry Murderer. Or the Jingle Bell Butcher." Her eyes danced. "Wait, no. The One-Horse Open Slayer. Get it? Sleigh-er?"

He swallowed the laugh building in his throat, not so much at what she'd said as how she'd said it, with such open delight. This unstressed, post-finals Hazel had an entirely different energy from the past several weeks—more like how she'd been in high school. Her playfulness sparked a little flame in his chest, a small flickering thing.

"You think we get a lot of murderers in here?" He dropped his voice, nodding to the knitters by the back window. "Sweet old Edna?"

"You never really know people as well as you think."

"I think I could take her." He gestured at his comparatively bigger frame.

One corner of her mouth twitched. "I don't know. She's pretty spry. She could get a knitting needle to the jugular."

"You've given this some thought before now, haven't you?"

"Anything to get you out of my chair."

There was a long silence when Ash could have asked the obvious question. It wouldn't be that weird to bring up her plans for the break. He made similar small talk with the other regulars. But she'd already watched him scramble for a ride last night and said nothing. As far as he knew, she never went back to Lockett Prairie. He'd never seen her on breaks, and her old friends, whom he occasionally ran into there, never knew more than he could glean from her Instagram himself.

Plus, she'd made it pretty clear their first week of college that coming from the same hometown didn't make them friends. He could have pointed out that, with as many times as he'd driven her and Justin around so that his ex-best friend wouldn't drink and drive, as far as rides were concerned, some might argue she owed him. But that was only an argument if she were already headed home.

When their mutual silence turned awkward, Hazel tucked her hair behind her ear and said, "So, no luck on all your posts?" just as he said, "Semester's over. Shouldn't you be—"

She motioned for him to go ahead.

"Shouldn't you be sleeping off a hangover or something?"

"That's how undergrads celebrate. In grad school, you just eat a cheeseburger in the bathtub and watch a movie on your precariously balanced laptop, hoping it doesn't fall in and kill you."

He huffed a laugh.

She looked half surprised, like she hadn't expected him to reward her with his amusement, mild as it was. Holding his gaze, she walked backward to the old green chair and settled into its high back, twirling one of her dark curls around her finger. "As it happens," she said airily, "I am here for pleasure."

His brain went straight to unauthorized places. Hazel, in that chair, wearing that ridiculously long scarf—*only* the scarf—

"What?"

She waved a paperback at him. "Yesterday was work. Today, pleasure. Plus, I knew you were working this morning and couldn't take my chair."

"You do know it's creepy that you've memorized my schedule."

"You say creepy. I say resourceful."

"Maybe the real wacko serial killer around here is you. The Scarlet Scarf Strangler."

She gave her scarf mock-serious consideration, and the basest parts of his brain jumped right back in.

"Coffee?" He bolted for the counter, needing the distraction of pouring her a cup.

"I want the mug with all the cats licking their butts," she called.

And thank God for that competing image.

BY NOON, ASH HAD TWO LEADS, THE SKETCHY MOVING TRUCK DRIVER from Craigslist who was coming through town on his way to Big Spring and a student headed to El Paso from the rideshare board, who'd texted to say she'd like to meet him first and came straight over.

When he offered his hand in greeting, she pushed back from the counter. "Wait, you're a guy? I thought Ash was short for, like, Ashley." Only then did he realize that in his few text messages he hadn't made his gender explicitly clear. He didn't blame her for rescinding the offer. If one of his sisters were in her position, he assumed they'd do the same.

But it left him with the mover, Buddy. Ash called to give him directions to the café and nail down a departure time. He could practically smell the smoke in the man's gravelly voice, which was periodically cut off by a hacking, wet cough. Ash pulled the phone away from his ear.

"I don't stop," Buddy ground out, "so if you're gonna need to eat or piss, you'd better bring your own supplies."

Ash's gaze darted unintentionally to Hazel. She was watching over the top of her paperback, shamelessly eavesdropping, her nose scrunched up in distaste. He turned away.

"And just so we're clear, the ride ain't free. You gotta help unload in Big Spring. That's part of the deal."

Ash rubbed his forehead. At this rate, he wouldn't reach Lockett Prairie before his family went to bed. Still, it was a way home, and he wouldn't have to touch his savings. He started to ask if Buddy would at least drive him the rest of the way, or even just to Midland, after they unloaded the truck, but a hand snatched his phone away.

"Sorry," Hazel said. "His plans have changed. Have a nice day, Buddy."

"What are you doing?"

She was shaking her head at him with a look of—what? irritation? disgust?—while tucking his phone protectively against her chest. Which drew his eyes to the snug fit of her fuzzy gray sweater. Christ, this recent sweater weather was going to be his undoing. He forced his eyes back up quickly, but her knowing squint said she'd caught him. Well, fine. If she didn't want him to check her out, she shouldn't hold his personal property hostage.

Her chin tipped up defiantly. "I can't watch you do this."

"Make a phone call?"

"Take a water bottle into some stranger's truck so you have something to drink *and then pee into.*"

She had a point. But, damn it, that had been his last option. "Thanks for the concern"—frustration made his jaw and hands clench, screaming the opposite of gratitude—"but unless *you're* gonna drive me home, which we both know you're not, I need to call this guy back."

"You're pretty certain, considering you haven't even asked me."

Hope lifted in his chest, but he tamped it down, already too frayed to risk the letdown if he was wrong. Hazel never went home. He didn't think she was *that* petty, but he couldn't discount that she was simply fucking with him. All those times he'd refused her the chair . . .

"Are you going home?" he asked carefully.

"It just so happens—" She crossed her arms and heaved a sigh, and he wondered what on earth she had to be so annoyed about when *he* was the one who would have to beg Buddy for a ride if she wasn't offering. Hazel started again, raising an eyebrow at his impatience. "It just so happens, I have been summoned to Lockett Prairie."

Still not an offer. She was impossible. But he didn't have it in him to play their game, act like he didn't care. "What are you saying? You'll drive me?"

She groaned, apparently agonized to have to say it. "I could be persuaded."

That balloon of relief floated up in him, untethered. Despite her absolute refusal to just say an explicit *yes*, he wanted to wrap her up in his arms and twirl her. Instead, he said mildly, "So, all of this"—he circled his finger to indicate the extraordinary measures she'd witnessed him taking since yesterday evening—"was just too entertaining for you to put me out of my misery?"

"Oh, there's going to be misery." She trudged back to the green chair and flounced into it. "I wasn't planning to leave for a few more days, and I thought you'd figure something out before then. If you'd asked, I would have told you that."

He dropped into the wobbly, wooden chair across from her. "I'll cover gas."

"I don't want your money . . ." She trailed off. "But I do have conditions."

"Fine. What are your conditions?"

She ran a chipped, mint-colored nail down the length of the chair arm. "For starters, I want this chair. For a month. Anytime I walk in, you have to give it up, no questions asked."

"Yeah, fine."

She frowned. "A whole month."

"I heard you."

"You're not even going to negotiate?"

"You know I'm desperate. What leverage do I have?"

"Why *are* you so desperate?"

A heavy weight pressed down on Ash's chest. He fought for a nonchalant shrug. "It's Christmas."

"You must really like your family."

That liking one's family appeared to be an unfamiliar concept to Hazel piqued his curiosity. Even under normal circumstances, he couldn't imagine a Christmas without his parents, all his sisters, his nieces. But this year, his need to get home went beyond just missing them. It was a melon baller, slowly and methodically scooping out his insides. He needed to be there, to see for himself just how bad things had gotten.

"I won't contest your terms," he said, "if we leave today."

She shook her head. "Tomorrow."

"Please?"

"NOAA is predicting a big storm for half the state tonight. We'd be better off waiting until morning."

"Who's Noah?" he joked. When she opened her mouth to explain like he was a complete idiot, he cut her off. "Or, if we leave soon, we can beat it."

Hazel pulled out her phone and opened a radar image that he couldn't immediately interpret, already squaring her shoulders for a fight.

"Please, Hazel." He tried not to sound too pushy, to keep the desperate edge from his voice, but it came out low and serious. He reached for something true, an explanation that might garner some understanding. "I promised my niece I'd be there tonight. She's four. I really don't want to disappoint her."

The front door of the café opened then, and Elise came in for the midday shift, signaling the end of his own. He could leave any time. He tugged off the rag he'd slung over his shoulder and raised his eyebrows at Hazel.

"*If* I say yes, I pick the music," she countered. "And I get the chair for the whole semester. You're right, you have no leverage."

She bit her lip, but he didn't protest.

"Okay," she said.

"We leave today?" he confirmed, hopping up.

She heaved herself out of the chair. "I swear to God, if this makes you so insufferable to me that we can no longer coexist—"

He laughed at her melodrama, already running through what he still needed to pack.

Her hand snagged his elbow, utterly serious. "If anything changes between us, I get it all. The whole building."

"You want me to . . . give you the café?"

"The whole building," she repeated.

"Uh . . ." The fierce spark in her eyes gave him pause. He worked here. And lived here. He needed some clarification.

"And stop doing that." She pointedly glared at his hands. He was popping his knuckles.

"Fine. Whatever. Yes. How soon can we go?"

Hazel said she still had to finish packing and gas up but could be back in an hour. Before she left, though, she added, "I'm serious. Nothing can change, Asher."

This time, he didn't correct her. Before she could throw in another condition or change her mind altogether, he gave her a quick salute, said, "Wouldn't dream of it," and headed for his loft.

Three

For all his insistence they hit the road immediately, Ash wasn't anywhere to be found when Hazel returned to the café. Maybe he expected her to come up to his place? Annoyance flared. She didn't even have his number, or she'd have texted him to come down. Grumbling that they hadn't agreed on this white-glove, front door concierge service, she marched up the stairs to his door, through which loud, bassy music thrummed. When she knocked, it swung open from the force of her fist. God, why couldn't he just be ready? Why did she have to debate whether to let herself in like some nosy creeper or stand awkwardly in the hall until he graced her with his presence?

She pressed her cheek to the doorjamb, peeking into his apartment. His place was small. The music was coming from a wireless speaker on the coffee table. He had a futon, a standing lamp, a tiny TV. A kitchenette occupied the far left corner of the room, and a bed took up the back right. A standing rack partially divided the sleeping area from the living area, all his dress shirts and slacks, as well as his collection of whimsical ties, hanging perfectly spaced. Over the music, she could hear water running behind the only door in the place. The bathroom, she guessed.

"I hope you're decent because I'm coming in," she announced, waiting a few seconds before she crossed the threshold.

All around the room, wooden models of buildings cluttered

what little space was left. She crouched for a closer look at the one on the coffee table. Its front open like a dollhouse, the long, ranch-style home had wooden shingles on the roof and a pebble-fronted fireplace inside. In a pink-and-purple room with a bed and a toothpick crib, tiny childlike art hung on the walls. A cotton-ball beanbag chair sat in the corner. Every room was furnished, down to rugs made of patterned fabric and stamp-sized framed portraits.

The next model, between Ash's futon and a bookcase, jolted her with recognition. Its lower level was full of fake plants and café tables, a newspaper-strewn farm table, her green wingback chair. Ash had re-created his own apartment in the loft with mind-boggling detail. He'd painted everything nearly the same colors of their real-life counterparts, stacked tiny books on the coffee table, hung a gray dish towel over the top of a kitchen cabinet, just as one hung there now in reality.

Hazel was squinting at the picture on the mini bedside table when the door opened right behind her. A yelp—"Jesus fuck!"—pierced through the music. She ducked and covered, emitting her own strangled sound of surprise, then twisted around to find Ash clutching a toiletries bag to his chest and gripping the knob of the bathroom door.

Hazel slapped her hand over her mouth to stop a laugh. It came out as a giggle and then a loud snort, which made her laugh harder. "That sound. I thought you were a little girl with a filthy mouth."

He huffed. "I didn't know you were here."

"I knocked." Another wave of mirth spilled over as he frowned deeply and leaned against the doorframe, his jaw tight. "I called out. Your door latch sucks, by the way. It swung right open."

"And you came right in."

She turned off the speaker. "Maybe if you had this at a normal volume, you would have heard me. Or if you were ready on time after demanding that I—"

"I was ready. I just wanted to brush my teeth."

"Aw," Hazel deadpanned. "For me?"

"Anyway," he said with put-on weariness. He strode past her to stuff his toiletries into the duffel by the door. He was dressed but freshly showered, hair still damp. The scent of his soap wafted out with the humid air from the bathroom. Hazel hated that she wanted to rub like a cat into the source of that fresh, earthy lemongrass smell.

After carefully lowering the ranch house model into a large box, Ash held it under one arm, grabbed his sweatshirt and duffel, and nudged her ahead of him into the hall. Downstairs, he cut a wordless detour through the café to pour to-go cups of coffee and stick two blueberry muffins into a bag. Then, they were off.

Or they would have been. But before she could pull out, Ash objected to the route Hazel had chosen. He "didn't trust" Google Maps and claimed perpetual freeway construction would add at least a half hour to her route on top of holiday traffic. Hazel had never made the drive back after moving here, so she had no clue if he was right.

"There won't be that many holiday travelers," she said. "Christmas isn't for a week."

"But all the schools just got out."

"Well," Hazel said, reselecting her original route and setting her phone into the cradle on the dash, "I'm not sleeping in my car in some cow pasture when we run off your little two-lane, farm-to-market road because of bad visibility."

He shook his head but dropped it.

They made it approximately two miles before he pulled her phone back out of the cradle and asked her to unlock it.

"Why?"

"I want to see your playlist."

"We agreed I pick the music."

"Yeah, but seriously, is this all so depressing?"

"Sorry it's not your beloved *Now That's What I Call Music: Deep Synth Volume 3*."

His unfiltered laugh, throaty and full, surprised them both. "Beloved," he repeated.

"It was all you ever played."

He laughed again, shaking his head.

"What?"

"First of all, get your subgenres straight. That was *Now That's What I Call Music: Psychedelic Space Trance*."

"*Oh*, okay."

"And secondly, that mix CD was stuck in the player when I bought my car. The radio didn't work. It was the only thing I could play until I replaced the stereo." He swung his gaze out the front windshield, a wry smile creeping from one corner of his mouth to the other. "You really thought I drove around just *vibing* to that?"

"You played it *every time*. Loudly. Never talked to me, just scowled all broody in your rearview mirror and cranked it up."

"Broody," he mused. His smile faded. "Yeah, well, as I recall, there wasn't much talking happening in the back seat."

Hazel's cheeks burned. She checked her side mirror just for the excuse to turn her face from him. When she looked back, he was scrolling again through her playlists. He read, "'We'll Have to Muddle Through Somehow.' What's this? More sad girl acoustic?"

"That's Christmas music."

"Wow. Dark."

She knew he was joking, but it stung. She wasn't a dark person. "It's from 'Have Yourself a Merry Little Christmas.' That's a line from the original version, the one Judy Garland sings in *Meet Me in St. Louis*. Fun fact: there was also supposed to be a line that said, 'This Christmas will be our last,' but she thought it was too depressing to sing to the kid in the scene, and she made them change it."

"Thank God for that," he said, back to scrolling.

Hazel itched to snatch back her phone and talk about anything else besides her apparently depressing taste in music. "So, you make dollhouses?"

"Models," he corrected. He selected a ukulele version of "I'll Be Home for Christmas" before returning the phone to its cradle then nodded at her back seat. "That one's for my nieces. It's just a hobby."

"Just a hobby? It's so detailed. They all were."

He laughed uneasily. "How long were you in my apartment?"

"Long enough to know you made one of your own place. Who's that one for?"

He rubbed his eyebrow with one finger. Was he embarrassed? Okay, she'd said it teasingly, but she was genuinely impressed. Each model must have taken dozens of hours. They had so many tiny pieces. She pictured him with a headlamp and tweezers, bent close over his work area, his tongue peeking from one corner of his mouth like it did when he was deep in concentration. When Hazel wasn't working, she mostly just rewatched entire TV series and blocked out the world.

Ash said, "That one was just going to be the café, but I figured why stop once I finished the downstairs. I don't know. I don't have, like, a purpose for them. I get tired of doing everything in 2D. I draft all these plans, but I never see them built."

"The floor plans you're always drawing on your laptop?"

"Yeah. At my internship, I mostly submit plans to the city and run errands, and the pay is crap, so I take extra jobs whenever I can. I make a little money doing freelance drafting on the side."

"I thought the floor plans were for school." His fancy, business-casual wardrobe made more sense now that she could imagine him in a cubicle at some architecture firm. She knew what time he arrived at the café every day, but it had never occurred to her that he came from another job. She'd always assumed he made all his money working for Cami. "So, you have, like, three jobs on top of your program?"

She winced at the surprise her tone betrayed, but she couldn't help it. In high school—at least, during the one semester she was aware enough of him to notice—Ash had been flaky, apathetic. He arrived late to their homeroom, fell asleep during class, even lost his starting catcher position on the school baseball team for missing too many practices. His own best friend blamed Ash's lack of focus and drive for their disappointing senior season. Not to mention the very first time she met Ash, when he bailed early on the volunteer field day she'd organized for at-risk kids. She couldn't help but wonder, where was this work ethic back then?

"The internship will pay better once I graduate," he said. "They'll let me do more, and the hours will count toward my license requirements. The models just . . . help me unwind."

"Lot of unwinding," Hazel said.

"I assume you have a more exciting life away from the café."

"Sure. Grad school is a riot."

"You're a TA, right? Actually teaching, not just doing grunt work for a professor?" He laughed at her suspicious side-eye. "What? You've stalked my schedule, but I can't notice that you make your lecture PowerPoints on Thursdays?"

"Technically, I'm a *research* assistant for Dr. Sheffield, but he doesn't like to teach on Fridays, so I usually fill in for him in Intro to Psych. It's one of those mass lectures with two hundred students. Plus tutoring. Plus whatever else Dr. Sheffield dumps on me. So, it's more like lab work, teaching, *and* grunt work for a professor."

"I bet you're a good teacher. You've got a knows-her-shit, takes-no-shit vibe."

"Well, the whole job *is* a shit show, but . . ." She'd lost any sense of healthy boundaries with the students ages ago.

"You work hard." At her dismissive shrug—frankly, she wasn't sure how to take him being so openly *nice* to her—he doubled down. "You do. I've watched you sit in that chair for five hours straight without taking a break."

"Maybe I'm just keeping you from stealing it."

"At least you did your undergrad here, so you don't have to navigate a new campus, make new friends."

She covered the scoffing sound that escaped her throat with a cough, but just barely. Though she'd been there for four years already, the shift from undergrad to grad school had unmoored her. She'd tried to make friends with the other students in her program, but at the first department mixer, she'd overheard some of them speculating about which first-year student had been awarded the coveted Benning Scholarship and answered too brightly, "Oh, that's me. I'm Hazel." They murmured strained hellos and immediately abandoned the dessert table to re-congregate in a far corner as though she'd announced she had Ebola. Dr. Sheffield didn't help matters, tacking "our illustrious Benning Scholar" onto every utterance of her name all semester, cementing her outsider status.

Even her lab team was more contentious than expected. Co-led by Zach, a fourth-year student, their meetings frequently involved the most competitive "brainstorming" sessions she'd ever seen.

Not that she had time for socializing anyway. She'd had to extend her tutoring hours to accommodate Sheffield's freshmen, pushing her own work behind all the other tasks he'd dropped on her desk.

The real breaking point was when she'd wasted a week transcribing the wrong set of audio files—a mistake that had invited a full dressing-down from Zach in front of the whole lab team—and, simultaneously, Sheffield's students started finding her outside her office hours. She realized she needed a hideout. And thus—not to be too dramatic about it—her self-imposed exile from school grounds.

"Maybe," Hazel hedged. "It's different, though. I didn't live alone before."

"Ah. Me, too."

"You haven't always been squatting alone above the café like some attic troll?"

"Cami let me crash there. It was supposed to be temporary. That was . . ." He scratched his eyebrow again. "Almost two years ago. To be clear, I do pay rent."

"What happened two years ago?"

Ash watched her for a beat before finally giving an easy shrug. "Breakup. Couldn't afford our place on my own."

"You lived with a girl?"

"I have four sisters. I've lived with girls pretty much my whole life."

"Yeah, but a girl you were . . ."

"In love with?"

Hazel was going to say *sleeping with*. "So, it was serious? You lo—" She tripped over the word, had to clear her throat. "You loved her?"

Ash laughed at her clear discomfort. "I don't know." He turned and drew a spiral in the foggy side window with his finger. "Doesn't everything feel serious when you're in the middle of it?"

Not if you don't let it, she thought. If she didn't crave touch like oxygen, she'd have entirely given up on dating a long time ago. Which explained why, lately, she jumped at the tiniest innocuous touches, the surprise brush of skin when a grocery clerk handed over her change, an accidental jostle on a crowded bus. She was *starved* for contact. But at least she was safe.

Ash seemed uninterested in talking about his ex and instead told her about his four sisters—Maggie, the oldest, three years his senior, who taught high school French in Kansas; June, an adventurous middle sister trying to make it as an actress out in California who had been two years behind him and Hazel in school; and Laurel and Leanne, seventeen-year-old twins.

"Wait, the cute blonde who was in all the theater productions and came to your baseball games?" Hazel asked. "I thought she was your girlfriend for a while."

Ash shuddered. "I'm going to pretend you didn't say that."

He told her the ranch house model in Hazel's back seat was a Christmas gift for the oldest sister's two daughters and grumbled lightly about his family being overrun with girls, but the way his eyes lit up at the mention of his nieces totally undercut the complaint. He hadn't seen them all since summer, the last time he went home, and she could *feel* how long that stretch had been for him. He was in the middle of showing Hazel a picture on his phone of a little dark-haired girl in a pink, feathered dance costume when the line of cars ahead slowed into an ever-compressing string of red brake lights.

"Is this the construction you mentioned?" she asked.

"It's usually further along, but yeah." He had the grace not to say they should have taken his route, but his fond, heart-eyed affection for his nieces was now shuttered.

For forty-five minutes, they crept through the bottlenecked stretch of highway. The traffic finally sped up again, but not for long. Rain dotted the windshield. Hazel calculated their slow progress against the weather models she'd checked before leaving. Not to give her father too much credit, but he'd taught her a bit about forecasting. The type of storm they were driving into was notoriously difficult to predict, but rain wasn't a good sign, and they were still five hours from Lockett Prairie on a good day.

"It's just rain," Ash muttered, shaking his head at the line of cautious drivers.

"We might want to consider a plan."

"A plan for what?"

"If we have to wait it out." Just then, they passed a sign with the distance to the next town. Seventeen miles.

"It's getting cold. If it freezes, it won't thaw until tomorrow. We'd have to stop overnight."

"Preferably in a hotel."

"No." He shook his head adamantly. "We should keep driving. If all these people would speed up a little—it's just rain."

The car ahead of them slowed. Hazel tapped the brakes, and her tires skidded before they caught. She squeezed the steering wheel, cutting a glare at Ash.

"We'll go slow. I'll drive if you want."

"I know you really want to get home—"

"Yeah, and for whatever reason, you don't."

"I'm not causing the weather!" She flung a hand at the windshield. He was squaring his shoulders, ready to fight, but her heart had skipped a beat with that skid, and her arm hair stood on end, and she didn't let him interrupt. "You think it's fine because it's not snowing yet, but that's only because there's a warm wedge of air beneath the upper atmosphere temporarily thawing the snow into rain. The ground temperature is already freezing. This is only going to get worse."

"And that's your weather, folks," Ash said, his voice dropping into a low, rich register. "Take care out there."

Hazel's lips parted, and her eyes widened in surprise. "What are you— Stop it."

He leaned forward, forcing his way into her periphery. "I'm Dan Elliot, and you're watching Channel 2," he said, smooth and lilting like her father's on-air voice, "the Permian Basin's most trusted news source."

She slugged his shoulder, and he slunk back against his door, laughing, rubbing his arm. "Don't ever do that again," she said.

"Oh, come on. You sounded just like him with all that 'warm wedge' and 'upper atmosphere' stuff."

"Understanding basic weather terminology does not make me my father." Her chest clenched with irritation, but the sound of her own petulant tone short-circuited her bad humor. She huffed a reluctant laugh and muttered, without any heat, "Shut up, Asher."

"Ash," he corrected, probably a mindless habit by this point. Then, quieter, "And I know this isn't your fault. I'm sorry."

She did feel weirdly responsible, though, like her resistance had somehow conjured the bad conditions. In other circumstances, she might have rejoiced at the unforeseen delay. But after hearing how excited Ash was to see his nieces, the proof in the elaborate model in her back seat, part of her wished she could snap her fingers and clear their path for him, even if it brought her home sooner herself. His quiet apology despite his frustration spoke to a goodness in Ash that she doubted she possessed.

It was an hour before they spotted the first signs of a small town—an old Texaco station, McDonald's arches. Their side of the highway was deadlocked with brake lights as far as Hazel could see except when, periodically, someone peeled off from the line, bounced over the grassy median, and came back their way. Eventually, the traffic started moving again as a steady stream of people bailed, taking an exit ramp into the town. The sky darkened. The rain became a wintry mix, lightly tapping on the roof and windshield.

Ash was scrolling on his phone. "There's ice on an overpass at the next town. They're only letting one car cross at a time. That's why we're stuck here. I can't believe I'm saying this, but—" He rubbed his jaw. "We should stop."

"Are you sure?"

"I agreed to give you the café if this trip makes me intolerable to you, and if we end up stranded in a cow pasture tonight, you'll never get over it, so." It was clearly an attempt at humor, but he sounded dejected.

By the time they inched into the tiny town, Ash had found two places to stay, a Motel 6 and some bed-and-breakfast called the Roadrunner Inn. Hazel pulled into the packed parking lot of the Motel 6 just as the **NO** lit up on the **VACANCY** sign.

The Roadrunner Inn it was. The old, pale blue two-story Victorian house sat at the end of a pothole-riddled road. Its much smaller parking lot was also full, and Hazel was already calculating their next move as she parked on the street. Drive on to the next town, where surely everyone who hadn't stopped here would be looking for lodging? Or head back the thirty or so miles to the previous one? She indulged, briefly, the voice that said, *This is a sign. You shouldn't have come at all.*

In the lobby, an enormous fire crackled. With a teeth-rattling shiver, Hazel looked longingly at the couches angled in front of it and the cart with cookies and coffee, her hands shoved into a thin fleece jacket that would have made her father shake his head. Nat King Cole played softly over speakers. The wood floor creaked with every last step to the counter, where three college-aged guys blew into their hands and shifted impatiently.

"Do you have a cot or something?" one of them asked.

Hazel eyed Ash in a wordless panic. If there weren't any rooms left, she was prepared to wage a sit-in on one of those couches.

Ash reached for her arm, and she lurched away on instinct. He caught her gaze for a long moment as if reading a wild animal before reaching again, slowly, and squeezing her upper arm.

The contact was surprisingly ... steadying. Her gaze dropped to his hand, but she quickly refocused on the taxidermied mallard duck in mid-flight on the wall. Uncertain what else to do with her body when Ash was touching her, she hugged her middle, then regretted it when the motion made him let go and push both his hands into his hoodie pocket.

The three guys were given an old-school metal key. At least for them, there was still room at the inn. Hazel and Ash shuffled forward.

The man holding their fate in his hands was tall and spindly with a disarrayed, feathery tuft of hair atop his head. In less dire circumstances, Hazel would have found his likeness to a road-runner amusing, but nothing about this could be funny until she knew she had a warm place to sleep for tonight. He spoke abruptly in a decidedly unbirdlike baritone. "Got one room left. It has a queen bed. And no, we don't have any cots."

Before they could respond, the door opened behind them, and a middle-aged couple tromped in, shivering from the cold, tension all over their grim faces.

One room left? Too bad for them, but over Hazel's dead body would those two get it. She slapped her credit card on the counter. "We'll take it."

Four

What the guy at reception had not mentioned was that their room had a name. Ash stopped short at the brass sign on the door that said: **THE LOVEBIRD SUITE**. Beside him, Hazel let out a soft snort.

Just ignore it, he decided. It was just a room. Just a place to sleep before getting back on the road tomorrow. They didn't even really need to address the issue of the lone, queen-size bed because of course he would insist she take it.

But when he pushed open the door, the casual line he'd rehearsed on the short walk upstairs dissolved under the assault of mustard-yellow bird wallpaper on every wall, a peacock-feather-patterned comforter, brass flamingo bedside lamps, and a gallery of pink-and-teal picture frames holding crudely drawn bird sketches. He jumped back when he realized even the carpet was a sea of alternating right-side-up and upside-down bird silhouettes.

Hazel pushed past him and turned in a slow circle in the center of the room. "This is . . ."

"Disorienting," he said. "Oppressive. A hell custom-designed by Lisa Frank."

"Amazing." She dropped her bags just past the entryway, where Ash was still standing, then threw open the closet, gasped, and yanked a robe off a hanger. Immediately, she pulled it on over her gray sweaterdress. It was a muted spa green on the outside, but the lining had colorful parrots printed all over it. She cinched the belt and pulled a second matching robe out for him.

"Uh, no."

"Put it on, Asher."

"*Ash.* And you look ridiculous." Ridiculously cute with her bright eyes and open smile, but whatever. She was swimming in the material, and he was pretty sure she'd taken the man's robe and was offering him the slimmer-cut woman's version.

"Well, I like it." She tightened the belt for emphasis and trust-fell onto the bed.

Aaand he'd missed his chance to get ahead of the bed conversation. Her shoulders tensed as she sat up and studied her hands against the peacock comforter. "So, how should we . . . ?"

Ash let the door close behind him. The room became way too quiet. "Uh, you paid for the room, which—I'll add it to your gas money. But I can just sleep on the . . ." He gestured aimlessly at the floor, where the endlessly flip-flopping birds made him feel like he was swaying. He crossed to the closet, hoping for an extra blanket, but found only three extremely flat pillows. He grabbed them anyway, then turned and collided with her.

"You don't have to pay me back," Hazel said.

Shaking his head, he dropped the pillows into the narrow space between the bed and the wall. He suspected the manager had jacked up the price when desperate people began turning up. "I'm paying my half. It's not your fault there was a warm air wedge."

"If you're paying for half, you should get half the bed." Uncertainty flitted across her face, but she committed. "I mean, you should. We can be adults about it, right?"

Ash expelled a tight laugh. "Yeah, no problem. We are adults."

But he'd already spent several hours in her passenger seat trying to look at anything other than her thighs in her smooth leggings, her soft curves in her dress, the low neck of which kept slipping down and exposing her right shoulder. Multiple times, when she'd gone quiet, he'd fallen into a daydream-like state and vividly saw himself leaning over to *kiss* that little curve of exposed shoulder.

At some point, she was going to sleep in something else entirely. Who knew what Hazel Elliot wore to bed? He didn't want to know.

Actually, now, he desperately wanted to know.

Ash yanked the comforter off the bed like a matador with a cape. "I'll take the top half."

"What?"

"Yeah." He tossed it into the corner. "You take the mattress. That middle blanket looks warm enough. And I'll take the comforter." A completely sane plan.

"That's not what I—"

He folded the blanket in half like a sleeping bag and lay down on top of it, crossing his arms behind his head.

"Are you sure?"

"Yep." And because he was nothing if not committed now, he closed his eyes.

A moment later, the bed creaked as she shifted above him. "Hey, Asher," Hazel whispered.

He cracked one eye open to find her face hanging over the side of the bed inches from his own. "Ash."

"It's only six o'clock."

Well, hell.

"We should eat." She opened the nightstand drawer. "Do you think they have room service here?"

Ash sprang to his feet. He needed *out* of this room. "I saw a diner down the street. My treat."

AFTER WATCHING A CAR SLIDE ACROSS THE INN PARKING LOT AND T-bone a truck, they decided to walk the two blocks. The almost painful shock of the cold was also a relief. Already Ash's head was clearing from the dizzying spell of that room, which was ten percent Technicolor chaos and ninety percent *bed*.

The thin jacket Hazel had thrown on over her sweaterdress seemed to be doing nothing to block the frigid wind, but despite her violent shivering, she snagged his sleeve just short of the diner. "Wait. Look." She tipped her face up to the sky.

He'd *seen* snow. West Texas got a dusting every few winters, occasionally a few inches. But not like this. The fine, icy precipitation had turned into genuine, fat Christmas movie snowflakes that were already sticking to the sidewalk. Ash wasn't sure if the sudden flurry in his stomach was from the novelty of *real* snowfall, or the pretty way, when Hazel opened her arms and turned in a careful circle, the flakes caught in her dark hair, on her lashes, her scarf. Lamplight bathed her cheeks golden.

As it turned out, even the biting cold sneaking down the back of his collar couldn't completely freeze out the heat that had ignited under his skin in that room.

"Look *up*," she insisted again.

He squinted up into the falling snow.

"It's pretty," she said.

"It's pretty," he agreed.

But the awkward thickness that blanketed his voice must have sounded like sarcasm because she huffed, "Fine," and left him standing there.

According to the half-burnt-out neon sign above the door, the diner was called, simply, **DINER**. Hazel tilted her head, considering the **No Shoes No Shirt No Service** sign. Someone had Sharpied *No Animals* at the bottom and, below that in blue pen, *This includes hamsters, Keith!*

"Wait," Ash said. "Is it no service if you bring an animal, or no service if you *don't*?"

"So many questions," she murmured, opening the door for him. He caught the top of it and nudged her through.

The smells hit him first: maple syrup, burnt bacon, very burnt coffee. The dining room was empty, two rows of booths to the left and a short counter to the right, split by a narrow walkway to the kitchen. Meat Loaf's "I'd Do Anything for Love (But I Won't Do That)" played from behind the swinging doors, accompanied by someone confidently belting out the words off-key. Whoever was back there hadn't heard the bell jingle with their entry, just kept shout-singing the chorus.

Hazel opened the door again, rattling the bell a second time, and the music abruptly stopped, followed by a clatter and a sharp curse. An older woman with a neck tattoo and her gray hair in braided pigtails burst through the kitchen doors like a bull out of a chute. Her breathing was labored like she'd been on a table doing air guitar back there, but her stern glare made absolutely no acknowledgment that they'd walked in on her mid-power-ballad. "Y'all never been here before." Unclear if this was a question or a statement.

"No," Hazel answered, scooting closer to Ash.

"Take a seat," the woman barked, chest still heaving. "Dial nine when you're ready to order."

"Dial . . . nine?" Ash asked, scanning the dining room again. Flickering fluorescent lights. Pepto-pink walls. Framed art, all wrapped for the holidays in green paper with armadillos wearing cowboy hats. Which was weirder than if they'd had Santa hats. At least that was ostensibly Christmassy.

"It ain't even a rotary phone. Shouldn't be that hard to figure out."

He saw it then. A cream-colored telephone, grimy from what looked like *decades* of diner guests' greasy hands, mounted to the wall above the nearest table. And more phones at all the other tables.

"Don't tell me you're one of these young Z-boys who's afraid to talk on the phone," she snapped, hooking her thumbs behind a longhorn belt buckle the size of a dinner plate. She was still panting, still pretending she wasn't.

"Z . . . what?"

Hazel choked on a laugh and turned abruptly to hide it. She was so close he could smell her mint gum. Her eyes were wide with joyful desperation, checking that he was fully absorbing *all of this.*

Pop Rocks sparked through his entire body, cutting through the fog of disorientation that was apparently part and parcel of this town. He *liked* this—her looking to him, being on the same side of the joke.

"Gen Z," Hazel squeaked. "I think she means Gen Z."

He rolled his lips between his teeth to contain his own laugh since no one was shielding *him* from the woman's impatient glare.

"We call," he said, "from the table?"

"Why else," she huffed, "would it be called the Phone It In Diner?"

Was it called that? Nowhere in all the other signage had that phrase appeared. Before he could say as much, Hazel shoved him into the nearest booth and buried her face in an enormous menu.

When the woman retreated to the kitchen, Hazel grabbed his wrist across the table, eyes still enormous, and said, "What *is* this place?"

"Well, obviously, it's the Phone It In Diner. Didn't you see the enormous sign?"

"Is that a *theme*? Phones?"

"Yeah, the classic diner theme: call a scary stranger on the phone."

Hazel laughed, and he liked that, too—*making* her laugh. She slumped back into the booth, apparently exhausted from holding it in. "She was kind of right, though. We do fear that."

"I can't tell if the phone thing is nostalgia, or if this place has been here since the telephone was boldly futuristic." He pushed spongy stuffing spilling from a gash in the vinyl seat back in.

"Either way, I'm not calling that lady. You're gonna have to do it."

Shit. Speaking of calling . . . Ash sent a quick text to Maggie to let her know he wasn't going to make it tonight after all.

Hazel checked her own phone, mumbling an apology then holding out her palm. "Give me your pen."

"My pen?"

"You always have one."

He dug it out of his pocket, and she wrote the date on a napkin, then held it under her face and took a selfie. "My old roommate, Sylvia, randomly demands proofs of life."

"Like . . . a hostage situation?"

"Yep. Watch, she's going to say it's not legit unless it's a newspaper."

"Well, sure. Everyone knows that."

She smiled when the text came in and showed him—That date could have been written a week ago just to throw me off!—then turned her phone down on the table.

"So, you said you've been summoned home." He opened his menu. "For Christmas?"

"And a wedding."

"Whose?"

She forced a smile. "Channel 2's own Dan Elliot."

"Your dad? You're . . . not psyched?"

"I don't have strong feelings one way or another," she said as she straightened the salt and pepper shakers. Then she scratched aggressively with her nail at a spot of dried syrup on the table.

He watched her over the top of his menu. "Touchy subject?"

"Nope. I haven't even met her yet."

"Have they not been together long?"

"He moved in with her and her kids last spring, I think."

"You think," Ash repeated.

"I didn't commemorate the event in my diary."

Ash smiled at her mild petulance. "She has kids?"

"Two."

"And you've never met any of them? Have you at least FaceTimed or something?"

She cringed at the sticky gunk now caught under her nail and grabbed a napkin. "Why would I FaceTime with them?"

"They're about to be your family, right?"

Hazel balled up the soiled napkin then turned her full attention to the menu, which was so long it would give a CVS receipt a run for its money. "Technically. But I won't ever see them."

"Because you never go home?"

She narrowed her eyes at him, clearly growing impatient with his questions.

Ash rubbed his forehead, unsure whether to keep pushing or to drop the subject. But he was curious. He didn't know anyone else who hadn't returned home at least once since high school.

College is for new experiences, not old baggage, she'd told him once.

He'd thought a lot about that party freshman year, before she'd all but told him to go bother twenty thousand other girls instead of trying anything with her. Part of that night had been all right. Good, even. Until she remembered her shitty ex was his best friend. She had no idea of the fight Ash and Justin had that summer or the rift that remained, nor how utterly *disloyal* to Justin his thoughts about Hazel were that night. How she looked edgier, *sexier* with her new, shorter hair. Or how, for the first time since they'd met, she didn't look past him to search the room for Justin. How he'd thought, briefly, things could be different.

But *Justin's friend* was all she'd ever really seen him as. Justin's *broody* friend, apparently. The guy who ferried her and her boyfriend around to a handful of parties senior year because otherwise Justin would drive drunk. Ash's reward: getting to watch them make out in his back seat.

"Afraid you'll run into Justin or something?" Ash guessed.

Hazel pressed her mouth into a tight line but otherwise didn't react. He couldn't quite tell what was real with her. Mild annoyances flashed, fiery and unfiltered, in her eyes, and she could tap into biting sarcasm on a dime, but other times, she was freakishly cool and impassive. He found himself swinging to the same extremes around her, mirroring her energy, trying to stay on even footing. But holding his every reaction in check had been exhausting enough in high school. It took even more out of him now. He knew why he'd done it as a teenager—he wasn't trying to steal his best friend's girl—but he wasn't sure why he'd started doing it again when she walked into his café two months ago. Except that, because she couldn't totally read him, she kept trying to.

The epitome of casual, Hazel asked, "Is Justin back in town?" And maybe she was *always* hiding something. Maybe her first instinct was to cover her real reaction until she calculated the risk and *decided* to have it.

"Yeah, he tore his rotator cuff sophomore year, lost his scholarship. He works for his dad."

"Huh." Ash caught the glimmer of concern in her pinched brow, the same little kick he felt when he pictured Justin's dad barking orders at him again, only now without Ash or a coach to buffer.

"So, he's not the reason you never go home?" Ash asked.

She closed her menu and folded her hands atop it. "I'm ready to order. Are you?"

Clearly, he'd pushed as far as she intended to let him.

In addition to the menu being a novel, someone must have been high when they named the items, because each was more ridiculous than the last. He wasn't dying to order the Big Bubba's Belly Blaster Burger or the Dreamy Creamy Broccoli and Cheese-y Soup. "What are you getting?"

She shrugged, a little too casual, and said, "Dial nine."

He lifted the receiver and pressed the button. A shrill, piercing tone rang out just behind Hazel's head, and she ducked, startled. The kitchen doors swung open, and out charged the same woman to lift the phone from the wall by the counter. She stood no more than four feet from Ash and, making aggressively direct eye contact, snapped, "What?"

"Uh, we're ready to order." He eyed her name tag. "Emeline."

"It's pronounced Eme*leen*."

Hazel slunk even further down into her seat and probably would have melted right onto the floor in a laughing fit if he hadn't reached under the table and squeezed her knee. At his touch, she yelped, lurched back, and banged her elbow against the wall.

"Go on then," the woman said. "Into the phone."

Something about her intense eye contact at such a close range made Ash's palms sweat. He forgot what he'd planned to order and opened his menu again, squeezing the receiver between his shoulder and ear. It slipped and clattered onto the table, and Hazel made a strangled sound. He glared first at her and then at Emeline in a silent plea to let the phone thing go and just take their order like a normal person.

She pointed her pen at his receiver.

He lifted it back to his face. "I'll have the chicken and waffles."

"The what?"

He closed his eyes, breathed in through his nose. "Chicken and waffles."

"That's not on the menu."

He pointed at the photo right there on page five.

Her eyes stayed locked on his, refusing to let him weasel out of saying it.

Pushing his shoulders back, he enunciated slowly so he wouldn't have to repeat himself. "The Mother Cluckin' Breakfast Platter."

"You want it with Granny's Sloppy Tots?"

"I . . . do not."

"What else?"

Hazel snaked a hand forward and pressed her fingertip halfway down the page.

"Really?" he snapped, covering the mouthpiece as though this woman couldn't both perfectly hear him *and* read his lips at this proximity.

Hazel squeezed her eyes and mouth shut and nodded.

He turned a polite smile up to their server. "She'll have the

Rootin' Tootin' Fruitin' Flapjacks." Quickly, he added, "No sides. And coffee for both of us. Creamer and twenty sugars for her."

Emeline hung up the receiver so hard it dinged, dropped an extra bucket of creamer and sweeteners onto their table, and left without a single other word.

Laughter tripped out of Hazel. Twice, she tried and failed to speak before wheezing, "I wanted those tots."

"Be my guest," he said, extending the phone to her.

A lingering tremor of amusement shook her shoulders. "Okay, because you were such a good sport with that," she said on a happy sigh, gesturing vaguely at him, "I'll bite."

Ash had entirely forgotten what they'd been talking about.

"You want to know why I don't go home?" She made a thoughtful face, then straightened and pushed up her sleeves. "Have you ever moved? Before college, I mean."

"No."

"Okay. Well, my parents got divorced when I was eleven, and after my mom left, my dad and I moved two streets away. It wasn't like going to a new city or something. Our old house was still *right there*. Only, this new family lived in it, and they changed all these things—repainted the door, took out the hedges. They had a boy, and I remember thinking he probably put *Star Wars* posters on my walls."

Ash scoffed in disgust on her behalf.

She sawed her teeth into her bottom lip. "You know what bugged me?"

"What?"

"My parents used to mark my height on the wall in the kitchen. Does your family do that?"

He nodded. "On the back of the laundry room door."

"When we sold the house, we had to paint over all the marks.

And then in the new place, my dad forgot. Or maybe it would have been weird to start a new one halfway up the wall."

"Sure. I guess."

"I don't know why I thought of that now." She pushed up her sleeves once more and laughed self-consciously. She was quiet a moment, then, "Whatever. Anyway, I used to make my dad drive by the old house all the time so I could see it, and he would, even though he hated going there. And then I'd regret it because I'd see the other family or the things they'd changed, and I'd feel sad. I remember wishing it had burned down or been bulldozed. Eventually, I stopped going back. Even years later, when I got my license, I drove the long way around so I wouldn't have to see it."

A vise tightened in Ash's chest. He hadn't known her at eleven but had at seventeen and could picture her back then, with long hair she used to straighten and an easy, sweet smile. She hadn't yet wrapped herself in so many defensive layers. She'd fallen for his best friend, who was fun and charismatic, sure, but also reckless and selfish. Those facts about Justin never bothered Ash until Hazel was under his arm. He'd felt pulled to shield her, though from *what* exactly he didn't interrogate too deeply.

Then again, vague worry had always been a default setting for Ash.

He imagined teen Hazel driving herself on a wide detour, neatly cordoning off her old street and house and all the complicated feelings she had about them. "That must have sucked," he said.

She refused his sympathy with a firm single shake of her head. "The point is, no, I don't want to run into Justin. But that's true of pretty much everyone in Lockett Prairie. I didn't keep in touch with anyone." She shrugged. "I'm just not that great with afters."

"Afters?"

"After moves, breakups, quitting a job. Once I leave, I don't go back. Ever."

"That's—"

"I know it's crazy."

He frowned. He was going to say it seemed sad, though what he'd really meant, on second thought, was lonely. "So, relationships are . . ."

"Fine while they last. Then, it's—" She made a cutting motion with one finger across her throat. And with that gesture, he saw the exact moment when she locked up the brief access she'd given him. "You're probably still friends with all your exes, right?"

"Sure, we're cool, I guess."

"Even the one you lived with? What happened with her?"

Ash half groaned, half laughed into his hands.

"What?"

"She cheated."

Hazel's eyebrows shot up. "And you're still friends?"

"We're . . ." He searched for a word to encompass his feelings about Brianna. "We just weren't a good fit. She said my world was like this little shoebox, safe and cozy. Then, I guess, not so cozy. She said she cheated because she wasn't feeling it anymore, but I kept trying to fix everything. She didn't see another way out."

"Wow, she really overshot on that one."

Still, his feelings had never quite swung from hurt to hate. His sisters had blown up a group chat with so much vitriol toward Brianna that he'd ended up talking *them* down instead of the other way around.

"The guy she cheated on me with cheated on her, so . . ." He shrugged. "Karma took care of it."

"Sure. Karma." She slapped her palms on the table, leaning across the table at him. "No, Asher. She cheated on you. Karma doesn't 'take care of it.'"

"It was a long time ago. Now she's engaged to one of the trainers for the basketball team. Got me tickets to a few games this season."

Hazel covered her face and mumbled into her palms, "Oh my God."

The kitchen door swung open, and Ash straightened at the sight of Emeline bringing their food, braced for another discomfiting exchange. "It's hot," she barked, slapping his hand hard. Then, she set everything down with record speed and quite a lot of noise and left.

"I think I'm witnessing you develop PTSD in real time," Hazel remarked.

"And enjoying it."

Despite the terrifying service, the food at least looked good. He drizzled syrup over his chicken and waffles and passed the pitcher to her.

Hazel scraped all the fruit off her pancakes before drowning them in syrup.

"Hold on. There were regular pancakes on the menu if you didn't want the fruit."

She beamed at him. "I know."

He shook his head and cut into his chicken. "So, what about you?"

"What about me?"

"Any relationships since high school?"

"Nothing serious." She lifted an enormous, dripping bite into her mouth and hummed a throaty moan of approval that tickled the hairs on the back of Ash's neck and made him reach for his water.

"So what do you do for human contact when you're not third-wheeling it to basketball games with your ex and her fiancé?" she went on, oblivious to the distress she'd stirred in him.

"I can get my own dates." At her skeptical squint, he added, "It was easier when I had more classes outside architecture. I'm barely on main campus. And I'd feel weird asking out someone at the café or city hall."

"So, how do you date?"

"Apps a couple times," he admitted. "Maggie and June occasionally play matchmaker with their friends. And friends of their friends. I'm kind of a project for them."

"Your sisters want you to sleep with their friends?"

He was mid-sip, and the water shot straight to the back of his throat, down his windpipe. He coughed and sputtered, eyes watering.

Hazel laughed delightedly and thumped his back. Once he recovered, she said, "I tried apps, too, but between the dick pics and knowing Sheffield's students might find my profile, every new DM gave me hives."

"So, how do *you* date?"

She ducked her face. Was that a flush climbing up her neck? Ash leaned his elbows on the table on either side of his plate, more curious now than when he'd lobbed the question back at her.

"I haven't in a while," she said, wary of his interest. "I see Sheffield's students all over the place. I don't go to bars anymore, or restaurants, or movies. I—" She shook her head. "God, why am I telling you this?"

"Tell me."

"You'll think I'm weird."

"I already think you're weird, Hazel." At her scowl, he raised his palms. "In a good way."

"Fine. But you can't judge me."

He crossed his heart.

"I told you Intro to Psych has a ton of students, right? I know a lot of them now because I've tutored them one-on-one, but I haven't memorized the faces of all two hundred. I definitely couldn't have picked most of them from a lineup back in October. Also, I used to have this . . . casual thing with a friend. But he moved after graduation, so it had been a while since . . ."

She shot him an uncertain glance, gauging, he guessed, his reaction to her having a fuck buddy. He rolled his hand over at the wrist. "You're a normal, hot-blooded twentysomething. You have needs."

"Gross."

He laughed. "And what happened? You swiped right on a student by accident?"

"Worse." She groaned dramatically. "Okay, so I went to the Fox one night, and there was this guy. He had just gotten this ridiculous tattoo of a pug with an overbite. Its face frowned deeper when he flexed his arm."

"Classy," Ash deadpanned.

"It was funny. And he was cute. We danced." She shrugged. "He was cute," she said again.

"Hold on. Are we talking dimples-and-muscles cute or, like, vulnerable-kitten cute?"

"Do you want to hear this or not?"

"Sorry. Go ahead."

"We made out, and I was going to leave with him. But I went to the bathroom, and when I came out, he was gone. The next day, I was collecting quizzes in class, and there, to my shock and horror, was Pug Boy."

"Yikes."

"So, not only did he ghost me, but he was also a *freshman*. I made out with basically a child. After I panicked about whether or not I could get fired or kicked out of my program or, I don't know, charged with a crime, I realized that, even though I didn't recognize him, he absolutely knew who I was. Not only do I sub in on lectures, but every other class, Dr. Sheffield has some technical problem and beckons me to the front to fix it. He makes this awful joke about how he'd be lost without his trusty teaching assistant and how the *T* and *A* stand for tech and audio. You can imagine how the boys have latched on to that."

"I can." Well, that was gross and terrible.

Unbidden and immediately undercutting his moral authority over a bunch of eighteen-year-old idiots, an image intruded: Hazel striding into the café in one of her Friday outfits. He had pieced together, after several weeks of observation and blatant eavesdropping on her conversations with Cami, that Friday was the day she often taught this professor's class for him. On those days, she wore black pencil skirts with fancy tops that tied in a big bow at the throat or had sheer sleeves or lace and tiny buttons up the back of her neck. She swept her hair up in a bun and wore glasses, as well as black tights with delicate patterns on them. She was probably aiming for professional and off-limits to undergraduates, but the whole look checked just about every box of the hot-teacher fantasy.

"Guys are dicks," he said apologetically. "Some of us less than others, though."

She shoved another huge bite of pancakes into her mouth with a look like, *We'll see about you.* "The other issue," she added, "is that I run into Sheffield's students constantly. You'd think my office hours were a Disney attraction—just a constant line outside my door for tutoring. A while ago, I extended my hours because I didn't want Sheffield to think I wasn't keeping up, and *more* of them came. Then, they'd find me at the library or after my lab. And *now*, it's all over town. The gym, Starbucks, my bus stop. They *find* me. I know it sounds paranoid, but I'm half convinced they've developed some kind of sophisticated system for tracking my movements."

"They find you," he echoed ominously, amused. "You're right. That does sound paranoid."

Hazel threw her balled up straw wrapper at his forehead. "Just wait until you're the one at H-E-B buying wine and a cookie cake in your pajamas, minding your own business, and some freshman makes you explain Kohlberg's theory of moral development on the spot while openly judging your purchases."

Ash raised his palms at the defiant edge in her voice but did nothing to stop his grin from spreading. "Hence your attachment to my café."

She raised an eyebrow at that possessive pronoun.

"So, no younger men," he summed up. "Hey, if you get desperate, you said yourself Frank seems lonely. I bet he'd take you out."

She watched him carefully, and he wondered if that little fantasy of her in her teacher clothes had been visible on his face.

"I can't date someone from the café. When Frank and I break up, which we would eventually, I wouldn't be able to go there anymore. And like I told you, it's the one place where I can work in peace. Or relative peace, aside from this one obnoxious barista."

She'd insisted nothing could change between them, coerced Ash's promise to cede the entire building if this trip made her hate him, and in his desperation for the ride home, he had agreed without really thinking. But now he understood how serious she was about the pact. She had cut out old friends, an ex-boyfriend, her entire hometown. When she left, she left all at once and all the way.

"Well." His swallow took surprising effort. "In that case, I will dissuade Frank from asking you out. But I've seen rom-coms. A lot of meet-cutes happen in cafés."

"Watch a lot of rom-coms, do you?"

"Four sisters," he reminded her. "But I guess you probably don't believe in all that. True love, second chances. You're already breaking up with Frank, and you haven't even given him a first chance."

She rolled her eyes. "I don't *not* believe in love. As for second chances, I think people stay longer than they should in most relationships because they see quitting as failing. But if I didn't believe in second chances at all, I doubt we'd be sitting here."

"Because . . . ?"

"It's no secret you didn't like me in high school, and we haven't exactly had a better run the last couple months."

A pang of regret cut through him. Back then, it had been easier to let her think he barely tolerated her than to open himself to her bright smiles, knowing he'd want more of her. He ached to correct her interpretation of all those scowls.

"But here we are," she continued, steering a bite through her lake of syrup, "having a civil dinner together in the strangest diner in Texas."

She glanced back through the window, back out at the thickest, most magical snowfall he'd ever seen, and this whole situation, this strange town, seemed like time outside of time. Some entirely alternate reality where the rules didn't exist anymore. And if he tried to recount any of it to his sisters tomorrow, he knew it would sound as unreal as a dream.

"If this is really a second chance," he said, "we could actually get to know each other. For real." The line landed with an earnestness that made his ears burn, so he added, "You know, like, more embarrassing Pug Boy stories or whatever."

"I can't believe I told you that. You're disturbingly easy to talk to."

"That's a bad thing?"

She bit her lip, a flash of wariness in her eyes. It triggered his own impulse to guard himself, but he fought the urge.

"I don't usually dump on people like this," she said quietly, ducking her chin. "I guess it shows that I haven't had anyone to—"

He could *feel* how it unnerved her, to leave the abandoned confession hanging between them. Here, he was supposed to reach for their usual teasing, to lob some borderline insult back, keep them riding the safe surface of mock-hostility. But this tiny admission of hers was real, just like how she felt about her child-hood home and all that stuff about *afters*, and he didn't want to do what they always did.

She narrowed her eyes at his refusal to play along, tugged at her dress. The wide collar slipped down her shoulder again, and whatever she'd reached to say died in her throat as she followed his gaze to her bare skin. Her foot, which had been tapping for the last several minutes, came to a rest. Everything between them sharpened, the soft husk of her exhale, the little dip above her upper lip, his own loud swallow.

He should have disguised the momentary snag of his attraction to her. But that dress. What on earth was the purpose of a dress like that, long-sleeved and cozy everywhere except one delicate swath of collarbone? He couldn't tear his eyes away, despite feeling like she'd caught him stealing something.

Then, as if in some cosmic admonishment, the restaurant went dark. Through the window, the streetlamps blinked out.

The kitchen doors banged open, and a flashlight beam cut through the darkness. "Don't you dare dine and ditch," Emeline warned, her ghostly lit figure appearing behind Hazel. "Cash only."

Ash pulled more than enough from his wallet. "Keep the change."

Hazel was rewrapping her red scarf around her neck, scooting to the end of the booth, that invisible line between them neatly severed.

Just as well. Whatever had sparked was probably best to quell before they made it back to that nightmare of a room.

Hazel pushed out into the dark night but immediately spun back into his chest, knocking him back on his heels. His arm instinctively wrapped around her. As soon as he had a hold on her, though, she took a big side step, saying, "Sorry. Jesus, it's cold," and huddling into herself, giving him space he did not want. And just like that, all logic about being sensible, about not feeding into the electricity between them, went fuzzy.

"Hazel." He held his arm back out to her, chest tight from the cold and the possibility that she'd refuse him. "Come on. I'll be your human windshield."

Wind whipped her ponytail across her face. She smoothed it back with both hands, holding it there while she deliberated. Already, her teeth were chattering. She sniffed, nodded once, and ducked neatly under his arm.

« CHAPTER »
Five

She'd said too much. Way too much. Her old house? Her parents' divorce? *Pug Boy*? What was wrong with her?

And what was up with all of Ash's probing questions, that almost commanding way he'd insisted, *Tell me*, like her life story was some high-stakes thriller he couldn't put down? She hadn't even told Sylvia some of it, hadn't wanted her to feel sorry about Hazel going to bars alone or feeling overwhelmed in her program. But two minutes of Ash's undivided attention, and a river had rushed forth—one she'd dammed up for too long, apparently.

Hazel felt like a puzzle all mixed up in the box. She needed to regroup. She'd hoped to escape into a nice, long shower, but the power was out at the inn as well. The bird man at reception didn't expect it to be restored any time soon. There was a reason Hazel's father said ice was a bigger headache than snow. It made roads dangerous, but it also coated power lines, froze pipes, weighed down tree branches until they snapped, left vulnerable people stranded, sometimes for days. God, what if she and Ash got stuck here longer than one night? Already, cold seeped into the old Victorian.

They stood on opposite sides of the Lovebird Suite, both retreating into their phones in resolute avoidance. Sylvia had texted again, asking if Hazel had decided to go to her dad's, or if she wanted to crash another Delgado family Christmas. It was said in jest—*crash*, an intrusion—and Hazel knew Sylvia's gaggle of relatives would welcome her warmly, just as they had the last three Christmases, but the reminder that she wasn't actually part of Sylvia's family, that for two years Sylvia's grandmother had thought Hazel was an *orphan*, made her close her messages without replying. She'd been doing that more and more lately.

She switched on her phone's flashlight, intending to locate her bags, and the beam lit up the comforterless bed. Ash was planning to sleep on the floor, leaving her with that flimsy, lightweight blanket. That wouldn't work now.

He followed the beam of light. She could already see his breath in the air when he said, "Yeah, I know."

While Ash remade the bed, Hazel quietly panicked. They were going to sleep there. *Together.*

"*The Office*," she blurted. "I downloaded all the Christmas episodes just in case."

"Just in case ... what?"

At the time, she'd anticipated being trapped in her father's unfamiliar house with unfamiliar people, hiding out in a guest bedroom. What if their Wi-Fi was spotty? She needed *something* to pass the time. She was pleased with herself for such smart preparation until she remembered: no power, shitty laptop battery. "Never mind. My computer won't make it through one episode."

"I have a portable—" He cut off abruptly. She could hear the soles of his shoes slide across the low carpet, his knuckles pop.

"A portable what?"

"Um ... charger."

"Wait, you have—"

"I know," he said defensively. "I have a portable charger, so I don't need the outlet by your precious chair. But just think, because of me, we can watch those Christmas episodes, so really, you should thank—"

"Then why do you even need the chair?"

"I never said I needed it. I *like* it. I can see everyone when they come in. I can hear all the conversations from the counter to the back windows. It's the perfect spot."

Her flashlight was still on, lighting up a patch of the bird carpet, and she turned it on him. "So, it has nothing to do with the chair or the outlet? You just like to eavesdrop?"

He threw an arm up to block the light, and she lowered her phone. She couldn't see him well in the dark, but the general shape of him looked sheepish. Good. He remained quiet as he rummaged through his bag for the charger.

They scooted up against the headboard with her laptop between their legs. Halfway into the first episode, Hazel began to shiver, compounding the ache in her lower back from sitting in the car all afternoon. She adjusted her pillow, but it didn't help.

Ash raised his arm like he was going to put it around her. "You can—"

"What?"

"If you're cold, you can come closer. Unless your spite for me won't allow it."

"Just trying to get comfortable."

He lowered his arm back down. When he'd done the same on their walk home, wrapping his arm tightly around her shoulders to shield her from the wind, a crazy thought had latched on to her lizard brain: Why were they wearing so many damn layers of clothing that she couldn't fully absorb the contact? She *had* felt the heft of his arm, though, its comforting press like a weighted blanket. Only better because he was a *man*. When she'd tucked in closer, playing it off like she was just cold, he'd tightened his hold, like she might float away. She *could* have floated away on the giddy uprush.

"I mean . . . are you sure?" she asked.

To her surprise, he got up, tugged the comforter from under her legs, and resettled beside her, pulling the covers over them and slipping his arm behind her back. His hand found her hip over her flimsy fleece jacket, and he tugged her closer into his side. Her belly swooped at the maneuver, not exactly *manhandling* her, but not exactly *not*.

"Good?" he asked, face directed at the screen like dragging her against his side was a totally normal thing for an acquaintance to do. In a bed. In the dark.

"Uh-huh."

The episode was a blur to Hazel. At one point, the sound of her own breathing, the way it made her chest rise and fall against him in the little space she'd curled into, felt excessive and unnatural. Hell, he was going to think she had a breathing problem. Or that she was huffing him. She breathed shallowly, overcorrecting until her lungs demanded a full yawn. It did not help that she could smell the faint, crisp note of lemongrass from his shower earlier. It also did not help that the tip of her nose was freezing, and his neck would be the perfect warm place to press it.

Then, Ash laughed, giving her a new sensation to puzzle over—the gentle rumble vibrating from his chest into her body. It was doing things to her. Things that made her want to squirm closer. But *that* made her want to scoot away. So what if Ash Campbell smelled good and was like a portable heater? He was only here because he needed a ride. And not *that* kind of ride. If she made any move, she'd basically be taking advantage of him. She lifted her head from his shoulder, wondering if she'd already crossed the line.

But then, his hand was still anchored to her hip, like he might pull her into his lap at a moment's notice, and she realized, with a confusing little thrill, she . . . might not hate that.

He murmured, "Need something?"

Yes.

She shook her head. Whatever she might be feeling had nothing to do with Ash. She was just touch-starved. That was all.

He looked down at her, distracted at first, then questioning. In the glow from the laptop, his lips parted, eyes flitting down to her mouth then back up. She could kiss him. They could blame the storm, the power outage. Whatever happened in—what was this tiny town called again?—could stay here.

Except Ash wasn't the kind of guy who hooked up and moved on. The momentary satisfaction of finding out what his mouth felt like on hers, his hands on her skin, would not be free of consequences. They still had the rest of the drive tomorrow and another long drive back after Christmas.

Hazel scooted over, putting a good six inches between them. He pulled his arm from behind her without a word.

SHE CLOSED THE LAPTOP ON THE FINAL EPISODE'S CREDITS, CASTING them into almost total darkness. They'd drawn back the curtains, but with all the streetlights out and clouds blocking the moon, it didn't do much to brighten the room.

Ash let her use the bathroom first. Hazel brushed her teeth, pulled flannel pajamas over her leggings, and swapped her dress for a hoodie. At least the cold made deciding what to wear to bed with Ash—God, there was a phrase she'd never get over— a lot simpler. When she tried to wash her face with the icy water from the tap, she couldn't hold in an anguished shriek.

"Okay in there?" he called.

She toweled off quickly, opened the door, and there was the shadowy mass of him, one hand on the doorjamb. He was leaning above her, head cocked to the side, his other hand drawing up to scratch his bicep. She didn't know why that particular movement snagged her attention—she couldn't even make out much more than his silhouette—but it did, and now she wanted to put her own hands on his arms, feel the firm muscles there. *No. Nope.* She took the first distancing tactic that came to mind and pressed her freezing fingers to the side of his neck.

Ash jumped, hissing at the contact. But he caught both her wrists as she tried to dart by him. "You—" he said on a jagged exhale. "That was cold."

She held her breath. What was he going to do to her? Throw her over his shoulder? Toss her into the icy shower?

He moved his large hands so that they encased hers entirely, just . . . holding them. She felt more than saw his eyes on her face, everything dark and shadowy. He seemed to sway closer, dip his chin just so, and sirens blared in her head. Her breath caught, and her blood sang with anticipation. He was going to kiss her.

After an eternity, his face dipped lower. A warm puff of air ghosted long and slow across her knuckles. With the next breath, his lips brushed over her skin—unintended contact, she was sure, but *God.* Something turned deep in her belly, a windup toy, ratcheting tighter and tighter. "Warmer?" he murmured.

She nodded, and he let her go. Then he passed by her into the bathroom and shut the door.

"Nope," she whispered into the darkness, panic-pacing in the tight space. "Nope, nope, nope, nope, nope." She could not— *could not*—sleep next to Ash after *that.* Not with the soft, barely wet brush of his lips a permanent brand on her skin.

That's just a natural physiological response to stimuli, she reasoned. Helpfully, her brain flipped through a deep catalog of relevant research. Skin-to-skin benefits for NICU babies. Blind-barrier studies where subjects communicated emotions solely by touch. Humans couldn't directly sense wetness by touch, only discern changes in temperature and texture that the brain interpreted as wetness. The fingers were the most sensitive area of the body. People could discern two close but distinct points of contact there that, on less sensitive parts of the body, felt like one point. She had felt *both* of Ash's lips, the humidity of his warm breath . . .

When Ash emerged from the bathroom, she was already cramming the spare pillows under the comforter. "What's this?" he asked, voice laced with a smile.

"Pillow barrier," she said coolly, not at all spiraling at the thought of his mouth on her skin. "Just to be safe."

"Safe from what?" When she didn't answer, he slid into the bed and said, "Don't worry. I'm not going to spoon you."

Hazel eased into her side and pulled the comforter up under her chin. "Okay, good night, Asher."

His soft chuckle danced around her in the dark, warm and a little raspy. He had a really nice laugh, nicer somehow in the disembodying dark.

The bed jostled as he rolled one way, then back, every move rustling the blankets, making a spring creak. Hazel tugged the comforter back at every little pull as he shifted. Once he finally settled, she closed her eyes and willed herself to fall into the most sudden sleep of her life—a non-drunk blackout, and she wouldn't remember any of this tomorrow. The silence grew like a dense fog, hanging there. No hum of a heater to mask their soft breaths. The whisper of the sheets. The hollow wind stirring nothing outside, everything frozen. She could hear her own heart thrumming in her ears. She was pretty sure she could hear the tiniest taps of snow hitting the window.

"I can hear you thinking," Ash murmured, already sounding half asleep.

"I can hear *everything*," she blurted, pulling the blankets over her face. "How can quiet be so *loud*?"

"It's nice."

"I thought you loved noise," she said, throwing the blanket off and rounding to the foot of the bed. Her teeth chattered at the sudden rush of cold air, but she pushed through, yanking the end of the sheet from under the mattress.

"What are you doing?"

"I can't stand my feet feeling stuck."

He gasped. "You just expose them freely to the monsters under the bed?"

"What are you, five?" she asked, climbing back in and covering her nose with the covers.

"I'd sleep in a straitjacket if I could," he confessed.

"A bean in a burrito," she said before she could stop herself.

He laughed. "That's cute. Is that a saying?"

She rolled onto her side, hugging her knees tightly to hold in more warmth. Her back was so stiff and achy from stress, the drive, the cold. She felt a decade older than twenty-three. "How does this not bother you?"

"I need noise to focus, not to sleep."

"I didn't *think* I needed noise to sleep," she grumbled.

The bed moved subtly, and that spring whined. It wasn't until the third whine, the rhythmic jostle of the mattress, that she realized Ash was doing it on purpose. Her voice went high and tight from the intrusive sexual images that followed: Ash hovering over her, sliding her hands above her head ... "That's not helping."

She squeezed her eyes shut, felt her cheeks burn with embarrassment despite the veil of darkness. This was too much. Her chances of ever falling asleep next to Ash Campbell tonight were on par with getting struck by a meteorite—which, actually, she'd welcome at this moment.

That soft, sleepy chuckle washed over her again. "Want me to talk to you?" he asked. "Bore you to sleep?"

"No." Several long seconds dragged by. Hazel sighed. "Fine."

Ash shifted, and when he spoke, even though she was turned away from him, she could tell he'd rolled onto his side facing her. His voice was sleepy and close. The hairs on the back of her neck rose to attention. He said, "Did you know the size of an architectural space can affect how you think?"

"I'm sure it can, but explain," she said.

"Higher ceilings make people feel freer and think more abstractly. Lower ceilings make people feel grounded and focus more on fine details."

Hazel's mind pounced on the idea, imagining her cramped apartment compared to the spacious one she and Sylvia had shared, the airy five-star hotels her mother lived in compared to this intimate, busy room that, coupled with the darkness, mired Hazel in every tiny sound and movement.

Ash shifted again, and the pillow barrier pushed into her back as if he'd scooted up against it. She was grateful for the darkness hiding them from each other, though the darkness itself also sharpened *everything*. Her other senses were so heightened, they were distorting reality, the opposite of the warning on a car's side mirror—*Objects may seem closer than they are.* She felt his low voice murmuring right into her.

"There was this study," he went on, "where they made small-scale models of existing spaces and had people mentally tour the model space. They were supposed to do it for thirty minutes, but there wasn't a clock. They had to guess when the time was up. And they found that people's perception of time is directly proportional to the scale size of a space. Smaller scales make people think time is passing faster than it actually is."

If only she could climb into the model of his sister's house, then. Cut the endless night ahead of them in half. "The psychology of architecture?" she said on a yawn. "Far too interesting. Be duller."

Ash laughed. "Okay. Want to hear the starting lineup of every Major League Baseball team from the 2017 season?"

"Perfect."

HAZEL BLINKED AWAKE TO DIM MORNING LIGHT AND AN ENVELOPING warmth. All was well. Better, in fact—soft and cozy and still.

Until she spotted the unfamiliar flamingo lamp on the bedside table and remembered. The icy roads. The power outage. The bed.

Her dream flashed back—a car drifting across a center line, her reaching from the back seat to correct the steering wheel. Every last inch of her skin prickled with panic. The pillow beneath her face was too solid, too warm. In her clenched fist was smooth flannel—Ash's *shirt*, his warm stomach rising and falling with even breaths beneath it. His shallow exhale stirred the fine hairs around her face, chin pressed firmly to the crown of her head. She hadn't just breached the pillow barrier. She was *on* him, her cheek resting on his chest, her *thigh* over his *knee*.

She had to *move*. Unfisting his shirt, she initiated a controlled roll. The blankets rustled, and she froze partway, her knee hovering above his still form. When nothing happened, she resumed her stealthy escape, successfully unpeeling her body from his. All she had to do was scoot back over the pillows, and it would be like this had never happened.

"Morning." His voice was scratchy and low from sleep. "Let the record show that *I* wasn't the one who needed the wall of pillows."

Hazel flopped onto her back. "I didn't know what I was doing. I was asleep."

Grinning, Ash rolled onto his side, propping his head up in his hand. His eyes were still half closed, his features sleepy and soft. His hair fell across his forehead in unkempt waves. Reflexively, Hazel finger-combed her own mess of curls back from her face.

"I'm not complaining."

Hazel rolled her eyes. "Survivor's instinct. I was cold."

"If you say so." He dropped back against his pillow. "Power's back."

She registered the low hum of the heater and the bedside clock blinking the wrong time. Desperate for an escape from this moment, Hazel lifted her phone from the nightstand, but a text from her father wondering when he could expect her was another trap. She hadn't told him she was leaving yesterday, nor that she had gotten stuck halfway home. She swiped his message away. "We should check the roads. I assume you want to get going as soon as possible."

Ash grunted softly in agreement before rolling out of the bed. He shuffled toward the bathroom, yawning and stretching his arms over his head—like a little boy, she thought. Until he scratched at his stomach and subtly adjusted his sweatpants.

"Gonna shower unless you need to pee," he said over his shoulder.

She'd started the morning draped on top of Ash. Now, she

couldn't block the thought of *what* needed adjusting in his sweatpants. Could this morning get any weirder?

"Hazel?" He turned in the doorway to face her.

"Huh?" Her eyes dropped straight to his crotch. "Sorry. What? Sorry."

Instead of bolting into the bathroom like she'd have done if she were a guy sporting morning wood in front of a girl he wasn't dating, Ash propped both hands on his hips. "I said," he began slowly, lips quirking, fighting back a smile, "do you need to pee?"

"Nope."

"Okay." He turned, stopped, and faced her again. "This isn't because of you."

"I didn't think—" Hazel closed her eyes and breathed deeply. "Asher."

"Ash."

She chucked her pillow at him, but he ducked inside the bathroom, and it hit the door.

"I'll be quick," he called.

"Take your time," she shot back way too brightly.

Yep, this morning had gotten weirder. She flopped back and yanked the comforter over her face.

Six

"Y ou're quiet."

Only when Hazel spoke did Ash register the absolute silence they'd been driving in for the better part of an hour. She wasn't even playing any music.

They'd traveled through the pine-dense and hilly parts of the state yesterday. Now, the West Texas plains stretched for miles all around them, gentle snow-dusted slopes that would continue to flatten throughout the five-hour drive, a lone oil pump seesawing lazily in the distance. Ash's thoughts swung up and down just like it, imagining awful scenarios he might walk into at home, then reassuring himself with his mother's refrain: *Everything's fine. No need to worry.*

"Sorry," Ash said. "What do you want to talk about?"

"Anything. What are your parents like?"

Ash picked at a hole in his jeans, forcibly extracting himself from mental quicksand. "My mom used to be a painter. She teaches middle school art."

Hazel nodded at the model of Maggie's house in the back seat. "You get that from her?"

"Yeah, probably."

"And your dad?"

"He's a mail carrier."

"Is he totally swamped right now with all the holiday mail?"

Ash let his eyes go unfocused on the mesmerizing rows of snow-sprinkled winter wheat through his side window. The furrows between the plants remained uncovered, making repeating outward avenues, one stark runaway line after another across the field. "He's taking some time off this year."

"Oh, that's nice," Hazel said.

Ash swallowed. He could just tell her that his dad wasn't on vacation, that he'd fallen from a ladder while cleaning the gutters the day before Thanksgiving. Two sentences maybe.

Except he didn't want to open the door to having to say more, whether the fall was an isolated, freak accident, as his mother insisted, or a sign of deterioration, the benchmark of "normal" nudged back another yard or ten or fifty. With his father's type of MS, they never knew when a relapse would hit, how long it would last, how severe the symptoms would be, though at least he still recovered between them. Relapsing-remitting MS tended to transition to progressive MS. In that stage, his father would never regain lost neurological function or mobility. Ash wasn't particularly superstitious, but his stomach went leaden at the thought of speaking about it before he could assess his father for himself.

"We should eat there," Hazel said as they passed a sign for the next town.

"Sure."

Silence descended around them again until she said, "Did I snore last night? You seem tired."

He turned his back to the window, willing himself to stay focused on her, to stop drifting. "Do you usually snore?"

"I don't think so. Sylvia claims I talk sometimes, though."

That morning, when he'd lain perfectly still half under her, he could have sworn she'd told him to *do something*. He thought for sure she'd woken up. Before he could ask for clarification or, hell, exact instructions, she'd grabbed his shirt and pressed herself against his hip, and he'd waited for her to make another move, pressing his itching palm flat against the bed so he wouldn't sink his fingers into her soft thigh. He wouldn't touch her unless he was sure she wanted it. But her breathing had stopped abruptly, and her body went rigid. Then, she rolled away.

"Crap, did I?" Hazel asked. "Like I didn't word-vomit enough at you last night."

"Lovely image."

"How do you do that anyway?"

"Do what?"

"Jedi mind trick me into telling you things. I'm not usually so . . ."

Warmth filled his chest at the cute way she wrinkled her nose in embarrassment. "Forthcoming?" he said.

"Pathetic."

"I don't find you pathetic, Hazel. Not at all."

Taking the exit into the tiny town, she held his gaze for a few seconds before returning her focus to the road ahead. "Looks like our choices are Whataburger or mystery Tex-Mex."

"Whataburger. That place looks like it still has a smoking section."

The parking lot was riddled with potholes, and the restaurant's iconic white-and-orange stripes were in desperate need of a power wash.

"The good news is," Hazel said, climbing out, "soon we won't be stuck together, and your voodoo won't work on me anymore."

Ash wanted to admit he didn't feel *stuck* with her, but his thoughts were derailed at the door to the restaurant by a fluffy tuxedo cat snoozing below a **LOST CAT** sign. The name, Fitzwilliam, was written above a picture of the exact same cat.

"Is that the missing cat?" Hazel asked the pimply teenage boy behind the counter, thumbing over her shoulder.

"Nah," he said.

"Are you sure? It looks just like the picture."

"That's just Toast."

Hazel shot Ash one of the same private, amused glances she'd cast his way in the diner last night.

Her comment about their impending separation weighed on him as they ordered and settled into a corner booth. He'd been focused on getting home, hadn't thought beyond the drive, but now it hit him. Once they arrived, this new, cozy bubble forming around them would pop. At the café, in their regular life, he saw her nearly every day. And now that they'd had real conversations, now that he knew what her body felt like pressed against his, *now* it wouldn't be enough to pour her coffee and get a rise out of her over that stupid chair. A week with no contact at all? He didn't like it.

He gestured for her phone on the table. "Let me give you my number. We still haven't nailed down when we're leaving."

She tapped in her passcode but held on to it, side-eyeing him. "Day after Christmas. Early, preferably."

"Seriously? That soon?"

She sighed, finally handing her phone over. "I have things to do, next semester to prepare for. You knew I wouldn't want to hang around Lockett Prairie for the entire break. Don't you have to work?"

"Not until the twenty-ninth. We could leave on the twenty-eighth."

Her gaze flitted to the door, where a trucker stomped in with the tuxedo cat tucked under his beefy arm. "Found your cat," he announced.

"Every freaking day," the teenager grumbled.

Ash slid Hazel's phone back to her, smiling at her little laugh. "This is why we should have each other's number," he pointed out. "We can figure it out later."

"Fine." She stole one of his onion rings, as though it were payment for her dropping the subject.

"Help yourself," he deadpanned.

She bit into it, holding his gaze defiantly. Flaky breading caught on her lower lip. His fingers twitched, moving to brush it away, but he stopped himself. She popped the last bite into her mouth, and then her eyes fell to his milkshake.

Ash pulled the cup to the edge of the table. "Nuh-uh. You should have gotten your own."

"I don't want a whole one."

She reached slowly across the table, eyes dancing playfully, daring him to stop her. He didn't, only said as she stole his cup, "You know this isn't normal dining behavior."

With a shrug, she lowered her lips to the straw, never breaking her gaze. He knew she was just seeing what she could get away with. And as she smacked her lips in exaggerated satisfaction, he worried the answer was *everything*.

"WHAT DO YOU EVEN *DO* AT HOME?" HAZEL WANTED TO KNOW LATER, as they neared Lockett Prairie.

"Hang out with my family. See friends. Eat."

"But don't you feel different?" She was tapping the steering wheel, all nervous energy.

"Different how?"

"You're an adult now. What do you and your friends *do* together?"

"I don't know. We hang out. We drink."

"At your parents' house?"

"No." He laughed. "Some of them have their own places. Or we go to bars."

Hazel gaped at him. "There are bars in Lockett Prairie?"

"Of course."

"Where?"

"Downtown. Vintage Square."

She snorted. The joke about downtown was that the tallest building in its skyline was the four-story First National Bank, and Vintage Square, the adjacent district, was no more vintage than a fifth grader. Someone's idea of a quaint town center with a gazebo and quirky antique shops, it had been developed just over a decade ago. But the last oil boom around the same time had set off massive growth in Lockett Prairie, and new modern subdivisions and chain restaurants pulled the sprawl to the other side of town before all the colorful Vintage Square shops were even leased. Teens back then, and still, wanted brand-name clothing stores and Starbucks. Ash wasn't surprised Hazel had never spent time there.

"Do you ever run into old teachers?" she asked.

"Buying a cookie cake at H-E-B in their pajamas?" he joked.

She rolled her eyes. "Or friends you stopped calling, and now it's super uncomfortable to face them? Asking for a friend."

"Ah." He supposed Justin somewhat fit that description, but he didn't want to talk about Justin.

"Junior year," she said, glancing sidelong at him and chewing her lip, "I went around town selling candy bars for a fundraiser, and randomly, Mr. Newton answered a door without a shirt on in these tiny yellow shorts. I swear the entire universe turned inside out and never went back again. He had a happy trail and weird nipples and a *thigh* tattoo. A full-color tiger."

"Jesus." Ash grimaced. "Why would you tell me that?"

"Because that's basically what I fear about this whole trip. Some equivalent of my old math teacher's nipples around every corner."

"I have never seen any of my old teachers' nipples," he assured her, laughing into his palms. "Christ, Hazel."

"Yet," she corrected with a slap to his knee. The touch, already over before he could even register it, made him turn to the window to hide his grin.

Soon, they passed the oil fields, the sun low in the late afternoon sky and casting long shadows from all the metal pumps. Hazel wrinkled her nose. "Still stinks."

A sulfur smell hung in the air, thick and cloying. Her shoulders visibly tensed as they passed the sign welcoming them to Lockett Prairie. Ash wanted to massage the strain back out of her muscles, but she'd probably startle and run them off the road.

Minutes later, she pulled into his driveway. He opened her back door but hesitated before lifting the model from the seat. She was going to drive away, and he wouldn't see her for days.

Hazel peered back at him in the rearview mirror, blowing a curl out of her eyes.

"Listen," he said. "I know you're not thrilled to be back, but you really saved my Christmas."

She shrugged. "I had to come anyway."

"Yeah, but you didn't have to bring me. And you were right about that storm. So, if there's anything you need this week—" He felt weirdly out of breath, palms clammy, like he was asking her for a date. He cleared his throat. "If you end up needing to talk or—"

She opened her mouth, but he pressed on before she could get a word in.

"Or if you need safety in numbers rounding all the unpredictable, dangerous corners in town, you should use my number."

She turned forward in her seat and gripped the gear shift. "I'm not going to bother you while you're with your family."

He tried to suffuse his words with gravity, a force she couldn't so easily brush off. "You're not a bother to me."

In the rearview mirror, the lines between her eyebrows deepened, and he wanted to shake her for whatever uncertainty about him remained. He was home, finally, and he'd been dying to run up the walk, burst inside, and hug his family, but he needed her to get this. "At least copy me on your next proof of life to Sylvia, so I know you haven't peaced out and ditched me here."

She smiled into the mirror and gave a shrug that turned into a nod. That was enough. "Merry Christmas, Asher," she said.

"Merry Christmas, Hazel."

Seven

The house was dim and quiet. And cold. A glance at the thermostat on his way through the foyer surprised Ash. It was sixty-four degrees in here. The fireplace was empty. Two space heaters faced his father's recliner, but they weren't running. A full, squat Christmas tree stood in its usual place by the front window, its branches burdened with handmade ornaments, ribbon, and lights—unplugged.

"Hello?" he called, crossing the living room. He dropped his bag and set his model down on the kitchen counter next to a battalion of orange medicine bottles. He lifted one to read the label. As if an unfamiliar drug name would reveal anything. Something simmered in a Crock-Pot, its savory scent mixing with a hint of the cinnamon candles his mom favored during the holidays.

A door whined open down the hall. Muted footfalls approached. "Took you long enough," his mother said, voice soft with sleep, crossing to hug him.

"Where is everyone?"

She went straight to the refrigerator and began pulling out Tupperware containers. She was wearing an oversize sweater and a turtleneck underneath, jeans, and thick wool socks with slippers. "The little ones got stir crazy. Maggie and the twins took them to the park. June will be in late tonight. Says she'll Uber from the airport."

"What time? I'll pick her up."

"Eleven-thirty. Now, minestrone or meatloaf? I've got stew for dinner, but I'm sure you're hungry."

He wasn't, but he wouldn't pass up his mother's cooking. "Meatloaf." He meandered back through the living room, knelt to plug in the tree lights. The rainbow bulbs instantly illuminated the whole room. Now it felt more like home, but he couldn't ignore the cold. "Is something wrong with the furnace?"

She shook her head. "It was doing that clicking thing again. Someone's coming to fix it tomorrow."

"What clicking thing?"

"Happens every couple of years, and they have to come out and replace a switch. It's fine. It's under warranty."

"Mom, there's snow on the ground out there. You haven't been able to run the heat at all?"

"We've got the space heaters. Go turn one on if you're cold." She popped a plate of meatloaf into the microwave and ducked back into the fridge for orange juice.

"What about the fireplace?"

She raised one eyebrow at him, a warning.

"What?"

When she reached for a glass from the cabinet, he beat her to it. She had a stool that she slid around the kitchen because she was too short to reach the top shelves, but it was over by the pantry. Shaking her head at him, she took the glass and poured the juice. "I know what you're doing, and I wish you wouldn't."

"What am I doing?" he said, defensive, though he didn't know why.

"All your questions."

"All I said was what about the fireplace? You're dressed for the Arctic."

For a moment, she stared at him, stubborn. Evading. He hadn't yet attached meaning or judgments to his observations, but now, concern solidified.

"A friend of your father's had an old tree that died. He gave us a few cuts of it for firewood. They need to be chopped into smaller pieces, but of course no one around here is up for splitting wood, so it's been sitting out there." Her tone was offhand, casual.

"You can buy firewood, Mom. Go to any gas station. There was a guy less than a mile from here selling it on the side of the road."

She flicked her wrist as if shooing a fly—it was settled, no point debating it. When the microwave beeped—saved by the bell—she pulled the steaming plate of meatloaf out and set it in front of him, then nudged him back to pull a fork from the drawer he was blocking. "You know your father won't pay for firewood when he already has it for free in the backyard."

"That's ridiculous. You can't use it."

She laughed, loud and hearty. He was preaching to the choir.

"Are you guys okay for m—" He didn't finish the question. His mother, usually a broken record insisting everything was always fine, had let some truth slip in one of her late-night calls. They'd started his first year of college, but the last one had been as recent as September. On these calls, she would hit him with a barrage of questions, wanting him to keep talking about his classes, his friends, football games, girls, work, until finally, she'd go so quiet he thought she was falling asleep, only to surprise him by saying, "What if this relapse is the turning point?" Or she'd say, "Your sisters. If he can't walk at their weddings . . ." Or, "If he won't take care of himself, what am I supposed to do?"

But in all these moments of unmasked worry, the one subject she never brought up was the financial burden of his father's condition. He could dig for details about a lot of things, but money wasn't one of them.

He turned his full attention to cutting into his meatloaf, watching the steam ribbon out. Did she know about the money he'd sent his twin sisters last month? He'd made Laurel and Leanne swear, one at a time on the phone, not to tell.

"Like I said," his mother went on, "the furnace will be fixed tomorrow. For now, the portable heaters work just fine. In fact, go turn them on. The kids will be back soon."

Ash rebuttoned his coat and strode to the sliding back door. "I can chop that firewood."

She yanked him back by his sleeve. "Your food will get cold, and I won't get a word in once everyone else comes back. We haven't really talked in weeks."

"If you already know what's wrong with the furnace, I can probably fix it." He flung a hand at the dormant space heaters and the tree that he knew had at least eight strands of lights threaded through its branches. "I'm surprised you haven't tripped a breaker."

She prodded him back to the island and his food. "If you tinker with it, it could affect the warranty. We will survive until tomorrow."

"Fine, but after I eat, I'm gonna chop some wood," Ash said, shoveling in a huge bite. It was still hot, and he had to suck in air to avoid burning his mouth.

"At least wait until your dad wakes up. And please, Ash, try not to rub it in."

Ash chewed slowly.

"You know how he is."

Yeah, Ash knew too well how his father was. Rather than tell anyone that he'd fallen off the ladder and hurt himself, the guy had army crawled across the front yard and into his truck, driven himself to the hospital, and waited until the broken hip was confirmed with X-rays to finally call and tell his wife where he was.

"He's taking a nap?" Ash was fishing, and he knew she saw right through him.

"I told you, he's fine. The pain meds make him drowsy."

"I'm just—"

"You're not telling me anything I really want to know. Like, if you've got someone special—"

He groaned and shoved more food in his mouth, burning his tongue all over again.

"Fine, then tell me how your internship's going. They still planning to keep you on after you graduate?"

Ash shrugged, but not because he didn't know. It was practically a done deal. "Yeah, probably."

"The money will be better?"

"Yep."

"Then you can quit the café? All your running around, you're like a chicken with its head cut off."

His back tensed. He didn't want to talk about this. He knew the point of all this school and his internship was to start his actual career, but the café was the only thing lately that offset the isolation of living alone, working in a cubicle and freelancing remotely, delivering plans to city hall clerks who were usually too immersed in their jobs to make eye contact. He made enough money to cover his expenses without his café shifts, but he needed the security of that financial cushion. More than that, he needed to feel like a person.

He also felt possessive of his regulars. The old ladies who gossiped while they crocheted. Frank with his crosswords. Hazel in her chair. Ever since she'd come back into his life, he'd been alternately taking advantage of every small moment shared with her and trying not to get too attached.

Although . . . who was he kidding?

But, sure, he wouldn't work there forever. He knew that. He'd take the next logical steps. After all, Ash was the stable one. Maggie's husband traveled too much, sometimes to remote and dangerous places, leaving her to parent Cosette and Isabel on her own. June had bailed on college and lived with three other people in a two-bedroom east Los Angeles apartment, her audition-to-rejection rate nearly one hundred percent. The twins were typical roller coasters of teenage emotions. And his father . . . Well, Ash didn't have the full picture of his father yet, but at the very least, the man was recovering from a hip replacement. Ash lived the way he did, saving what he could, following his plan, because he expected to be responsible for all of them at some point.

"You know," his mother said, "if you had a nicer place to bring a girl back to . . ."

"Mom."

She clutched nonexistent pearls. "Don't look so scandalized. I was young once, too, you know."

Ash groaned around another bite of meatloaf before rummaging through his duffel bag for the pound of fresh coffee he'd brought from the café. His father was content with Folgers, but his mother appreciated the good stuff. When she reached for it, he held it up over her head and, with his other hand, pulled out the filter basket on the coffeemaker.

"I finished Maggie's house," he said, nodding over his shoulder at the model on the counter. A shameless diversion from the previous line of questioning, it had the added benefit of keeping her from waiting on him.

"Oh," she gasped. "It's beautiful. The kids are going to love it."

Then, as if she'd summoned them, young, joyful laughter rang out from the front walk. Boots thudded up the porch steps. His mother lifted the flaps on the box, but they wouldn't cover the top of the model, so she hoisted it off the counter, arms barely reaching all the way around, and motioned for him to intercept his sisters and nieces at the door. "I'm not done talking to you," she said before she ducked backward into the laundry room.

ASH TRIED. HE REALLY TRIED, FOR HIS MOTHER'S SAKE, TO LEAVE THINGS alone.

But after several rounds of flinging his nieces up in the air until his shoulders ached, and after Maggie and his mother took them for a bath because they were cold and muddy, and after his twin sisters left to meet up with friends, Ash found himself alone and unable to ignore everything that was wrong: the huge water spot on the hall ceiling, the weather stripping coming off the back door, the carpet peeling up from the floor outside the bathroom, which he nearly tripped over, and about twenty other ways the house was falling apart.

He chopped enough wood to start a fire, then went in search of tools. When he came in from the garage, his father was hunched over a walker, about to ease himself into a seat at the kitchen table. He stopped, turned the walker as though he meant to cross to Ash instead of sitting. "Hey, son. Where you been?"

"Dad. Hey. Wait," Ash said, distracted by the tapered gray sweatpants his father was wearing in lieu of his usual khakis. His polo shirt was tucked in—an attempt, if Ash knew his dad, to not completely let his image go. Still, the sweats and the walker threw Ash. He set down the toolbox, heart pushing up into his throat. "Let me—"

Before he took a step, his dad plopped roughly into the padded chair. "Something wrong with that old car of yours?"

Swallowing, Ash glanced at the toolbox. "I noticed the front door isn't latching right."

"The cold makes it do that."

"I know. I was just gonna . . ." His eyes fell once more to the walker. A cloth bag hung over the top bar. A pair of glasses stuck out at the top. "You finally get your eyes checked?"

"When you fall off a ladder, people think it's because you can't see or something."

"Looks like people were right." Deteriorating eyesight was a sign. Ash and his father both knew this. But all the questions Ash wanted to ask came saddled with too much baggage. Aside from the walker and sweats, his dad looked like his dad—clean-shaven, a recent haircut, good color in his cheeks.

"Come over here, wiseass. Leave my tools. Come give me a hug."

Ash did, and when he half-assed it, his father pulled him in tightly, like he had something to prove. "You're skinny. You eating?"

"Been running is all. And you're one to talk."

His father laughed and palmed Ash's head, giving it a playful shake. Ash darted out of his reach and dropped into the nearest seat. The melon baller feeling was back, hollowing out his stomach, but his father's old playfulness eased it some.

Down the hall, the bathroom door opened. Tiny feet pattered to the back of the house, high-pitched squeals followed by Maggie's stern voice calling, "Walk." Another pair of footsteps came toward them—his mother's. That these sounds, these footfalls, these nearly intangible familiarities of home, hadn't changed in his absence brought Ash another whisper of relief.

His father leaned across the table conspiratorially but didn't lower his voice. "Your mother's taking advantage of the situation." He patted his hip. "She put all the good snacks up high. Got me on this diet against my will since I can't take myself to a drive-through every once in a while."

His mom emerged then, sleeves pushed up to her elbows, drying her hands with a towel. She dropped a kiss on top of his father's head. "A girl could feel unappreciated hearing that kind of talk, you know."

Ash's father turned to catch her mouth in a kiss that went on a touch too long for Ash's comfort. He cleared his throat.

"How was the drive?" his dad asked once they pulled apart.

"Not bad." Ash rubbed his neck. "Actually, a friend was heading this way, so we came together."

"What friend?" his mother asked, her voice rising with interest.

His chest filled with breath, like he planned to deliver an important proclamation or a monologue instead of merely the name, *Hazel Elliot.* Clenching back an involuntary smile, he peered out the kitchen window and caught the bright white glow of the neighbor's Christmas lights, the bare eaves overhanging their own house. "You haven't put up your lights yet."

His mother did a poor job of pretending not to have noticed then offered a weak explanation. "I thought we'd go more minimal this year."

Ash wasn't sure if this new stance of hers was about not wanting to hurt his father's pride, or if it had to do with being stretched thin herself. She still worked, still volunteered, still cooked and cleaned, still mothered her kids and delighted in being a grandmother, and even before his father fell, she was involved in his appointments, the lifestyle measures that kept him well. It took time. Regardless of the reason, here she was, covering for him, claiming it was her own idea not to hang the lights when everyone at this table knew her personal philosophy regarding Christmas: the more, the merrier.

Cosette raced into the living room in underwear and a shirt with a pair of pajama pants on her head. She was laughing in her infectious, breathless way, running from Maggie, whose face was tight with frustration, though she fought for a patient smile. Ash liked his brother-in-law but noticed the dark circles under Maggie's eyes, how quickly her playful tone turned to exasperated with her kids, and wondered what toll Nick's frequent absences took on her.

Ash lurched after Cosette, who squealed when she saw him. He scooped her up. "Hey, monkey," he said, tickling her side. She squirmed and laughed and threw her arms around his neck.

Maggie put her hands on her hips and blew hair out of her eyes. "You've got this one?"

"Yeah, I've got this monkey." He lowered her to the floor then tugged the pants off her head and held them open for her. While she stepped into them, he said, loud enough for his parents to hear, "Hey, Cosy, I couldn't help but notice our house is the only one without any lights outside. Did you notice that?"

She looked out the window, then turned back, nodding gravely.

"Don't you think we should have lights, too?"

"Yes!"

"You think I should go out there before it gets too dark and put them up?"

"Yes, yes, yes!" she sang, twirling and clapping her hands.

"All right. If that's what you think, I trust you. I want you to come out later and inspect my work. Got it?"

She low-fived his outstretched hand hard enough to sting

before racing across the room and launching herself into his mother's lap. "Grandma, Uncle Ass is going to put up the lights!"

His mother hugged Cosette to her body then carried her toward the bedrooms. She held his gaze as she passed, a weariness there. "Uncle *Ash* thinks he's pretty clever," she said into Cosette's damp hair in a singsongy voice, "but Grandma sees right through him."

« CHAPTER »

Eight

After dropping off Ash, Hazel texted her father to say she was on her way. Immediately after sending the message, though, she panicked and added, Be there by dinner.

He replied, Can you pick up a few cans of soup? Doesn't matter what kind.

Was he seriously sending her on a grocery run after she'd driven all the way here? She made him wait a few minutes before she sent a simple K. Then, she bought a coffee and took in how different Lockett Prairie was. Entire shopping centers and manicured subdivisions where there had once been scrubby fields. A lush green golf course. A medical center, whose towers made the start of a real skyline. An AMC movie theater. The main boulevard that ran north all the way through town had been widened in places, but still the traffic was slower than ever, the sheer number of people beyond anything she remembered. It was practically a city now.

Hazel turned off her music, overwhelmed by all the new sights, a little worried she'd get herself lost. Finally, she recognized some landmarks as she reached the older part of town. Lockett Prairie High School with a new electronic marquee out front advertising the Winter Festival. The city pool. The ocean-themed Putt-Putt place where, as teenagers, her old friend, Franny Bowman, made them take the same suggestive selfies everyone else did at the clamshell hole. The old five-dollar movie theater—closed now.

She wound up in the parking lot between the library and her old elementary school. Despite the chill, a handful of kids were running around the school playground, red-cheeked and shrieking, their parents chatting on a nearby bench. The playground was smaller than she remembered. The school, too. On cold days like this, she and Franny spent recess huddled inside the log tunnel, their backs curved against opposite sides, feet propped by the other's face. Except on Thursdays, when Hazel went to Ms. Hatcher's office to draw trees and cats and nod that, yes, she understood her parents' divorce wasn't her fault.

"I have to go see Ms. Hatcher again," she'd complain to Franny, but she secretly loved those meetings. Ms. Hatcher gave her hot chocolate in a real, adult mug, and her office had a comfortable couch, warm lamps, a closet full of art supplies. Once they got the first part out of the way, where Ms. Hatcher asked if she had any new feelings or questions about her mom leaving, they talked about other things—her friends, school, concerns about how lockers would work in junior high. Hazel felt very grown-up, talking and sipping from her mug.

It wasn't until an upper-level college psych course that she understood what that school counselor had really been doing— talk therapy disguised as casual conversation and play. But it made an impact. Those Thursdays in Ms. Hatcher's office inspired Hazel to develop a volunteer program pairing struggling kids with high school mentors and led her to major in psychology and pursue her PhD. She wanted to help kids. Not in clinical practice, but more broadly, through research that would inform better interventions, programs, and frameworks.

The work she'd been doing in Sheffield's lab hadn't turned out to be quite so life-changing. She could see the importance of their study on language development in toddlers, but she'd spent all semester mindlessly transcribing audio files. All that typing felt inconsequential, the research questions not urgent enough.

What *did* feel urgent was Dr. Tate's upcoming study on children separated from their incarcerated mothers. Hazel had attended Dr. Tate's brown bag talk and followed up during her office hours with possible research questions she hadn't been able to stop thinking about. She'd read articles on innovative family reunification programs, even studied the protocols at the women's prison where the study would take place. Dr. Tate asked about her work with Sheffield and, after Hazel stumbled over a diplomatic answer, offered her a spot in her lab in the spring. "It may ruffle feathers," she'd warned, "especially with him. But if it's what you want, you have a spot with me."

Hazel couldn't bear another semester of transcription and Machiavellian lab politics when Dr. Tate was inviting her to do such important, hands-on research, but after busting her ass to impress Dr. Sheffield, it killed her to know he would interpret her request to switch advisors as wishy-washiness, a failure to follow through, or worse—a slap in his face. Never mind the awkwardness if he said no. She wasn't sure she could do it.

The kids left the playground as Hazel finished her coffee. She considered how soon her father and his family would eat dinner, when she would have to make the final drive across town. A few hours yet. She wouldn't go until she absolutely had to.

She could at least write the request to transfer, even if she wasn't ready to send it.

Ah, there wasn't much that was more pathetic than only facing her Sheffield problem when it delayed her from facing her father problem.

But Hazel had decided, and there was power in having a

plan. She trudged into the library, found a table by the window looking out at the melancholy gray winter sky, and plugged in her laptop.

HAZEL FORGOT HER FATHER'S STRANGE REQUEST FOR SOUP UNTIL SHE was already driving past the last grocery store before his neighborhood. Honestly, she reasoned, if they needed soup so badly, they could probably pay someone to fetch it for them.

She knew next to nothing about her father's fiancée, Val, only that she did a lot of philanthropy. What kind of philanthropy remained a mystery. So did her job, if she had one. Last year, out of curiosity, Hazel had looked up her father's new address, and the Google Maps street view revealed a modest mansion. Her father made decent money now that he was the lead weather reporter at his station, but not that kind of money. Hazel had come to think of Val as a rich, Stepford wife type—beautiful, blonde, and Botoxed. A divorcée whose money came from some oil baron ex-husband, maybe. She'd probably met Hazel's father at a black-tie event in Midland and been drawn in by his minor celebrity status, his camera-ready smile.

Hazel was at the gated subdivision entrance now, passing a lit sign that read **Emerald Hillcrest Estates**. Which had to be a joke since this whole area was naturally flat and full of brown, scrubby brush. She joined a line of cars waiting to get into the neighborhood and searched her sparse text history with her father for the gate code. But the gate wasn't what was holding up the line. This was a whole damn procession, past the gate, down the main road, and winding from one street to the next. It snaked toward the back of the subdivision on one side and around to the front on the other. Through the line of windshields, Hazel could see that on their way into the Estates, drivers kept passing items to a security officer.

"Happy holidays," the officer said flatly when she pulled up. "Food or clothing?"

"What?"

He bent to peer in her window. "Admission to see the Christmas lights is three cans of food or an item of winter clothing."

Ahead, it looked like Clark Griswold had decorated every house. She had to squint to take in all the lights. "My dad lives here. Dan Elliot? It's his fiancée's house, actually. Val . . ." She trailed off, blanking on Val's last name. "I can tell you the address."

"Most residents just donate something when they come home at night, given . . ." He gestured past the gate. The lights on the eaves highlighted that the homes all had two stories and some had columns, Juliet balconies, or double front doors. Even in the dark, she couldn't miss the extensive landscaping—young trees planted along the entry drive, lush winter florals surrounding the security booth, sprawling lawns with grass that was likely green in other seasons despite the arid soil—that all made good on the promise of the neighborhood's name. She got the guy's meaning. The people who lived here could stand to toss in a few cans of peas on their way back to their Estates.

"I don't live here. My dad does."

"If you don't have a donation, you'll have to pull in here and turn around."

Seriously? She gripped her open window, wincing against the wind. "I drove for two days to get here. I'm just a grad student. I don't even have three cans of food in my pantry right now."

"I need to keep the line moving."

"What if I bring you six cans next time?"

He pointed at a sign propped against the large donation bin. "It's a food *and* clothing drive."

Hazel's fingers found her chunky, red scarf. It was her favorite. "Would you take cash?"

He crossed his arms.

She unwound the long scarf from her neck and folded it over twice before reluctantly passing it through the window.

"Happy holidays," he said, already walking away.

Hazel was trapped in the line of cars for the next fifteen minutes before she finally reached her father's street and parked in front of the detached three-car garage at the end of the long driveway. Then she trudged back around to the front door and knocked, aware that everyone inching by to take in the lights could see her standing out here, waiting to be let in. Or maybe in her black leggings and jacket, she looked like she was casing the place. Impatient, she pressed the doorbell.

A muffled voice called out inside, "Come in!" For the second time in as many days, she let herself into someone else's home, feeling like an absolute intruder.

"Hello?"

"In here! Come in!" a woman called again. Something crashed to the floor around the corner. Voices overlapped with a jumble of directions—"Grab it! Stop her! Over there!" A scrambling, scratching sound, then several thumps, and another crash.

"Hazel!" Her father. "Get in here!"

Hazel dropped her bags and closed the door, breathing in the delicious aromas of baked chicken and fresh bread. The living room was spacious and tastefully maximalist with colorful patterns and plants everywhere—and a massive, toppled Christmas tree, its ornaments strewn across the tile floor. The room opened around a corner into a large kitchen, where a teenager was blocking the wide opening, half crouched, her arms wide.

Beyond her, Hazel's father held a baking pan with an entire golden-brown chicken above his head. A green leash was wrapped tightly around his legs, attached to an enormous dog.

The dog's focus darted between the chicken, a spread of sugar cookies across the center island, an overturned basket of dinner rolls on the floor, and a white cockatoo pacing and squawking on top of the refrigerator. Every time the dog lunged, Hazel's father teetered.

Val—she assumed this was Val—was rising from the floor, rubbing her elbow. Paw prints and streaks of mud ringed the island. A plant had been overturned, the pot cracked in half and soil scattered. It was clear the dog needed to be contained first, so Hazel took the baking pan from her dad's hands.

He muscled the dog into a bathroom down the hall, calling over his shoulder, "Hey, kiddo. Glad you're here."

Val was decidedly not Stepford-looking: bronze-skinned and dark-haired, the tips dip-dyed red—a match to the teenage girl's full head of festive, poinsettia red. Val's jeans and knotted T-shirt were covered in muddy paw prints. She wore kitschy Christmas lightbulb earrings, a full set of silver studs outlining the shell of one ear. When she swiped her hair out of her face, Hazel spotted her engagement ring—not an enormous diamond but a modest green gem on a simple, thin band. With a self-deprecating laugh, Val said, "Not the impression I was hoping to make, but welcome, Hazel." She approached, arms opening as if for a hug, and Hazel lifted the pan of chicken to say, *I would, but my hands are full*. Val took the pan with another laughing apology, then turned off the stove, where green beans were on the verge of charring in a skillet.

The teenager, presumably Val's daughter, stretched up on her toes below the bird on the refrigerator. "It's okay, Maddie," she cooed. It bobbed and squawked and paced some more before finally hopping onto her crooked finger. Full of disdain, she said to Val, "I told you his dumb dog would try to eat her."

His dog? Did she mean Hazel's father?

"I will talk to your brother," Val said.

Sibling bickering, then. Hazel's shoulders eased down.

She could hear her father down the hall, running water in a tub and threatening the animal in a way that sounded amused, not angry. She'd wanted a dog growing up. She'd thought when her mom left, her father might relent on a puppy, but he'd told her he didn't have the time or energy to be a good pet owner. He hadn't been wrong.

The girl petted the bird gently, both of them visibly ruffled. On her way out of the kitchen, she paused to say politely to Hazel, "Hi, by the way. I like your boots."

Val began putting cookies in Tupperware, and Hazel smoothed her palms down her thighs, willing the clammy nervousness away. She found her voice and offered to mop the floor, half expecting Val to say no, she was a guest. But Val nodded toward the closet. "That'd be great."

And so, she went from feeling like an intruder to doing chores. Hazel got to work on the trail of mud from the back door around the kitchen island and into the living room, where the Christmas tree lay. After putting their dinner in the oven to stay warm, Val swept up the broken ornaments. Eventually, Hazel's father took the now-clean dog to a bedroom then returned to help Val right the tree. It was artificial, and its center pole had cracked, so they disassembled it instead.

When they finally sat down to eat dinner, a boy arrived. He looked about the same age as Dr. Sheffield's students, baby-faced but confident, on the cusp of adulthood. He wore a Lockett Prairie High marching band sweatshirt. "Sorry I'm late," he said, breathless. "I forgot the cans. The guy at the gate was a dick."

"Raf," Val warned.

"You were supposed to be back an hour ago to walk your stupid dog," the girl said. "He nearly killed Maddie."

"Lucy," Val said. Then she straightened. "Oh, we didn't do introductions. Hazel, these are my kids, Rafael and Lucia. I'm Valentina, but everyone calls me Val."

Both the kids corrected her with the nicknames she'd already called them, Raf and Lucy.

"Just Hazel," she said. "No nickname."

The name her father used to call her, Hazelnut, bubbled up. Was he thinking of it, too? Because of all the chaos, they hadn't even hugged when she'd arrived, and now he was seated two chairs away. His hair was shorter, and he'd stopped dyeing it. He'd told her he was going to when she last saw him at graduation in May, self-consciously chuckling about his vanity, and new gray streaks cut through his nearly-black brown hair. He looked older, but relaxed, comfortable in his skin, in this house.

During dinner, everyone interjected and talked over each other but somehow maintained the various threads of conversation, passing side dishes around. Hazel lacked instincts for how and when to speak up herself, like entering a game of double Dutch. She worried if she did, everything would grind to a halt.

Then, like it was a standard procedure, they all pulled up calendars on their phones to discuss their schedules. Lucy had extra rehearsals for a choir concert. Raf was starting a dual credit mini-mester at Midland Community College. Val was taking cookies to a nursing home. Hazel's father had his last day of work at the station until two days after the wedding.

"You have Christmas off? Like, *off* off?" Hazel asked.

He nodded, but his gaze dropped. He took great care to stab several green beans with his fork before removing them and grabbing a bite of chicken instead. Maybe he knew what she was thinking. That he'd never once taken *days* off during the holidays. If he had Christmas morning off, he worked Christmas Eve. Even then, an ice storm within a hundred-mile radius could pull him out into the field all day for a spaced-out string of two-minute updates, or to the station to pore over models and reports. Rather than use the single dad card, he'd left her with babysitters or, once she was old enough, alone. On *Christmas*.

Hazel supposed some rookie reporter got those holiday assignments now.

"That's great," she said, quiet.

Dinner lasted a full hour. Afterward, she felt like she'd extroverted for a whole day, so when Val suggested they help her take her things to her room, she sagged a little at the impending relief of being alone.

The guest room was anything but the HGTV-neutral, bland one she expected. Opposite the door was an enormous photo print of a foggy, tree-dense mountainside. The wall color was moody, dark teal, which should have made the space feel small but somehow had the opposite effect, like a bottomless well. The L-shaped room featured a nook with a window seat and leafy plants. Her eyes flitted from one detail to the next, unable to take it all in at once—a vintage library catalog in the corner, a white desk topped with a set of mint-colored hardback reference books, eight framed illustrations evoking inkblot tests but with vibrant colors and textures, a bright yellow typewriter. The same maximalist aesthetic as the rest of the house, but moodier and somehow exactly her taste.

Then, she saw the framed photo of herself at about ten, doing her best impression of a French sophisticate, her hair tucked under a forest-green beret so it looked cropped, a pale pink scarf knotted at her throat, pencil propped between her fingers like a long cigarette. She cringed at the thought of anyone seeing, let alone framing, this photo. Wasn't this a guest room?

"We should let you get settled," Val said.

Her father, who hadn't quite made it all the way into the room, drummed his fingers on the doorframe and stepped back to let Val squeeze out. He turned his shoulders but not his feet after his fiancée. They still hadn't hugged. Was he waiting for Hazel to reach for him? Most fathers didn't need their daughters to reach out first, did they?

"The room is really great," she said.

His chin dipped in acknowledgment. "Okay. Holler if you need anything."

Holler if she needed anything? He didn't crack a smile or give any indication that he'd said this with irony.

He did, however, step into the room and bend to loop his arms around her. It wasn't a tight embrace, but for the few seconds of contact, Hazel's senses were soothed with the hard-wired, familiar scents of Carmex and his clean aftershave, the light scratch of his short hair against her cheek, and the exact way that she fit with him, always small, always safe. She brought her hands up to loosely clutch his arms until he cleared his throat and stepped back.

With a rap of his knuckle against the door, he asked, "Open or closed?"

"Closed."

« CHAPTER »

Nine

Hazel awoke to the smell of bacon and a bright, midmorning beam of light spilling across her face. Voices drifted down the long hall. She burrowed deeper into the most comfortable bed she'd ever slept in and allowed herself another five minutes before she got up.

Her father was scooping scrambled eggs onto everyone's plates at the table. A fifth plate already waited for her. "She's alive," he said. The old familiar greeting stopped her short at the threshold of the kitchen.

She took the seat that she guessed was hers for the week. "I didn't mean to sleep so late."

"It's a great bed, right?" Val said. "Our room had one in Italy, and I'd never slept so well in my whole life. I had to order them for all our bedrooms."

Next to Hazel, Lucy, immersed in her cell phone, let out a groan. "Children present. No talk of beds."

"Luce is right. It's two things on the list," Raf said around a mouthful of eggs.

Hazel looked to her father. "List?" She would not ask the bigger question: *When did you go to Italy?*

Lucy leaned in. "All the topics they're not allowed to talk about. Sleeping. Kissing. Italy. Any description of food that's remotely sexual."

Hazel's cheeks warmed. "Oh."

On his way back to his seat, her father bent and pressed a kiss to Val's cheek. "We shouldn't traumatize the children."

Hazel searched her memory for a scene like this from her childhood and came up empty. For one thing, her dad had missed a lot of meals. His schedule was all over the place, different from one week to the next. But he and her mom weren't a kiss-hello-and-goodbye couple, not even in Hazel's earliest memories. She'd always assumed that was just their preference. But maybe this was what her father looked like in a happy relationship. Hazel had no other points of comparison because he'd never dated after her mom left, at least not while she still lived at home.

"Hazel?" her father said like she'd missed a question.

"Huh?"

"Did you want to go with Val today?"

"After the nursing home, we could do something fun. Manicures?" Val suggested. Hazel thought she kept her face neutral at this, but when she looked from Val to Lucy, their matching hair dye jobs, Val quickly amended, "Or grab coffee, browse a bookstore?"

"I'm at the station late," her father said, "but y'all should go out to eat, too, after Lucy's rehearsal."

It was one thing to have to act like she was part of this family when he was around, but it was a whole different situation to have to do it when her dad wasn't even there. What would they talk about? What would be the point? "I, um, might have plans today, actually."

"Oh." Her father set his fork down. "All day?"

"Maybe? I don't know. I'm waiting to hear from some friends." She couldn't look at him, just scraped butter across every last bit of the craggy surface of her toast.

"Who?"

She could feel red splotches blooming in her neck and cheeks. "Well, there's Franny, obviously. And . . . Justin."

"Justin, huh? You two are still close?"

"We're . . . friendly." *Another lie.* "He's working for his dad now," she added, grateful Ash had given her one tidbit.

She risked a glance. Her father was watching her intently. He didn't seem outright suspicious, but he clearly had an expectation of how this visit should go, despite them never discussing it, and that expectation wasn't her having her own plans, her own priorities.

"Sorry." Her voice came out harsh, verging on sarcastic. Instantly, she wanted to take it back. She wasn't even angry. Anger required feelings, and hers were not that easily tapped, let alone hurt.

Although, if she really did have plans with old friends, could he honestly hold that against her? He'd asked her to come and assumed she'd be able—would *want*—to slip into the rhythms of his new family. But *he* hadn't been like this before, either. For them, he was so *here*. He took holidays. He cooked and joked and let them have pets. He didn't, for example, come home from work late, struggle to come up with a few questions about their days, and shut himself in a bedroom full of unpacked boxes.

"I figured you'd be working," she said carefully. "You didn't say I would be needed for anything right away."

Her father smiled tightly. "I suppose we have the whole week. Maybe you can keep a few windows open? Lucy's concert, for one. On Thursday at Winter Fest. And the station holiday party on Friday."

The station party, like she should know about it.

"The wedding on Saturday," he added, "and Christmas on Sunday, obviously."

She forced a bright smile. "Absolutely."

HAZEL MADE SURE TO LEAVE THE HOUSE BEFORE VAL TO SELL THE LIE
of having plans. Then she parked at a McDonald's and ate luke-
warm chicken nuggets. Despite what she'd told her father, she
definitely would not be calling up Justin. Or Franny.

She wished instead that she'd brought Sylvia. The thought
hadn't even crossed her mind. Sylvia had holiday plans, and it
wouldn't have made sense at all, but Hazel also knew, if she'd
asked, Sylvia would have come. And after growing up in Houston, she would have found a million things to marvel at in a
town that felt to Hazel like a too-small coat. She would have
demanded a trip to the sad windmill museum that Hazel went
to for *three* school field trips, would have bought the souvenir
shirt that matched the welcome sign: **Unlock Your Dreams
in Lockett Prairie**.

Hazel supposed she could kill a few hours at the library again.
Or go see a movie, a luxury she hadn't had time for in months.
But guilt wriggled in. Maybe it wouldn't have been that awkward
to join Val at the nursing home. She didn't know why, given all
the other ways she bent over backward to please people, pleasing
her father felt impossible today. And because of that, she'd boxed
herself into a corner, nowhere to go, nothing to do.

She listened to a podcast about brain science until she finished her food and the car got cold. Again, she thought of the
study Ash had mentioned about time passing more quickly in
small-scaled spaces and wished to crawl into one of his models
for the afternoon.

Yesterday, he'd told her to use his number. Just being polite,
of course. He was *so* excited to see his family, he wouldn't want
to leave them. But he'd really been quite insistent.

She wouldn't use it. Just to see, though, she thumbed through
the A's in her contacts. And was surprisingly let down when his

name wasn't there. She checked the C's for Campbell. Nothing. She started again from the top and scrolled until finally she found *JUST ASH* in all caps. And then, forgetting entirely that she didn't intend to use his number, she started texting.

HAZEL: You have no idea how long it took me to find your number, Just Ash.

HAZEL: I'm sure you're busy with your family, so if you tell me to get lost it won't hurt my feelings and we can pretend this never happened, but do you want to hang out?

HAZEL: Again, you can say no. In fact, I'm expecting you to. Or nothing at all since you're probably with your 17 sisters and nieces and not checking your phone every 5 minutes.

Cool. She sounded unhinged. Hazel searched "how to un-send texts" on the off chance this was possible. It wasn't.

HAZEL: Never mind. Please strike these messages from the official record, thanks.

JUST ASH: Come pick me up.

JUST ASH: You still there?

HAZEL: Not if you're making fun of me.

JUST ASH: Cross my heart. My mom is kicking me out of the house.

HAZEL: See you in 10, Asher.

———

ASH WAS ON THE PORCH WITH A BLONDE ABOUT THEIR AGE, WHO WAS huddled under a big quilt, holding a coffee mug and a cigarette. A sister? The girl perked up at the sight of Hazel's car and moved to come down the walk, but Ash blocked her. They exchanged some words. He plucked her cigarette and stubbed it out on the cement, and she flicked his ear. He jogged over, and just as he opened Hazel's passenger door, the girl drawled suggestively, "Hey, Ash's *friend*."

"Shut up," he called back before dropping into the seat.

"Why did she say it like that?"

"No reason. Please, go."

"Was that June?" she asked.

"That was June."

"She's so grown up. And pretty."

"Pretty annoying," he muttered, but as they left his block, he angled his body toward her, a pleased smile spreading. "So, what happened? Not a fan of the new fam?"

Hazel rolled her eyes. "I could ask you the same thing. How'd you get kicked out already?"

He unbuttoned his jacket. It was different than the gray peacoat he wore over his business clothes and the hoodie he'd worn on the trip here. This one was faded denim with a faux shearling collar. On anyone else, she'd think it was an ironic nod, nostalgic-trendy like corduroy overalls or a fanny pack. On Ash, though, it felt earnest.

"Where's your scarf?" he asked.

Hazel touched her bare throat then curled her fingers into air quotes. "I 'donated' it." She explained about the price of admission into her father's neighborhood.

Ash shook his head, seemingly as disappointed by the loss as she was. Hazel appreciated that. After a few minutes of silence, he said, "I may have exaggerated about getting kicked out."

"You just wanted to see me, huh?"

"My mom told me if I couldn't stop fixing things, I had to leave."

"What were you fixing?"

He blew out a long breath and turned to the side window with a shrug. "It's an old house. I was just trying to— I wasn't saying they weren't keeping up with things, or if they weren't that they didn't have a good reason to let stuff slide."

"What reason?"

His face whipped back around, and for a second, he seemed confused by the question. His fingers tapped on his thigh. "Just, uh, they've been busy. Holiday errands. Maggie's kids."

Hazel didn't buy that answer, not for a second.

"So, where are we going?" he asked.

She'd given it some thought on the way over. Guilt had fully settled into the space below her ribs, every breath pushing against the mass of it. Guilt and worry that she was coming across like a disgruntled, displaced daughter when that couldn't have been further from the truth. She needed to show her father just how *fine* she was. They were clearly all under the illusion that she needed to be included. So, to get through the week without them resorting to team-building activities and trust falls, she decided to perform a decisive, preemptive gesture of good will.

"We're going to get a Christmas tree."

"Okay," Ash drawled, clearly not expecting this.

"The one at my dad's was fake, which is just sad. Then there was this whole thing with the dog, and it broke."

"They sent you for a replacement?"

"It's a gift. Also, an excuse to leave." She pressed her palm to her chest. "But it's from the heart."

Ash laughed. "Presents instead of your presence. Interesting strategy."

When he put it this way, it didn't sound like such a grand gesture. But she had already made up her mind. She was not going back there without a tree.

"You're in luck," he said. "I worked at a Christmas tree lot one winter. I'm an expert."

"Of course you are."

"SO WHAT ARE WE LOOKING FOR?" ASH ASKED, FOLLOWING HER INTO the pop-up tree lot at the outer edge of a shopping center parking lot. "Wait, let me guess. You're a scrappy, *Charlie Brown Christmas* kind of girl."

She peeked over her shoulder at him as he pulled his sweatshirt hood out of his jacket and over his messy hair. It struck her then that this Ash—Home Ash—was different from Café Ash, both the one who stole her chair and wore whimsical ties and the one who charmed people behind the counter. He wore worn jeans, shitkickers, and the denim jacket, and she'd bet there wasn't a drop of product in his hair. He looked tousled, simultaneously softer and rougher around the edges. Cozy.

He reached for a scraggly, four-foot tree. It shed half its needles when he tapped its trunk against the asphalt.

"A pity tree?" She hugged her arms around herself. She'd opted for her favorite thick cardigan instead of a warm coat because the elbow patches matched her ankle boots, but without her scarf or a hat, the chill permeated straight to her bones. She headed for an aisle between two rows of trees, hoping they would block the wind.

He leaned the sad tree back into its slot. "All right. Not a pity tree."

"I want something tall and full." She spread her hands apart to indicate height then width. "Straight. With a good top. Something . . ." She thought of the enormous living room where the tree would stand, the shiny tiles she'd mopped last night. "Something stately. A great, big, thick—"

Behind her, Ash choked on a laugh. He waved off her confusion at the interruption. "Sorry. Go on." But his smile broke across his face again, wider, and his shoulders shook with laughter.

Realization burned through her. "Oh my God, Asher. I'm talking about a *tree*."

"Nothing wrong with knowing what you want. Something stately it is."

"That's not what I meant. I'm not a snob about—I mean, I wouldn't automatically reject a—" She gestured at him vaguely.

Ash clutched his chest. "Hold up. I'm not a pity tree."

"I didn't mean you, specifically. I have no idea what you've got going on—"

"It's not *A Charlie Brown Christmas* in there, I can tell you that."

A vision of him in the Lovebird Suite, his sweatpants tented by his morning erection, made Hazel cover her face with her freezing hands. "Oh my God. Why are you like this?"

"What am I like?" When she uncovered her eyes, he was still smiling, his dark eyes burning amber.

She rubbed the waxy needles of a nearby branch between her thumb and forefinger. "What's this one?"

He watched her for a moment, refusing to follow her subject change. What did he want her to say? Between the models and his ambitious workload and the music he'd only ever played because the CD was jammed, she didn't *know* what he was like, not like she thought she did. He reminded her of a magic trick she'd seen as a kid: a book with totally blank pages, suddenly filled with black-and-white images, then colorful ones with two simple waves of a wand.

He licked his lips, made her wait before his gaze finally shifted over her shoulder. "That's a Leyland cypress. Nice shape. Doesn't really have a smell."

Hazel leaned in and breathed deeply. He was right. It had no scent. She faced the opposite line of trees. Ash hadn't been totally off the mark about the kind of tree she would have chosen for herself—small and unique. But for her peace offering she needed something impressive.

"You're the expert," she said. "What's the most classic tree?"

"Can't go wrong with a Douglas fir." He pointed at the end of the walkway, where a batch of trees leaned against the outer wall of the lot.

She could smell the sweet, earthy aroma before she reached them. Yes, this was the Christmas smell she was after.

"They've got sturdy branches. Good for decorating."

"This is more like it." She muscled one out and stood it up. But it barely surpassed Ash's height, maybe six and a half feet. She leaned it back and righted another, then another. "They're all short."

The lot wasn't as full as the ones she remembered wandering through as a kid, tugging her dad along behind her. But maybe that was because everything looked bigger from a kid's vantage point. Then again, they also usually got their tree well before Christmas.

Ash confirmed her suspicion. "The best ones go early."

"So, these are all the leftover trees no one wanted?"

"No," he said slowly then again with more confidence. "No, sometimes the good ones are hiding behind all the basic, traditional trees that everyone picks first."

"You just said the best ones go early."

"I meant the ones everyone thinks are best."

She squinted, blinded by the midday sun behind him. "Are you saying there's some weird, artsy, emo tree with quiet, overlooked beauty tucked in a corner? Hair in a bun, dorky glasses?"

He grinned. "Yes."

"I don't know, that still sounds like a pity tree to me."

They wandered to the other side of the lot, where a teenager emerged from a trailer and asked if he could help them find anything in a tone that begged them to say no.

"We're looking for a tree that would be into Sylvia Plath," Hazel said.

"Actually—" Ash pointed at a menu on the side of the trailer and pulled his wallet out of his back pocket.

She laughed. Even his wallet was duct-taped.

"Can we get a couple hot chocolates?"

"You don't have to pay," she said, remembering his tight finances. "This is my errand I dragged you on."

He passed over a five, and the boy ducked back into the trailer.

"It's cold," Ash said simply, gesturing at her nose, the frigid tip of which she assumed looked like Rudolph's. "And I didn't get dragged here. I wanted to come."

"Right." She followed him to a nearby picnic table and sat across from him. "For a guy who was so desperate to get home, you have to admit it's a little weird you're not there."

"I told you. My mom kicked me out."

Hazel narrowed her eyes. He'd already walked that back. "You were fixing things," she prompted.

Ash drummed his fingers on the table, looking longingly at the trailer. When the teenager didn't immediately emerge with their drinks, he relented. "My dad is a big DIY guy. All my life, he's made me help fix things. Once, he made me help replace our entire roof in the middle of summer. But now, I'm supposed to do nothing while all these things are clearly—" He shook his head, pursing his lips.

"Broken?"

He eyed her, a silent debate warring across his features. She wanted to pounce, to say, *Tell me.* She'd revealed all kinds of personal things to him already. It was only fair. She sat up straighter, ready to say as much, when the kid came out with their drinks.

"Do you remember that party freshman year?" Ash asked, removing the lid to let it cool. "Right after the dorms opened but before classes started."

"Vaguely." Hazel's nerves hummed to life. "Why?"

"You had cut your hair since graduation, and you looked really..." He trailed off, scratching one of his thick eyebrows. "It was just off your shoulders."

"Yeah, I did the cliché girl thing and chopped off half my hair after Justin and I broke up."

One corner of his mouth tipped up. "Part of your 'fresh start,'" he recalled.

She crossed her arms. "I didn't invent wanting a fresh start in college."

"Didn't say you did."

"Then what are you saying?"

"I'm saying—" He laughed into his palms, raked both hands through his hair. "Why do you always assume I'm picking on you?"

She shrugged and shook her head like, *Aren't you?*

A deep trench formed between his eyebrows. "This is exactly my point."

"*What* is your point?"

"Nothing."

"No. Go on." She learned her elbows on the table. "You saw me at the party, and I looked like Audrey Tautou in *Amélie*— that was my hair inspiration—and then what? Something happened?" A lot had happened at that party, and while she couldn't remember all the specifics, the bits and pieces that stuck had *really* stuck. She picked at a splinter on the edge of the table.

"You were *real* happy to see me," he said with a dark laugh.

"Did you think I would be?"

Ash peered past her into the trees, shrugged.

Tensing under his silence, Hazel said, "In my defense, someone had spilled beer on my shoes, Sylvia disappeared five minutes into that party, and I dropped my ID through the patio slats, so *you* turning up right then was just—"

"'Shit icing on a shit cake,'" he quoted.

Hazel winced.

"It was also the first time you called me *Asher*."

"I was drunk."

He laughed. "Oh, I know."

The few times she'd tagged along with Justin and his friends to parties in high school, she'd easily declined every cup and joint passed her way. But everything had changed that summer before college. Old Hazel had been too *passive*. Things wouldn't happen *to* College Hazel. *She* would make things happen.

So, she'd tried a beer, just to see if she liked it. But the noise and congestion inside the apartment sent her out for fresh air, only for the soupy August heat to plaster her short hair to her forehead and neck. Bored and hot but determined to make it at least one hour at her first college party, she drank more. When Ash stepped through the sliding patio door, the extra syllable tacked itself onto his name. But it also sounded weirdly right. *Asher*. An uptight chauffeur, judging her in his rearview mirror.

"When I saw you," he said across the picnic table, pressing a palm to his chest, "I thought, *Thank God I don't have to recite my hometown for the hundredth time*. But *you*. You were like, 'Just fucking great. Forty thousand students at this school, and you had to come to *this* fucking party?'"

"I didn't swear that much."

"Hazel, you swore like a damn sailor from the moment you

saw me. At one point, you turned to some random girls on the lawn, shouted, 'Hey, this guy is the fucking worst' and got them all to boo me."

"Well!" she said, defensive. Then . . . nothing because she had no good argument or explanation for herself. She *had* been annoyed to see him. Her first college party had seemed like a great opportunity to try on the new, improved version of herself. But a new haircut and a borrowed skimpy top from the roommate she barely knew hadn't automatically banished Hazel's old ways. When that guy spilled beer on her, *she'd* apologized to *him*. And instead of drunkenly yelling the school fight song or making out on the lawn like the rest of the partygoers, she'd spent her time texting her lost roommate, fretting about how to replace her dropped ID, regretting her new ponytail-resistant haircut, and slapping futilely at mosquitoes.

Ash's arrival was a cosmic taunt, a barb from the past hooking her. He'd lurked in the periphery of her relationship with Justin, and now, everything she'd spent the summer trying to forget slammed back into focus. Justin had lied to her about losing his baseball scholarship, let her think they were still coming to college as a couple. So, she'd fallen that last bit in love with him, *slept* with him, only to find out at graduation, when the principal announced everyone's post-commencement plans, that he'd landed a walk-on spot with a school in Missouri she'd never heard of. And that was that. Her first love: over. He'd expected her to still join him at a graduation party that night and to "make the most" of summer before they parted ways, but she'd ended it in the parking lot, not yet free from her scratchy commencement robe.

"You wanted your fresh start," Ash said, turning his hot chocolate cup in circles on the picnic table, "and apparently, you couldn't do it with me around."

"I told you. I didn't keep in touch with anyone after I left home. I wanted to be different in college. I thought it would be easier without any ties to people who knew me before. Especially someone who never liked me to begin with."

He nodded, thoughtful. "I'm not sure when you decided that."

"What?"

"That I didn't like you."

Hazel didn't realize she had a guffaw in her repertoire, but welp, there it was. "You literally used to groan when you saw me coming. When Justin started talking about us all going to college together, you acted like I was some parasite who'd glommed on to your best friend, like you dreaded having to put up with me for a minute longer. I got early admission, for Christ's sake—*before* we'd even started dating. I might have stupidly believed we'd last, but I was never just following him."

"I didn't think you were a *parasite*."

"Once, I overheard you ask what he saw in me because I wasn't even his type."

Ash's leg bounced erratically under the table. He didn't speak, apparently had no defense on that point.

"Yeah, that was pretty harsh," she said.

"You *weren't*." He shook his head, nostrils flaring and jaw clenching. Finally, he looked directly at her, his dark eyes stormy. "You were sweet and smart, and you didn't care about baseball or being cool or any of the dumb shit that whole crowd was into. You cared about school and those kids you mentored. You planned that whole sports day for them."

Hazel nearly interrupted to point out that at that event—a field day for little kids with tough upbringings, which she'd convinced the baseball coach to make a mandatory volunteer day for his team—Ash had bailed early. She'd even thought he was kind of cute at first. The other guys had shown up hungover and tired, complaining about giving up their Saturday morning, but he'd seemed excited to meet the kids and amused by her whistle-blowing to rally the lethargic group. Fifteen minutes into the morning, though, he was glued to his phone. Then he walked out without an explanation. Justin had been the one to horse around, his energy and attention for the kids boundless. Both had made a strong impression.

"You weren't Justin's type," Ash insisted, "but that wasn't criticism, just fact."

He lifted a stern eyebrow, as though asking if she was getting this statement through her stubborn head, and she swallowed, feeling weirdly chastened.

For the first time, she wondered if Ash and Justin were still close. After the breakup, Hazel had left Lockett Prairie earlier than planned to visit her mom in New York, wanting to nurse her broken heart as far away as possible, but rumors of a fight between the guys had reached her. She'd never learned the specifics or whether they'd made up. She hadn't cared at the time.

"What," she asked quietly, "does any of this have to do with that party?"

"Because for a minute that night, I thought—" He cupped his hot chocolate carefully. "For just a minute," he repeated, cautious, "it was . . . fun."

"What was fun?"

"Talking."

"*Us* talking was fun?"

He laughed. "I mean, yeah, at first you were pissed I was there. You wanted to divide campus into your side and mine so we'd never cross paths again. Which, come to think of it, is kind of a recurring theme for you."

She glared at him.

"But then . . . I don't know. It shifted."

Hazel racked her brain for details from that night. Sweat.

Mosquitoes. Grit on her knees from kneeling on the patio. The drunk, floaty feeling that rolled through her just as Ash opened that sliding door. And later, after she laid into him for reasons that amounted to *she was drunk* and he was a symbolic extension of her ex, he'd egged her on.

"What else?" he'd challenged, a chuckle shaking his shoulders. "What else is wrong with me, Hazel?"

"You're flaky. You have terrible taste in music. You crack your knuckles constantly. You don't take anything seriously—school, baseball, anything. The way you drive is annoying."

"The way I *drive*?"

"With your wrist flopped over the top of the steering wheel like, 'Oh, I'm so cool.'"

"Didn't realize you cared so much where I put my hands."

"I don't— That's not—" She rolled her eyes. "I don't know why I'm talking to you anyway. College is supposed to be my fresh start."

"Fresh start?"

"You know, clean slate. Hazel 2.0."

"And what exactly is going to be so different about you, other than your hair?"

She'd heard it as more criticism—her *wild* hair that she'd expected to look so sophisticated but, in actuality, curled up in all the wrong places and puffed out like a poodle in the humidity. "Everything."

"Specifically, though. Is there a list?"

She cocked out a hip, refused to let him belittle her plan. "One: I drink now."

"I see that."

"And B: I took a self-defense class over the summer, so I know, like, three different ways to incapacitate you."

"I'd like to see that."

"I'm sure you would."

"What else?"

"Yoga."

"Show me some yoga."

She didn't hesitate. She straightened abruptly, slapped her palms together high over her head, and tucked one beer-soaked flat to the inside of her other knee. "Tree," she announced, like he should be very impressed. She only bobbled a little, covered it up by stepping back into a deep lunge. "Warrior one."

"Incredible," he said, helping with a hand around her bicep when she had to pull on the railing to get back up. "You might also be a little drunk there, warrior."

When she looked up to tell him he could let her go, *thank you very much*, his face was much closer than expected—his *body* was much closer than expected—and he was *smiling*. Not smirking, not sneering, but actually smiling at her.

It hit her like sun breaking through blue-black West Texas thunderclouds—a thought so ridiculous she knew it meant she was drunk. At this proximity, she could see little gold flecks in his dark brown eyes. She'd raised her hand to touch the white scar cutting through one of his thick eyebrows but stopped herself when his gaze caught her hand hovering there. Still, she let him take more of her weight as that heady, swimmy feeling rolled over her again.

"And you can't do all of this fresh start stuff," he said, licking his lips, "if I'm around? Who knew I had so much influence?"

Hazel ran her tongue over her lips, too. She nodded very seriously, raised her beer—third? fourth?—for another sip.

"Did it ever occur to you," he murmured, his breath laced with cinnamon gum, "that if you can change, I could also change?"

That had *not* occurred to her. And between the beer and his sudden proximity, she felt like she was bobbing, rudderless, pulled by some unseen tide.

Grasping for an anchor, she found Justin. His *best* friend. "You know," she said, shuffling back against the patio rail and wiping a bead of sweat from her neck, "he screwed you, too. Justin? You guys were supposed to be roommates."

Ash shrugged it off. "Actually, I ended up with a friend from this baseball camp I went to a few years back."

"You were able to pick your roommate that late?"

"It wasn't that—" He stopped, turned to look out into the dark lawn, drummed his fingers on the rail.

"They sent roommate assignments back in June. How did you change yours?"

He didn't face her as he said, "I changed it in April."

Even though she was drunk, she'd gone over the timeline enough to have absolute clarity on at least this one thing. At the beginning of April, Justin had pitched a bad game, started a fight on the field. That night, he'd told her he loved her—but *not* that the college coach in the stands had rescinded his scholarship and spot on the team. Two weeks later, after prom, she'd slept with him. Then, for five more weeks, he'd kept quiet, let her look up the best dining hall, avoided her questions about his course load and which parking lot he planned to get a permit for, all the while knowing they weren't going to go to college as a couple.

And if Ash had had time to request a different roommate—

"You *knew*?"

Ash squeezed the back of his neck. "Hazel—"

"So, the whole time I was going on and on about doing our laundry on weekends and riding home together at Thanksgiving, you *knew* he wasn't coming to school here. God, you must have thought I was so stupid. You spent all those weeks just, what, laughing at me?"

"I wasn't *laughing* at—"

"Bro code?" she went on. "That's what that was?"

"No." He reached for her, but she pulled away.

Only, the patio was beginning to tilt, and she stumbled. He caught her by the waist before she could face-plant off the step down to the lawn. "Hazel, I think you're pretty drunk."

Hazel wasn't yet versed in the transitions from tipsy to fun drunk to not-fun drunk, but she supposed this seesawing feeling meant she'd gone too far. But she'd be damned if Ash Campbell was right about anything, drunk or not. She shoved him. "I'm fine. Leave me alone."

He'd raised his palms in surrender and backed off. "Just— Do you have a ride home?"

"That's not your concern." She power walked across the small lawn, into the parking lot.

He followed, and when she stumbled again, he grabbed her elbow. "Will you just stop?"

"Why?"

"Because you're headed directly for the train tracks."

"Now you *care* about me?"

"Christ, Hazel. Yeah, I care if you stumble in front of a train."

They stopped under the orange glow of a halogen light, moths circling frantically above them. Cicadas shrieked in a continuous chorus. Hazel wanted to join them, just scream at Ash until he went away.

"*Why?* Because we went to high school together? College is for *new* experiences, not old baggage, Asher. There are, like, twenty thousand other girls here for you to bother. Just because we're from the same nowhere town doesn't mean we have to be anything to each other."

"Fine, but I'm not leaving you out here."

"Oh my God. Why? What is this? First, you hate me. Now, you can't leave me alone?"

"Would you please just let me drive you home?"

Hazel laughed in his face. "What, like, to hook up? *This*"— she waved a hand between them—"is *never* going to happen."

His face twisted. "You think I'm *hitting* on you?" The vehemence in his voice pressed a bruise deep inside her, even though she couldn't have made her own feelings any clearer. She was either going to cry or vomit and couldn't focus past breathing down the sickening lump in her throat.

Only later did she piece together that he'd taken her phone, texted Sylvia until she came, and ordered them a ride back to their dorm.

Now, across the picnic table, the chilly December breeze carrying the sweet, earthy scent of Christmas trees blew a loose curl across Ash's forehead. He shook the hair out of his eye.

"Part of that night was fun," Hazel said, echoing him from before.

"Yeah."

"And then . . ."

"Yeah."

She pulled her hands into her lap, confused by the gulf between how she'd seen him back then and how she was seeing him now.

"You avoided me after that," he said.

"You avoided me, too."

"Only once I realized you were always speed-walking around corners when I saw you."

She gave a helpless little shrug.

"Four years." He sawed his teeth into his lower lip, shaking his head. "I wanted to tell you— I thought I'd get the chance, some other time when you were sober, to let you know I really did just want to make sure you got home okay. I wasn't"—his face screwed up with something dark—"trying to take advantage."

Remorse wormed through Hazel. She didn't blame herself for not knowing, for not realizing Ash was *good,* but she wished all the same she'd seen him more clearly then. "I know," she said.

He pressed his lid carefully back onto his drink. "And I was never laughing at you. I told Justin a hundred times to come clean. He kept saying he would. You don't know this, but we fought that summer, after you left town. Not just about what he did to you, but that was part of it. When I saw you at that party, and you acted like we couldn't be friends because I was Justin's friend, I hadn't spoken to him all summer."

He held her gaze, his eyes boring into her, like he had so much more to say. She found herself holding her breath, wanting to hear it. Long seconds passed. The breeze rustled the trees and blew that same errant curl back across his forehead.

Finally, he said, "I guess I just wish it hadn't taken you four years to come into my café."

She would have huffed at that possessive pronoun, but she felt strangely breathless, like time had lurched forward and she'd fallen out of step. There was something knowing and steady in Ash's face now, as though this conversation had lifted a weight from him, but Hazel felt newly burdened, like she'd lost something. Time, maybe. Or a possibility.

Ash sipped his hot chocolate and hummed in approval. Then, he nodded at a batch of trees leaning against the side of the trailer. "What about those?"

White tags fluttered on their branches. "They look like they're reserved."

Ash hopped up from the table. "This close to Christmas," he said over his shoulder, "I bet some of these won't even get picked up."

For reasons she couldn't pinpoint, she wanted him to turn around, to gather her into a wordless hug. Instead, she wrapped her arms around her middle and followed him.

She had to jump back as he hauled one tree out from the group and dropped its trunk to the asphalt with a thud, its unbound branches bouncing from the impact, shaking some needles loose. They both leaned back to see the top of the tree. It had to be eleven or twelve feet tall. The aroma of Christmas surrounded her. And despite having been crammed in the middle of the group, its branches were full and uncrushed.

"You want this tree," Ash said, not a question.

It was perfect. But she lifted its tag. It was very clearly reserved for an *M. Conway*.

Ash peeked around the tree, then behind her, then over his shoulder. He tore the name from the tree and toed it back into the mess of needles under the other unclaimed trees.

"What are you doing?"

"If that kid comes out, ask him to show you where the blue spruces are."

"Asher—"

He pushed her toward the front of the trailer. As she rounded the corner, she ran right into the teenager in question and blanked for a few long seconds before blurting, "Blue spruce?"

After making the kid pull out every last scraggly tree from the blue spruce section of the lot, Hazel apologized for taking up his time. Back by the picnic table, Ash stood with the enormous tree, looking mildly aggrieved at how long she'd taken. "You're not gonna believe this, Haze," he said, selling his excitement.

Haze. Her insides flipped. "Wow, where'd you find that?"

He pressed his lips together, gave a slight shake of his head at her too-enthusiastic acting voice, and gestured at the back corner of the lot. "Behind those over there. Isn't it— What's the word? Stately?"

Her cheeks burned from the force of her smile.

Despite all of Ash's adjustments, the tree trunk stuck out past Hazel's back bumper, and the top flopped down onto the windshield. Ash tied it as securely as he could with twine then joined her in the car, where she was cupping her hands around the heat vent. "Sure you're okay to drive? We could always come back in my dad's truck."

"And let someone steal my tree?"

"They'll hold it for you."

"Yeah, I see how effective that is."

He frowned at the branches obscuring the upper windshield. "Will this even fit in your dad's house?"

"The house is a mansion," she said. "It'll fit."

"That's what she said," he mumbled. "Sorry. That was—"

"*So* mature."

She was still teasing him when, a mile from the tree lot, a cop pulled them over. Hazel turned an apologetic smile up at the officer, who pointedly lifted a branch out of the way to lean in the window. As Hazel retrieved her license, the officer bent even lower. "Ash Campbell?"

He recognized her, a friend of his mother's. She asked after his family, and Ash asked about her son. More than once, Hazel shot disbelieving looks his way, still clutching her license to hand through the window.

"Is this beautiful tree going to the children's hospital?" the officer asked. "Your mother outdoes herself every year."

"Uh . . . you know how she is!" He was going to hell, probably.

After a few more minutes of his best small talk, the officer let them go with a warning.

Instead of pulling back onto the road, Hazel gaped at Ash. Her hazard lights clicked on and off steadily. "Is this what it's like coming back home regularly? You know everybody and get out of tickets?"

"Well, you have to be a little charming, too."

She snorted. "And where did this charm of yours come from?"

"I've always been charming." He flashed a grin.

"Not always. At least, not around me."

He was hyperaware of the way his smile faltered, tried to salvage it anyway.

"You're charming with people at the café. I thought it was an act before."

"An act?"

"Ash, the friendly barista. I thought maybe you were just angling for better tips."

"But now . . ." he prompted.

She shrugged. "Then I thought it was just me. Even in high school, you smiled at everybody. Just never at me."

This again. How could he make her believe he'd never hated her without admitting that, actually, he'd been kind of in love with her? "It wasn't because I didn't—"

She squared her shoulders to him fully. "I'm sorry for how I acted at that party."

"That's not why I brought it up."

"We're friends now, though. Right?"

"Yeah. If you want to be."

She nodded once. "I want to be."

He stuck his hand out, and she laughed, shaking it with an affectionate eye roll. But as quickly as her amusement rolled in, it ebbed away. "So, I should take you home."

It wasn't a question, but she sounded uncertain nonetheless. Did she not want to drive after getting pulled over? Did she not want to part ways just yet? Hope fluttered in his chest.

But when she checked her watch, the flutter died. It was only midafternoon. She just didn't want to go home yet.

"Come hang out at my place. I'll follow you back later with the tree in my dad's truck."

Even as he spoke, alarms rang out in his head. Inviting her back to his house was a terrible idea. All his sisters were there. His mother. He swallowed hard. He hadn't ever found a way to tell Hazel about his dad's injury, partly because he didn't know what he was coming home to, and partly because offering the half-truth that his father had broken his hip without the full context of his MS felt more explicitly deceptive than saying nothing at all.

Hazel played with her curls, uncertain but . . . hopeful? "You don't have to do that."

"You seem to think you're forcing yourself on me here. You're not, okay?" He squeezed her shoulder, intending only to reassure her, but his thumb swept of its own volition into the dip of her clavicle, and . . .

Damn, didn't he know by now touching her was dangerous? He was suddenly back in the dark Lovebird Suite, when she'd pressed her freezing fingers to his neck, and he'd grabbed her hands to warm them, emboldened by the cover of darkness. He'd rocked forward on his toes, barely stopped himself from crowding her back, all shadowy lines and curves in the blackout. She hadn't pulled away, hadn't cracked a joke to ease the pulsing tension, and he'd wondered, fleetingly, achingly, if she was waiting for him to do just what he'd barely managed not to before breathing warmth into her fingers instead.

He wondered it now, too, as her tongue darted out between her lips. Her chin dipped closer, like she intended to lean into the contact but caught herself, and that tiny move made him swipe once more with his thumb. She didn't retreat. Their bodies were twin flares: *Come to me. No,* you *come to me.*

The thing was, Hazel's problem with *afters* wasn't just an abstract concept to him now, wasn't just something she did with other people. Sure, he was relieved to finally clarify his intentions, both the night of that party and in the last weeks she'd dated Justin. But she'd avoided him all the same since, erased all the possibilities the last four years may have held. All this time, they could have been friends.

The other thing was, if she had any idea how he'd felt at that party, how freeing it was to finally relax, to be *himself* with her, she'd understand just how deep this went for him—well before she came to the café, before they'd even left Lockett Prairie. He thought the attraction simmering between them now was mutual, but new, reciprocal interest was an entirely different beast than one-sided lust that had been hibernating for years. If she saw *all that*, she might bow out of this little dance. She couldn't have made herself any clearer: nothing could change.

He dropped his hand from her shoulder. "I'll take the tree for you whenever, whether it's later or right now, but you want to kill some time, right?"

She looked like she wanted to disagree, or clarify some point, her head tilting to one side, mouth pinching. But after some thought, she said, "Okay." Then, she pulled back onto the road.

Toward his entire family of nosy, oversharing sisters, his mother who so desperately wanted him to find a serious girlfriend, and his walker-bound father.

"So, listen. There's something I should probably tell you."

My whole family knows I had a crush on you in high school.

"My dad had this accident at Thanksgiving. He broke his hip and had surgery, so he's using a walker." *Maybe indefinitely.* "Temporarily."

"Oh my God. Is he okay?" The sudden deep concern etched between her eyebrows told him that the *other* conversation about his father would be way too heavy.

———————————————

UNLIKE THE DAY BEFORE, WHEN ASH LED HAZEL INTO HIS HOUSE, IT WAS brimming with the loud, joyful voices of his entire family and upbeat Christmas music playing on the kitchen radio. Half of them shouted the standard Campbell greeting, an indiscriminate, "Hello! Come on in!" before they realized it was him.

He fidgeted under the collective double take from his mother and sisters at the sight of *a woman* trailing close behind him. Then, there was the silent but obvious "Is that *her*?" look from Maggie, and the "I *told* you" look from June, who had undoubtedly blabbed about Hazel picking him up that morning. *Ash's Hazel.* That was what June had called her in high school after *one* slip, one mention of the cute girl from the volunteer field day he'd had to leave early. He prayed June had the sense not to repeat it now.

He debated ushering Hazel straight back out the door until Cosette tore through the room and launched herself at him, her hands, arms, face, and hair dotted with glitter. She scrambled back down out of his arms just as quickly, and Hazel picked errant sparkles from the shoulder of his jacket. Maggie was the first to cross over to them under the guise of wrangling her child. "You must be Hazel."

"And you must be Maggie."

Maggie flashed an impressed look at Ash, straightening with pride at having warranted a mention. She reached to ruffle his hair, and he ducked away, his ears burning.

From their positions around the kitchen island and dining table, his family each greeted Hazel before resuming their various tasks. The little kids were making construction paper Christmas cards. The twins were stringing popcorn and cranberries on fishing line and arguing about the ratio of each while his father ate from the bowls. Ash's mother monitored the whirring KitchenAid mixer. June did a piss-poor job of tucking paper liners into muffin tins because she was watching Hazel and Ash, likely plotting an ambush.

"I didn't realize you guys were having a party," Hazel said apologetically.

Ash's hand settled at the curve of her lower back. To his surprise, she shuffled closer.

His mom held out a perfectly golden blueberry muffin to Hazel. "Oh, this is just the usual Campbell chaos. The more, the merrier."

"Mom, give her a minute before you force-feed her," Ash complained as Hazel stepped out of his touch to take it.

Hazel moaned. "Wow, this is delicious, Mrs. Campbell."

"Oh, please, call me Annie." Food compliments were the surest way, after adoration of her children and grandchildren, to Ash's mother's heart, and she pulled Hazel over to the other counter to have her weigh in on the next batch.

Ash watched from the living room until his father said, "You gonna join us or lurk in the corner?" and he shrugged out of his coat.

"Hazel Elliot. I remember you." June was suddenly right beside

Hazel and cast a mischievous glance at Ash that screamed, *I'm totally going to fuck with you.* Everything in Ash tensed with adrenaline. "He used to talk about you all the ti—"

Ash chucked a marshmallow from the open bag on the counter at her face, cutting off her comment. She retaliated by pelting him with chocolate chips.

"All complaints, I'm sure," Hazel said with a nervous laugh.

If he weren't on the verge of tackling June, he would have addressed this persistent misconception of hers.

"I remember you, too," Hazel added. "You played Sandy in *Grease*, right? You were so good."

June smoothed her hair and smiled, pleasure diverting her from her devious plan.

Until Cosette piped up from the table, "Are you Uncle Ass's girlfriend?"

June's face brightened in triumph, and she rewarded Cosette with the remaining chocolate chips in her hand. "Good girl."

Maggie—good, protective, oldest sister that she was—pointedly snatched the chocolate chip bag from June and said, "Well, it's nice to meet a *friend* of Ash's." Maggie's refusal to conspire made June pout, but she dropped—for the moment—her mission to mess with him, sitting down with Isabel and Cosette to help cut construction paper trees.

Ash started a fresh pot of decaf while his mom and Maggie pulled Hazel into conversation. She was nervous at first, hugging herself and nodding politely. She smiled gratefully at him when he interrupted to hand her a mug of coffee with cream and way too much sugar, the way she liked it. He ignored Maggie's raised eyebrow and then his mother's subtle swat at Maggie's shoulder with her dish towel, confirming that she, too, knew this was the Hazel that June had teased him endlessly about in high school.

They asked about grad school, and soon, Hazel relaxed, encouraged by their genuine interest. Ash was still on guard for June's shenanigans, but the tableau of Hazel here in his kitchen, talking warmly with his family while Christmas music lilted in the background, was some kind of magic. He didn't bother to disguise his rapt attention.

Hazel was telling them about her lab's study on language development in toddlers. He hadn't even known what she was working on and appreciated Maggie pressing for details about how they studied toddlers—the children wore vests with a recording device in their homes—and if they were studying bilingual households—they were. Ash realized Maggie's underlying concern when she asked what parents should do if their toddler communicated in more grunts and gestures than actual words.

Hazel must have realized it, too. She followed Maggie's glance to where Isabel was babbling excitedly but incoherently in June's lap and squeezed Maggie's wrist. "The best thing you can do is continue to be so responsive. Anyway, I don't want to bore you all. I'm actually hoping to transfer to a different lab next semester."

"What's the other lab?" Ash asked.

Everyone's eyes cut to him, as though they'd just remembered he was there. It broke the spell of Hazel being casually folded in with his family, and she blushed, waved her hands as if to say she'd already monopolized the conversation too much, but he kept her on the spot so she couldn't weasel out of answering. "The one you're wanting to switch to."

"Dr. Tate's. She'll be studying children separated from their mothers due to incarceration. We already have a pretty good idea of the negative development outcomes for kids. They're basically collateral damage, and it's unjust and unnecessary—

these women are mostly nonviolent offenders. But through the study, Dr. Tate hopes to identify policy changes that might better preserve attachment between the moms and kids and support family reunification."

As she launched into specifics, the physical shift in Hazel was magnetic. Her whole body became involved, eyes bright and open, a passionate flush in her cheeks, hands emphasizing her words. She exuded competence. And that competence, at once both admirable and a little intimidating, was *unbearably* sexy. A brain and a heart like that were completely unfair in a body like hers, which on its own made him stupid with want.

"Won't that be kind of depressing?" June asked over her shoulder, helping Isabel press her paint-covered palm onto paper. "Will you have to go to a prison?"

Hazel shook her head, not in answer but because going to a prison clearly didn't daunt her. "I'd take it over transcribing scratchy audio files any day."

Ash's father rose from the table. He was stiff, his movements deliberate and slow. On instinct, Ash crossed the kitchen to help just as his mom grabbed one of the orange pill bottles on the counter. His father held up a hand to stop him, but Ash fetched the walker just out of his reach and set it before him. "You tired?"

Everything continued around them, this choreography of care nearly invisible, the way his parents preferred it.

"She's got a good head on her shoulders, that one," his father said quietly, nodding at Hazel. Pride surged through Ash. If the comment was an attempt to distract him from assisting his father, he let it slide.

He looked back at Hazel just in time to catch her gaze on him. She didn't falter in whatever she was telling Maggie, but he clocked her interest in his dad, the concerned little furrow between her eyebrows. If he hadn't jumped to help, if he'd let his mother handle it alone, Hazel probably wouldn't have even noticed his dad's achy shuffle to the recliner in the living room. She thought it was just the hip, of course. But Ash considered whether he could have told her about the MS, too. He'd thought it would be too heavy, but then, most people wouldn't choose a prison study over toddlers. As much as she seemed to paper over discomfort in her personal life, she didn't shy away from it to help other people.

The conversation turned to embarrassing stories about *him*. His fear of horses—"*Distrust*, not fear," he corrected—after a carnival pony ran off with him when he was a toddler. Crying at his first T-ball game because, after he hit the ball, he thought everyone was yelling at him.

"I was a kid," he pointed out.

"You weren't a kid when you made the duct-tape vest," Maggie sang. As the big sister, her protection was selective.

"Wait, I have a picture." His mother rifled through the millions of photos and invitations on the refrigerator and plucked out a four by six of him at fourteen. He'd gotten bored one day and constructed a vest entirely out of duct tape and, unfortunately, put it on and paraded around in it. Other than a pair of boxers with dinosaurs eating pizza on them, it was all he was wearing, his scrawny, pale chest exposed and glasses sliding down his nose. Why that photo remained on the fridge after all these years, he'd never know.

Hazel's expression was pure joy. "This is kind of impressive, actually. You could have gone into fashion."

He snatched the photo and shoved it into a drawer.

"Wait, is this the origin of your whimsical accessories?"

"My what?"

"The floral ties."

Ash raked a hand through his hair, wishing he could steer the conversation to anything else.

"He actually wears them?" June asked. Her eyes looked almost feral with delight.

"Okay," he said. "It's not that big of a deal."

June turned to Hazel. "You should hear how he complains. 'I'm not your Ken doll,'" she mimicked.

Maggie cut in, "'I'm a person, not a project.'"

"They gave you the ties?" Hazel asked, loving this whole situation.

"Does he wear the rad two-tone wingtip shoes?" June asked.

Hazel nodded. "There's a very snappy herringbone vest, too."

Laurel and Leanne high-fived across the kitchen table.

Hazel covered her mouth, but not before a giggle escaped. "I thought a girlfriend was dressing him."

"Nope," Ash said, giving the melodramatic sigh they all wanted, "just a bunch of meddling sisters."

His mother invited Hazel to stay for dinner, and although Ash knew she was avoiding going home, he was still glad she accepted. The price for his family not fully exposing his old crush appeared to be roasting him more, but he took it in stride, glad to have her there, laughing along with them. For a while, he even forgot to worry about his dad, about his parents' finances, about the house and his sisters.

Later, he followed her home in his dad's truck, the tree in the back. At the gate, she spoke to the security guard for a long time before passing her sweater out the window. He remembered her story about losing her scarf and realized neither of them had come prepared with a donation. He was ready to offer his hat, but when he pulled up, the guard waved him through, saying the previous car had covered him. On her father's long driveway, Hazel waited for him to park, shivering.

"At this rate, you won't have any clothes left by the time we leave town," he said, hopping down from the truck. He pulled off his jacket and held it out to her.

She looked longingly at it but didn't reach out, so he moved behind her and draped it over her shoulders. She quickly slipped her arms into the sleeves and turned up the collar. With frequent stops, they carried the tree awkwardly, her at the top, him hoisting the substantial trunk. She peeked through the front door window, checked her watch, and whispered, "Shit." Wincing theatrically over her shoulder at him as she entered, she called, "Uh, it's just me." She tugged at the tree, and Ash lifted his end. The force of it knocked her forward, and they both stumbled into the enormous foyer.

She hadn't exaggerated when she'd called it a mansion. He felt like he was stepping into a palace, his boots scuffing too loudly across travertine tile. Alongside the contemporary elements typical of a newer build—open floor plan, soaring ceilings—the place had unexpected design specificity with arched doorways, wainscoting in the entry, and exposed rough-hewn beams in the living room. It was a shame that visitors came to marvel at the homogenous, somewhat boring all-brick exteriors, professionally decorated in the same excessive but classy holiday aesthetic while the most interesting details were kept private in highly customized, expensively sourced interiors like this one.

A woman and two teenagers—the stepfamily, he assumed—exchanged perplexed looks over their meal at the dinner table around the corner.

Hazel busied herself fluffing branches. "Sorry I missed dinner. After the other tree broke, I wanted to get you all a new one. Should we put it over by the window?"

The stepmother rose from her seat. "That's a real tree."

Hazel peered up at it, breath short from the effort of hauling it in. "Yeah, it's pretty big."

"No, I mean, it's real." She sniffed the air. "Your dad—"

"My dad what?"

The stepmom gave a pained smile. "He's allergic? That's why we had the artificial tree."

Hazel cast a worried glance Ash's way, brows knitted together, but she quickly returned to fidgeting with the needles. "I—" She shook her head, a flush climbing up her neck.

Footsteps came from behind Ash on the porch, and he had to shuffle out of the way to let Channel 2's Dan Elliot into his own living room.

"Whoa." Dan let out a low whistle. "Where'd this come from?"

Hazel tried block him. "I didn't know—"

He bent in and breathed deeply. "Love that Christmas tree smell."

It was almost comical how quickly he sneezed.

"We always had a real tree," Hazel said quietly. Ash wasn't sure to whom specifically she was saying this since he was closest and barely heard her. Louder, she said, "Every year, we went to the lot and picked one out. It was, like, the one thing we did."

Her father leaned back to take the whole tree in. He sniffled. "This is a great tree."

"But you're allergic to it."

He shrugged and shook his head, fixed on the tree rather than looking at his daughter. Hazel tilted her head and inched closer, trying to make him see her. He just kept looking up at the tree and sniffling, like he was waiting for a teleprompter to give him his lines.

"Dad."

"You always loved a real tree. I used to take extra allergy medicine."

Hazel pressed her lips into a tight line. Ash could see her mind at work, calculating. "Okay. Fine. We'll take it back." She leaned the tree back toward Ash, and he braced to catch it, but her father grabbed it.

"No. It's a nice tree. We'll keep—" A sneeze cut off his sentence.

"God," Hazel muttered.

"You always wanted a tree in your room," her father said. Confusion crossed his face briefly as he took Ash in for the first time.

"I got it for *them*," she said, tilting her chin at the family hovering around the dining table. "For all of you."

"It's so thoughtful," the stepmother chimed in.

Her father pulled at the tree. "We'll keep it. This is what allergy medicine is for."

She yanked the tree back. "That's stupid. Your eyes are watering. You're starting to wheeze."

He was, a little, and after attempting to deny it again, he told her to wait while he went to take a dose. Ash knew, though, that as soon as her father was gone, she would haul that tree out of the house by herself if she had to. Her eyes glittered under the crystal chandelier.

"Would your family want it?" she asked, not meeting his eyes.

"Too tall."

The stepfamily were still watching from the table, uncertain. Her father would be back soon.

"Let's just put it in your room," he suggested gently.

"Fine." She started dragging it before he could pick up his end, grunting with the effort.

To his credit, her father came back with a tree stand and handed it to Ash from the doorway. "I'm Dan, by the way," he said, holding up a used handkerchief as an explanation for not offering his hand. His teeth were blindingly white and straight, and from only a few feet away rather than on Ash's TV at home, he could make out subtle makeup in the creases by his eyes. "You're a friend of Hazel's?"

"Asher," he blurted. "Not Asher, actually. That's what she calls me. Just Ash." Then, for reasons unknown, he added, "Campbell."

"Glad to meet you," Dan said. No sign of recognition. It shouldn't have bothered Ash. He knew Hazel and her dad weren't close, and if she ever did mention Ash, she probably would have painted him as annoying at best. But he couldn't ignore the absolute gulf between his long-standing feelings for her, so poorly contained his whole family practically salivated at the sight of her, and her long-standing dismissal.

Hazel busied herself clearing a spot in the corner, and Ash helped her hoist the enormous tree into the stand, crawling under the scratchy, low branches to tighten the pegs. Sometime during this process, her father eventually drifted back from the door without another word.

While Ash crawled back out and took in the tree—leaning only slightly—Hazel sat heavily on the bed and covered her face with the too-long sleeves of Ash's coat. With caution, he sat beside her, sinking into the mattress and tilting her into him, hooking an arm around her back. His heart hammered. He wasn't entitled to hold her like this, but what else was he supposed to do? He couldn't just sit there.

"Don't look at me," she whispered.

"I'm not," he said, his heart tugging. "I'm looking at this adorable photo of you in a beret."

She tried to bolt from the bed, but he pulled her back. She'd uncovered her face, and he saw the tear streaks, the wet eye-lashes she'd tried to hide.

"It's so embarrassing," she said, sniffling and ducking her head.

He squeezed her shoulder, tucking her into his side. "It's cute as hell."

After a few breaths, her resistance gave. She pressed her cheek to his shoulder, blew out a shaky sigh. "You can go whenever."

He rubbed his hand up and down her arm. She smelled like mint and vanilla, and he hoped a trace of her stayed on his jacket. "I will. But not yet."

Eleven

How about this one?" Hazel held up a T-shirt with a sequined cat eating a donut.

Ash doubled back from a rack of sunglasses, many of which had been jammed in haphazardly or dropped on the floor by the frenzy of Christmas shoppers. He made a thoughtful face over the throng of people between them but shook his head. "Seems a little young. Lucy's fifteen, you said?"

Hazel refolded the shirt and tossed it onto the table, where another shopper immediately snatched it up. A mass of shopping bags clobbered her in the back, and as she attempted to extricate herself from the sea of people closing in around her, someone else stepped on her foot. She closed her eyes and breathed deeply.

Ash waved at her, then pointed at the front of the store. She met him outside.

"This is ridiculous."

He made a sympathetic face. "It's five days before Christmas."

"Did you find anything?"

"No. You?"

An entire family pushed their way between Hazel and Ash, making them stumble apart. Ash jerked his chin toward a landscaped alcove nestled between two candy-colored Vintage Square shops. The place was overrun with holiday shoppers and kids in sweaters waiting to meet Santa in the gazebo. She plopped down on a bench. "I don't know these people. How am I supposed to shop for them?"

That morning, Hazel had ventured from her bedroom late, hoping she'd missed breakfast and could fix herself something quick then retreat to her room, and instead, she found everyone gathered in the living room, assembling another artificial Christmas tree. A mountain of presents wrapped in brown paper with red ribbon covered the hearth and overflowed onto the floor beside it. Her name was written on several of the packages.

Five stockings had been added to the hooks over the fireplace as well, fancy embroidered ones similar to the Peruvian fiber art pieces she assumed were Val's in the formal living room. The one with Hazel's name on it had the same colors and motif of the others, though it looked newer, stiffer. It stopped her in her tracks. Someone had *made* hers to match. She assumed the elaborate stitching had been commissioned months ago.

Val perked up at the sight of her. "Oh, good. We were just going over today's agenda. I'm picking up our suits and dresses from the dry cleaners later, and I realized I should have asked if you need your dress cleaned."

"My dress?" Hazel said slowly.

"For the wedding."

"I didn't— I thought it was, like, a backyard thing." Hazel looked to her father, who was snapping the top tier of the fake tree into place. "I'm supposed to have a dress?"

"Ah, I may not have been clear in my email."

Email? Hazel pulled out her phone, scrolled through the mostly one-sided history of her and her father's communications.

Hey, kiddo. In case you don't get a spare minute to talk before finals, I'm passing along that the ladies' dresses should be cranberry for the wedding. Wear any style you like. Hope you're keeping your head above water. Dad.

"Oh," she said, too embarrassed to look up from her phone. She remembered this message, remembered skimming it quickly between tutoring sessions, irritated at the oddness of him informing her what "the ladies" were wearing. It hadn't even occurred to her that *she* was one of the ladies. "I'm sorry. I misunderstood."

Val smiled far too brightly. "It's okay. What do you have?"

Other than her gray sweaterdress, Hazel had brought a pencil skirt and a white blouse, staples of her teaching wardrobe. At some point she'd equated "small backyard wedding" with "courthouse wedding," for which she'd figured she could fancy the skirt and blouse up with jewelry and her faux-fur-lined cardigan with the pearl buttons. As she relayed this, Val kept smiling and nodding, not a single crack of disappointment showing. "Sorry. Is that not nice enough?"

"You don't need to apologize," Val said. "It'll be fine. The important thing is that we're all together."

Except if the dresses were being dry-cleaned, they were most likely fancy. Hazel would look like a photobomber, not a family member. She could tell Val didn't want to make a big deal of it. She was truly going to let it go. But Hazel's skin felt too tight with her mistake. If she hadn't been so irrationally irritated when she got that email, she would have paid better attention. She would have bought a damn dress.

Hazel's gaze fell once more to the packages with her name on them. There were at least seven, maybe more. She hadn't exchanged physical gifts with her dad in years. They always sent electronic gift cards to each other first thing on Christmas morning. She hadn't even thought to get him a real card this year, let alone anything for Val and her kids.

"I'll look for a dress today," Hazel said. "I need to do some shopping anyway."

"Do you . . . want company?" her father asked, a hopeful lilt in his voice. "I'm free today."

She slid her phone into her pocket, already edging out of the room. "I would, but I still have to get your gift, so I'd better go alone."

Now, hours later and nearly empty-handed on both the dress front and the gifts front despite hitting three shops already, Hazel rolled her head against the wall behind the bench to look at Ash. She'd found a few small things she could go back for—hair clips for Lucy, a set of cloth napkins for Val that matched the navy-and-gold kitchen cabinets. Ash had a single bag with a book light for his mom and a Taylor Swift phone cover for Leanne. "Maybe I could get one of those covers for Lucy."

"What kind of phone does she have?"

She groaned. She'd seen it several times but didn't know for sure. "How about for Raf? All I know is he's going to UT next year, likes dogs, and plays the tuba. How am I supposed to shop for that? What does a seventeen-year-old guy want for Christmas?"

"Honestly?" His lips twitched in a smile, and she rolled her eyes.

"Don't say a PornHub subscription. I'm just going to give everyone gift cards."

"Giving up already, huh?"

"I should have gone to Sylvia's."

He started to ask, but she shook her head. She didn't want to talk about it. She wanted to check "presents" off her list and get out of here.

"You said you need a dress. Why don't we focus on that?" He pushed up from the bench and held out his hand.

But she was getting too comfortable with him trying to ease

the weight of things for her. If she kept letting him, one day, she'd be used to him *being there*, offering a hand, lifting the other side of a heavy tree, putting his coat around her shoulders. If she got used to it and then he disappeared, it'd be so much harder to reset than to continue on as she always had.

She rose without his help and pushed back into the crowd.

WHILE HAZEL BROWSED RACKS OF DRESSES AT A SECONDHAND BOU-tique that was less crowded than the other shops, Ash meandered nearby, lifting and dropping price tags on clothing, necklaces, hats. He never ventured too far to call questions back at her, like whether she and her mom were close.

She told him about her mother's job, traveling all over the world to open new spas for a hotel chain. She'd started as a receptionist and worked her way up, earning her first big promotion right before the divorce, then relocating to Chicago. After that, she went to New York, London, countless other places, never staying long anywhere. The current stint was in Paris. Because of time differences and her mother's long hours, their communication had shifted over the years from spotty phone calls to even less consistent volleys of emails. They usually caught up around the time her mother wanted to share her next destination.

"You ever visit her anywhere cool?" Ash asked.

"New York. Summer before college. My luggage got lost for a week. There was always some crisis in the spa, so I spent the whole visit in the hotel room—she lives in whatever hotel she's working at. I think she thought I'd be impressed by all the TV channels and room service."

"She didn't take you to do touristy things?"

"I don't think *she* ever did touristy things, in any of the places she's worked. She stays busy. But the hotel gym had yoga and other classes. Those were fun."

"Ah, the start of your yoga journey," he said, grinning.

She laughed. "Shut up."

"Does she ever visit you?"

"The first few years after she left, I'd visit my grandparents in Colorado for two weeks in the summer, and she'd come to see me there."

Ash didn't speak for a long time, and everything she'd said echoed back to her. Hazel's mother probably sounded monstrous compared to his. She wanted to explain better, that her mom had never wanted to live in Lockett Prairie, that her parents had moved there for her father's job, and Nora had hoped eventually they'd leave. Resentments had built up. She'd lost herself in the mundanity of housework and childcare. She'd been completely honest with Hazel about this over the years, especially that summer in New York, when Hazel had turned up heartbroken. Never depend too much on a guy, she'd said. Never sacrifice your dreams or your freedom. And keep moving forward.

They never directly talked about Hazel's father—the implied culprit behind these lessons learned. Her mother's only acknowledgment of the impact on Hazel was to urge her to make the right choices before she had kids—*if* she had kids—because afterward it was much harder to choose your own health and happiness.

Hazel looked at it that way—that leaving had been the best thing for her mother—and most of the time, she left it at that. She didn't dwell on what might have been better for herself, didn't wonder if there could have been some acceptable middle ground that could have met everyone's needs. Hazel had turned out all right. Really, she'd made it out of childhood better than lots of people. So.

Eager for a happier subject, she offered, "The last few years, I've spent the holidays with Sylvia's family in Houston."

"Hmm," Ash said, wrapping a yellow-and-black striped scarf around his neck. It was a perfectly neutral syllable, which seemed intentional. "Does your dad ever visit you at school?"

She pulled a wine-colored dress with a drop waist and fringe from the rack and draped it over her arm even though she was likely too curvy for it. Even if the crowds weren't bad, dress shopping would have been enough to sour her mood. Hazel could buy tops and bottoms off the rack, but finding one dress to accommodate her whole figure—curvy with wide hips and thick thighs, a long torso, and narrow shoulders—was an uphill battle from the start. Her annoyance bled through when she replied, "I'm a stop on his way to other people."

"What do you mean?"

"He comes through when he has a conference or a friend to visit and I'm on the way. Buys me dinner, and gets back on the road. I think he was in town for five whole hours at graduation, and most of that was the ceremony."

"He never comes just to visit?"

Hazel stopped sliding hangers. Ash was at the next rack over, idly lifting the skirt of a cute black dress she might have worn to a New Year's Eve party. He was an expert at this, asking seemingly offhand questions that struck right at the profoundly personal. Underneath his question, she heard judgment, though it was likely all her own reflected back—First her mother, and now her father, too? *Why* didn't he come just to see her?

Because . . . that was just how they were. She hadn't ever *asked* her father to come. And she hadn't returned here to see him, either. Her already prickly mood had sharpened further talking about her mother, and now she was agitated, tension knotting in her shoulders and neck, a headache pulsing in her temples. *She* had opened this door by grumbling about her father's tacked-on visits, but the suggestion that there was more to it—that his priorities weren't normal and therefore said something about *her*—put Hazel on the defensive.

"We're looking for *cranberry*," she said, lifting the three total dresses in the entire store that matched her color and size needs.

He dropped the black dress and pulled out a burgundy one she'd missed. "I don't know what size you are."

She glanced at the tag—size four—and laughed. "Bigger than that. Shouldn't you be looking for your own gifts?"

Ash shoved his hands into his pockets and rocked back on his heels. "Eh."

"Eh?"

"I'm not exactly flush right now."

"Right. Sorry."

"I'm not actually *broke*. I have savings. I just try really hard not to touch it." He blew out a breath. "I mean, I know you've seen my shitty car and my tiny apartment—"

"Trust me, the people at *Apartment Therapy* aren't dying to do a spread of my place anytime soon."

He gave her a small, joyless smile.

Hazel gestured to the dressing room down a long hall at the back of the store. Ash followed, dropping into an upholstered chair right outside the two stalls. The area was vacant apart from the two of them, and rather than ending the conversation, the quiet allowed her to hear him clearly when he said, "After my dad's accident, my parents missed a tuition payment for the twins' dance class. They didn't want to bring it up and stress out our parents, so I covered it. Between that and my car dying . . . I get nervous when I have to use my savings. I can't come back here after every accident or hug June after a bad audition or babysit for Maggie, but at least I can send money. Unless some other shoe drops and wipes me out."

"You're a good brother."

"If my parents find out, they'll be pissed."

"Why?"

She heard him shift in the chair, aware that he could probably also hear her shimmying out of her jeans and pulling off her sweater.

"Same reason I'm not allowed to fix things around the house. They're the parents. I'm the kid. Never mind that I'm twenty-three."

It didn't sound so bad to Hazel, to have parents who still wanted to parent. She'd been used to her father's unpredictable schedule since childhood, but after the divorce, he'd become absent in a less obvious but more confusing way than her mother—there but disengaged. By fourteen, Hazel made or ordered her own meals, managed her own bedtime, checked her own homework. When Justin tried to get her to break curfew, she never told him it was self-imposed.

"They wouldn't even let me get a job in high school. Wanted me to focus on school and baseball, even when—" He cleared his throat. "Even when I got benched."

Hazel tugged the flapper dress on, meeting resistance at her hips. She pulled it right back off.

"I keep hoping they won't notice the dance payment, but I don't know. Maybe that would mean things are really . . ." There was a soft shushing sound like he was rubbing his hands on something. She peeked through the crack in the door but could see only half of him, the hunch of his right shoulder, his hand in his hair.

"How's it going in there?" he asked, his face lifting.

Hazel ducked back from the door. "Fine."

The second dress gaped through the waist. She reached back to pull the material tighter, listening hard for Ash, but he'd fallen silent. If she were him, she'd know the perfect probing question to get him talking again, to draw from him the kinds of personal confessions he pulled from her. Ironic, she thought, that she was the psychology student here.

Because that would mean things are really—bad? That was what he'd been about to say, right? Were the medical bills from his father's surgery not covered by insurance? Was Ash worried his father might be out of work for too long? Or was the problem even bigger than that?

"I'm sorry things are stressful," she said, assessing her reflection in the mirror. With no time for tailoring, this dress wouldn't work.

Ash gave a soft grunt, and she sensed that he wouldn't say more.

Did he not trust her with whatever was bothering him? Or did he just not need another friend to confide in? Unlike Hazel, Ash was surrounded by nosy sisters and loving parents. He maintained relationships—with family, with his cheating ex, probably with all his old friends. She didn't know how things had shaken out with Justin since that summer before college, but if either of them still held a grudge, she'd put her money on Justin being to blame. There were probably twenty people Ash could turn to before he would need her.

They *were* friends now, though. They'd shaken on it. But she had to admit it felt mostly one-sided, their conversations so often coming back to her. With barriers up between herself and just about everyone else—Sheffield's students, her classmates and lab team, even Sylvia more and more—she had been so starved for conversation, she couldn't seem to shut her mouth around Ash, to balance their give-and-take. She'd been aware of the shift when Sylvia left, how every little thought she would have texted, every anecdote she would have passed along suddenly felt too trivial, too *needy* to send across so many miles. It had hit her clear as day: Sylvia had sailed on, and Hazel did not want to be a barnacle, clinging until someone eventually noticed and had to scrape her off.

It was hot in the tight stall. The air wasn't circulating at all. Hazel didn't want to try on the last dress. She fanned her face and chest, wiped the dots of sweat from her upper lip. Her hair was beginning to frizz at her temples, and she gathered it up off her neck into a quick, messy bun.

Of course, if she went back to her dad's house without a dress, he'd think she hadn't really tried. Grudgingly, she tugged the third dress from the hanger and stepped into it, prepared for another bad fit.

But this one slipped over her hips without a hitch. The zipper in the back went up easily. She twisted in the mirror, and the slightly flared skirt draped over her knees in an objectively pleasing way. Her bra straps showed, so she elbowed out of it under the dress. Better. The lacy overlay and wide straps had seemed a little stuffy on the hanger, but she liked the texture, the pretty contrast against her skin. The real selling point? It had pockets.

"I guess we can cross 'find a dress' off the list."

"Yeah?" Ash said. "You gonna show me?"

She blew at a hair tickling her nose and clocked her reddening cheeks in the mirror. As well as the dress fit her—and the low, sweetheart neckline *was* flattering—the rest of her looked wild, skin shiny, hair already slipping from the hasty bun. "Nope. I'm just going to ch—"

No. Hazel twisted, trying to see her back. She tugged the zipper again. It was stuck. "Shit."

"What?"

"Nothing." She twisted the other direction, switched hands, bounced as she tugged. The zipper wouldn't budge. It wouldn't even go back up. It was stuck exactly where it was, two inches from the top of the dress.

Her fingers kept slipping on the pull. She pressed her palms to the cool metal of the wall, then her forehead. *Do not panic. Just because there's no air in here, and the dress is stuck, and the heat is suffocating—*

"Haze?"

God, she couldn't even relish the nickname. She blew out a defeated sigh. "I'm stuck."

"The door?" The handle jiggled, and she slapped her palm against the door even though it was locked.

"The dress. The zipper is stuck. I can't get it off."

"Oh," he said.

"I'm *stuck*," she repeated, her voice embarrassingly shrill. She could see it. Someone was going to have to cut her out of this dress, and it was the only one in the entire store that was the right size and color. Maybe it wasn't the right size, though, because now it was getting hard to breathe.

"Do you want me to find a salesperson?"

"I want you to come in here and get me out of this thing."

Did she? Too late. She'd said it. And now her insecurity about her wild hair and perspiration seemed trivial. Now, she was full-on panicking, and if she didn't get a real, complete breath of air, she was going to have to bolt from this stall and throw herself into the last sparse remains of snow outside.

There was a long silence on the other side of the door.

"Asher, for the love of God—"

"Open the door."

She did, and he was right there on the other side, ready. Only, he didn't step in right away. His gaze swung straight to the ceiling.

"You're going to have to look at me to help."

Slowly, his eyes tracked down to her face. They flitted lower, as if to close but his lashes didn't quite meet. Then, he was taking her in thoroughly, abandoning any attempt to avert his dark, dark gaze. He licked his lips. "It fits," he said, his voice oddly gruff.

"Please, get it off me."

Ash swallowed then motioned for her to make space. The backs of her knees hit the bench seat as she accommodated him in the tight stall.

"Turn around."

When she did, he squeezed in against her backside, jostling her against the mirrored wall to clear enough space to close the door. Already short of breath, Hazel held her sharp inhale until he stepped back and broke the contact.

Behind her, in the mirror, his shoulders and chest rose with a deep breath. Then, she felt his fingers at the upper edge of the dress, just below her shoulder blades. Goosebumps broke out on her skin despite the heat.

She felt him tug at the zipper to no avail. He cursed softly, and the hairs on her neck stood on end, her shoulders flexing back against the warm brush of his knuckles. His attention was laser-focused, eyebrows determinedly drawn together. His tongue licked out over his lips once more. Hers did the same, and she caught the movement in the mirror, her focus shifting to her flushed cheeks, her shallowly heaving chest. Despite the bright fluorescent lights above the mirror, her eyes were dark, pupils overtaking the irises almost entirely. She looked deranged. She itched to hide her discarded bra, which lay open in all its pink lacy glory atop the pile of her clothes, but he would find out as soon as he unzipped her just how naked she was under the dress.

"This zipper is tiny," Ash said.

"Can you get it or not?"

His mouth twitched up in the corner. "Patience, Hazel."

"I'm not good with small spaces."

"Small spaces," he repeated, like he was noting it in an official record.

"Or suffocating dresses."

He stopped working at the zipper to place one big hand over her bare shoulder and meet her eyes in the mirror. She expected him to make light of her outsize reaction, but there was no trace of mockery when he said, "I've got you."

Maneuvering her back a step closer to him, he gathered the fallen strands of her hair and tucked them over one shoulder. "The light," he said by way of explanation. This didn't explain, however, the slow stroke of his thumb down the side of her neck, down the ridges of her spine, his other fingertips trailing featherlight after, the scrape of a callous lighting a fuse under her skin. Her eyes snapped to his reflection, and that was when she realized he wasn't looking at the zipper but at *her*—her eyes, her mouth, lower. His throat bobbed with his swallow, and she felt it behind her.

He noticed her noticing him and cleared his throat. His next firm tug pulled her onto her heels, and she tipped back, her backside flush against his front, his hands dropping immediately to her hips. They both issued breathy apologies. Hazel was ready to just pay for the dress and wear it out of the store to escape.

Ash dropped a knee onto the bench, bringing his face closer to the problem. "I think it's just caught on the lining. Can I . . ."

She had no idea what he wanted to do, but she nodded anyway.

His hand slipped inside the dress, knuckles brushing a spot she had no idea was ticklish until now. She let out a little laugh as he made adjustments.

Finally, the zipper gave. He slid it down all the way to the curve of her butt, his hand stilling there. A desire to sway back seized her. Just enough to press against his fingers, just enough to let him know she wanted . . . What did she want? For him to touch her, here in a public dressing room? She wanted his body pressed against hers like it had been when he first squeezed into the stall behind her. She reached up for the lace straps of the dress, now loose, and held them, wondering, her heart hammering, breath halting, what he would do if she let them fall.

He met her gaze in the mirror, his eyes as dark as hers, jaw clenched. "There." The syllable scraped out of his throat.

She moved to let him pass at the same time he tried to get by. They continued the dance in the opposite direction, Hazel turning around to face him as they shuffled. She laughed, but the sound was cut short by his hand at her hip, first stilling her, then grasping her through the dress like he couldn't help himself. She backed up against the mirror and gasped at the cold against her shoulder blades. His body closed in the space between them, trapping her there.

"Don't move," he said, barely audible.

She could inhale, and their chests would touch. She could reach up and pull his face down to hers. His fingers were still gripping her hip.

Then, somehow, he let go, squeezing around the door and out of the stall without even a whisper of contact.

Twelve

H e could have kissed her. *Should* have kissed her. Her lips were stained cranberry red, and he could have devoured her mouth when he backed her against the mirror. He'd told her not to move, a last-ditch request that every fiber of his being wanted her to disregard. If she had, if she'd pushed forward even the tiniest bit, he'd have given in to the flash flood of desire. But Hazel hadn't moved. And he'd made an escape out of the dressing room stall before he did something he couldn't take back, like tug the loose straps out of her grasp to free her breasts, push that skirt up over her hips, press every aching part of himself against her . . .

"Asher," Hazel said, apparently not for the first time.

He was following her through the attached gift shop of a restaurant called Country Kitschin' while they awaited a table for dinner, but even a half hour after the zipper incident, he couldn't get his head out of that dressing room.

"So . . . no, then?" She waved her hands between them, indicating bright pink mittens.

"For your brother?" he teased.

"*Step*brother." She cast him a weary look as she dropped the mittens back into the bin. "My dad apparently told them all this stuff about me, but I barely know anything about them."

"At least they're nice, though. Sounds like they want you to be a real part of everything."

"If I were looking to expand my circle, sure."

"But you're not?"

"I just don't see why anything needs to change."

A little pang twinged in Ash's chest. She was a fortress, drawbridge always up, archers ready. Her father and his new family weren't the only ones who wanted in.

"There's a window for getting new siblings. Once you don't live at home anymore, it kind of doesn't matter. But they're putting in all this effort, buying me presents, wanting my dress to match in pictures—"

One mention of the dress and Ash was right back in that changing room. To get control of himself, he turned his attention to a shelf of mugs.

"Now I have to fake this closeness I don't feel. It's like I showed up for my first class on the day of a final, and everyone else has been going to extra tutoring, and they have a cheat sheet. It feels so unbalanced."

"What would make it balanced?"

Hazel lifted a mug and handed it to him before winding through the tight display area. The mug read *TALK NERDY TO ME*. "Speaking of talking."

"There's a segue," he deadpanned.

"We always end up talking about me."

He hadn't missed her agitation earlier when he asked about her parents. But as uninterested as she seemed in letting people in, she was actually pretty forthcoming, like she *wanted* to talk to someone. Then she seemed to regret it—or regretted that she'd shared those things with *him*. "What do you want to talk about?"

She slipped a headband behind her ears. A unicorn horn jutted out from her forehead. She raised her chin, daring him to tease her. "Your hopes and dreams. Darkest fears. Deepest desires."

Desires? Nope. Not doing that in the Country Kitschin' gift shop.

He plucked it off her head and slipped a different headband into its place. She reached up and patted at the sprig of faux mistletoe dangling above her, then pulled it off to look at it. "Oh," she said softly. She turned to put it back in the bin, stopped, considered, and finally dropped it in.

Before she could think too hard about it, he said, "We should buy all our Christmas gifts here and be done with it."

He was joking, but it wasn't a terrible idea. Necessity was the mother of invention and all that. The shop sold a bit of everything—kitschy trinkets, games and nostalgic collectibles, Christmas decor, clothes, housewares, artsy ceramics, candles.

"Make it a competition?" she challenged.

"You sure about that? I actually know and like my family."

She released a real, spontaneous laugh. "Okay. Terms. If I find a gift for everyone on my list, you have to tell me a secret. Something personal."

"And if I get everyone on my list?"

"What do you want?"

You.

He scratched his eyebrow. "I need to think about it."

For the next twenty minutes, they searched the cramped gift shop. By the time he made it to the cash register, she was already collecting several bags from the counter. The hostess called his name, and Hazel went ahead to their table while he paid.

When he entered the dining room, Hazel was dumping sugar into her coffee. He smiled, warmth blooming through him. The room was packed and loud, and he had to squeeze between the tables. A sudden urgency to reach her edged out the warm feeling, a sense that the evening would end too soon.

"I did it," she said as soon as he sat down.

"You got everyone?"

"Check this out." She presented a wood and glass object that looked like a snow globe. "It's a storm glass—basically an old-school barometer. It's probably wildly inaccurate and not actually antique, but my dad will think it's cool." She pulled more items from her bags. Bamboo bracelets and a beaded purse with a white bird on it for Lucy, a University of Texas collectors' set of dominoes for Raf, and a macrame plant hanger and hand-painted alpaca salt and pepper shakers for Val. "She likes alpacas," she said triumphantly, like she'd cracked a code.

"Not bad," he agreed.

The server came to take their order, and when she left, Hazel leaned across the table. "Well?"

"Looks like we tied."

"Does that mean we both win? You never told me what you wanted."

The middle of a crowded restaurant, their server interrupting at any moment, didn't feel like the right setting for a confession. "I'm still thinking about it."

"Well, I still want a secret."

"Fine. What kind?"

She thought about it for a moment. "Something you're afraid of."

He didn't know what he'd expected her to want. Maybe an embarrassing anecdote, like her Pug Boy story. But being afraid was exactly his problem right now. Because if he somehow maneuvered them through their budding friendship and into something more, it would start a clock, ticking down to the inevitable *after*, when she would cut her losses and move on. For all he knew, as soon as he admitted he liked her, they'd already be in *after* territory. He had to tell her something else.

The next pressing fear, though, was about his father. A sick weight dropped in his stomach. Ash rubbed his neck, looking for the waitress.

"There," she said. "Whatever you're thinking about right now."

"*You* scare me a little," he admitted, stalling.

She rolled her eyes. "Be serious."

"I am."

Hazel crossed her arms, mirroring his own defensive backward lean, willing to wait him out.

His feelings for her were off the table for now, and if he told her he didn't want his father to deteriorate before his eyes, this whole evening, light and flirty and warm, would stop dead in its tracks. That was the last thing he wanted.

"Geese," he said finally, an absolute cop-out. "They're mean as hell."

The light in her eyes dulled. "Geese. Hmm. I guess that's true."

She moved the conversation on to other topics. To the untrained eye, she looked like a young woman with a friend or on a date, smiling, talking with her hands, nodding when he spoke. But something small had shifted underneath. A switch from the Hazel he'd been getting to know—the Hazel who had cried in front of him last night despite how hard she worked to appear unfazed, the Hazel who was afraid of *afters* and small spaces and, he suspected, giving her whole heart to anyone without an escape hatch—to surface Hazel. Still warm, still friendly. She made eye contact with the waitress when she thanked her for a refill. He liked that about her, that she was always courteous, always gave her full attention to servers. But that was also how she was now looking at him, with polite, distant friendliness.

"Okay, you want a secret?" he said once their plates were cleared. "The place I intern for is going to offer me a job after I graduate."

She smiled that same ninety-percent-Hazel smile.

He made sure she was looking at him and added, "What I haven't told anyone is that I might not take it."

And now that smile was down to seventy percent. She was humoring him, but she looked disappointed, like this revelation still didn't seem particularly personal. "Why?"

"I thought I wanted to do all this cutting-edge, green tech stuff. A lot of it is pretty cool. But I shadowed an architect on a restoration last summer, a protected landmark. They can be tricky. You have all these constraints. It would have been cheaper and easier to demo it and rebuild from scratch. But the challenges made it interesting, and there's this art to it, and . . . I don't know, it was pretty satisfying to save something with so much history."

There it was—her full Hazel smile. "You're sentimental," she said. It didn't sound like criticism.

"If I don't take the job at my current firm, I'll have to find someone to take me on for the postgrad hours toward my license. Sustainable architecture is a growing field. There are more job opportunities, better security. It makes better sense long term."

"You can't worry about that," she said immediately. "You have to do what you love. Don't settle before you even start. Besides, isn't restoration architecture still pretty green? So it's not like you're abandoning your principles and contributing to overconsumption."

"True." If he didn't have to worry about the future—that the twins could afford college, that he could bail out June when too many auditions didn't pan out, ease the burden on Maggie when Nick was on assignment, make sure his mother didn't have to work until she died—he would have already decided on it.

Hazel didn't know all these considerations. Maybe that was another reason he still hadn't told her about his father's MS and his role as his family's security net, because he wanted her to say exactly what she'd said. She spoke with such conviction that it made doubting her—in turn, doubting himself—nearly impossible.

"Like you love working for Dr. Sheffield?" he challenged. "What about Dr. Tate and her prison study?"

She shrugged.

He laughed. "Why are you shrugging? That's what you *want* to do. You gave an entire TED Talk on the unjust collateral damage of incarceration in my kitchen yesterday."

She pulled a curl over her shoulder and mindlessly twirled it. "You should have rescued me from all their questions."

"You didn't need rescuing."

She shook her head, but she couldn't suppress a tiny, pleased smile. "I wrote a request to switch labs, but I don't know if I'll submit it."

"Why the hell not?"

"For one thing, Dr. Sheffield is going to be pissed. I still have to take classes with him, see him around the department. Plus, like I already told you, I can barely keep up with my assistantship as it is. I've always been able to handle everything academic with no problem, but this semester has been a shit show. I'm not sure that I'm—"

"What, cut out for it? That's ridiculous."

She laughed, surprised. "It's not ridiculous. I've slipped up. I transcribed twelve hours of the wrong audio files one week because I misread an email. Twelve hours. I *kissed* a student."

He waved these off. "You're human. Those aren't major mistakes. Doesn't everyone in grad school go through crippling self-doubt at first?"

"I don't know," she said sarcastically, but not meanly. "Do they?"

"Pretty sure it's a widespread phenomenon. Imposter syndrome. You're not an imposter."

She made a skeptical sound in her throat.

He waited for her to meet his eyes again before he threw her comment back at her. "You have to do what you love, right? Don't settle before you even start? Even if it means upsetting some old guy you don't want to work with anyway."

"Fine, I guess it's not as simple as I made it sound."

But maybe all of this—choosing a career, going for what he really wanted—*was* that simple. That new possibility swelled within him, until they were outside in the parking lot, loading their bags into her car. When Hazel closed the trunk and turned for the driver's seat, he stepped into her path.

She looked at him expectantly, hair blowing across her face. He tucked it back behind her ear, a gesture that came so naturally he didn't even register the intimacy of it until he saw the change in her face, the slight furrow of her eyebrows, the parting of her lips.

"Campbell?"

Ash turned reluctantly to find Travis and Derek Cline, old friends he'd have been happy to see any other time than right now. He went through the motions of introductions, though they all vaguely remembered each other. Every second of it pulled him further from what he'd wanted to say, that he knew what he wanted for his prize—to see her every day, here and back at school after their trip, and not just because he happened to work at her favorite café.

Travis and Derek were headed to the bar across the street and invited them to come along.

"If you want to go, we can," Hazel offered.

"You don't need to get back?"

Travis and Derek stood by in awkward silence, shoulders hunched against the cold.

"*Please*," she said, "my entire purpose in life right now is avoiding that place. I don't want to keep you from whatever you would normally do. If I weren't here, would you go with them?"

"I can't promise you won't see someone you know," he said, grasping at straws. He didn't want to share her.

"Someone in particular?" Travis cut in.

"Anyone we went to school with." Silently, he willed her to take the out. "Mr. Newton, shirtless."

Travis and Derek exchanged perplexed looks.

Hazel lifted her chin, eyes flaring. "I'm a big girl," she said, then spun on her heel and charged forth.

THE BAR WAS CROWDED AND STUFFY. WITH ALL ITS DARK WOOD, GREEN wallpaper, and a constant soundtrack of Dropkick Murphys and Flogging Molly, it was a typical Irish pub, except for the back wall dedicated to West Texas taxidermy—a handful of bucks, two pheasants in flight, a vicious-looking javelina, a set of long-horns, and a mounted squirrel—all adorned with Santa hats and white twinkle lights. While they waited for their drinks, Ash shouted over the noise that the pheasants reminded him of the Lovebird Suite.

"Hmm?" Hazel's gaze flitted to him distractedly from Derek Cline, who was rubbing the cuff of her sage-green sweater between two fingers and using the crowded bar as an excuse to move in closer.

"I like this color," Derek said, plucking at her sleeve. "I just realized it matches your eyes, too."

Christ. Ash was in hell.

"Wow. This is smooth. Are you seeing this, Asher?" Hazel asked.

Derek released her sweater, raising his palms and turning to Ash. "Sorry. Are you two a thing?"

She arched an eyebrow at Ash, a challenge in her eyes. Maybe she was annoyed that he'd called her out for worrying about seeing people she used to know in front of them. Or did she want him to stake a claim? *Just try. I dare you.* As enlightened as he liked to think he was—raised by sisters, privy to their complaints about guys, sometimes even a target for their lectures on toxic male behavior—the desire to wedge himself between Hazel and Derek, to wrap his arm possessively around her waist, to say, *Keep your hands off her,* was a primal vibration in his bones.

"Seems like a question for her," Ash finally said.

She looked impressed by the side step and told Derek, "Save your lines. Maybe for those ladies over there." She nodded to a group that had just walked in.

Because she was into Ash, or because she *wasn't* into Derek? He saw the same question pass over Derek's face. It hung there, unanswered by Hazel, until the bartender set their drinks on the bar.

Travis thumped Ash's back in a way that felt consoling and directed the group to a spot between a boisterous table of men and a group playing pool.

Soon, Ash was three drinks in, literally backed into a corner, ducking the occasional jab of pool cues from the table they were vulturing, and sulking while the Cline brothers regaled Hazel with a story about running their dad's tractor into a ditch. Just over a year apart, Travis and Derek had no shortage of such stories. While Travis primarily contributed a droll punch line here and there, Derek knew how to spin a yarn and loved to be the center of attention. To Ash's annoyance, Hazel was riveted.

"Wait, why were you naked?" she wanted to know.

Derek waggled his eyebrows. "That, sweetheart, is a whole different story."

"Jesus Christ." Ash tipped the last of his beer into his mouth.

Just then, the rowdy men to Ash's right abandoned their table. He snagged the round two-top and indicated for Hazel to take one of the stools underneath. She hitched up one hip to perch on it, but the stool teetered. On instinct, he reached out. He meant only to keep her from toppling over, but now, as her eyes darted down to where his hand gripped the front edge of the small seat, he realized he'd grabbed it directly between her thighs, the soft denim of her jeans brushing against his wrist.

She straightened, bumping her back into the table, thighs closing around his hand. Why was he still holding the stool?

"You drunk already, Hazel?" He aimed for a teasing tone, but his voice came out low and hoarse.

"It's off-balance." He barely heard her over the music, all breathy and flustered, her cheeks and neck awash in a pretty pink blush.

"Here." He tugged the stool out from the table to give her more room. Her eyes snapped to his in surprise. His hand was *still* between her thighs. The stool rocked onto its shorter leg again, and her hand shot out to clutch his forearm.

A whole montage of untimely, intrusive images played before his eyes.

He dropped down to shove a wad of napkins under the short leg, and while he was there, Ash thought of taxidermy, snow down the back of his shirt, one of the Cline brothers belching loudly somewhere above the table. When he finally rose back up, she looked dazed, and he wondered if she was struggling like he was. "Better?"

She crossed her legs. "What? Yep. Yes."

Mercifully, Travis and Derek had missed the entire exchange. Hazel tugged her hair down over one shoulder, and her mouth twitched into a little smile that rocketed through his veins. Then, she pressed the smile away and yelled over the noise, "These dudes are never giving up their table." She meant the four guys occupying the pool table, who had just started another round.

Travis nodded toward the back wall. "Dartboard just opened up."

They came to a quick consensus. Hazel, smaller and more able to squeeze between the crowd of mostly men with a flash of smile and a cheery, "Sorry! Excuse me!" reached the board quickly and began plucking the darts from it before anyone else could claim them. Derek lagged, having already started flirting with some older women in the brief minute they'd been at the table. Travis followed close behind Ash and, when they were halfway across the room, yelled over the noise, "Say the word if we need to get lost."

"What?"

"So y'all can hook up."

"We're not hooking up. We're . . ." He stopped the word *friends* in his throat.

"Something wrong with your—"

"No, nothing's wrong with my dick, asshole."

Travis laughed, hands raised. "All right."

"I'm working on it."

"Well, here's some free advice. Work faster. Pull the trigger."

"Yeah, okay," Ash said sarcastically, jostling around men

who had parted politely for Hazel but were immoveable boulders for him. "It was super helpful that you invited us here where I can't even talk to her, but sure, I'll just 'pull the trigger,' whatever that means."

Travis laughed again and clapped his hand hard against Ash's shoulder, shaking him roughly. "That's always been your problem."

"What's my problem?"

"You think too much. You into her?"

Ash sighed. There was no point in denying it. "Yeah."

"So, do something about it. Teach her how to throw a damn dart."

"I'm not doing that."

"Why not?"

"Because it's a fucking cliché. She won't be into it."

"Man, every girl is into that shit. In fact, if you *don't* do it, you're pretty much saying you're *not* into her."

Ash figured it was pointless to clarify that he didn't want only to hook up with Hazel. "Just so we're clear, your brilliant advice is to mansplain darts to her. Revolutionary, truly."

"Pull the trigger, Campbell." With that, he shoved Ash the last few steps, right into Hazel.

"Sorry." Ash removed his hands from her hips, where he'd caught himself. "I think we lost Derek to those cougars."

"But what a way to go."

"So." He scratched his arm. He felt Travis's smirk beside him but blocked it out. "Have you played before?"

Hazel raised an eyebrow. "Why? Are you going to teach me how?"

Travis barked a laugh and said something about the restroom.

"Do you want me to?"

She squinted at him. "What if I'm actually a professional dart player? Bet you'd feel pretty dumb trying to teach me my own sport."

"Are you a professional dart player, Hazel?"

"I've never thrown a dart in my life. But—" She pressed a fistful of darts against his chest. "Are you any good at this? Because I don't want to learn from someone with terrible form."

Ash shot one. It landed in the ring around the center.

She looked impressed then forcibly unimpressed. "I guess you'll do."

Somewhere in the shadows, Travis was probably laughing his ass off, but Ash decided to go with it anyway. He'd seen enough rom-coms to know how this part was supposed to go. "Shut up and turn around."

She gaped at this. But then . . . she straightened and did it.

He slid in close behind her, nudged her heel forward with the toe of his boot, shifted her hips. Leaning in close, he murmured in her ear, "Not so tense," as he pressed his palm flat to one shoulder blade. Reflexively, she rolled back into his touch. He positioned her elbow then reached around to adjust her grip on the dart, his fingers curling around hers.

She looked from their fingers to his face and chuffed a breathy laugh. They were dangerously close to breaking their cover, the flimsy charade of it all. She knew what he was doing, and he felt borderline stupid doing it. But he didn't flinch at her scrutiny, and instead of rolling her eyes at him, she bit into her full lower lip and leaned ever-so-slightly back against his chest.

"I think she gets the idea," Derek said, coming up behind them.

Ash stepped back. She threw the dart. It landed closer to center than his own, and her hands flew up in victory, smile breaking wide.

Travis returned, and they split into teams. He'd have liked to team up with Hazel, but he was beginning to understand that her preferred method of flirting was trash talk. "Maybe I should be teaching you," she crowed. He feigned exasperation, which made her smile. A dance they knew the steps to.

Despite being in competition, Ash managed to stay close to Hazel. Their arms brushed as they waited for Travis and Derek to shoot. She swatted at his chest when he gloated, which he did only because she wanted him to, because it made her green eyes flare with something fierce and free. After a bad throw, she chucked him under his chin and said, "Aw, better luck next time, Campbell." And by their second game, after Hazel and Derek won the first, she was openly cheating, nudging the toe of her boot into the back of his knee or reaching around to cover his eyes with her hands.

"Get a room," Travis hollered, and she didn't blush or hide her face, just openly stared at Ash so long he nearly asked, *Should we?*

Something unreadable passed over her expression, like he'd actually said this out loud, and she grabbed a fistful of his shirt, dragging him into the hall that led to an ancient payphone, the bathrooms, and an emergency exit.

It was finally happening.

Hazel backed herself flat against the wall and yanked him in against her, leaving no question that she wanted it, wanted him. "Damn it," she breathed. She pressed her face into his neck, right under his chin, a puff of warm breath tickling his throat. "Ash."

He laughed—he felt just as wild-eyed as she looked—but it came out as a grunt. He braced one hand on the wall above her shoulder, skated the other from her hip up her side, catching the hem of her cropped sweater, ghosting warm skin, and continuing up to her neck, where he threaded his fingers into her hair and tilted her face up to his. No more dancing around each other. No more toeing the line. They couldn't pretend any longer that they weren't dying to rip each other's clothes off. He dipped down and caught her mouth in a firm kiss.

Years he'd waited, studying that sexy little dip of her cupid's bow, wondering what her mouth would feel like, taste like, and the answer was *perfect*. Peachy and sweet from her drink. Soft and a bit tentative. Then, he felt her whole body melt further into the kiss, into him, and he couldn't help himself, couldn't believe this was finally happening, couldn't go slow anymore— and maybe never again. He deepened the kiss, a little reckless, a little rough, until a groan in the back of her throat snapped him to his senses.

When he pulled away, already breathing hard, already aching to kiss her again, a whole emotional journey passed over her face—surprise, confusion, hesitation, then clear as day, desire.

She released his shirt and pulled his mouth back down to hers. The first kiss seemed to have caught her off guard. Maybe she'd expected him to swerve to safety at the last second yet again. But this time, she came for him confidently, greedily, her tongue exploring, her hips tilting into his. He couldn't keep his hands off her, pulling her to him at every possible point. He wanted to be all over her. He wanted to somehow envelop her so completely that she became a part of him.

"This—" He tore his mouth from hers to kiss her cheek, her neck, her collarbone. He cradled her face. "This is what I wanted."

Thirteen

wanted you in that dressing room." His words came breathless and broken in her ear.

Hazel pressed herself shamelessly against him, hooked her hands up over the backs of his broad shoulders and tugged, needing him closer.

"In that bird room the other night," he went on. "Christ, in that dress that never stays on your shoulder." He yanked the neck of her sweater over to mouth at the skin beside her bra strap. The soft, velvety warmth and scratch of stubble made her head swim.

A toilet flushed from behind one of the bathroom doors.

Ash buried his face into her shoulder and groaned. "So many better places we could have done this." Drawing in a slow, deliberate breath, he straightened to search her eyes. His thumbs drew up either side of her neck, the touch melting her even as he gently moved her back a step from him. He was tense all over, fingertips pressing impatiently into the nape of her neck, then releasing.

Hazel wanted to kiss him again for it, for how he showed that he wanted her, for how he wanted it to be right. But she also couldn't look at him, dread slowly ebbing in.

"You okay?"

She toed up and pressed her lips to his cheek, stalling.

He leaned back on his heels. "Talk to me." His voice was stronger now, nearly back under control.

She still felt entirely out of control. "You surprised me."

"A bad surprise?"

"No." She felt her face flush. "Not bad at all."

Two young women spilled out of the bathroom, and Ash gave Hazel another foot of space, nodding politely at the pair, who took one look at her, feral and breathless, and giggled. Hazel forced herself not to track their path into the bar, back to the figure that had sent her fleeing down this hall in the first place.

Why *hadn't* she dragged him into this dingy, dark corridor to kiss him? She'd wanted to. She'd been so worked up all evening, turned on by his playful teasing, the private brushes of his hand at her back, on her hip, down her arm in the middle of the crowded bar. But it wasn't her boldness that landed them here. She was a coward through and through, and in a few seconds, he would realize it.

She edged toward the heavy exterior door at the end of the hall. "Is there an alarm on this door?"

He scratched his forehead. "Not sure."

She gave the bar a tentative push, and cold air licked inside the gap. No alarm.

"Your jacket," Ash said.

"Don't need it."

He reached around her and pulled the door closed. "What's going on?"

One second was all it took, one quick glance over his shoulder. He froze, didn't turn back to her.

Hazel tried to be subtle, scooting strategically so his body blocked hers from everyone in the bar. And, more importantly, from Franny Bowman, who had just walked in.

He was silent for a long moment. Then, "Wait, is this why

you—" He gestured at the wall they'd been pressed up against, then dragged his palm across his mouth, eyes wide. "And I—"

"Ash."

"Christ, I was all over you."

"I was all over you back." She tugged at his shoulders, willing him to see in her eyes that she didn't regret the kiss, even if it hadn't been her intention.

He scrubbed his hands over his face, into his hair, making it stand up at odd angles that would have made her laugh if he weren't so distressed. "I thought you were—"

"I was."

"No," he said. "You were hiding."

"At first. But then I was into it. Couldn't you tell?"

He leaned a shoulder into the wall, looking at her from the corner of his eye like it was the only way he could manage it. When Hazel shuffled two steps over to remain obscured behind him, his jaw tightened. She couldn't hide anything from him. "What happened to 'I'm a big girl?'" he said, throwing her over-confident claim from earlier back at her.

She shrugged, defenseless.

"You were really going to bolt?"

"Maybe. I don't know." She hugged her middle. "Yes."

"You used to be friends. What's the worst that could happen?"

"I don't know, okay? I'm not like you. I don't comb through the wreckage looking for something salvageable. I find somewhere that isn't already wrecked." Her voice was climbing, edged with anger. God, she sounded like she was attacking him rather than trying to defend herself.

"I'm not the one who wanted to come here," he pointed out.

"I know. I know." She petted at his shoulders, his chest, wanting to go back to when he was all over her.

"I feel like an asshole."

"Don't. Please. I'm the asshole." Her fingertips grazed up his neck to his hair, coaxing his eyes back to her.

He breathed in deeply through his nose then gave a resigned shrug. "What now? I get your jacket, meet you in the alley?"

"You'd do that?"

He hooked one finger into a belt loop of her jeans and tugged, relenting. Sexy. Reassuring. Bless him.

Hazel peeked around his shoulder to track Franny's movement through the bar, assess the situation. But Franny turned at the exact same time. A squint, another quarter-turn, and recognition flared across her features. Her hand lifted in a wave, then she was weaving through the crowded room, towing a very tall, well-groomed man along behind her.

"Too late," Hazel said.

Franny's face was unreadable as her heels clicked toward them on the tile, her oversize wool poncho swaying with every step. Glossy and manicured, she moved like she was on a catwalk, not in a grimy hallway that smelled of disinfectant. Hazel braced herself. Maybe Franny had been waiting for this moment to unleash everything she hadn't said in the trickle of voicemails and texts that marked the death of their friendship, the ones Hazel simply hadn't answered. For a wild moment, she wondered whether Franny might slap her.

About four feet away, Franny stopped, waited for her companion to catch up, and said, "Hazel."

"Frances."

Franny's frown was slight, but it was enough for Hazel to correct herself. "Sorry. I don't know why I called you that. Hi, Franny."

Silence descended. Hazel fought the impulse to blurt another apology. Besides, how did you apologize for falling off the face of the earth? Certainly not like this, standing awkwardly post-kiss, next to a bathroom.

Ash extended a hand to the other guy, jump-starting a round of introductions. God, he was a savior. Franny referred to Hazel as her "first best friend" without a trace of bitterness. "And this is Cedric, my fiancé." She wiggled her fingers, an enormous diamond refracting the dim light, then leaned in to hug Ash. "How are you? How's your dad?"

"You two are friends?" Hazel asked.

They spoke at the same time, and Hazel gleaned that they'd crossed paths a few times since high school, kept up with each other on Instagram. Last she'd checked, Franny's account was private, a closed door Hazel would rather die than knock on. A jolt of possessiveness consumed her, though she wasn't sure which territory felt threatened—her relationship with Franny or with Ash.

Ash said his dad was recovering well from his surgery, which only seemed to confuse Franny. "Surgery? Was it related to the—"

He shook his head with a strange urgency, like the bobble-head armadillo that still sat on the dashboard of his old car. "Just a freak accident."

Hazel felt like she was missing some insider information, but before she could figure out how to clear things up, Franny leaned in to hug Hazel. They embraced lightly, the equivalent of a dead-fish handshake.

How many of these halfway hugs could Hazel stand? First with her father, and now her oldest friend. *Ex-friend.* She remembered the easy physicality they'd had as girls. She'd had it with Sylvia, too, that cozy intimacy. Her stomach dropped.

They relocated to the bar, and the guys hovered behind them, already talking casually about sports. Hazel couldn't remember a time when she'd ever had to *think* about what to say to this girl. She started and abandoned a dozen questions in her head, and when their drinks came, she sucked half of it down before Franny finally said, "This is so awkward, right?"

"Yes," Hazel breathed.

"I thought I might hear from you after the invitation." Franny waved a hand. "I mean, it's okay. I know we haven't talked in forever."

"Invitation?"

"To my wedding."

"You invited me to your wedding?"

There it was, the agitation. Franny's nostrils flared, and she picked at her cocktail napkin. "Of course I did."

"I'm sorry. I didn't get an invitation. But I moved last summer. I have a new apartment."

Franny's expression remained severe for another long moment. Then she reached for her handbag, her eyes guarded but something hopeful in them, too. "It's in August. Do you want to see the venue?"

A pressure valve released inside of Hazel. "Yes."

She swiped through the pictures on Franny's phone. Each one led Franny into another story about the wedding planning, and the weirdness between them began to dissolve.

"This is all so you. Exactly what I would have pictured."

"Well, some things are different than I planned."

Hazel remembered then—they'd agreed once to be each other's maids of honor. She swallowed thickly.

"I was supposed to marry Noah Centineo."

"Oh God. Specifically, Noah Centineo playing Peter Kavinsky in *To All the Boys*," Hazel clarified. She laughed harder than the moment warranted, the last of the tension finally breaking.

It set Franny off, and soon they were clutching each other's arms, mirthful tears in their eyes. Of all the ways Hazel had imagined such a reunion going, laughing so hard she cried had never been an option.

"So," Franny said, pitching her voice low, "you and Ash Campbell? What's going on there?"

Hazel tried to shrug it off, but her usual ability to rein in her feelings had apparently been compromised by the reunion with Franny, or by the alcohol, or by the sudden flash of Ash gently biting her lower lip, his unfiltered low groan as he pulled her closer in the hallway earlier. A wide smile broke free, and she dropped her face into her hands. "I don't know," she admitted, the words anguished.

"Holy shit," Franny said. "You're really into him."

Hazel turned, resting her cheek on her arm across the bar. "Am I?"

"You're bright pink right now."

"He kissed me right before you came in. Don't—" She hooked her arm through Franny's. "Don't look at him. I don't know what to do."

"Was it good? The kiss?"

Hazel had to bite the inside of her cheek to get her smile under control. "Yes. Doesn't matter. I told him before that nothing could change between us."

"That's stupid."

Hazel snorted. "Okay."

"He's a nice guy. You could do worse. You *have* done worse." She didn't say Justin's name, but her meaning was clear.

Justin, Hazel sensed, was too fraught a topic for them to tackle at this point. She had forgotten that when they'd broken up, all Franny's true feelings had come out. In retrospect, part of the reason Hazel had pulled away from Franny, ironically, was guilt about neglecting her best friend for a boy.

"I owe you a massive apology," she said, forcing herself to meet Franny's eyes. "I'm sorry I disappeared."

Franny nodded, shrugged, then said, "Thanks."

They coasted on safer waters until Cedric reminded Franny that they had to meet friends across town. This time, the hug Franny pulled her into was real.

HAZEL AND ASH ENTERED HIS HOUSE TO THE AROMA OF BAKING COOK-ies, the glow of a roaring fire, *The Grinch* on the TV, and several demands to come sit down for the movie. Ash's older niece peeked inside the corner of one of Hazel's bags, and June pulled her, giggling, back onto her lap. Mrs. Campbell rose from the couch to get them cookies.

Ash ruffled his niece's hair, then June's, laughing when she slapped his hand away. "We've got to wrap these presents because you're all too nosy." His smile grew even bigger at June's melodramatic protest, and Hazel's insides flipped at the pure sunlight that emanated from him when he was like this. *Happy.* How had she ever thought him broody and apathetic?

He dropped a loud, smacking kiss on his younger niece's plump toddler cheek. As they passed through the kitchen, his mother tucked cookies in a paper towel into his jacket pocket.

Right at that moment, here with him, Hazel realized, she was happy, too.

She stopped short when he opened the door to the laundry room, which led to the garage and an upper-level addition. Names and dates were scrawled in pen up one side of the door, Ash's at the very top. She pressed him back against the door and leveled her hand atop his head, comparing it to the mark there. "Someone fudged his last measurement. Either that or you've shrunk half an inch."

Ash straightened, nudging her hand up.

She made a skeptical sound in her throat. The next thing she knew, he'd spun her around into his place. Her heart leapt at the thought of a replay of their kiss at the bar. But he pulled his pen from his pocket, nudged her heels flush with the door, and scratched a line above her head.

"What are you—"

"There." He waited for her to move, then added her name and the date.

She was right between Maggie and June. A quick scan confirmed that this was not some communal record for just anyone who passed through the Campbell house. The only other names belonged to his siblings, his parents, his nieces. "You can't just put me on here."

"I can just," he said and started for the stairs. "Come on."

Inside his bedroom, Ash toed off his shoes by the door while Hazel surveyed his space, part of an add-on to the original house after the twins were born, he'd told her. Clearly, in his absence, it had also become a storage space. Two large plastic bins were stacked under the single window. File boxes lined the wall opposite his typical-guy, blue-and-green-plaid-covered bed. But Ash's fingerprints were all over the elaborate Popsicle stick chandelier hanging above, as well as a pair of concert posters on the wall—Hippo Campus, Bad Bad Hats.

"I'm getting you one of my 'sad girl acoustic' posters for Christmas," she said, then lifted a pair of black, square-framed glasses from his nightstand and smiled. "So, you *do* still wear glasses."

"Only at night."

"I want to see."

He shook his head but slid them on.

"Oh, my," she said. Hazel didn't even have a thing for glasses, but she *did* have a thing for Ash in glasses. He was easily ten percent hotter, all scholarly and serious-looking. He was also blushing under her open appreciation.

He pulled them back off and set them on his dresser. "That's enough of that."

"There will never be enough of that. Why is it that in movies with makeovers they always take the glasses *off* to make the lead sexier? They've got it totally backward."

Ash leaned back against the closed door, popping his knuckles. She strolled through his room some more. Did her snooping bother him? She couldn't tell. Still, she turned her attention from his walls to their gift bags. "We could wrap these later if you want to hang out with your family."

At the reminder, he popped out into the hallway and returned with an armload of supplies.

"I've kept you all day," Hazel continued. "Besides, I like them. They're . . ."

"They're a lot." He lifted the paper towel pouch of cookies from his pocket as if it were evidence and tossed them to her.

A burst of laughter drifted up to them.

"I see why you need the noise at the café. It's never quiet in this house. Impossible to feel lonely."

"Impossible to *be* alone," he corrected, but he said it with the same affection that accompanied all his empty gripes about his family.

Hazel placed her boots beside his shoes, then selected shiny red paper for her gifts and sat on the floor. He sat across from her, his outstretched foot nearly touching her own. For a few minutes, they wrapped in silence, the voices and TV from below coming to them in bursts. She imagined Ash in this room as a teenager, his boisterous family always present in this subtle, steady way, and felt a pang of longing to have spent time here back then, even just once. She pictured staying over for noisy family dinners instead of ordering takeout or making sandwiches for herself, his mother pressing a container of leftovers or cookies into her hands as she left. Maybe she and Ash would have come up here to listen to music.

Maybe, in a totally alternate reality, they would have come up here to make out on his plaid bed.

"About earlier," he said, breaking the silence.

She smoothed a piece of tape more thoroughly than necessary. They hadn't talked about the kiss yet. In her car after they left the bar, she'd filled the silence babbling about Franny's wedding plans, mainly to keep from offering to find some secluded park to finish what they'd started like horny teenagers.

"It was—" she began just as he said, "Let me expl—"

"No, please. I was—" she started again.

"Just listen," he said.

She set the tape dispenser down.

"It was . . . great."

Hazel breathed out a sigh. "Agreed. No regrets."

"Good. So, I wanted to assure you nothing has to change." At her confused expression, he added, "We were drinking. We were having fun. It doesn't have to be a whole thing."

"A whole thing," she echoed slowly. They hadn't had *that* much to drink. And that kiss had been more desperate and, frankly, way hotter than some random, casual fun.

"Look, I think at this point I just have to say that I find you . . ." His eyes trailed from her face to her cropped green sweater and down her jeans to where her socked foot nearly touched his. When his gaze returned to hers, Hazel shivered. There was his studious, borderline serial killer look again. His Adam's apple bobbed. "I find you incredibly sexy, Hazel."

He gave her name gravity. The effect on her was the opposite, floaty, heady.

"If I'm being totally honest, it's not a new thing for me. At the café . . ." He gave a single-shouldered shrug, one corner of his mouth lifting. "But it never stopped me from pouring your coffee. We can have this . . ." He rolled his wrist, indicating a back and forth between them.

"Attraction?" she supplied.

"Yeah. Which I'm hoping is mutual?"

"It is." Her voice came out thready. She cleared her throat, tugged her suddenly itchy sweater collar from her neck.

"Christ, between your little off-the-shoulder number and now that," he said, pointing accusingly, "I'm going to develop an unhealthy fixation on your neck."

After the last few days of dancing around it, she hadn't expected him to come right out and state his attraction to her. It was almost businesslike, this clarifying of terms and conditions, and yet there was still a charm to the way he seemed to have abandoned being cool or coy. Her heart felt like a shaken-up Coke can.

"Anyway." He closed his eyes as if trying to refocus. "What I'm trying to say is: it can be a physical thing without changing anything else, whether it's just the one time, or only while we're here, or whatever."

He placed a set of bracelets onto a square of paper and folded the edges around it, so casual, like he'd just offered her the muffin of the day at the café rather than . . . what, exactly?

"Friends with benefits?"

Ash didn't look up from his wrapping. "I wouldn't even call it that."

"What would you call it?"

"Just . . . Okay, so, we can kiss if we both want to. We can stop whenever. You don't have to worry that I'll get attached. I won't 'get weird' and make you avoid the café." She heard the air quotes he put around *get weird*, his mildly sarcastic recall of what she'd said when they'd agreed to carpool home.

Her stomach went oddly leaden at how easily he brushed off the prospect of an emotional attachment. "We already agreed that if things *get weird*, I'm not avoiding anything. I get the café."

He smiled, an amused, genuine smile that broke a little bit of the tension. "Sure. And since I live and work there, you can trust that the very last thing I want is for anything between us to get complicated."

Hazel narrowed her eyes. "Just physical. And you can do that, Mr. Still Goes Out with His Ex and Her Fiancé?" Why did she want him to admit that it would be a struggle, that he didn't really feel so cavalier about her? When he'd kissed her at the bar, pressed his entire frame against hers, she'd felt like she was bursting at every edge of herself. A supernova. *This is what I wanted*, he'd said, and it had felt like a door opening.

"You want me to put it in writing or something?" He raised his palm. "I, Ash Campbell, swear not to catch feelings from making out a few times with Hazel Elliot."

"A few times, huh?" She settled back against the bed, smiling despite her nagging unease. It *would* be easier to know they could act on their attraction without complications. If they were straightforward with each other, if they established clear boundaries, wasn't that better than this wild attraction driving them to do something reckless and messy?

Yet she couldn't help but think of seeing Franny after all this time, how avoidance had made her lock their friendship in a box and throw away the key. All this time they might have had, all this loneliness Hazel had been drowning in since . . . well, before

Sylvia even moved away. If she hadn't run into Franny tonight, she never would have realized that maybe burying the past and avoidance weren't her only options.

Ash drew up onto his knees and prowled across their wrapping area, crinkling the paper under one hand and then the other as he leaned in, a cute, playful smile on his lips. "A few make-outs. A thousand. Whatever you want." He waited for her to tilt her chin up to him, then brushed his lips softly across hers.

Threading her fingers into his soft curls, she tugged and deepened the kiss. He fell on top of her, right into the open V of her legs, the paper underneath him surely getting destroyed beyond use. She didn't care. When he dropped his lips to her neck, all thoughts beyond their bodies and how good his mouth felt flew right out of her head.

His warm, broad palm slid around to the middle of her back, pressing so she arched into him. They were at awkward angles, his other hand propped on the bed behind her shoulder, his body still too far above her, up on his knees. She had nowhere to go, boxed in by the bed, and as far as she arched, she couldn't get the contact she wanted. They expelled frustrated sighs at the same time, and he sat back on his heels, ran a palm down his face. "Haze," he said, half agonized and half laughing. The nickname zinged through her.

Bed. Bed, now, she thought, the rest of her vocabulary beyond grasp. She wanted to unbuckle his belt and shove his jeans down, wanted to wrap her legs around his waist and koala-hug him, let him palm her ass and lift her up. To fall onto the bed, finally bearing the full, satisfying weight of him on top of her.

His eyes danced back and forth between hers, reading her, debating. Just when he seemed to have settled on a decision and his hand ran down to the curve of her butt, a muted thud came from the hall, followed by a hissed, "Shh."

Ash's hand paused. "Someone there?" he called hoarsely. More shushing came, then a louder, indignant little girl's voice, accusing, "You walk too loud, Aunt June."

He groaned. "I'm taking their gifts back for interrupting this." He tucked Hazel's hair behind her ear, then rocked back on his heels and went to the door.

When he flung it open, June and Cosette thudded loudly down the stairs, shrieking. Then came Maggie's voice, laughingly admonishing June for setting a bad example.

"I'm keeping you from your family," Hazel said as Ash tried to smooth the mangled wrapping paper. "We should go down there."

"Yeah, just—" He licked his lips, his eyes still heavy-lidded with want. "Give me a few minutes." His eyes dropped, and hers followed, landing squarely on the bulge in his jeans.

That he was still very turned on made her want to go again. She swallowed. "Good idea."

She checked her phone for a distraction and sobered at a text from her father reminding her that they were all going as a family to the winter festival tomorrow for Lucy's choir performance.

"I suppose they still do Winter Fest at the high school?"

Ash nodded. "Are you going?"

She tossed her phone onto his bed. "Looks like. Lucy has some choir thing."

"Yeah, the twins have a dance recital, too."

Hazel perked up. "You'll be there? What time?"

He shook his head, smiling. "I'd be flattered if I didn't know you just need a buffer from your family. What time do you want me there?"

She opened her mouth to protest, but he threw her a look that said he wouldn't buy it. "Eleven."

He talked about the twins' small but constant competitions

with each other over dancing, school, friends, June's disappointing go at breaking into acting in L.A. When he moved on to
Maggie and his nieces, she saw genuine concern there. Everyone
was trying to make this Christmas a little more magical for
them with the little girls' father away for work.

"And your dad," Hazel said.

He stilled.

She'd only intended to empathize, but she sensed she'd said
something wrong. She recalled his response to Franny at the
bar, the same sudden straightening of his posture, the darting
eyes, the weird feeling that she was missing information. "His . . .
surgery?"

"Right, yeah."

Hazel couldn't pinpoint why the energy between them had
changed, but soon they ran out of gifts to wrap, and he was back
to normal. Ash descended the stairs behind her, carrying presents, and as she opened the laundry room door, her name and
height marked there in his assertive handwriting, he hooked his
free hand around her waist and whispered in her ear, "I won't be
able to do this in front of them." Then he dipped his chin over
her shoulder to kiss her. It was firm but quick. Before she could
respond, he squeezed past her and out into the kitchen.

They watched *While You Were Sleeping* with Ash's family,
and the coziness of so many bodies all squished together on the
sectional and sprawled across the floor in the dark, all their
laughter, all their mild complaints about someone hogging the
blanket, someone's cold toes, *everyone* talking too loudly, enveloped Hazel. She was hyperaware of the warmth here, already
aching at her inevitable departure even as she tried to stay in
the moment, wring every last drop from it.

Only the two of them and June managed to stay awake to the
credits, the rest of the family all lightly snoring, heads tipped

back or resting on someone else's shoulder. Unlike Ash, all four Campbell sisters so strongly favored Annie, with matching strawberry blonde hair, freckles, and blue eyes, that the actual identical twins among them barely stood out. But like Ash, they'd also all inherited their dad's height. With their willowy limbs sprawled across each other on the couch, their close bonds, both genetic and emotional, were impossible not to notice.

It was after eleven, the fire nothing but embers. Hazel considered feigning sleep. Maybe Ash would let her stay. But when June extracted herself from the little kids and slipped out back to smoke, Hazel resigned herself, stretched, and said, "I guess I should go," embarrassed by the last-second upward inflection that turned it into a question. Even more embarrassed when he said, "Yeah, sure."

Just as she climbed into her car, he said, "Wait, I forgot," and ran back inside the house. He returned with a box under one arm and a small tower of soup cans in his other hand. "For the gate, so you don't have to give them another sweater."

She tried and failed to suppress her smile. The gate stopped charging admission so late at night, but she decided not to tell him that. "What's in the box?"

"Ornaments. You said you didn't have any for your tree, and as I'm sure you saw, the grandkids' have taken priority around here."

"Asher . . ." She stared up at him in awe, unable to speak for a long moment. "Your mom won't miss them?"

"It's just a few of the literal hundreds I made as a kid. Cinnamon dough stars. Popsicle reindeer. Very amateur. And I was pretty generous with the glitter on a few of them, so it's honestly more a burden than a gift."

Hazel got out of the car, reached up on her toes, and kissed him hard.

Fourteen

Ash's first thought upon waking was *Hazel*. Kissing Hazel. Holding her. She smelled minty and sweet, sweet like the excessive sugar she required in her coffee, and he was beginning to understand that addiction. He didn't even care that he couldn't sleep past five-thirty. The promise of seeing her at Winter Fest propelled him out of bed, humming "Joy to the World" through a quick shower and heading downstairs to join his mom for coffee.

When he reached the kitchen, though, he stopped short at the sight of both his parents seated at the table, his mother applying a Band-Aid across his father's forehead. Icy dread trickled down his spine. "What happened?"

"Nothing." His father pushed at the hands smoothing the bandage and tried to rise, only to fall back into his chair. Ash's mother reached for his elbow, and again he brushed her away, pulling on the edge of the table to erect his obviously stiff body. He listed to one side and, after two shuffling steps toward Ash, apparently thought better of walking and leaned against the counter.

"Nothing, huh?" Ash asked, catching his mother's eye.

She shook her head in warning. "He tripped by the fireplace."

The bandage was one of the big ones with wide wings, right

over his left eyebrow. Ash could see dark blood already absorbing into it.

"What was he doing?" Ash stalked to the fireplace and noted the fresh logs stacked for their next fire.

"*He's* standing right here," his father complained.

"Leaning," Ash couldn't help but correct him.

"We need coffee." His mother set about making some, adding, "It's more of a scrape. It's not serious. You know head wounds bleed like a stuck pig."

"Forgive me if I don't trust your opinion of a serious injury at this point," Ash muttered. Then, he asked his father, "How'd you trip?"

"If I'm gonna be interrogated, I guess I'll sit back down."

"Probably a good idea."

"Ash," his mother warned.

"How'd you trip? Are you having an attack?" He scanned for the signs. Clenched fists. Pained grimace. Sensitive, squinting eyes.

"It's not an attack." His father shot his mother a hard look, as though they'd taken bets on Ash's reaction, and she needed to pay up.

"One of the kids left their shoes on the floor," she said in a placating tone.

"Overexertion, not enough sleep, stress—" Ash ticked off his fingers as he ran through the list they were all familiar with of common precursors to a relapse.

His father slapped his palms on the table. "I tripped on a goddamned shoe."

Ash froze, surprised by the burst of anger. His mother mouthed for him to *Calm down*. He knew he should. But what was this if not proof that things were not *just fine*? His father could be difficult, but not usually in this way, raising his voice, pounding on the table. Ash felt vindicated, relieved even, for uncovering the truth, or at least moving in that direction. He'd known better. He'd *known*. But being right also came with the spike of fear, the drop in his stomach that he'd so far managed, with his mother's flimsy optimism, to hold off.

"We're calling the doctor." He directed this to her, bypassing the stubborn patient.

Before they could protest—and they would—the front door opened with a cheery jingle of wreath bells, and June stumbled inside. "Oops," she said when she saw them. She closed the door with a wince and tiptoed through the living room like she might still sneak by. He could smell the smoke on her clothes from here, see smudged mascara under her eyes.

"June," he barked.

She rolled her eyes. "Can I shower before the lecture?"

Ash's gaze swiveled from his sister to his parents. They didn't say a word.

"You were here when I went to bed. When did you leave?" he asked.

She frowned, clocking the bandage on their father's forehead. "What happened there?"

"Oh, he fell, but it's okay because, according to the two of them—not actual doctors or anything—it's not serious."

Her eyes widened. "Someone's salty this morning."

"Where were you?"

"Dude, relax."

Ash threw his hands up. "The problem here is not how unrelaxed I am. Is this what you're doing in L.A.? Partying every night?" He didn't wait for her to respond before turning on his parents. "And it's not just the *head injury*. You could have hurt your hip when you fell. Why am I the only person who remembers the protocol here? A fall means you see your doctor."

"Fine," his mother said. She watched coffee drip into the glass carafe, and Ash knew she was avoiding his father's eyes. "You're right. I'll call when the office opens."

He itched to push for the after-hours line or a trip straight to the hospital. Was this how they'd been handling his father's MS? Pretending it didn't exist? Hoping for the best? He should have come back at Thanksgiving, should have been here the whole time. The twins were too young, too sheltered to step up, and with Maggie and June both out of state, his mother was the only person who could manage his father. It was why he'd offered to stay home another year instead of going straight to college, but his parents had insisted they could handle it without him.

Anger burned at the litany of all his mother's phone calls over the last four years, all the times she complained about his father's refusal to take better care of himself, only for her to downplay what was really going on the rest of the time. How could Ash help when he didn't have all the facts?

"I'm coming with you to the appointment."

June shot him a look that said to *just stop.*

Ash's mother slid his father a mug of coffee, paired with two pills from the orange bottles on the counter and a book of crosswords from the pouch on his nearby walker. With a grunt, he reached out a hand, and she remembered the glasses he now needed, handed him those, too. When she set her hands on his shoulders, he squeezed one back, sliding the glasses on.

She marked the dosage in a notebook, then poured two more mugs and set one of them before Ash. Her eyes were tired, chastened. "I know," she said.

"Know what?" That he shouldn't have to push for the doctor? No shit. They all knew that.

"You think you can't trust what we've told you."

"Yeah," he admitted. "Seems that way."

"So, come and see for yourself then."

BY THE TIME THE DOCTOR'S OFFICE CALLED BACK, SOME OF THE MORN-ing's urgency had dulled. Dr. Griggs had directed them to the hospital at the mention of a head injury, but the long wait and no obvious signs of illness chipped away at Ash's certainty. His father wasn't speaking to him, either, sure this was all a waste of time.

The rest of the family had been equally frosty. They'd planned to all go skating and still could have gone, but Maggie insisted it would be hell without their mother helping with Cosette and Isabel. The girls were particularly wild that morning, and Maggie was short with them. June was no help, sleeping off her hangover. The twins were practicing their dance routine in the living room, nitpicking each other's form and snapping that they couldn't turn down their music when he suggested it might be contributing to the chaos.

Ash tried to wrangle his nieces while his mom made breakfast and Maggie took a call from her husband, but things went from bad to worse. Nick's first flight, a remote charter that ran just once a day, had been canceled, throwing his entire travel schedule up in the air, so he might not make it on Christmas Eve after all. Maggie relayed this news like Ash was somehow personally responsible. While that was bullshit, he was relieved for a little space from all his sisters, despite the all too familiar mix of anxiety and abject boredom that made time move backward in hospital waiting rooms.

When a nurse arrived to take his father back, Ash followed

his parents, intending to get the truth straight from the doctor's mouth. His mother flipped through two notebooks—a medicine log and another with detailed symptoms—to supply exact answers to intake questions. "So, no real changes since the tenth," the nurse summed up, checking boxes on a computer.

"Nope," his father said. "I was fine then, and I'm fine now." His tone was pointed. He'd gone through a full workup following his surgery.

When the nurse left, the room fell silent, and Ash pulled out his phone to find a slew of text messages from Hazel.

We're by the ticket counter. Are you here yet?

Help, my dad has left me to "bond" with Val over coffee. Please tell me you're here somewhere.

Asher??

He'd lost track of time. It was eleven-thirty, and his father still hadn't gone back for an MRI yet.

"Another emergency?" his father muttered.

Ash had risen from his chair as if to leave. He sank back down, tucked his phone into his pocket. "I didn't know they'd send you here," he argued weakly. "I thought your doctor would just see you in the office."

"I knew. And I didn't want everyone worried about nothing four days before Christmas."

Ash swallowed down the anger that balled up in his throat. He didn't think he could hear one more time that nothing at all was wrong. It didn't feel like nothing was wrong. It felt like his parents' house was falling apart, their finances were strained, and his father was deteriorating right in front of them. "Dad—" he started.

"What's going on with your car?"

"My car? What does that have to do with anything?"

"Making conversation. We've got time, after all," he said, looking pointedly at the clock above the door. "You're so concerned about everyone else. I want to know what's going on with your car."

"Nothing. It's old. It's not reliable enough to drive across the state. Had another option, so I took it."

"About time to get a new one, don't you think?"

"Sure, I'll go test-drive a Tesla later."

His father shook his head at Ash's sarcasm. "You hurting for money?"

"No," Ash said immediately. "It's funny, though, you telling me what to do about a situation you don't know anything about when you're the last person to take advice."

"Well, that's simple. You're the kid here. It's my job to give you advice. It's not supposed to go the other way."

Ash scoffed. "Okay."

"I'm not sure when you got it in your head that you know better than everyone else, but I'm a grown man. I don't need you looking for everything wrong with me and the house like it's all proof I'm halfway into the grave."

"Jesus. I don't think you're halfway into the grave, Dad."

"But you can't accept that my health is *my* call. Not even when you think you know what's best."

Ash threw his hands up. "Most parents would be glad when their kid helps out, but fine. Whatever you want."

"Sure, son," his mother interjected gently. "Take out the trash, load the dishwasher. But this . . . this pushing about your dad's health, lecturing June, spending hours lugging tools around the house instead of just spending time with us?" She raised a severe eyebrow, making sure he was paying close attention when she added, "Giving the twins five hundred dollars without checking with us first?"

Ash's skin pricked with guilt. He crossed his arms, fixed his gaze on the mottled linoleum floor. "Fine. I hear you."

But fuck, it burned. All of it. He wasn't sorry for stepping up. He didn't feel bad for pushing when no one else was going to do what needed to be done.

"You know what?" he said, pushing up from his chair. "How about you guys decide exactly when and how you want my help and let me know? Because this"—he spread his arms to indicate the exam room—"this might all be fine today, but what about when you relapse? Or worse? You know that's a *when*, not an *if*, right? When is it still my job to get you to bed because you'll hurt Mom if you fall on her, and when does my help make me an asshole? I'd really like to know."

"Ash," his mother snapped, eyes darting between his father and the closed exam room door. She didn't want the staff to overhear, didn't want anything, ever, to appear to be wrong.

"If this is really what you want," Ash pushed on, something tangled and filthy unclogging in his chest, "then don't make me help hide your episodes from the girls, and don't ignore your limits to the point that Mom has to call me, crying about how you won't take care of yourself."

His father's eyes cut to his mother, a remark dying on his parted lips. He looked genuinely stunned. Betrayed.

And that righteousness burning like magma in place of his blood cooled immediately. He never meant to hold those phone calls against his mother. More than that, he never wanted to expose her calls to his father. And as true as the sentiments were, long as he'd stuffed them down, he regretted immediately that the lid had come off now, like this, in anger.

He lost a bit of steam. "It's not— Shit. I'm not saying don't call me."

"That's enough," his father said, so quiet Ash might have imagined it.

Then someone in scrubs swung the door open and ushered them back to radiology. Ash and his mother followed silently to another empty waiting room.

"Was that Hazel on your phone?" she asked once they were alone.

It took him a moment to backtrack. She meant Hazel's texts. Ash swallowed. He wanted more than anything to stop fighting, but leaving it unresolved didn't sit right. "Mom, I'm—"

"Is something wrong with Hazel?"

"I was supposed to meet her earlier."

"You should go." She didn't sound angry or dismissive, only tired. He shook his head, and she raised a palm to cut him off. "At least let her know where you are."

He couldn't tell Hazel where he was because he hadn't said a word about the MS, and now it felt like he'd been lying to her, when all he'd meant to do was keep things as uncomplicated and light as possible, to not scare her off. Just like he'd given her that ridiculous speech last night, insisting they could have a purely physical relationship without any feelings threatening their equilibrium. She'd been completely fine with that proposal, which only proved it was a smart move if he wanted to keep kissing her. And he did.

"I'll text her," he relented. "But I still want to hear what the doctor has to say."

"Ash."

"You're asking me to back off. I need to hear the truth before I can do that."

She shook her head, gearing up to argue, but finally said, "Fine." Then, "About the money you gave the twins . . ."

He swallowed.

"I need you to understand we are not suddenly incompetent or destitute."

"I never said—"

"We didn't miss a dance payment. That's what they told you, right? They wanted expensive winter formal dresses. I gave them the same deal as Maggie and June, a reasonable budget and chores for anything extra, but they decided it was easier to lie to you. And instead of checking with me, you gave it to them."

Ash sighed. He could throttle his sisters for playing him, especially for how it cut him off at the legs now. "Why is it such a big deal that I gave them money?"

"Your car is twenty years old. Your apartment is a storage space. You're barely scraping by when you could have a comfortable life. Honestly, as your mother, it drives me crazy."

"I'm doing fine, Mom."

"See, when you tell me that, I believe you." He doubted this was entirely true, but he got her point.

"Sorry," he mumbled. He wanted to mean it. He didn't quite though. He still felt right. Still felt a current of anger tugging him back.

"Don't leave that girl waiting," she said, turning to look down the long, quiet hallway. "I'm going to see if I can rustle up some coffee."

Hazel didn't respond to his text. In fairness, he'd been vague: Sorry, got caught up with a family thing. Thirty minutes. Hour, tops.

He heard for himself from his father's neurologist that there were no indicators of anything serious—no concussion from the fall, no lesions related to the MS. The hip was also in good shape, so his father was cleared to return home to rest.

The good news was met with passive-aggressive sighing and muttering from his sisters, who claimed to have known all along none of this was necessary.

"It's not like I *wanted* there to be a problem," he muttered, rushing them out of the house. He was so late meeting Hazel.

His happy anticipation from this morning had been fully hijacked by the familiar, whole-body tension and anxious restlessness he'd fought to mask back in high school, during the onset of his father's illness. Back then, Ash turned inward to contain it, pulled his energy back wherever he could, from school, from baseball, from his best friend whose plans for their future suddenly sounded trivial. *That* was the version of him that Hazel had first met. Constant worry exacerbated by his futile pining. And because of it, she'd read him as apathetic, selfish, *broody*. Thought he'd hated her.

He couldn't go to her like this.

But he couldn't stand her up. Which meant, instead, he was going to have to explain. All of it. Somehow.

« CHAPTER »

Fifteen

Hazel was hiding in the girls' locker room at her old high school, and she didn't care if that made her a coward.

Ash had blown her off. The place was swarming with semi-familiar faces. And her father had dumped her on Val, who meandered through the Winter Fest craft fair in the gym while telling Hazel about her father's two botched proposals before the one that stuck. "He never even said he loved me before the first one. When I pointed that out, he tried to tell me I was mistaken," Val said, laughing. "Like a woman might forget a declaration of love. But you know your dad. He thinks just because something's obvious to him, it must be obvious to everyone."

When a text came from Ash saying he'd be a while yet, Hazel had hastily excused herself to pee, and now she was sitting alone on a hard bench in an alcove with beat-up lockers at her back and a mix of cheap perfume, hair spray, and stale sweat in the air. Across the room, two sinks dripped in mismatched rhythms, the mirrors above them dirty with kiss smudges.

She reread Ash's brief text. No explanation. No sense of urgency. It didn't mesh with the guy who, just last night, gave her his childhood tree ornaments. Even though his proposal of an uncomplicated physical relationship had taken her by surprise, he hadn't been weird or gross about it. In a way, it was the very thing she'd told him she wanted.

She checked her school email to find a message from her lab listserv. Zach, the combative fourth-year, wanted everyone's spring schedules to establish a new weekly meeting time. If she didn't suck it up and submit her transfer request to Dr. Sheffield, she'd be dooming herself to work with *both* of them for another semester or more. She vowed not to chicken out, to just send the document tonight.

Dreading going back out to the festival, Hazel took a picture of herself under the Lady Bulldogs mural by the door. She'd brushed off four texts from Sylvia since arriving in Lockett Prairie, and if she'd learned anything from seeing Franny again, it was that unresponsiveness was a slippery slope. She didn't want the same thing to happen with Sylvia.

P.S. I'm alive, she texted. But I welcome death. Am being forced to bond with my father's fiancée. At my old high school, no less.

Sylvia's immediate reply was a GIF of a guy dragging a stubborn bulldog down a sidewalk. You can do hard things! she added.

Hazel smiled at the platitude, intended to make her groan, from her relentlessly positive friend. Hazel loved her for it. She considered confiding to Sylvia her frustrations with school and her disappointment that Ash was late, but it'd require so much background she didn't know where to start. Besides, Sylvia was probably with Dave, or working at the restaurant . . .

These sounded like excuses. Censoring, withholding, avoiding being too needy. So instinctual she hadn't realized she was doing it. But she realized now. She would open up to Sylvia. Soon.

Hazel replied, Live, laugh, shove me off a cliff. Gotta go. Wish me luck.

LUCK!

On her way out of the gym, a bright blue sandwich board sign stopped Hazel short. **Lockett Prairie PALS: Partners in Academics, Leadership, and Service**. It was the same one she'd hand-painted nearly seven years ago when the group consisted of her, an advisor, and three other students. Two girls were selling ornaments, and a banner behind them listed all the elementary and middle schools they partnered with now—easily triple the number from Hazel's days. She wandered closer, warmth spreading in her chest.

"Oh my God," one of the girls said, her hand pressing over the acronym on her T-shirt. "Hazel?"

Hazel's phone fell with a clunk onto the table as the voice and face clicked together. Her braces were off now, that adorably crooked front tooth pulled into alignment, and her hair, once kept in sectioned twists with plastic barrettes on the ends, curled tightly in a mature pixie cut. "Amaya?"

Amaya squeezed between the tables and threw her arms around Hazel. The embrace was tight and long, and when Amaya pulled back to explain to the other student, "Hazel was my Big when I was a Little," pressure pricked at Hazel's eyes.

"You're a Big now?" she asked, her voice tight.

"President, too." Amaya tapped an enamel pin on her shirt.

"That's amazing."

"I can't believe you're here," Amaya said. "My mama just left. She'll flip when I tell her."

"She's home?" Hazel asked.

"Three years now."

"That's amazing," Hazel repeated, prevented from saying more by the lump rising in her throat. Her smile was so huge her cheeks hurt. Pride overwhelmed her at the young, confident woman before her, though pride maybe implied a personal contribution to her development, and all Hazel had ever done was crawl under a picnic table with the timid little girl and draw pictures in the dirt with her.

She pulled out her wallet. "Let me get an ornament."

BOOSTED BY SEEING AMAYA AND HEARING ALL ABOUT HER COLLEGE plans, Hazel tried harder to put in a real effort, smiling and playing all the carnival games with her dad and his family. It wasn't terrible. But by the time Ash turned up, she had a stomachache from eating too much caramel corn, a headache, and a questionable fruitcake from the cakewalk, the one game she'd won. Ash scuffed toward her, hands in his jacket pockets, head bent.

He'd left the rest of his family by the ticket booth, his father in a wheelchair, his nieces tugging Maggie in two different directions. Hazel gestured to him to stop. She wanted to say hello to his family. But he shook his head, kept walking, and his family peeled off in the opposite direction.

"Hey." He eyed her cake dubiously. He didn't take his hands out of his pockets, didn't lift his gaze to hers. Though she'd rallied and made the most of the morning without him, his subdued greeting reminded her that he'd stood her up for two hours. And he didn't look particularly excited to be here now.

"Hey," she said back.

"That looks gross."

"I won it."

"You sure you won?" His grin faltered, and the quip fell flat.

An awkward silence stretched between them. She'd expected him to immediately explain, to apologize for something that, admittedly, wasn't that huge of a transgression. She trusted he had a good reason for being late. But he didn't explain. He just stood there. The irritation she'd quelled earlier reared its head.

"We could have gone with your family."

Her father, Val, and her kids were two carnival booths down, attempting to topple snowman cans with softballs. Ash moved to close the gap. "Nah, I need a break from them for a bit."

"Why? Your dad's in a wheelchair. Did something—"

"It's a lot of walking. Chair's easier. Come on." He nudged her toward her father.

Dark circles marred the skin under his eyes. His shoulders were tense. She'd seen him tired at the café when, at the start of an evening shift, he'd move his laptop to the other side of the counter and keep working during lulls. But even at his most stressed, when he pulled his attention from his work to bug her, refill her coffee, take her sandwich plate, a playful spark usually glinted in his eyes. She'd chalked it up to him taking pleasure in annoying her. The spark wasn't there now.

She grabbed his arm. "Are you okay?"

He laughed, but it sounded hollow. "You're stalling."

She hadn't been. Not this time.

The tendril of concern that had begun to stretch toward him doubled back on itself. By the time they reached the snowman game, her defensive hackles were back up. Had she seriously asked if *he* was okay? If anyone had a right to be closed off, it was *her*.

She grabbed his arm again just before they joined her father.

There was a flicker of emotion in his eyes, a word on the tip of his tongue, muscles on the verge of release. He looked raw. Just as quickly as the glimmer of vulnerability appeared, though, it vanished. He performed polite greetings with her father and the others and accepted an invitation Hazel only half registered to enter a gingerbread house competition.

She heard herself say, "Great. I'm with the architect," and looped her arm through his, as though she were completely fine, as though he were a boyfriend she'd brought home to meet her parents. Sometimes, it came so easily to plaster over imperfections, to sell an image. She hated herself for it a little bit.

Her father had probably intended for them to build the gingerbread house together, as a group, rather than in competition with each other, but he smiled his TV smile and clapped a hand to Ash's shoulder. "Architect, huh?" He cast her an approving look, which immediately soured her on the entire concept of introducing any boyfriend to him ever.

"Not yet," Ash said modestly.

"Lot of school for that. You two study a lot together?"

When she didn't respond because she couldn't uncross her emotional wires without tripping a bomb, Ash rescued them. "No, not together."

Not together. She was only half following the conversation, having some kind of out-of-body experience, and she thought Ash was telling her dad they weren't in a relationship. Which was *true*. But him clarifying it so quickly and easily stung a little.

Ash's easy grin reappeared now, for her father. "She's very focused. In fact, I don't exist while she's working. I just keep her caffeinated and wait for her to resurface." He looked teasingly down at her, like she might jump in all, *Ha ha, funny story, guys*, and explain about their rivalry over the green chair and the outlet, like some meet-cute in a movie.

She could imagine a scenario where she did explain about the chair and the way, now that he'd mentioned it, whenever she finally leaned back from her laptop screen and stretched, Ash was nearly always already rounding the counter with a refill, like he'd been waiting for his cue. Even when she'd been single-minded about their rivalry, Ash had been something else. There. Attentive. Thoughtful. Which was why it hurt, this little charade, putting his best foot forward with her father—not so different from the charade she played with her father herself—two seconds after he'd been closed off with her.

Val said, "Well, you may have the official training, but I know my way around some gingerbread."

Hazel slipped her arm out of Ash's. He hadn't responded when she'd taken it, and he didn't respond when she let him go.

"I THOUGHT YOU'D BE GOOD AT THIS," HAZEL SAID WHEN THEIR GINGER-bread walls collapsed yet again.

"Why would I be good at this?"

"You make dollhouses for fun." She squirted a giant glob of icing between two cookie slabs.

Across the large tent, her father and Val were already paving their roof with candies while she and Ash couldn't get two walls to stay up. Lucy and Raf had declined to join, which Hazel hadn't realized was an option.

After his performance with her father, Ash had gone right back to quiet and tense and, frankly, kind of miserable, passing her icing and sprinkles without comment, leaving her to do most of the work. She'd tried to catch his eye, to make him laugh, especially when the kids at the next table started jamming jelly beans in each other's noses, but he was in his own world.

"I make *models*. With *glue*." Ash pointed out, grabbing her hand.

"Hey—"

He turned her wrist. She'd smeared icing along her thumb. His dark eyes held hers for a long moment. When he lifted her hand like he was going to lick it off, her heart stuttered in anticipation, wanted that playful, cute version of him back at the table.

But he swiped the icing with his finger instead, popped it into his mouth, and grumbled, "Gingerbread houses are actually really annoying."

His guardedness coupled with his unexplained delay left her adrift where, at least lately, she'd grown used to a strong foothold. Her stomach clenched, and it wasn't from the caramel popcorn.

Just two things she'd needed from him today: to show up when he said he would and to make a damn gingerbread house.

"What was that?"

Apparently, she'd said this out loud.

"Are you mad at me?" He was quiet, resigned, like he was already far too burdened for her slip of frustration.

Well, *that* made her kind of mad. "No," she said. "Why would I be mad at you?"

"So, you are." He ran a hand down his face and back up, raking his fingers harshly through his hair. "I'm sorry I was late, all right?"

She laughed. "Fine."

"Don't do that."

"Don't do what?"

"Get pissed and then deny it, like I can't read you at all."

"Maybe you are misreading me. Ever consider that?" After all, she couldn't read him right now, not even a little.

"Just like you're mad at your dad and this whole situation," he said, even and controlled.

"I'm not mad."

"But you bend over backward pretending everything's fine."

Her cheeks burned.

"Don't do that with me," he pleaded. "Hell, you've never had a problem telling me how I'm bugging you before."

This was true, at least after she'd broken the seal on her

grievances with him at that party freshman year. Never in her life had Hazel spoken so honestly, with such unfiltered aggression to anyone. But that had been because she'd had nothing to lose—he already didn't like her.

"Speaking of bending over backward," she said, "you sure turned on the charm back there. My dad was so impressed. An *architect*. I don't even think he knows what I'm studying."

"You're the one who told him I'm an architect. And, I'm sorry, I happen to be good with parents. Isn't that what you wanted, for me to be a buffer from your family? Who are, by the way, perfectly nice people who just want to include you."

He must have realized he'd hit a sensitive mark because he shook his head, ducking his face with remorse. "I didn't mean to leave you hanging. I'm— Something came up."

Still so vague. He hadn't thought up even the barest bones of an explanation in the last two hours. "Right, a family thing," she parroted from his text. "It's whatever, Ash."

"It isn't, actually." He sucked his teeth, shook his head in frustration. That controlled, even tone finally gave way to a flare of heat. "I feel like you should know by now I wouldn't bail on you if I could avoid it. I *hoped* you wouldn't still think I'm that kind of asshole."

The two kids to their left gasped, their wide-eyed shock at his swearing made ridiculous by the jelly beans bulging from each nostril. Even this didn't break through Ash's wall. The parents scolded the kids, and he mumbled his own embarrassed apology, squeezing the back of his neck.

Hazel didn't know *what* she knew, besides the fact that something was really off with Ash. *I wouldn't bail on you if I could avoid it.* Nice words, sure, but he still hadn't *explained*.

"So, what kept you then?" she asked.

Ash tensed even more, if that were possible. Quietly, he said,

"I don't really want to do this here. Can we just get through this and talk later?"

Somehow, this was worse than *a family thing*. This was an escalation from something so minor they didn't even need to discuss it to something so big it couldn't be discussed until later. *Later* was for difficult conversations, things you said in private so the other person wouldn't make a scene or feel mortified in front of a bunch of strangers.

Something drastic had changed since last night. He'd pursued her yesterday but could barely meet her eyes today. He couldn't muster even half the enthusiasm for her that he showed her father.

Oh God, did he even need space from his family like he'd said, or did he not want her around them, getting more attached? It had to be obvious she envied their closeness. She'd stayed so late last night, so happy to be with them. When she'd said, "I guess I should go," she'd even hoped he might say, "No. Stay."

Pathetic little barnacle. She hadn't even realized she'd latched on. But he obviously had. He'd just told her no strings, no expectations, and her very first move was to overstay, to imagine a place for herself, not just in his arms or bed, but in the core of his life. His family. As if writing her name on that laundry room door meant something.

Suddenly, every part of Hazel wanted to slam doors and turn their locks. She let the two slabs of gingerbread slump apart.

Shaking his head, he righted them. "We're so bad at this."

He was talking about the gingerbread, she thought, but he just as easily could have meant their non-relationship. She shuffled back from the table.

"What are you doing?" He twisted to look at her. "Hand me that other bag of icing. This one's too runny."

"We don't have to do this."

"What, just give up? Let them win? You hate to lose." He made a grabby gesture, moving right on from their spat back to the task at hand.

"We said if one of us wanted to stop, we'd stop."

His thick eyebrows drew together. He looked from her to their disaster of a gingerbread house and back. Finally, understanding softened his brow. "Last night, you mean. We said . . ." His back straightened. He let the slabs list to one side. "Okay. Uh . . . is that what you're saying? You want to . . ."

If he was just going to say it *later*, then yeah, she was saying it now, first. "I'm—"

"Hey, loser. Hi, Hazel."

June skipped around the table, her blonde hair in a braided crown, Fair Isle sweater tucked into high-waisted jeans, effortless and way cooler than Hazel could have ever pulled off. Across the tent, the rest of Ash's family were settling in before a fresh gingerbread kit. Annie waved cheerily at them. Hazel lifted a hand.

Ash closed his eyes and drew in a long, slow, bracing breath through his nose. "We're kind of in the middle of something, June."

"In the middle of what? Not building a gingerbread house." She eyed the mess before them, patently unimpressed.

"None of your business."

June rolled her eyes. "I see someone's still in a terrible mood. And still shit at this. I figured this was the last place we'd run into you guys. He didn't tell you about the Gingerbread Meltdown of 2009?"

"June," he warned.

She raised her hands. "Fine. Don't be a baby. Give me the icing." June lifted her chin and boasted to Hazel, "I'm the reigning

Campbell family gingerbread champ. Didn't even need five years of college to do it."

"We don't need your help," he said.

But Hazel saw the opportunity for what it was. Ash had been her buffer from her father, and now June could be her buffer from Ash. She could just keep inserting other people into every tense situation until, eventually, no one was left. Which, okay, that was depressing.

Hazel passed the icing to June, who smirked victoriously at her brother. He stuck around for a minute, eyes boring into the unresponsive side of Hazel's face, until finally, he gave up and left the tent.

"You'd think the guy would be a little nicer after freaking out and ruining our morning."

"Freaking out?" Hazel asked.

June bent to get a better look at her work, which was coming along surprisingly well after all of Hazel and Ash's failed attempts. "Oh, he didn't tell you he doesn't trust anyone to make medical decisions for themselves?"

Hazel gripped June's wrist. "What happened?"

"Dad fell, and Ash was convinced it meant he'd relapsed or something. We were supposed to go ice skating this morning, but instead, we all had to sit around while they went to the hospital, worrying about something that wasn't even wrong."

"Relapsed?" Hazel felt like an idiot having to ask for information that June clearly thought she already knew.

"Dad's MS. What, Ash didn't tell you?"

Hazel shook her head. "MS . . . multiple sclerosis?"

"Oh. That's surprising. He's kind of weirdly high-strung about it. Or maybe that's why he didn't," she offered gently, as if this might soften the blow.

That was why he'd seemed tired, why the glint was gone from his eyes. He'd been through something stressful—not *a family thing*, a family *crisis*. And she'd assumed it had been about her. God. *God*. She'd been snippy with him. She'd maybe even ended things.

"Your dad's okay, though? It's not a relapse?" She searched for Ash and June's father across the tent and found him seated in his wheelchair behind his family. He was holding Ash's younger niece in his lap.

"Yep. Just my dumb brother overreacting, as usual."

ASH DIDN'T RETURN TO THE TENT. JUNE AND HAZEL MADE A RESPECT-able gingerbread house, then followed several paces behind her father and Val in a group migration to the performance area. The seats filled in quickly, but Hazel spotted her father, Val, and Raf in the front row with a pair of seats beside them. She was saying, "I should sit with my—" when an elderly couple shuffled into the row beside her father, and rather than telling them the seats were saved, he checked over his shoulder, the minutest of scans, before gesturing for them to sit.

"Sit with us." June pulled her to the back of the crowd. They took seats between Maggie's crew and their parents.

"What about Ash?" Hazel asked.

June placed the fruitcake Hazel was still carting around at the end of the row for him. He turned up midway through the choir performance, taking the saved seat on the other side of Maggie's kids. He had just enough time to frown at the fruitcake and slide it under the chair before his smaller niece reached for him, and he pulled her into his lap and bounced her idly on his knee. Over the top of her dark curls, his eyes swung to Hazel's.

She looked away. When she risked another glance, he was still fixed on her, unreadable but strangely insistent, as if willing her to understand something he wasn't saying.

Like . . . she shouldn't be sitting here with his family.

Let me explain, she willed back. *After. Later.*

She turned from him first, afraid that in two more seconds he would break his silence and tell her to leave.

Students passed out programs as the choir took the stage in angelic-looking white gowns. They would sing a medley of Christmas carols, followed by a handful of jazz and tap numbers by the dance team. Lucy was short, so she stood in the front row. Directly across from her, Hazel's father held up his cell phone. She could partially see it from here, Lucy singing on his screen, red light recording. It came on suddenly and sharply—an ache in Hazel's throat, stinging behind her eyes. She refused to blink, willing the chilly air to dry out the brimming tears.

The transition to dancing came as a relief, and soon enough, the show was over. Hazel waited patiently for Maggie to usher her kids out of their seats and, in the other direction, for Ash's mother to unlock the wheelchair. Now that she had the chance to speak to Ash, she wished she'd spent the last forty-five minutes preparing *anything* to say. He stood to one side, holding her stupid fruitcake. That seemed like a good sign.

She strode toward him just as her father came down the center aisle from the front seats, nearly running into her. He did a double take. "Oh, you *were* here."

She turned a cheery smile on Lucy and somehow managed not to sound as incandescently angry as she felt. "You were great."

Lucy chirped a quick thanks before running off to join her friends. Val and Raf wandered ahead. But Hazel's father lingered a moment before rubbing his neck and echoing Lucy's thanks in a far more subdued tone, clarifying, "For coming." He squeezed her upper arm, and she couldn't help it—she flinched away.

Thanks? As if she were some stranger returning his grocery cart for him? As if, after she'd driven hundreds of miles, lost half her wardrobe at his entrance gate, and played her part in their little father-daughter charade, this performance had been optional?

Had it been? Not once had he asked if she wanted to come or even officially invited her. Hazel wasn't sure which was worse, to be obligated without the courtesy of an actual request—she would have said yes, obviously—or to be thanked for doing something she hadn't really minded. It cheapened it somehow to be thanked.

"Kiddo," her father said.

"Of course." She flashed a feeble smile. "I have plans this afternoon. I probably won't be back in time for dinner."

"Okay," he said.

She hadn't noticed, but Ash had meandered closer, stood just a few feet away. He offered his hand in a simultaneous greeting and goodbye to her father, his *I'm good with parents* smile. When her father left, Ash faced the parking lot beside her and said, "That was shitty." She knew what he meant—the awkward thank-you, the seat her father hadn't saved.

Hazel blinked, and the first tear fell. She didn't wipe it away, didn't turn from him or try to hide. She knew she should apologize to Ash, should tell him she hadn't meant to fight—and she would.

But for now, there was something cathartic about not saying, "It's fine."

« CHAPTER »
Sixteen

M y car wasn't made for off-roading," Hazel said, bracing on the dashboard as Ash drove over a bumpy set of hardened tire tracks between an old pecan grove on one side and a goat pen on the other.

Back at the festival, he'd asked for her keys, and she'd handed them over without a fight. He hadn't planned at the time to bring her here, but when he impulsively took the highway east of town, it made a simple kind of sense. Here, he could talk to her, come clean about this morning, his father, everything. He just hoped he wasn't too late.

Ash parked by the big, whitewashed barn. He unlocked the heavy doors with a long-memorized combination and slipped inside. The lights flickered on. He tasted dirt and rust in the air as his movements disturbed the space, which was half work-shop, half storage. What he needed was right where he expected.

When he emerged back into the daylight, Hazel squinted du-biously and crossed her arms. "What are those for?"

"Come on."

She did not fall into step behind him for a few stubborn sec-onds. Then, he heard her boots crunch through the short scrub.

Near the barbed wire fence marking the edge of the property, Ash set down his loot: a crate of golf balls, a seven iron, and a handle of Jack Daniel's that was down to its last inch. He stomped down weeds that had sprung up since the last time anyone had done this and pushed a tee into the ground.

"Explain," Hazel said, impatient.

He pointed at a slowly bobbing oil pump on the other side of the fence. "We're aiming for that."

"That's got to be a hundred yards away."

"Give or take."

Hazel let out a heavy sigh, arms still crossed. For a second, he worried he'd pushed her too far, brought her out here when she'd meant what she'd said earlier about wanting to stop what they'd only just started. But she nodded for him to go ahead. *Do it, then*, said the clench of her jaw. *Hit it.*

He knew his first ball wouldn't land anywhere near the pump. His shoulders needed to warm up first, his body had to dial into the right force. He was better with a bat than a golf club, but golf balls were cheaper than baseballs. He swung, and the ball soared in a long, low arc and fell somewhere in the mid-distance, a small puff of dirt kicking up where it landed.

He handed her the club.

"I don't know how."

Before he could offer to show her—for real, not like their flirtatious charade with the darts—she stiff-armed him. "Can I just say—"

"After you swing."

She opened her hand for the club, and he passed it to her. Then she eyed the whiskey, and he gave her that, too, tamped down a smile when she made a face at the taste. "Don't tell me how old this is. Or who else's mouth has been on it."

She teed a ball, swung, and hit a huge chunk of earth through the barbed wires. "Don't laugh." She shoved the club back at him.

"Try again."

"I don't want to golf." She bent to replace the ball on the tee anyway. "I'm trying to tell you I'm sorry."

Ash saw his mistake now, stalling and giving her the chance to speak first. She was going to tell him she was sorry they'd started this, sorry she wanted to call it off already. He could feel it. Even so, her palpable irritation was some kind of kryptonite for his dumb heart. Despite everything, one corner of his mouth twitched up. What did it say that he felt most at ease when Hazel was annoyed with him, even now?

She huffed and shouldered the club. She took a slow practice swing, eyes fixed to the ball at her feet.

Ash sipped the whiskey to keep from saying anything else. He didn't have a plan here, only broad strokes. Take her somewhere she couldn't easily run off. Do something to keep his hands busy—another club would have been nice. And alcohol. Because if he was going to tell her about his dad, he was going to need some help.

But now that they were out here, where he'd talked and drank and whacked the shit out of these balls with Travis so many times in the last several years, the flaws occurred to him. One: they'd eventually need to drive home, probably sooner rather than later, so he couldn't get drunk. And two: he'd taken her to the middle of nowhere like some kind of axe murderer.

Hazel chipped the ball a good several yards. He said, "Nice," right before she said, "June told me about your dad."

That was not at all what he'd expected her to say. Forgetting that he'd just decided not to get drunk, he took a long pull from the bottle. It seared his throat.

"The hospital this morning. His MS. I'm sorry. I feel like such a jerk for earlier. I thought you'd . . ."

"What?"

"I don't know. You were acting weird. I thought you'd changed your mind."

They switched places. She capped the Jack and set it in the dirt. He fumbled with a ball before successfully teeing it. He was afraid to ask but had to ask, "Changed my mind about what?" as he took his swing.

She watched his ball cut through the sky. "Me, I guess."

"I thought I was pretty clear last night that I want—"

"But then you showed up late today and didn't say why, and something was obviously wrong, but you wouldn't say what. Now I know, but you kept brushing me off. I thought you were trying to figure out how to break it to me gently."

He was holding out the club, but when she reached for it, her meaning crystalized, and he pulled it back. "Wait, is that why you brought up stopping this? You were beating me to it?"

She reached again for the club, eyes boring into his until he released it. "You said we needed to talk later."

"Yeah, I was going to explain about my dad."

"Oh." She tucked her hair behind her ear then busied herself with several practice swings before finally, finally hitting the damn ball. "Why didn't you just say you'd been at the hospital? I thought you didn't want me around."

He wanted to shake her. "Why would I suddenly not want you around? Haven't I come every time you've asked me to? Haven't I told you repeatedly that I *want* to be around you?"

"You *didn't* come, though. And then you were squirrelly and quiet. If you were going to break up with me—I mean, not *break up* break up. I know we're not—" She blew out a frazzled breath. "I was taking the hint."

"It wasn't a hint."

"Well, it felt like one."

"Are you really that—" *Insecure*, he wanted to say, but didn't.

Another flaw to bringing her out here: he'd given her a weapon. She nearly threw the club at him. Her chest rose and fell with sharp breaths, and he realized he was doing the same, getting worked up. If he wasn't careful, he would go too far, just like he had at the hospital with his parents.

"It wasn't a hint, okay? I didn't want to dump all my family stuff on you in the middle of Winter Fest. That's why I wanted to talk later."

"It wasn't just at the festival, though," she said. "I've been to your house, met your family. I've told you all kinds of personal things. Why didn't you tell me about your dad before? June thought I knew. And last night, Franny was asking about him, wasn't she? Not his hip, but the MS?"

Reluctantly, Ash nodded.

"So, what, you can talk about it with Franny, but not me?"

"That's not it at all. She knows because people around here know about it now. I haven't *talked* to her, not in any deep way."

"If people around here know, then why keep it a secret from me?"

He swung hard, and the ball sailed out and up, suspended for a long moment, the small white sphere nearly vanishing in the washed-out sky before its arc broke. The ball bounced off the top of the pump with a distant *ping*.

"Why?" Hazel pressed.

"Honestly?" He teed up another ball, ignoring that it was her turn. "Hazel, I've been trying to figure out some foolproof way to be with you and not scare you off."

He swung again. He reached for the next ball as the last hit its mark. "You told me nothing could change. You don't do afters. Hell, you made me promise you the café because, if *anything* went wrong, you'd be done with me."

Another swing. Another hit.

"I—"

"It was always just a matter of time, wasn't it, before things got too serious? I thought if I could keep things easy and uncomplicated, maybe I could hold on long enough for you to see that I'm—"

A gust of wind blew his next ball off the tee. He scrubbed his face in frustration. "Maybe I should have told you about my dad sooner. But look what happened the first time things got remotely difficult. You panicked and tried to bail. Because God forbid you have to admit you have feelings about anything."

"That's not fair."

"It's not?"

Her shoulders hunched in, and her lip quivered before she bit it. As soon as he registered how hard his words had landed, she thrust her hand out for the club. He barely jumped out of the way before she was planting her feet and rounding back for a big swing. "You're the one who said this was just physical, that you could stop on a dime and go right back to pouring my coffee."

Her ball shot wide, ricocheted off the fence post with a loud *crack*, and zinged back, nearly taking out Ash's knee.

"Shit, I'm sorry, I'm sorry," she cried, flinging the club away.

A harsh laugh scraped out of his throat, part relief and part indignation. "What was I supposed to say, Hazel? That I'm so fucking gone on you I'm already dreading the end of this trip? When we go back to regular life, and coffee is the only thing you'll need from me?"

"You're— Ash."

He turned. He couldn't look at her. This was exactly what he'd been trying to avoid.

"*Ash.*" The remorse woven into his name made his chest tight. Her fingers brushed his knuckles, his wrist, and squeezed. He could hear the catch in her throat behind him when she tried to speak but stopped. Then, "All I've wanted these past few days," she said, her voice so quiet the wind nearly carried it away, "is to get as close to you as you've somehow gotten to me."

He turned around, and she shifted back to maintain the space between them, a buffer. He clasped his hand over hers to keep her grip on his wrist, keep her right in front of him. "That true?"

She blew out a breath. "Yes."

He didn't let her duck her face, tipped her chin up. She held his gaze as long as she seemed able to stand it before the dark fringe of her eyelashes fluttered closed.

"Haze, I need you to tell me if any part of you wants to stop. For the record, I don't. At all. But if you do, I'll figure out how to—"

"Pour my coffee?" She came back to him with more confidence this time, her eyes open and bright. With a resolute shake of her head, she toed up and kissed him, firm, closing the door on that avenue of thought. She stayed close, her breath ghosting across his lips. "I don't want to stop, Asher."

It was that stupid, playful nickname, after all her harsh, angry intonations of *Ash*, that made him cradle her face and pull her mouth back to his. "I kind of hate that you've made me like that."

"What?" Her hands slipped up under the back of his jacket, fingertips pressing against his flannel shirt. He inched closer, and she made an approving sound in the back of her throat that made him want to do anything, everything she wanted.

"You do know my name really is just Ash, right?"

She laughed and pecked his cheek then his neck, pausing to say, "I feel like I'm going to need to see your birth certificate."

Her fingers delved under his shirt at his lower back. He hissed at her freezing touch, reached behind to take her hands in his, covering them, keeping her wrapped around him.

"You're always warm," she murmured, burying her nose into his chest.

They stood like this for a moment, the wind licking her hair up and making her burrow even closer. It wasn't nearly as cold as a few days ago, lower fifties and almost pleasant in the sun, but the wind still bit. With shuffling, rocking steps, he walked her back toward the barn to block it. "I'm named after a tree. We all are."

She looked thoughtful. "Maggie . . . Magnolia?"

He nodded.

"And . . . Juniper?"

"Yeah, but don't ever call her that. She hates it. Leanne is short for Oleander, and then Laurel."

"Why trees?"

He crowded her against the wood siding of the barn. "My parents got married on Arbor Day."

"That's sweet."

"Yeah, until you're a scrawny kindergartner on a school bus with the name Ash."

"Oh." She winced. "Poor boy."

He chuckled. "Why am I telling you my childhood embarrassments? Not very manly."

"I beg to differ."

"Oh, yeah? My getting picked on is a turn-on? That doesn't surprise me, actually."

She nodded, dead serious. "It's only fair after everything I've told you. There's even a theory in psychology about this—social penetration theory."

He tugged her belt loop. "I'm listening."

"The theory is that people grow closer through an intensifying series of self-disclosures, beginning with superficial things like favorite bands or TV shows and moving toward more personal stuff." She gulped as his lips brushed lightly down the side of her neck. "Like childhood traumas. But it requires reciprocity, or else one person winds up more vulnerable."

"Reciprocity, huh? Like, I'll show you mine if you show me yours?"

"Basically."

"Who knew psychology was so hot?"

She tugged him closer. He caught himself on the wall above her shoulder, but not before stumbling into her, chest to chest, his knee wedging between hers. He tried to push off her, but with a bright laugh, she wrapped her arms tighter around him and kissed him again. He was already hard and fought the desire to rock against the soft lower curve of her stomach, but just barely. Breathing was no longer a vital concern. He could survive on gasps of secondhand air between kisses. Her foot hooked around his calf, agreeing, warning, *Don't you dare pull back.* The almost painful dig of her nails at his back made him twist and give in, give her what they both wanted. When he grinded against her, she rolled her hips into his.

Ash wanted to touch every inch of her, but so much of her body was covered up, and at every point his hands settled—her neck, her collarbone, the stolen spot of warmth at her hip beneath her sweater—he had to resist squeezing too tightly. But when his fingertips grazed up over her stomach, her ribs, and finally met the satin band of her bra, the control he'd managed so far nearly broke.

He groaned, pulling his mouth from hers only to smother his face into her shoulder. He bit playfully at the material there, chuckling at how crazy he felt, how badly he wanted to sink his teeth into *her.* "Hazel . . ."

He didn't even know what he was trying to tell her. He wanted to savor and devour at the same time. Through his in-

toxication with her, the sensory overload, her smell—so fucking
sweet and minty and something he couldn't name—he felt a
vague imperative to not push any harder than she did. Whatever line she set, he would not cross. But damn, he would walk
right up to it.

Her fingers slipped through his hair and gently scratched his
scalp before tugging at the roots.

"Tell me if you—"

"I don't want to stop," she said.

While he nuzzled the neckline of her sweater down with his
chin, kissing the swell of skin just above her bra, his hands rev-
erently spanned her rib cage, then cupped her breasts, thumbs
finding her nipples through the thin material. He brushed one
and peered up to watch her eyes close, her teeth bite into her
lower lip. He brushed it again, this time with more pressure, and
she shivered.

"Is it too cold?" he whispered, hoarse.

"No." Her fingers were still frigid where they settled at the
nape of his neck, her nose and cheeks pink. A mass of clouds
crowded out the weak midday light, casting them in shade.

Ash reluctantly slipped his hands from her sweater.

"Why are you stopping?" she demanded, borderline whiny.

He pecked the tip of her nose, grinning at her immediate
scowl. Then, he tugged her to the front of the barn.

<< CHAPTER >>

Seventeen

Hazel's skin was cold, but inside, she burned.

While Ash opened up the barn, she had to hug herself to keep from wrapping her arms around him. If that made her desperate, so be it. She was. Every sensor in her touch-starved body had fired back online. It had been so long since anyone had put their hands on her, and the brief loss of contact while he went around flipping on lights, closing the door, and plugging in a space heater, tested her self-control.

The inside of the barn didn't match its rough exterior—fully finished with warm gray walls, and insulated, she guessed, from the complete hush of the wind outside. The wood-plank floor was a bit nicked and scuffed but swept clean around neat rows of boxes. And though the rafters were high, a loft ate into half of it with a circle staircase leading up. Big, rustic wagon-wheel chandeliers lit up the space.

"Are we trespassing?" she asked suddenly.

He shook his head, then moved in close behind her and rubbed warmth into her arms. That wasn't much of an answer, and this was clearly private property—they'd passed a house on the way in—but she lost her conviction as soon as she felt him at her back. She tried to spin around, but he stilled her. One hand slid across her stomach, the other to her hip then her butt. He nipped at her ear as his hand dragged up to her breast. Just like outside, she thought she might collapse from the relief of that wide, warm palm.

"God, your body," he murmured. "Don't know where to touch you first."

The heater hummed, low and steady, an echo of the thrum of blood in her ears. It was either incredibly efficient, or she was so turned on she could no longer register the chill.

All Hazel could do in this position was receive his hot, open-mouthed kisses on the back of her neck, the electric promise of his fingers tracing her waistband, dipping just inside to skim the top of her underwear. She endured the agonizing bliss of it until, finally, desperate, she turned in his arms.

She was struck by how beautiful he looked right now, watchful and intense, his eyes dark, locked on her. Even his eyebrows did something to her, thick and a little unruly, that sexy scar. Hazel kissed one, pulling a soft laugh from him. She kissed the other, then his cheek, his chin, his throat, the dip where his neck met his shoulder. Her kisses turned to sucking, and she pressed her palms to his chest, his stomach, working them under his layers of shirts to feel his sun-hot skin over ridges of lean muscles. Oh, yes. This. She wanted this body on hers.

"Take this off," she said, trying to pull apart the halves of his flannel.

He laughed. "They're buttons, not snaps."

"They're annoying."

He shrugged his jacket off then worked the shirt buttons quickly, and she yanked it down his shoulders. Next came the Henley underneath and then—

"Jesus Christ, this is the clown car of shirts." She shoved the last undershirt, a threadbare tee, up and off, and there he was, bare and lean, his chest rising and falling. She tore off her own sweater and shirt in one quick movement, not caring where they fell, and melded her body to his.

Then her hands were between them, working at his fly.

Ash groaned and walked her backward until her backside hit a ledge. A workbench, she realized, just as he bent to catch the backs of her thighs and lifted her onto it.

She'd managed to get his zipper down, and now that her face was just above his, she had the perfect vantage point to see his pleasure pass across it when she slipped her hand in and palmed him over his underwear. He swayed involuntarily into her touch and pulled her face down for a kiss that immediately turned rough, his tongue probing into her mouth, teeth catching her lip.

Her mind snagged on the unexpected image of Christmas trees.

Ash pulled away, panting, eyes dark with want. "Are you laughing with your hand down my pants?"

"You told me you weren't working with a *Charlie Brown Christmas* tree in here." She couldn't get it out without a giggle. "You weren't lying."

He opened and closed his mouth, at a loss. "If you utter the word 'stately,' I'm out of here."

"It's a compliment."

He shook his head, trying for stern, but he was breathless, eyelids heavy, and very hard against her hand.

Then, an unexpected touch at the seam of her jeans pressed right at the part of her that had begun to ache, and she squeezed her thighs around his hips, heels at the backs of his knees begging him closer. His mouth dropped to her collarbone. Before she could get used to the delicious wet warmth there, he moved lower, lips dragging over her, tongue darting out to lick just above her bra. He tried the clasp at her back for two seconds before giving up, hooking his fingers into one cup, and tugging it down. His mouth covered and then sucked her nipple, a moan vibrating straight to her heart.

She didn't recognize her own voice, but yes, that was a whimper, and it had come from her. She was a live wire from months of deprivation and loneliness. But this—*he*—was something else. She was losing control a lot faster than usual, writhing into him, nearly hyperventilating. She wanted him so badly she could cry.

Hazel shoved her hand inside his waistband, wrapped her fingers around him.

He groaned at the contact, rocked forward into her grip as she began to work him. "Fuck. Wait." Ash tilted his face up to the open rafters of the barn and then back down, kissing her more gently this time. "If you keep that up," he murmured against her lips, "this isn't going to last as long as either of us wants."

She smiled and knew he felt it because he grumbled, "Don't be cute. I want this to be good for you."

Every inch of him screamed restraint. His shoulder muscles, his abs, his jaw—they were all rubber bands about to snap. Couldn't he see she felt the same, practically bursting through her own skin? She wanted to see him lose control, but not at the expense of his pride, even if her own had left the building.

She released her hold on him, ran her palms up his back to the smooth plane of each shoulder blade as he snaked a hand into her pants—when had he gotten them open?—and stroked the damp heat of her underwear, making her jump and then grind shamelessly into his touch.

After a few rolls of her hips, he stopped to work her jeans down over her butt. The wooden workbench was cold under the backs of her thighs. The shock of it wasn't entirely unwelcome, though, one extreme swinging to its opposite, just like her warring desires to race ahead and to savor this.

He pulled her closer to the edge so she was perched there, one hand clinging to the back of his neck, the other planted behind her for leverage. His fingers were finally on her without a barrier, gently stroking her slick heat then circling right where she wanted him.

"Ash," she panted.

"What do you want?"

She wanted everything—his fingers, his mouth, him pushing deep inside her. She wanted the sweet release that was building, but also for this to never end.

"Don't go quiet on me now," he teased. He stroked her entrance, thumb still circling, and she shuddered in anticipation.

"Ash," she said again, his name a harsh intake of breath, broken and needy.

"God, you're too much." In any other context, she might have taken this as a complaint, but his voice was so raw and wanting.

He yanked her underwear down her thighs, tilting her back so her shoulders and head met the pegboard for tools on the wall. On the other side of the table, something clattered down and fell to the floor with a metallic *clunk*. She covered her head, laughing, but then his face was between her thighs, and he was licking into her, and she forgot everything else except the hot velvet press of his tongue.

When she clutched his hair, he pushed a finger into her, withdrew it, and immediately added another, the stretch and fullness almost pushing her over the edge. She felt unmoored, swept up in a huge swell about to break.

"Condom?" she managed to say.

He shook his head then pulled back. "I don't—"

"What?"

"Hazel, I didn't bring condoms to a family festival." He brought his mouth back to her like this wasn't the worst possible news he could give her right now.

"Whose barn is this? There was alcohol. Maybe there are condoms."

The rumble of his laugh against her core made her eyes flutter closed. "Do you want me to stop and look?"

Yes. No. God, she didn't know anything right now, except that she wanted more of him, all of him. His mouth was already back to work.

"I'm close." It came out like a complaint.

"Good."

If she was going to fall apart, she wanted him right there with her. "Reciprocity," she said, unable to articulate anything more.

At first, he kept his steady pace against and inside of her, but when she tugged helplessly at his hair, he relented, rising back up. "Okay, okay." He tongued at her free breast again and caressed and massaged the other. Every part of her body clenched with the insane pleasure of it, and she wasted no time getting back into his boxer briefs.

Soon, his teasing at her nipple turned aimless as he rocked his hips, pushing himself into her grip. Even his mouth fell away when his breathing turned ragged. He curled over her, their chests touching, their wrists and hands brushing with each pull and thrust. He was right there, almost where she wanted him, so tantalizingly close. His weight now resting more heavily on her, fingers still filling her, pushing deep while she ground hard against the heel of his palm, their bodies simulating what they were barely not doing, she could imagine the real thing, and she broke.

With a sharp cry, she buried her face into his neck, and somehow, in the midst of his own quickening, unsteady thrusts, he cradled the back of her head so sweetly, holding her to him. He saw her through it, her body shuddering, and then he followed, falling against her and groaning her name.

Eighteen

This is my best sandwich," Hazel said, dropping his mother's apron around her neck.

When she reached back for the ties, Ash pushed her hands away and knotted them for her. He lingered, sliding his palms over her hips. She gathered her hair to twist it into a bun, and he bent to kiss the back of her neck. He could do this now, see a part of her he wanted to touch and do it.

Less than an hour ago, in the barn, before his shaky breaths calmed, before the full-body shudder leveled back out, reality had flooded in—the cold, sawdust-covered table beneath Hazel's bare butt, the rusty wrench that had clattered down by his feet, and the mess between them, his fingers still curled inside her, her hand still loosely gripping him. He might have joked about the cringey convenience of blue, industrial strength paper towels within reach above the workbench, but he was still coming down, still too cracked open to say a word before he tore one off and set about cleaning them both up.

Had it ever been like this, after? This fragile feeling, like he'd break if she breathed a certain way? He couldn't remember. But then, he couldn't remember a *during* like they'd just had, either. Never had he felt so desperate to worship every inch of a partner before he chased his own need. And then, Hazel had demanded *reciprocity*—not a plea for her own pleasure but for *his*, for him to fall apart with her—and the vulnerability in her eyes had snapped something in him, whatever final thread of restraint had allowed him to savor her while keeping himself at bay. All of this with only his hands and his mouth. How would it be when they managed to get where they both so desperately wanted to go?

Hazel had let him wipe at her stomach, sighing contentedly back against the pegboard.

"Sorry," he muttered, self-conscious when she took over with a fresh paper towel.

"For what? That was . . ." She shook her head slowly, abandoning the search for words. She bit into one side of her kiss-swollen lip to stop a grin, and the gesture was so sweet and reassuring, he wanted to thumb her mouth free so he could see the full force of her smile.

Instead, he zipped up his pants and searched for the rest of their clothes.

"Now that *that's* out of the way," Hazel said, "whose barn is this?"

Ash was grateful for the question, light, pushing them straight past any awkwardness. He pulled his T-shirt back on, keeping his body half turned in case she needed privacy. "Travis and Derek's."

He heard her hop down off the table, her zip rise. "Okay, now I'm certain we could have found condoms in here."

"But we would have had to stop what we were doing."

She made a sound of reluctant agreement and touched his shoulder, prompting him to turn. She took her clothes from his hands. "Rain check, though. Right?"

She was so goddamned pretty, swollen lips, unruly hair, skin still flushed from her cheeks down to her— Ash had to physically retreat to keep from escalating things again. "Absolutely."

Now, she was preparing to make him a sandwich in his kitchen, and he was almost dizzy with the fact that he got to be with her here, like this, unfiltered, unrestrained, so achingly *casual*. He was most at home here—a thought that made him huff a laugh against her skin. Of course he felt at home, it was his literal home. But it was more than that. She *belonged* here.

"So, tell me about your best sandwich."

"It's not that fancy," she warned, setting a skillet onto the stove. She broke their contact as she fetched things from the fridge and their grocery bags, and he gave her space, leaning back against the counter.

"Don't downplay it now, Hazel."

"I shouldn't have built it up."

"My expectations are very high."

"You're the worst."

He nodded solemnly. "Can I help?"

"No. The main thing going for it is that it's unexpected. So, if you watch, it'll lose its mystery."

Ash laughed. "Okay, but just know that this is still a lot of buildup."

"Do you want to . . ." She spread butter across four slices of bread, and he felt how intentionally she didn't look at him. "Do you want to stand over there and not watch me cook and finish what you were saying before? About the golf balls?"

Earlier, once they'd dressed, and he'd returned the golf balls, club, and nearly empty bottle of whiskey to their place in the corner of the barn, she'd asked, "So hitting that oil pump is something you guys do for fun?"

"No, not for fun."

And then a silence opened up that she waited for him to fill. He'd brought her out there for exactly this—this chance to explain in the only way he'd ever really known how to talk about his father. It was time. But her stomach had growled loudly, and he had promised to talk once they'd had lunch.

Even now, he wanted to stall again. But for how playful she'd been before, explaining her psychology theory, the need for reciprocal disclosures, he understood she felt the scales were out of balance when it came to this.

"Travis and Derek's dad sold their mineral rights to some oil company about five years ago. It was a bad deal for them."

Hazel hummed sympathetically as she sliced into a block of sharp cheddar.

"Around that time was when my dad . . ." He drummed his fingers on the counter behind him. "He wasn't diagnosed right away, but he was having symptoms, seeing doctors, running tests. They initially thought it was ALS. That was senior year."

"When we met?" Hazel asked, surprised.

He nodded and chose to ignore the little frown she cast at the cutting board.

"From pretty early on, he'd lose feeling in his feet, his balance. Once, my mom tried to help him to his bed. You've seen their height difference. He was heavier back then, too. He knocked her down, and she broke her wrist."

Hazel's hands, now arranging precooked bacon on a paper towel, froze.

"After that, I did most of the physical stuff. His legs would go numb, or he'd be so fatigued, I'd have to haul him to his bed. They were still trying to keep the worst of it from June and the twins. Maggie was away at college, and my mom wouldn't let us tell her. And we weren't supposed to stress him out because stress can make it worse, so we just . . . didn't talk about it."

Ash's jaw clenched as if in residual resistance. He'd stood in almost this very spot the day of the broken wrist. His mom wrapped an ice-filled towel around her arm, her back to him at the stove, then cracked eggs one-handed into a skillet for breakfast while June overslept and the twins bickered through the bathroom door. "Are you hurt?" he'd asked, and she'd turned around, blotchy-faced and teary but with a cheerful smile. "Everything's fine. Eggs?"

Only once he was away at college did she talk—in those panicky, breathless dumps over the phone, like she could only admit the full scope of her fear with distance, her worries so much heavier than she'd ever let on in person. Although he wanted to know the truth and wanted to help, some part of him walled off at her crying.

Again, he regretted the way he'd thrown this like a weapon at his parents in the hospital earlier.

"Anyway," Ash said, realizing he'd gone quiet. Hazel had assembled two sandwiches, and the butter on the bread sizzled in the skillet. "I went over to Trav's one night, and he and Derek and their dad were hitting golf balls at that pump and getting trashed, and it seemed like as good an idea as anything else to deal with how—" He clasped the back of his neck, the word stopping in his throat. He swallowed. "How angry I guess I was. And then, for a while, when I felt that way, I went and tried to hit that pump. Sometimes, when we drank too much and couldn't aim for shit anymore, we'd talk."

"You and Travis?"

"He's got his own stuff. I guess everyone does. But yeah, he knows more than anyone else what things were like back then."

"Even Justin?"

Ash hesitated. He still wasn't sure how sore a subject Justin was for her. "You know my dad coached all our Little League teams growing up?"

"No."

"Justin was good. Natural talent. But his dad also pushed him hard, got rough sometimes."

She nodded. "He yelled a lot at games."

"Yeah. He was worse when we were little, if you can believe that. Justin spent most of his time at my house, avoiding him. He would talk my dad's ear off about baseball. We'd run drills in the backyard. We were practically brothers. I mean, every memory I have from childhood, he was there. With so many sisters, it was nice to have another guy around. My mom used to call us peanut butter and jelly. I was a shy, careful kid. He was always looking for fun, or making it himself." He nodded at Hazel. "*You* know. He brought out some different sides of me, and I kept him mostly out of trouble. But when my dad got sick, he stopped coming around, just like that. He didn't get why I was distracted, why I quit the club season right before senior year."

Ash swallowed. He never talked about this. "Early that summer, my dad had one of his first bad episodes and, uh . . . wet himself during a game. I saw it from home plate, my mom trying to help him down the bleachers. Justin didn't notice until my dad wasn't there for our usual postgame breakdown. He was such an ass about it. I was trying to get ahold of my mom to find out what had happened, and Justin was mad my dad wasn't there to heap praise on him."

Ash shook his head, the frustration of that day fresh. "I got it. His dad backed off when mine was around. But he wasn't . . . there. For us. For me."

"I hate him for that," Hazel said quietly.

Ash didn't like to think about it.

"When everything came out at graduation," he said, meaning Justin's college plans, "and you guys broke up, we went to a party a couple weeks later. He acted like he'd done nothing wrong, and I lost it. It was just *everything*, all year. He never got what was going on with my dad, or me. He only cared how it affected his game. When I got benched for missing practices—because my dad was having these flare-ups—and he pitched that bad game—"

"When he tackled his own catcher," she recalled.

"Yeah. And that coach rescinded his verbal offer, Justin blamed me for not playing. Said he would have pitched better to me. Even if he didn't, I would have kept him from losing his cool. And I actually felt guilty about it. I mean, shit. He didn't have other options. College ball was his dream since forever. I guess that's why I kept quiet for him with you, even though I didn't like it. But I snapped at that party. We beat the shit out of each other, didn't speak again all summer. When I see him here, we pretend it never happened, but we're not close."

"I'm sorry," she said quietly.

"*I'm* sorry."

She shook her head. "Don't. You didn't owe me. He made his choices." Then, "It's hard to talk about? The stuff with your dad?" Her voice was achingly tender, sweet.

"It's not that I didn't trust you with it."

"You were afraid it would feel too serious."

"I *was*," he began, quiet around an ache in his throat. "But not just because you might pull away. The opposite, actually. I knew if you saw this . . ." She turned, spatula hovering, and he gestured feebly around them at his home. "I was the one who would want to hide out until I had it handled. I'm just now realizing I'm not actually very good at this part."

She tilted her head, sympathy and confusion both in her eyes. "What part?"

"Talking about it before it's okay. My parents don't— My dad doesn't like to be managed, and my mom doesn't like to dwell on anything negative, so we just silently handle the situation and then . . . move on."

"Like the other day when your dad got up to go to the living room," Hazel said. "Suddenly you and your mom were there, helping him, like you guys had this sixth sense."

"Yeah, I guess we do." He sat for a moment with that—that she'd seen something even his own sisters barely noticed, that she'd been paying such close attention. "I'm not used to talking about it much at all, but especially when I don't know what's going to happen. Or I didn't, before this morning." Then, out of habit: "Everything's all right now."

That his father had been cleared today should have made it easier to tell her all of this, but everyone's frustration when Ash had pushed to call the doctor, then the fight in the exam room, the fact that his father still hadn't looked at him since and the rest had barely spoken to him, even his mother, made his chest ache.

"I overreacted this time. June told you, right? But it's frustrating. Sometimes, they want me to step up and help. Then they don't. They're the parents, I'm the kid."

"Like they didn't expect you to manage it with them when you were just a kid."

"I'm not complaining."

"I know. But you were seventeen with all that on your shoulders? I wish I'd known. Those nights you drove us around, I thought you were annoyed I was tagging along. When you fell asleep in class and missed practices, I thought you just didn't care. You must have been so stressed out." She turned the burner off and faced him, a deep furrow in her brow. "God, you were helping take care of your dad, your sisters, your mom, even Justin and . . ." She didn't say *me*, but he saw the realization on her face.

He clutched the back of his neck.

"*Ash.*"

"It's nothing."

"It's not nothing. All of it, everything—" She gave a frustrated huff. When she spoke again, her voice was so soft it needled straight into his heart. "Who was taking care of you?"

"Come on," he said with an attempt at a quick, reassuring smile. "I was fi—" But his throat finally succeeded in sealing itself off. Pressure built behind his sinuses and then his eyes, and blinking it back brought it instead to the surface. Tears—fucking tears—gathered.

She took a half step, opened her arms, but stopped. "Can I?"

He shrugged because to say that, yes, he wanted her to cross the short distance and hug him felt embarrassingly weak, but this was all she needed to push into his space, to wrap her arms tightly around him until the ache in his throat released and the sting behind his eyes passed. After a while, he murmured, "Our food will get cold."

She squeezed tighter, breathing him in. "One more minute."

"THIS IS REALLY FUCKING GOOD."

Hazel tossed her napkin at him.

"I'm serious. I'm adding this to the café menu when we get back. 'Hazel's Best Sandwich.' It'll be a bestseller."

"You'll have to pry the turkey and Swiss from Frank's cold, dead hands first."

"Dark." Ash smiled around another big bite. "What made you think to put pears in a sandwich?"

"Actually," she said, something sparking in her eyes, "that wasn't me. After the divorce, my dad didn't know how to cook much of anything. He used to order pizza or buy these awful premade meals. We lived on those and PopTarts and cereal forever. After a while, I got so annoyed that I basically yelled at him for not feeding me a real meal and sitting at the table to eat it together. He had no idea how to do the things my mom used to do. I'm talking basic cooking, cleaning, laundry. He didn't unpack the boxes from our old house for *months*."

She cleared her throat, sat up straighter. "I mean, I'm sure it was all a lot—feeding me, coordinating babysitters around his crazy work schedule—"

Ash caught her wrist across the table. She did this a lot, this downplaying and redefining of things she hadn't quite meant to say.

She took a breath and started again. "The day I lectured him about food, he pulled out all the ingredients we had, and we came up with this. A pear and bacon grilled cheese."

"It's delicious."

"Thanks."

"So," he said, hesitant to bring up what he'd witnessed that afternoon at the festival. Ash had watched her watch her father filming her stepsister's performance and felt helpless to reach her across his family sitting between them. That her father really thought she'd no-show after everything Hazel had done to show up gut-punched him as sharply now as it had in the moment. He'd wanted to whisk her away, to rewind time and not be such an ass about the gingerbread house, to not have walked out when she started to shut down.

"What?" Hazel prompted around a delicate bite of her sandwich.

"Why'd you come home?"

Her stare was pointedly blank, like he was being obtuse. "I was summoned."

"Yeah, but you had a choice."

She mulled this over. "Didn't really feel like a choice."

"You've never come home before. Not for holidays. Not for summer breaks. Pretty typical times when you're expected to visit, but you always chose not to. And it sounds like your dad doesn't make much of an effort to come see you, either. So, why now?"

"He's getting married."

"Yeah," Ash said carefully, "and you told me you don't need any more people in your inner circle."

She shook her head, less a denial and more of a helpless flail. "If I didn't come, it would seem like it was *about* the wedding. Like I had a problem with it."

"Which you . . . don't?"

"I don't." Hazel wiped her mouth with her napkin. "It doesn't affect me at all."

"You've said that. A lot, actually."

She narrowed her eyes. "What are you getting at? That I'm protesting too much? That I'm a big baby, and it hurts my feelings that he's suddenly this great dad to someone else's kids?" Her voice dipped into a mocking sneer on the last bit.

Ash opened his palms on the table. He wanted to close them around her hands, but she pulled them into her lap. "I think if that's how you were feeling, no one would call it childish. If you were hurt or angry, it would be justified."

"It's not like it's some huge burden to be here."

Ash wasn't sure about that. For one thing, she had resisted it so vehemently from the beginning that, even if she didn't think it *should* be a burden, it clearly felt like one anyway. For another thing, Ash had wanted to come home, chosen it freely, and he still felt burdened by the position his parents had put him in, sometimes responsible for their problems, sometimes shut out like he was being controlling instead of concerned. At least their relationship could survive the discord. His father wouldn't let him leave without speaking to him again, no matter how angry he was. From what Ash could see, Hazel felt obligated to come home, but that obligation ran in only one direction.

Hazel chewed on her lower lip and looked out the window. It was dim in the kitchen. They hadn't turned the lights on, and the feeble daylight was fading. He waited for her to say more, but she remained quiet. The thing about Hazel, he realized, was that when something really got under her skin, her usual fierceness and quick, combative spirit were nowhere to be found. She would fight for a chair in a café, or to follow her own driving directions instead of his, or to win at a silly bar game, but corner her on something real and she'd close right up.

He wanted more of her, not less. "Point is, I'm Team Hazel. That's all I'm trying to say."

She finally cast a tentative glance back at him. A little smile quirked the corner of her mouth, and she lifted her sandwich. "We should get you a team shirt then. It's pink. And sequined."

"Okay. Sure."

"And very fitted." Her eyes dropped to his shoulders and torso, and he watched her openly appreciate his body.

"I'm not scared." If he flexed a little, sue him.

"Good."

"Hey. Finish eating. I want to go upstairs with you."

"Wow." She laughed. "Subtle."

"Not for that. I mean, not *not* for that. I just want to . . ." He rubbed his face, chuckling into his palms. Why was he embarrassed, especially after what they'd already done in the barn? "I want to hold you. In my bed."

She chewed slowly, feigning deep thought, dragging it out.

"Haze," he groaned. A bubbling affection for her washed over him.

"You told me you didn't want to spoon me."

"When did I—"

She clasped her hands on the table between them, utterly serious. "In the Lovebird Suite. You said—"

Ash pushed back from the table and hoisted her out of her chair and over his shoulder. "I lied," he said, loving the loud laugh that burst from her.

She swatted ineffectually at his back, exclaiming in mock horror, "Oh my God, you *lied*? You were *dying* to spoon me?"

He set her down at the door to the stairs and smoothed her wild hair back from her bright, smiling, perfect face. He shook his head at her, pressed a firm kiss to her forehead. "You have no idea."

"Well, we'd better—"

The front door opened.

"Greet your family," she finished, amused at how he deflated against her.

"They can't see us. We could hurry up there. They'll never know we're here."

"Except for my car and all the dishes we left out." She kissed his cheek then laid a loud, hard slap on his butt. "Buck up, private."

Nineteen

It was late when Hazel returned to her father's house. She'd stayed at Ash's through board games, dinner, and a movie. When they'd finally ventured up to his room, he'd held her just like he said he wanted to, his body fitted to the back of hers, arms tight around her. If he'd rolled his hips, if his lazy finger strokes on her arm had ventured anywhere else, if his affectionate nuzzling on her neck ever turned to kissing, Hazel would have reignited like dry kindling. But she followed his lead, and after a while, an odd combination of sensations enveloped her, like falling and being caught, a sinking rock settling into a soft seabed. She'd snapped a photo of them on her phone, wanting to hold on to the feeling. "Proof of life?" he'd murmured, and although she didn't intend to send it to Sylvia, that phrase had been exactly, perfectly right.

She was still thinking about Ash's soft flannel comforter that smelled like him and his low, sleepy-rough voice in her ear, talking about small things—parts of campus they both liked, local events they'd attended, movies they'd seen, though none of them together—when she let herself through her father's front door.

The alarm chirped. It hadn't been set, and she wondered whether she should tell someone she was back or try to set it herself. Then, the panel beeped, and a flashing alert told her the alarm was reactivated—a keypad in the master bedroom, probably. In which case, her father or Val was aware she was sneaking back in at nearly one in the morning.

Did Lucy or Raf ever come home after curfew and tiptoe up the stairs to their room, mindful of every creaky place on every step? Hazel mused. Was it Val or Hazel's father, or both, who waited up to lecture them? A door opened. She lurched out of sight, only to catch her toe on a potted plant and fall hard to her knees on the tile floor.

"Hazel?" her father asked from his bedroom door across the living room.

She could crawl to her room. In the dark, she'd just be a weird shadow, and then she'd be gone. But if he saw her *crawling* away, that would be far more awkward than saying a quick hello and slinking off to bed.

"Yeah, it's me. Sorry."

As she struggled to right the plant she'd taken down, the foyer light flicked on. "What are you doing?"

She didn't know if he meant right at that moment, hoisting the heavy pot back onto its flat bottom, or if he wanted to know what she'd *been* doing. Or was it a broader question, some fundamental confusion about her as a person? She wasn't sure how to answer, which he apparently took to mean something was wrong because he eased the weight of the pot out of her hands and held her by the shoulders to get a good, concerned look at her.

Oh God, did he think she was drunk? She'd never once had this experience as a teenager, but now, as an adult, she was going to have to convince her father she hadn't broken any rules he'd never set.

"I'm out late a lot at school," she said defensively. "College towns don't really sleep." Suddenly, it felt imperative not to apologize. No one had asked her to be back by a certain time.

Hazel's father nodded at the throbbing knee she was absently massaging. "Do we need to amputate?" Maybe every dad told this one, even the ones who stepped back from the job of parenting, but she had clear memories of him saying it while she fought tears on a playground, a soccer field, beneath the big tree in their old backyard. It always broke through the pain, made her huff a little laugh.

"I think I'll live."

"Just in case, I know what will help."

The words came out before she even thought them. "Ice cream?"

"You still like mint chip?"

Part of her wanted to hug him. But then, remembering her favorite ice cream was a pretty low bar, wasn't it?

He offered her whipped cream and sprinkles, and she declined because she wasn't eight years old, but she relented to chocolate syrup because a third no felt like it would *mean* something. Was he as hyperaware as she was of all these tiny, unspoken negotiations? Was he making them, too, or was it completely one-sided?

She sat in the dining chair that had been unofficially assigned to her. He took the one beside her, Lucy's usual place. Then they ate in silence. Just *didn't speak*. And she didn't actually want ice cream, not all by itself.

Ash had asked why she'd come back here. It was true enough what she'd told him, that it hadn't felt like a choice. She'd *resisted* coming, but it was empty resistance. Ash didn't realize all those other usual times people their age visited home, she hadn't been asked to come, hadn't had to say yes or no. So, when her father sent a *formal invitation* to the occasion of his wedding, it felt like a big deal. If she said no to that one, another invitation may never come.

But now, eating ice cream too quickly to escape this silence, she knew some small part of her *had* hoped for something. She couldn't quite name what.

Right now, she wanted him to speak, to fall into easy conversation, into teasing like Ash's family did. She wanted this to be something they'd done a million times—late-night ice cream talks. She wanted him to ask questions—not to get to know her, but questions that came from knowing her, like how her final paper had turned out and whether she'd submitted her request to switch to Dr. Tate's lab. She still hadn't.

"Val wanted me to ask you about the Christmas Eve menu," he said. "Which I suppose is also the wedding dinner."

Hazel wished she'd taken her chances on crawling away earlier. "Whatever she has planned is fine."

"Tomorrow night will be catered. Italian," he went on, like this might help her form an opinion. She'd almost forgotten about his station holiday party.

"Val and her kids have always done enchiladas on Christmas Eve. I guess some families have traditional meals like that." He paused. "I know one year your mom spent hours cooking a ham. I remember because I got called last-minute to the station before it was done."

"I remember." She didn't add that her mother had protested cooking any big holiday dinners after that year.

Sylvia's family barbequed brisket and ribs on Christmas Day. On Christmas Eve, it was chicken-fried steak and root beer floats, which had some elaborate origin story of a blind date and a car breaking down before the intended destination. Technically, she'd eaten that meal more than any other on Christmas Eve.

"Enchiladas sound great," she said.

The last few years, when her father called on Christmas, that obligatory quick call not too early and not too late in the day, she excused herself to Sylvia's childhood bedroom to answer. She would stare at herself in the closet door mirror while they talked, calculating back to whenever he'd last come through town and noting the small changes in her appearance as he might have. He always ended the call too quickly, at the first lingering pause. "Well, I'd better not keep you," he'd say, like she was the one eager to hang up. She'd wait a few more minutes before rejoining Sylvia's family so it wouldn't seem too soon.

"I made Ash our famous pear and bacon grilled cheese today," she heard herself say, then tensed because—what if he didn't remember? Or, what if, like their real Christmas trees, he'd only let her think he liked it at the time?

"Those were dire times," he said with a self-conscious laugh. "I'm sorry. You know, I've learned a few basic domestic skills since then."

She did know. He'd helped with most of the meals since she'd arrived. Logically, she knew her parents hadn't divorced because of all the dinners he'd missed, but it had certainly been one of her mother's most repeated complaints. Ironic that the divorce had forced him into dealing with the tasks her mother had resented, and now, he was a more present and capable partner for Val. She would never mention this to her mother.

"Everyone likes the pear. My roommate—well, my *old* roommate—always used to ask for it when she was . . ." Hazel blushed. "Um, drunk."

"This is Sylvia?"

Hazel smiled, pleased he'd remembered. They had lived together for all of college, but still.

"You said she's in Houston now?"

Had Hazel told him that? Apparently so. "Yeah, she's opening a new location of her family's restaurant."

"I'll have to check it out next time I'm there. Maybe we could make a weekend of it."

"Sure," she said, though she wasn't sure if he meant he and Hazel or he and Val.

Her father pushed his ice cream away and patted his stomach. "I'd better stop before I regret this."

Hazel took their bowls to the sink. She wasn't sure what possessed her to ask, "Do you ever do this with Lucy?"

"Can't say that I have, no." He stood up, coming over to the counter.

"Okay." *Good*, she wanted to say. Like a child. Then, because she knew that was what she sounded like, she said, "It would be okay if you did. I was just wondering."

Her father leaned back against the counter. He opened and closed his mouth, and she attempted to rescue them both from the awkwardness, tried to edge past, saying, "Well, good night! See you in the morning!" But he clutched her by the shoulders, steering her directly in front of him. "Kiddo. Hazel."

He seemed not to know what to say after that. He looked determined and somber, and Hazel remembered Val, just that morning, recounting his proposal of marriage without ever having said he loved her. Finally, he asked, "Did I tell you how glad I am that you're here?"

"You don't have to . . ."

"Thank you for coming home. I am very glad you're here," he repeated, enunciating every word. It was different than his thank-you at the festival. Forceful and deliberate, like he'd practiced saying it. Like maybe he'd realized how painful that blurted thank-you had been, and he'd been waiting to get it right. Even if it was a little sad that her dad had probably rehearsed the line, he could have not bothered to say it at all.

"Sure," she said, because every response that came to her felt phony—*happy to be here, my pleasure, thanks for having me.*

He opened his arms, and she stepped into them.

Twenty

The next evening, after joining Ash's sisters and nieces for their delayed ice-skating outing—and accepting that she was not going to become an ice princess at twenty-three—Hazel was back at her dad's house, debating changing her outfit again. She was supposed to be leaving in a few minutes for her father's station holiday party, and she looked like an accountant in her white button-down and pencil skirt.

Hazel wasn't looking forward to spending the evening with a bunch of her father's colleagues, but he'd agreed Ash could come to the party.

As she buttoned and unbuttoned her collar for the third time, her phone lit up with a text from Sylvia. Tap, tap, tap. This thing on?

Hazel smiled. She'd meant to reply to Sylvia's latest proof of life request, but she hadn't trusted herself to take a picture while teetering on ice skates. She took a selfie and sent it, adding, Be honest. Am I going to look like one of the servers at this holiday party in this outfit?

SYLVIA: Undo another button and leave your hair down.

SYLVIA: Are you going to do a red lip? You should do a red lip.

SYLVIA: Is that an enormous Christmas tree in your bedroom?

SYLVIA: And who are you trying to impress by not looking like a waiter?

There was no time to explain everything before she had to go pick Ash up for the party. But the answer to Sylvia's last question—who was she trying to impress?—pulled a giddy smile across Hazel's face. She wanted to make Ash look at her again like he had in the barn. And a not insignificant part of her wanted to tell Sylvia everything about him.

But for now, she had to go.

HAZEL: Can't I just not want to be asked for cocktails all night?

THE EVENT HALL HAD A DISTRESSED BRICK FAÇADE, FAUX GAS LAMPS burning romantically on porch posts, arched windows in the upper level, and a gleaming red vintage pickup parked in the side lot.

While Hazel parked, she felt Ash crane around, using her seat for leverage to see out her back window.

"What's back there?" she asked.

The look he gave her was cautious, considering.

But before he could say anything, the front door of the event hall opened, and a woman in a sparkly blue evening gown and long wool coat waved urgently at them, beckoning.

"Hang on," Ash said. But as soon as she opened her door, the wind gusted and bit, and Hazel ran for the building.

"Come in, come in, come in," the woman said, practically shoving them inside and letting the door slam. "You just made it."

Hazel checked through the window, half expecting an apocalyptic dust cloud or a tornado touching down in the parking lot, but nothing was amiss, just her father's silver SUV turning into the entrance.

"Hazel," Ash began just as the woman said, "The family is arriving now," and prodded them toward another set of doors, which opened into a dim dining room. Sixty or more people sat at round tables with winter floral centerpieces and flickering tea lights, all arranged around a parquet dance floor. Was it her imagination, or did everyone deflate a little at the sight of them?

"We'll find your seats in a moment. For now, wait over here." She nudged them toward a string quartet already crammed into the corner and ducked back out to the foyer, leaving them standing in strange silence.

Hazel whispered, "Wait, is this a surprise party?"

Ash took her elbow. "Listen, I think—"

Someone shushed him.

"I could be wrong, but—" He tugged her farther into the corner, eyes darting about the room.

She laughed, an uneasy itch spidering up her spine. "What's wrong with you?"

Someone shushed them again. Greetings were volleyed in the foyer, heels clicking on the tile. Then, the big doors opened, and even though Hazel had figured it out, she still jumped when the entire room chorused, "Surprise!"

Right away, the hostess whisked her father, Val, Lucy, and Raf to a table across the room with the largest centerpiece and red sashes draped on each of the chairs. *Not red, cranberry*, she thought. Only then did Hazel notice a banner that announced **Congratulations and Best Wishes** and blown-up prints of her father and Val, some with Val's kids, propped on stands around the room.

When the hostess offered them flutes of champagne and

a toast, acknowledging their desire for a small wedding but insisting on the people's right to celebrate, Hazel's father made his own impromptu toast back to the room. He credited his colleagues for bringing out the best in him on-air, making him appear "decent enough" that Val overlooked how stilted and awkward his side of the conversation was when they'd met at some charity event. He could be stiff one-on-one—exactly what he was alluding to—but in a room full of people, something clicked on, carried over from his on-camera persona. Everyone laughed warmly at his self-deprecating speech.

"This is weird." Hazel bumped into a cello and apologized to the stony-faced woman holding it.

"Do you want to leave?" Ash asked.

"We can't leave."

"We can, actually."

"And say what?"

"Bye," he deadpanned. "Or nothing. Just slip out. Who cares?"

"A Hazel getaway."

"What?"

"That's what Sylvia calls it. Like an Irish goodbye?" He didn't crack a smile. "My dad will notice."

She didn't miss the flash of doubt that passed across his face before he said, "That woman didn't even know who you were."

"She's never met me."

"There should be pictures of you. And I only see four chairs at that table. Didn't they know you were coming?"

Hazel's cheeks flared hot with embarrassment. "I don't know, Asher. I didn't see the guest list."

He squeezed her hip, frustrated, she guessed, by her deflection, or sorry for calling attention to the slight against her. But she couldn't think too hard about it right now, not in front of all these people, not when she was so close—just the wedding and

Christmas the day after to get through—to escaping this week mostly unscathed. Not after last night in the kitchen with her father, when it had finally seemed like . . .

Best not to hope, not even in the safety of her own mind.

Right now, her father was making his way across the room toward her, pausing periodically to greet and thank people. "I had no idea about this," he said when he got to them. "We'll get an extra chair—two chairs. And another table. I added your name to the list, but they obviously had a whole other plan here. They didn't make the connection."

"They didn't connect the last names?" Ash asked.

Hazel pushed in front of Ash, gesturing back the way her father had come. "It's fine. They'll add a table. No big deal."

"Hazel, hold on," Ash said.

She marched after her father.

The situation wasn't really anyone's fault. Hazel's father hadn't expected assigned seating, especially not a table of honor for his family. If not for the surprise, a simple, overall head count would have sufficed, so he hadn't called attention to Hazel's late RSVP. It was all very understandable. No one had intentionally left her out. Besides, who could really be blamed when Hazel was never *around*? Unlike Lucy and Raf, who probably got dragged to these kinds of events, Hazel was always across the state, living her own life.

Hazel could tell Ash was biting his tongue to not point out that, still, someone should have said, *Wait, but isn't there another kid? His kid?*

"Let it go," Hazel sang through a smile while caterers slid a two-top against the larger round table. It was a slightly lower height and rectangular, but someone was already placing an extra floral arrangement in its center, and someone else was pouring ice waters for them.

"It's not just that. There was a truck in the lot. I wasn't sure, but— Hazel." He tugged her arm, making her stop helping arrange tea lights and look at him.

"What?"

"Justin's here."

"Justin . . ." she echoed dumbly. Her pulse kicked up.

He tipped his chin to some point over her right shoulder, but his eyes stayed steady on hers. "He's coming over here."

She felt leaden. Her usual fight-or-flight response simply never kicked in, leaving her with only freeze. She could feel every second with which she might have fled or devised a plan tick away.

It was fine. She'd seen Franny, and that turned out fine.

Ash was watching her, though, like maybe her face was saying something else. Like she looked *not* fine. Then his eyes darted just over her head, his expression morphing from serious to friendly just as Justin's familiar voice announced behind her, "Hazel freaking Elliot."

He turned her by the shoulders and pulled her into a tight hug, swaying her back and forth so one foot lost contact with the floor and then the other. When he set her back down, he didn't release her immediately, just kept crushing her body to his, his mouth tickling the shell of her ear as he murmured, "Been too long."

She squirmed free with a nervous laugh and an awkward pat on his shoulder. Reaching back, she latched on to Ash's wrist. His chest, steady against her back, grounded her as he reached around to offer Justin his hand.

"Campbell." Justin's eyebrows bunched together. "Uh, hey. What are you . . . ?" He looked to Hazel for an explanation.

She shot back the same question. "What are *you* doing here?"

"I was . . . invited? Didn't you—" He glanced at her father a few feet away. Shaking his head, Justin smiled, eyes scanning her from head to toe and back up her stretchy black skirt, her white button-down. His eyes didn't quite make it back to her face, a cocky smile kicking up at one corner. "Whatever. Look at you. You grew up nice."

That slow perusal and his lopsided grin sent Hazel further off-balance. But politeness reigned. She heard herself say, "Thanks. You, too."

His voice dropped into the confident purr she used to jokingly call his Casanova voice, the one he used when trying to get her to go skinny-dipping or to sneak him into her room after curfew. "No, I mean . . . damn."

She didn't thank him this time, crossing her arms over her chest.

"You been working out or something?"

"Um." She frowned down at her body. Yes, she'd been working out, at least before Dr. Sheffield's students ruined the gym for her. She suspected her new muscle tone wasn't what he meant, though. She swallowed loudly, fidgeting under his gaze, which she preferred to think was on her necklace, and not the extra button she'd left open at Sylvia's urging.

"You should let me give you a workout."

Hazel choked on nothing.

"I'm getting my personal trainer certification," he explained innocently, but the devilish smile that followed told her he'd intended it exactly as it sounded. There had been a time when his semi-lewd playfulness flattered and excited her. Now, it made her skin prickle with discomfort. He wagged his finger. "You've got a dirty mind."

Ash cleared his throat. He was still behind her, so she couldn't read him, could only feel the contraction of tendons in the wrist she was clinging to like a lifeline as his thumb popped each of his knuckles.

"I've been doing CrossFit," Justin offered, not so subtly flexing, his cocky grin spreading. "You getting to the gym at all these days, Campbell?"

Ash gave an amused grunt.

"Justin," Hazel's father said then, coming around the table to offer his hand. To her surprise, he added, "You made it."

"Hey, Dan."

Hey, Dan?

"Wait," she said. "You knew he'd be here?"

Her father clapped a hand on Justin's shoulder. "The invitation was a bit last-minute, so I wasn't sure, but . . ."

"You invited him? When did you— How?" Ordinarily, she would have swallowed such a shrill, tight question, would have opted for private confusion over appearing upset, but there was no containing her shock. What was happening here? What the *hell* was happening here?

"You said you were going to try to get together this week, so when I ran into him at the gym the other day . . ." Her father peered over one shoulder then the other. "A few other guys are around here somewhere. I invited the whole group."

Her brain couldn't compute all the jarring details at once. First of all, why would her father think she'd intended to see Justin? That was the last thing she wanted. Only . . .

Shit. Shit, shit, shit. She'd *lied* about having plans to see friends early in the week to get out of spending time with Val and her kids. She was still lost as to how merely saying his name led to him standing here before her, but she understood with a heavy weight in her stomach that she'd brought it on herself.

So, obviously, the most logical and pressing next question was, "You do CrossFit?"

"Oh," her father said after a beat. "No. Racquetball at the YMCA. The rec league tournament starts up after Christmas. The younger guys keep me on my toes. Justin and I wound up on a soccer team together last spring. Went head-to-head for the championship in softball last summer. Flag football, basketball . . ."

She cast a hard glare at Justin. Sometime after he'd led her on to sleep with her, he'd become her father's *friend*.

But Justin didn't notice her glare. He didn't seem to be paying much attention at all, working something out behind his cool blue eyes, his lopsided grin leveling to a nearly flat line. The confident swagger he'd worn like his high school letter jacket was gone.

"So, you guys are gym buddies." An unhinged laugh bubbled up in Hazel's throat. What could she even say? Her father didn't know Justin had hurt and humiliated her. She'd never told him.

As for Justin, he'd gone from his old confident, flirtatious self to a cold statue. His arms were crossed, eyes fixed on some point off to the side of the room, jaw tight. And suddenly, she knew why. His confusion when she asked what he was doing here, that big hug, the compliments and open perusal of her body—he thought she knew he'd been invited, maybe even thought she'd *asked* her father to do it. Now he knew she hadn't.

"Should I not have . . . ?" her father began.

"I'm just surprised." She smiled wider, her cheeks aching with the strain.

Around the room, caterers placed plates before the guests. Desperate for him not to ask any more questions, she said, "Oh, look, they're serving dinner. We should sit."

But when she slid into her seat, she caught the corner of the tablecloth. Everything on the table tipped. Ash caught the flowers, but he could do nothing to stop both glasses of water from flooding the table and running directly down her blouse and into her lap. She lurched back. The cold—a *thousand* needles—stole her breath. The screech of her chair legs cut through the

266 — MELANIE SWEENEY

din in the room. Everyone's eyes shot to her. She crossed her arms tightly, as much to hide her bra and pinched nipples through the now-see-through material as for warmth. Her wet shirt sucked against her stomach. The icy water ran down inside the waist of her skirt and into her underwear. Perfect. This evening just kept getting better and better.

An arm tucked around her back. Ash steered her out to the lobby and opened the restroom door for her.

Standing in the doorway, she plucked miserably at her shirt. "What am I doing?"

"Getting dry," Ash said gently.

"No. I mean, what am I doing here? What is *he* doing here?"

Ash gave her a tiny shrug. "We can leave."

She huffed. That wasn't an option, and he knew it.

"Then, we're doing what you planned. Getting through it."

"Sure," she said, doubtful. "Okay."

"Hey," he said when she still didn't go inside, catching her eyes. "It could have been worse."

"How?"

"The water put out the candles. So, you didn't set the place on fire."

Her laugh surprised her. "Can you imagine?"

"Nothing says happy to be here like a little light arson." He turned her around, squeezed the back of her neck with his warm, wide palm. "Go dry off."

Twenty-One

A sh's attention was split in too many directions right now, and this disaster of a dinner couldn't end soon enough.

Beside him, Hazel's knee bounced anxiously, his blazer pulled tightly across her chest. When she'd emerged from the bathroom, cheeks splotchy and clothes still damp, he'd draped the jacket around her shoulders, and she'd threaded her arms through the long sleeves, pausing to breathe in the collar. It had seemed to fortify her enough to return to their table, her head held high, smile back in place, if a little stiff.

But neither of them had expected, as salads were cleared and entrées were placed before them, that the evening's agenda would turn to speeches. No one tried to keep up the ruse of this being a holiday party anymore, offering their best to Hazel's father and Val like the toast portion of a wedding, only the worst kind, where the mic wasn't wisely limited to the immediate wedding party.

The woman currently holding the floor reminisced about Val and her kids touring the station early in their relationship, how everyone knew it was serious by the multiple emails Dan sent out beforehand, reminding people they were coming and suggesting interesting features of their various departments to show them. This, though, was better than the woman before her, who had claimed to have seen literal heart eyes the first time Val and Dan met, which had made Hazel stop eating.

And who could forget Justin lurking on the other side of the room by the bar? Ash had counted three times that he'd risen for another beer. His moody gaze had hardly left Hazel as he took long pulls. She was sure Justin thought *she'd* invited him here through her father. "*You grew up nice. Let me give you a workout*," she mocked under her breath. "Seriously?"

Ash wasn't sure what Justin had expected, but he knew that look—Justin's flared nostrils, his tongue periodically running over his lower lip and probing into his cheek. Ash, who had spent years across fields and down dugout benches from Justin, could recognize when the guy was sulking.

"Doesn't he look mad?" Hazel grumbled. "That's rich. He really thought I'd invite him? He thought I'd *want* to see him?"

"I don't know," Ash said. He'd suspected she had unresolved baggage with Justin, considering she'd never actually dealt with it, but he wasn't sure what to do with just how worked up she was. It felt familiar, her keeping her eye on Justin across the room, not really noticing Ash right next to her. He adjusted his tie, but it didn't relieve the tightness in his throat.

"Sorry." Her hand found his under the table. "It's not Justin I'm mad at," she admitted with a little shrug. Her gaze cut to her father then back. "It's just easier."

Someone new took the microphone, and Hazel perked up. "Oh, I know him. He used to come over sometimes to watch football with my dad."

The man introduced himself as Tom, a longtime friend and producer of Dan's. Hazel seemed more relaxed, and Ash rolled the tension out of his shoulders, hopeful that at least one person in this whole room might remember she existed as he waxed romantic about the happy family.

"I've known Dan a long time," Tom said. "He's always been an even-keeled guy. Not the life of a party, but easy to get along with. You'd never know if he was having a bad day, or a great day, for that matter. But in the last couple of years, I've seen him come alive. And I credit you, Val. You and Lucy and Rafael. I don't think he even knew what was missing all those years, but when he found you, you all just lit him up. You've made him a different, better man, truly. So"—he raised his glass—"to Val and the kids."

Hazel stopped chewing. Everyone was looking at the family and he could feel the effort it took to not let her smile slip, just in case someone's eyes should drift over to her, the forgotten daughter, the one who apparently wasn't enough all those years to light up her father.

Fuck. He hated this. He should have insisted they leave. He should have set her father straight at the start of this, before she'd begged Ash to let her overlooked spot at their table go. He palmed her knee under the table, aching to offer more. He half expected her to pull away, to fortify herself by retreating inward. But then her hand covered his. He turned his palm and threaded their fingers together.

Finally, the toasts ended. Desserts were passed around, and Hazel's father and Val were urged to dance on the parquet floor. They swayed to half of an instrumental version of "All You Need Is Love" before others joined them, and finally, finally, everyone's attention was occupied enough that Hazel let herself slump back against her chair.

He waited until her father left the dance floor to mingle before tugging Hazel up by the hand and leading her to it. He didn't have any words that would fix this, but he could hold her. In fact, he needed her close as much for his own benefit as for hers. Two steps onto the floor, she stopped. Patiently, he squeezed her hand, questioning, and she sighed, looped her arms around his neck, and shuffled closer.

"Hey," Ash whispered as the first song ended. "You okay?"

"It's fine."

"It's not fine."

"It can't be anything else." She ran a hand down his shoulder, finally looking at him as the quartet played what he belatedly recognized was "Matilda" by Harry Styles, which he only knew because the twins spent hours watching concert clips from his tour. "You're tense," she said.

"I hate everyone here."

Hazel laughed. It was soft but genuine. "I would have thought Justin being here was the worst thing that could happen tonight."

"I hate that he hit on you."

She studied him. "That bothered you? You played it so cool."

"Yeah, well. Just because I want to throw you over my shoulder and get you out of here doesn't mean it's right. I know that's some deeply problematic caveman shit."

"You were jealous," she mused, like it pleased her. And he was glad for anything that made her smile right now.

A visceral longing seized him, though—all those times he'd watched her in his back seat, all those times he'd wanted her to notice him, wanted her to choose him instead of Justin, even if loyalty to his friend stood in the way. He spoke before he could think better of it. "I always have been jealous, Hazel. Not just now. Always."

She tilted her head in confusion, but then her lips parted in a silent *Oh*. He fought the urge to take it back. He wanted it all, finally, out on the table.

"When I was with him . . ." she said.

"Yeah."

"So, at that party freshman year . . ."

"Yeah."

"And when I started coming to the café . . ."

"Even after four years of only seeing you as you rounded a corner," he confirmed. "I didn't want to want you again. I tried not to."

She slid her palms over his heart hammering in his neck, up to his jaw, into his hair.

"I know you didn't want things to change between us," he went on, mouth dry and stomach somewhere near the floor, "but technically, nothing's changed. I've wanted you this whole time."

With wonder in her eyes and a bewildered little shake of her head, she toed up and kissed him, and he guessed that was an answer of sorts to the question he hadn't asked. Was this still okay? Was she going to bolt? She nestled her cheek to his shoulder, dropped one hand to his chest.

Holding Hazel like this felt like a sudden melt into calm, everything rigid going soft and loose. His heart rate slowed, shoulders eased. He had her in his arms, and everything was going to be okay.

A FEW SONGS LATER, HAZEL'S FATHER FOUND THEM ON THE DANCE floor. "Sorry to interrupt. I'm told we're taking a photo. The whole family." Hazel looked down at her still-damp clothes. "You can keep the jacket on, of course."

"No, that's okay. I'm not dressed up enough anyway."

"No one cares about that, kiddo. You look nice."

She shook her head adamantly. "We'll have the wedding pictures in a couple days. I've got my dress for that. It's fine."

Her father glanced back across the room to Val, who was re-draping her shawl around her shoulders and reaching for her son's crooked tie. He faced Hazel again, gave a little laugh like her refusal made no sense. "You're here. It would be strange not to include you."

Hazel exhaled sharply. "*Now* it would be strange not to include me?" Her voice was suddenly tight and high.

Her father frowned. "Is . . . something wrong?"

"Is something wrong?" She directed this to Ash, and that melon baller came for another scoop of his insides.

He didn't know what to say. She hadn't wanted to make a scene, to tell her father how she really felt. Was he was supposed to back her up, finally help her say exactly what she'd been holding in for years, or calm her back down, prevent her from doing something she'd regret?

"I'm here," Hazel said, clenching her fists at her sides. "Isn't that enough?"

"I didn't know— I didn't realize you were upset," her father said, surprised.

"Of course I'm upset!" Her cheeks flushed, and a vein strained under her eye. She shook her head, struggling for words, and the longer she floundered, the more Ash itched to steer her away. He was supposed to be her buffer.

"I don't belong here," she told her father, tears brimming in her eyes. "Not at this stupid party. Not in your precious pictures. I don't even belong in this town. And it was fine. It was all fine until you made me come back."

She turned to leave, but her father reached for her arm. It all happened so fast. In her haste to get away from the growing attention around the room, from the confused but pained expression on her father's face, Hazel jerked from his grasp, stumbled to the side, and knocked into a table so hard it tipped. She went down with it. Silverware clattered. Glasses broke. Red wine splattered across the white tablecloth.

Ash and her father reached to help her up, but she refused them both, clutching her hand to her chest and wobbling to her feet like a baby deer. Then, she ran.

Ash turned to follow her winding path back out to the front entry, but her father barked, "Wait." At first, Dan was speechless under all the gawking stares. The instruments had whined to a staggered stop, and now dead silence hung over the room. Instead of addressing Ash, he directed a sheepish smile at everyone, a nervous laugh, and said, "Well, it's not a party until someone flips a table, no? Sorry for the disruption. Carry on, folks." To the musicians, he asked, "Can we get something upbeat?" as catering staff rushed in to clean up the mess.

Ash saw his opportunity and took it. He pushed through the doors, scanned both lengths of the empty foyer, then marched out into the cold night. "Hazel?" he called.

She'd been pleased earlier that her clutch with her phone and keys could fit stuffed into one of his jacket pockets, and he half expected her to have peeled out of the parking lot already, but her car was still there, and she wasn't in it. He retreated back inside and ran right into her father.

"Do you know what that was all about?"

Ash swallowed. "You should talk to her about it."

Dan threw his arms out helplessly. "I'm trying here. I really am."

Ash did not want to do this. He didn't want to hold her father's hand through processing her outburst. He also knew, despite what she'd just told him herself, Hazel wouldn't want Ash to expose any more of her feelings. After everything with his parents, he was mindful to help only in the exact way she wanted. But, God, if she and her dad would just talk, they could clear everything up. Once again, no matter which path Ash took here, he would hit a brick wall.

274 — MELANIE SWEENEY

"It's not my place," he hedged, but Dan blocked his path.

"No, none of that. I'm making it your place. I'm asking for your help."

That wasn't how it worked. His loyalty was to Hazel. But an intense pressure rushed up from his chest into his throat, and he couldn't hold it back anymore. "Justin wasn't good to her."

"To Hazel? She never told me that."

"I know," Ash said, pitching his voice low. He spotted a side door and stalked to it. "Because you don't visit her. You don't call her." He yanked open the door. An empty alley. He marched back in the other direction, remembering the restroom where she'd dried off earlier.

"Now, hold on," Dan said, jogging to keep up. "Just hold on a minute. I visit. I call every few—well, at least every month or so. I know she's busy. I don't want to smother her."

Ash clenched his fists. "Don't you get it? You *need* to smother her. I've practically forced myself into her company all week, and I think some part of her still doesn't believe that I *want* to be with her. And it's because nobody in her life has made her feel unquestionably, unconditionally wanted. I don't get how that's even possible. She's fucking inc—" He cleared his throat, shook his head. "With respect, sir, she's incredible."

Dan slumped as though Ash's words had physically hurt him. He opened his mouth to speak, face stricken, but nothing came out.

The noise of the party spilled through the doors as Val entered the foyer. "What happened? Is Hazel okay?"

Ash slipped into the bathroom as Dan turned to answer Val.

Hazel was at the sink, tears streaming down her cheeks, a wad of toilet paper clutched in her fist. He locked the door. "Are you bleeding?"

"It's just a little cut." Fresh tears spilled down her cheeks. "What is wrong with me?"

"Nothing."

"I knocked over a table. I ruined the party. My dad—" She grabbed the side of the sink and breathed shallowly over it. "Oh God. I ruined everything."

"You didn't ruin anything. The music is already playing again. People are dancing. Listen. They're half-drunk. No one cares."

She was shaking her head, spinning out.

He needed to get her out of here. He crossed to a frosted window, felt for a latch.

"What are you doing?" she asked.

"Time for a Hazel getaway."

SHE DROVE TOO FAST, KNUCKLES WHITE ON THE WHEEL, SWERVING IN-stead of braking for slow cars. She practically threw her cans at the security officer when they reached the neighborhood gate. And then they were inside the house, in her bedroom, and she began stuffing clothes into a bag.

"What are we taking?"

"Everything." She shoved an empty box at him and steered him toward the massive Christmas tree in the corner. "Get your ornaments."

"Hazel—"

"Just, please." She yanked her phone and laptop chargers from the wall. "And can I . . ." Only now did she stop, fidgeting with the cords. "Shit. Would your parents mind if I . . . ?"

He set the box down and stopped her in her tracks, held her face so she'd look at him. "Of course you can stay at my house."

She drew in a shaky breath, the first full one he'd seen since they'd left the party. Then, she pulled away to cram the chargers into her bag. "Get those ornaments now, or you'll never see them again."

They were in and out in five minutes.

She let him drive to his house. She leaned her head against the window, even closed her eyes at one point. He wasn't sure what she was thinking, but she was no longer crying or vibrating with anger when they pulled into his empty driveway.

"Where's your family?"

He scratched his eyebrow. "We probably passed them coming out of your dad's place. They took the kids to see the lights."

She huffed a laugh, which grew into a full fit, hovering right on the edge of something else. Tears leaked down her face, but through manic giggles, she assured him, "I'm not crying. It's just so ridiculous." She stepped out of the car and tried to sling her bag over her shoulder, but she dropped it with a hiss and sucked her palm.

Ash picked up her bag then ushered her into the house, straight up to his room, where she sat on the bed, holding her injured hand in her lap.

He turned on the bedside lamp. "Let me look."

The cut wasn't very deep and had stopped bleeding. Still, he rose to fetch supplies from the bathroom.

She caught his shirt. "I'll live."

"There could be glass in it."

"There isn't."

She pulled him down beside her on the bed. And then she was kissing him with the same urgency and desperation as her getaway from the disastrous party, her uninjured hand delving into his hair, tongue probing into his mouth. For a moment, it was all he could do to keep up. He braced a hand at her hip, but she took it as an invitation to scoot into his lap, her stretchy skirt riding up her thighs. When he tried to kiss her more gently, she deepened it.

"Hold on," he breathed. At her father's house, she'd told him to get his ornaments, or he'd never see them again, and only now did he realize what she'd meant. She didn't intend to go back. She was running.

But she wasn't running from *him*.

He wanted to fix everything, patch up every injury, seen and unseen. He wanted to kiss every hurt. And then he wanted to put his mouth on all the places that might make her feel better, feel good. He couldn't parse the parts of him that wanted to soothe her from the parts that wanted to do these far less tender, far less noble things.

With an impatient huff, she grasped his jaw to kiss him again. "Be with me."

"I am."

He shifted her off his lap, and she stood in front of him, brows furrowed as if to say, *Then why'd you just dump me out of your lap?*

Standing, he asked, "What do you want, Haze?" He peeled his blazer down off her shoulders, ducking to kiss her neck.

She exhaled a relieved sigh. "That's good."

"Yeah?" He gathered her hair back and gently tipped her jaw to the side for better access. "Do you want gentle?" He brushed his lips featherlight across her throat to the other side. "Or something with a little more . . ." He gave her a bite that made her squirm, then quickly soothed the spot with his tongue.

"Do I have to pick one?" she breathed, tugging his hips closer.

He smiled against her neck, fingers finding her shirt buttons. "No. You can have everything you want."

"What do you want?" she countered.

He didn't miss the evasion or the blush coloring her cheeks.

She wasn't there yet. So, he didn't press. He started undoing her buttons. "Want me to tell you?"

"Yes."

"I want to touch more of you than I did in the barn."

She yanked her blouse from the waistband of her skirt, then reached for the zipper at the side.

"Wait." He stilled her hips, slid his palms down over the sleek, stretchy material. He smoothed them down the outsides of her thighs until he reached the hem above her knees, flirted with the skin there, swiping his fingertips just under the fabric. "I've thought about this. A lot."

He lowered to his knees, and her eyes went inky black. "Thought about what?"

This wasn't the way he'd intended this to go, with him confessing his own fantasies to her instead of discovering hers, but now that he was here, he wanted to say it, and he was starting to think, from her labored, shallow breaths, that maybe hearing what he wanted worked for her, too. Slowly, he pushed her skirt up a few inches, pausing to look up at her. "Can I—"

She nodded emphatically.

"Every Friday, you come in wearing these hot teacher skirts." He pushed the skirt up another inch, drawing his thumbs up the insides of her thighs. Her eyelids fluttered, and she swayed, had to steady herself on his shoulder.

"And your hair all twisted up off your neck. And those fucking glasses."

"They're fake," she confessed, a wolfish gleam in her eyes as she peered down at him, watching to see what he would do next.

He pushed her skirt up to her waist and traced the lower hemline of her underwear with his knuckle. Not breaking eye contact, he swept one thumb across the damp center of the cotton. Hazel sucked in a sharp breath. Her nails dug into his shoulder, sending the hairs at the back of his neck to attention. When he withdrew the contact to skate his palms back down her thighs, her hips stuttered forward.

"Doesn't matter." He barely even knew what he was talking about anymore, mesmerized by the feel of her. How was her skin this soft and warm? "They're hot. Everything about you is so fucking hot."

He pressed a kiss to one inner thigh, then the other, nudging gently for her to step her feet further apart. Then he hooked one finger inside her underwear, tugging it to the side just as his other hand squeezed the smooth, full swell of her ass and drew her forward to his mouth.

<< CHAPTER >>

Twenty-Two

Ash's mouth should have come with a warning. Hazel hadn't had a lot to compare it to, since her limited hookups tended to skip this part entirely, but he had clearly tacked a specialty in oral onto his architecture studies. This was graduate-level work.

When he admitted he'd thought about this, pushing up her *hot teacher skirt*, she figured the fantasy would have gone somewhere more satisfying for him. This was all for her, wasn't it? *Her* pleasure? He'd gone down on her yesterday in the barn, too, had only stopped when she demanded he come back up, let her get her hands on him. She didn't quite know what to do with herself when all his attention was on her.

She reveled in the scratch of his stubble, the shape of him kneeling before her, the breadth of his shoulders, dark curls falling across his forehead, until she caught sight of them in the mirror above his dresser. And . . . *Oh.* She thought the view of him from above was a lot. *This* perspective made her lips part on a gasp.

After he'd roughly pulled her to his face, he'd hitched one of her knees over his shoulder, and she'd complied so quickly, she hadn't had time to consider how intimate this position was. Now, she was looking at herself, half climbing him, hips angled desperately toward the exquisite warmth and pressure of his mouth, her skirt up around her ribs. She was clutching his hair, his free shoulder for support. His hands worked in tandem with his mouth, one working into her while his other hand squeezed her ass cheek. She watched herself writhe against his face and—

It was enough to break through the haze of her lust, make her unhook her knee from his shoulder. He looked up at her questioningly, and she fought the urge to cover her face. "Too much?" he asked roughly, turning to kiss her thigh.

Not physically. Physically, it had been so good. Already, she'd felt the swelling ache and pressure of an orgasm building. But something else had come with it, a frantic, needy clawing in her chest. Her skin pricked with a feeling of overexposure.

"Tell me." His voice was gruff but not impatient.

His eyes flicked to her hand, which she'd drawn up to her collarbone, as if she could calm the internal clawing there. His awareness of her hand made the clawing worse, made it push up into her throat, a thick knot of emotion. God, where was this coming from? Her nose and eyes stung with the threat of tears—again—and she went to push her skirt down.

Immediately, Ash rose. He reached first for her face but seemed to second-guess touching her there and swept his palms down her arms, cupping her elbows. That wild, hungry, half-drunk look in his eyes vanished, replaced by sober concern. "Talk to me."

"Sorry, I don't know why—"

"Don't apologize. Just tell me what's going on."

He waited, but she didn't know how to explain something that she hadn't yet worked out for herself. She'd stopped him in the barn yesterday, too, when she'd been *so close*, when she'd needed him to come with her.

"We don't have to do this tonight," he said. "We can watch a movie or—"

"No." She wanted this, wanted him. There was just something

malfunctioning inside her, some faulty wiring that had never been up to code but had kept the lights on until now, until someone opened the wall and took a good look at the shoddy work in there.

He waited, and she swallowed down the blockage in her throat. How could she explain to him that his adoration made her feel like she was coming apart at the seams?

"I don't know how to let you . . ." She gestured between him and herself. "I'm not used to this." She was being entirely too vague, practically saying nothing at all. She didn't want to admit that sex, as rarely as she had it, was just another escape for her. She just closed her eyes and chased her release, and while she didn't jump into bed with just anyone, she didn't need an emotional attachment. In fact, the attachment she felt for Ash seemed to be precisely the thing making this harder.

"You're not used to someone taking care of you," he said.

This must have been true, too, because the sting of unshed tears sharpened.

Ash ran his hands back up her arms to cradle her face. "You need to know you're not in this deeper than I am? Not more out of control?"

She shook her head. She shouldn't need the upper hand. That wasn't how relationships were supposed to work.

"You know how good you were feeling before we stopped just now?"

Her cheeks heated, but she couldn't deny it.

"Do you have any idea how good it feels for me to do that to you? To see you like that?" He groaned like he was remembering, feeling it all over again, and kissed her. Staying in close, he said, "When you're like that, I'm like that, too, I promise. I'm just as turned on. More, probably."

When she didn't speak, still embarrassed at how greedily she'd rocked herself against his mouth, he pressed his hips into hers, and she felt the hard length of him. The warm firmness of his body molded to hers made the tension in her own body give a little. He was a weighted blanket in human form. And yet, under the calm that emanated from him, the feel of him still hard and pressed to her and the open desire in his words stirred her own need back up.

"As for the feelings part . . ." He tipped his head back just enough to look her in the eye and smoothed her hair back from her face. "I'm ahead of you there, too. I meant what I said. It's been a long time."

Earlier, when he'd admitted he'd been jealous of Justin, even back in high school, her reaction surprised her. She didn't feel trapped. It made her feel secure. Safe.

"I didn't even really know you then," he said. "Not like I do now."

"And now you're wondering what you were thinking?" she said on a watery laugh.

One finger swiped affectionately across her eyebrow and down to her jaw. "Pretty sure I'm falling for you." A half shrug, a little shake of his head. "Don't panic, okay?"

The swelling in her chest was different from the clawing, needy sensation that had made her pull away, the ache in her throat replaced by a stretch in her cheeks, a smile she couldn't tamp down. And the tears that sprang back to her eyes were of an entirely different kind. "I won't panic."

"Good."

If he hoped she'd say she was falling for him, too, he left no room for her to fumble over the words, covering her mouth with his. It was there, on the tip of her tongue. Something small. *Me, too.* But instead of breaking away to let her say it, Ash deepened the kiss, hands slipping down to her hips and flexing there, and soon she was following his backward shuffle to the bed.

She lay on the soft flannel bedspread and watched Ash toe off his shoes, loosen his tie, unbutton the collar of his shirt, and pull it over his head. She shimmied out of her skirt while he yanked off his belt. Once they were both in nothing more than their underwear, he sat by her hip and traced a finger across the top of her bra, over the swell of one breast, into the dip of her cleavage, and over the other. His hand continued around to her back, and she arched for him to unclasp her bra. This time, he managed it on the first attempt instead of desperately tugging it down. He gave her a victorious grin that made her giggle, giddy with affection for him as she lifted her arms to let him slide her bra off.

The grin vanished as soon as he got a full look at her. Thank God they'd turned on the bedside lamp because otherwise she would have missed that dark hunger in his eyes. That look could power a whole city block. *I want to touch more of you than I did in the barn,* he'd told her earlier.

Her nipples pinched into little peaks, aching for contact. "Touch me."

He didn't need any more invitation than that, covering one breast with his palm. She fumbled for his hips, tugging him to lie atop her, and he settled between her legs, pressing his erection right up against her. "You need me close? Right here?"

She wanted him even closer than this, but every point of their bodies that could be in contact already was, especially when he dropped his mouth to her neck. She nodded, then realized he couldn't see it. "Yes."

He was everywhere. Just when she got used to one sensation, he switched to another kind of touch, another part of her body.

His palm slipped into the back of her underwear, squeezing a handful of ass cheek and lifting her up against him, before he ducked to capture her breast with his mouth, teeth grazing her nipple, then closing his lips around it and sucking hard. He shifted his body back up to meet her again with a slow, hard grind.

She couldn't believe they both still had their underwear on. They were dry humping like teenagers. But God, it felt good. She could come like this, without even getting to feel him where she wanted him. The muscles in his arms and shoulders were threaded taut from supporting his weight, as if he didn't understand she wanted him to crush her. "Closer," she said. "You can come closer."

"I want to be inside you." The way he said it seemed to encompass more than just sex, like he had the same strange desire she did, to burrow through his skin, to curl up inside his chest.

She pushed his boxer briefs halfway down his ass, loving the hard muscles there, which flexed as he ground himself against her. When she didn't finish the task, he made an impatient sound in the back of his throat and pushed off her until she focused enough to shove his underwear the rest of the way and wriggle out of her own.

He was beautiful, stretched out above her to open the nightstand drawer, all lean muscle, long lines, and smooth planes. She ran her fingers down the ridges of his abs, making his stomach clench. His shaky laugh cut off into a deep groan as she wrapped her fingers around him and slid down and back up his length. He was in the middle of tearing a condom open but dropped his forehead to her shoulder, apparently too caught up to do anything else with it, so she took it and rolled it onto him. She slid her hands up his sides and urged him closer until his chest pressed firmly against hers, and he positioned himself at her entrance.

Instead of pushing into her, though, he lifted his face to look at her. His breathing was labored, the tendons in his neck strained tight, but the kiss he pressed to her lips was tender. He reached between them, and she jerked, surprised by his fingers on her again. Dear God, was he really going to keep teasing her? She would combust.

"Asher," she said sharply. "Get in me."

And then, with an amused huff, he did.

She wanted to cry from the relief of finally having him there, from the pressure and stretch of the welcome intrusion. He pushed in slowly. Too slow. She whined when he retreated, but he came back, pushed deep inside her. They both released shuddering exhales, husks of sound scraping through the silence.

Hazel was about to beg him to *move* when he began to rock into her, back muscles flexing under her palms, mouth open against her neck. "Goddamn, Haze," he said, both strain and awe in his voice. The pace was slow at first. She felt everything, every movement like shoreline waves crashing in and dragging out. Under her hands, his shoulders began to tremble—"You're shaking," she marveled—and he snapped his hips harder into hers, giving in to some needier drive.

She understood now what he'd been trying to tell her, that seeing her on the edge of losing it turned him on. She pulled his face up so she could see it again, that wild hunger, and when she did, when his impossibly dark, desperate gaze met hers, and she took in his kiss-swollen mouth, the tense crease between his eyebrows, the ragged sound of his breath, something snapped inside her.

She didn't know how he understood immediately what she was doing and maneuvered them, but quickly they were sitting upright, and she was straddling his hips. His head tipped back, letting her hold his face and kiss him hard as she rolled against him, staying deep, getting the pressure she needed. His hands hovered at her waist and then gripped tight enough to leave a mark. The thought of it, his fingerprints on her skin after, quickly morphed from a curiosity to a need.

"Fuck, I'm—"

She knew already. He was bucking up into her, giving her hips an extra pull every time she rocked against him. She was right there, too, tried to say as much, to assure him he could let go, that maybe she needed his release to get to her own.

"Haze," he panted. "Come with me."

The pressure deep inside her crested then tore through her. Every part of her clenched tightly around Ash as the waves of it kept coming, kept breaking. The night's ever-present tears stung her eyes anew, this time from sheer relief, like her orgasm was yanking open every door inside her, letting out every pent-up breath. She was only half aware that he came, too, his thrusts hard and fast up into her and then one last jerk.

They held each other, chests heaving, until Ash gingerly tilted her face back and swiped a tear from her cheek. His eyebrows furrowed, but then he seemed to understand these tears were different. "How?" he whispered. "How is it like this?" And his own eyes were intense with emotion that made her want to hold him forever.

"Pretty sure I'm falling for you, too," she answered.

He swallowed twice before he managed, quietly, "Thank God."

———

THE FIRST TIME HAZEL AWOKE, THE ROOM WAS STILL DARK. ASH'S arms were wrapped around her from behind in a full-contact cuddle. He stirred shortly after she did, pressed a kiss to the back of her neck, and soon they were grinding against each other under the warm blankets, pausing only to grab a condom from the bedside table.

The next time she awoke, the dark night outside was just beginning to turn, an undertone of blue bleeding through. She extracted herself carefully from Ash to tiptoe across the hall to the bathroom, hoping since they were the only ones up here in the addition, she wouldn't run into one of his sisters or nieces. When she returned, she stopped in the doorway to watch Ash, curls brushed across his forehead, T-shirt sleeve twisted up around his shoulder. She had designs to pull the covers down, wake him with her mouth, but something began buzzing. She pawed through the pockets of Ash's blazer on the floor until she found her phone.

She had seven missed calls, four voicemails, six texts, all from her father.

"Get back in here," Ash murmured, eyes still closed. When she didn't, he pushed up on one elbow. "What's wrong?"

She held up her phone.

"Your dad?"

"I don't want to look yet."

"Don't then. Give it 'til morning."

She nodded at the window. "It is morning."

He pulled the covers back. "Five more minutes. Then we'll figure it out."

Hazel was pretty sure you couldn't snooze anxiety, but she relented. He took her phone from her and tucked it behind him where she couldn't fixate on it, and he held her in the cozy warmth of his bed until, somehow, her adrenaline and dread leveled off.

"It's going to be okay, you know," he said after a while.

"I acted like a freak."

He made a sound of protest in his throat.

"I flipped a table. And the things I said . . ."

"I think you needed to say them."

Regret burned through her. "I should have had more control. Now it's all just . . ." She closed her eyes. Her breathing was shaky.

"You did the hardest part," he said, kissing her shoulder. He stroked her arm. "Now you guys can talk it out."

Hazel flipped over to face him. "There's no coming back from this. Now he *knows*."

"I know," he said gently. "I know it feels like that. But it's a step forward."

"No, it's like ten thousand steps back. It undoes *everything*. The whole point of this week was to *not* do any of this. No steps forward or backward. Everything was supposed to stay the same."

"But things don't just stay the same. I understand you didn't want to tell him how you really feel, but—" He squeezed her wrist gently. "What you guys have been doing all these years isn't a real relationship. Isn't that what you want, something better? Isn't that, deep down, why you came back?"

Hazel opened her mouth to deny it but couldn't.

"You don't want to change anything so you won't risk losing these scraps he's given you."

She sat up, and he barely dodged her shoulder. "You don't get it."

"What am I not getting?"

"That I fucked up. Things can never go back to how they were. I didn't want this."

"You're right, they can't. They have to change. But I'm telling you, it's going to be for the better. When you took off, he wasn't angry or annoyed or whatever. He was concerned. He wanted to understand."

"What are you talking about?"

"When you went to the bathroom. He had no idea what he'd done wrong. I mean, Christ, Hazel. He didn't know about Justin. He thinks if he tries even a little, he'll smother you. He's not just on a different page than you. He's in a completely different fucking book."

"What did you tell him?"

"I told him he needed to talk to you." Ash groaned, dragging a hand down his face. "And I said what anyone with a shred of sense would have known after two minutes around you, that he should see this incredible person right in front of him, visit you, call you."

Her eyes went wide. "*Why* would you tell him that?"

"I was trying to—" He tried to stroke her arm again, but she pulled it away. "Look, I know it wasn't my place. I know I shouldn't have said anything, and I'm sorry. But, Hazel, him not knowing how you feel about anything doesn't protect you. It only hurts you. And I really hate seeing you hurt."

"That's funny," Hazel said without a shred of humor and pushed herself off the bed. "Nothing hurt until I came here. Until you started digging around in my business."

It felt at once not quite true and the absolute truest thing she'd ever said. *He* was the one who'd been so incensed by her exclusion at the dinner last night, who just couldn't let it go. She'd given in to her hurt feelings after *he'd* stoked them. Not to mention all their other conversations this week, his badgering questions, how openly *not right* he judged her relationship with her dad to be. And now he'd gone and compounded her outburst, revealed more that she wouldn't be able to claw back.

She gathered last night's clothes from the floor and dropped them next to her bag, which she unzipped so hard, the teeth caught the canvas. She had to yank it several times before it gave. Then, she pulled out jeans, a sweater, and jammed her legs into the pants.

At this, Ash rose from the bed. "What are you doing?"

"Getting dressed."

"I see that. Why are you doing it right now?"

"Because I don't want to have this conversation naked."

"Can you just—"

"What?"

"Slow down and talk to me."

A bitter laugh scraped out of her. "Maybe I don't want to talk. Maybe talking is the whole fucking problem."

"I don't think that's true," he said quietly.

"Well, you don't know everything," she snapped. "Maybe you're one of those people everything just works out for. Maybe you can count on people wanting you around, even after you fuck up. But people aren't falling all over themselves to be with me."

He pressed a palm to his chest. "*I* am."

"Well, you shouldn't!" She felt wild. The clawing in her chest was back, and she rubbed the spot, felt her heart pounding back. "God, you shouldn't have to work so hard for something that isn't going to last anyway. Everything eventually falls apart. Everything. The only difference is whether you know that and accept it, or you let yourself hope it'll be different this time."

Ash shook his head, letting it hang. "Don't do this," he said. The resignation in his voice stopped her short. He didn't mean just to stop spinning out, to stop talking herself out of a reasonable outlook on her relationship with her dad. He was two steps ahead, even of her own self-awareness. And now she was catching up. He was resigned because she was talking herself out of a reasonable outlook on her relationship with *him*.

The realization sank in her stomach. She didn't want to do

this. She wasn't ready to do this. But it was always going to happen.

"If I don't do it, it's not like you will. You'll keep driving the same shitty car until it dies, stay friends with a guy you don't even like."

His face was strained when he looked up. "So, this is a favor? Is that it? You think you're saving me from some future pain by ending it now? Because you're too goddamned late, Hazel. If you leave now, you will fucking break my—"

He stopped himself short as she looked away. Hazel's rib cage was too tight. She couldn't get a full breath. Her eyes stung and blurred, so she stooped to zip up her boots, anything to not have to look at him.

His voice was thick when he continued. "Won't it hurt you, too?"

She shoved the remaining clothes into her bag. Just like last night, she forgot about the cut on her palm, and it stung when she lifted the strap. This pain was what finally made the tears spill over. She was so damn tired of crying.

She held out her uninjured hand, eyes cutting to her phone on the bed beside him.

He picked it up but didn't give it to her. "Don't leave. Not like this."

"Please, give me my phone."

He shook his head again, kept shaking it, like this was the only gesture, the only thought available to him—*no*.

Hazel pulled the phone from his grasp and shoved it into her back pocket. She turned to his door. "It hasn't even been a week. We barely even started this."

"So, what? Shit got a little uncomfortable, and now that's it?" He came up behind her, pressed his hands flat to the door on each side of her shoulders, caging her in. He wasn't touching her, but she felt the warmth of his body behind her. How many times had she wanted him to press against her like this, wanted the relief of that contact? If he wrapped his arms around her again instead of just holding the door shut, she didn't know if she had the strength to resist.

She felt his breath on her ear when he asked, "Last night you were falling for me, but now you'll just turn it off?"

She shook her head, helpless.

"Hazel." A plea. Her body wanted to stay, wanted to sink into his arms. Her heart begged her to turn around.

"Hazel, please."

She grabbed the doorknob, willing him to unblock the door. Willing him not to.

"Fuck," he said, voice brittle. He rocked his weight into his palms, making the door creak on its hinges. He stayed there for long seconds, trapping her.

Every moment that passed cemented her words. *Take it back*, she thought. *Don't let this happen.* But she couldn't speak. She needed *out*.

Finally, Ash pushed himself back. His bare feet shushed across the carpet, away from her.

"I just need some space," she whispered.

"Yeah," he bit out from somewhere behind her, bitterness in his voice. "I'm sure that'll fix everything. Thousandth time's a charm."

"You know me so well," she agreed, matching his cold tone. "I guess you should have seen this coming."

Then she opened the door and walked out.

Twenty-Three

I n the minutes after Hazel left his room, Ash paced. He texted, knowing she wouldn't respond. He paced some more.

The blazer Hazel had worn last night lay rumpled on his floor. He balled it up and threw it into his closet. The soft impact was completely unsatisfying. He threw his shoes in after it, and they smacked against the closet wall.

Then, he hoisted up the box of ornaments he'd taken back from her house and let it fly. It sailed into the wall above his nightstand, contents raining down onto the table, his bed, the floor. A plastic ball ornament rolled across the carpet and stopped at his feet, his ignorantly happy eight-year-old face on the inserted picture beaming up at him. He kicked it, and it shot straight at the water cup he'd filled for Hazel last night.

"Fucking great," he muttered at the wet spot on the carpet. Destruction of his own belongings would not extinguish the burning anger in his chest. Some part of him knew this. But the tiny release of so much pent-up, suffocating tension promised more relief. He spotted the wooden baseball bat propped in the corner.

Ash hadn't held one in years, hadn't even played intramural softball in college. He lifted it, rotated it in a circle with a simple turn of his wrist, tucked it to his shoulder. It felt good. He was strangely ahead of himself, warning, *Do not put a hole in a wall*, while also drunk on the weight of the bat, how it seemed to have been left there for this exact occasion.

And then he looked up at the Popsicle stick chandelier he'd made the year before he met Hazel, before his father got sick, before he'd ever really wanted something he couldn't will into existence. He swung. The sticks burst from the impact, a candy-less piñata raining splinters down over him, scattering across the carpet. For one heartbeat, it was deeply satisfying, this breaking.

In the next moment, however, on his reckless follow-through, the bat smashed into the model of Maggie's house on the dresser, crunching through Cosette and Isabel's meticulously rendered pink-and-purple bedroom and sending the whole thing onto the floor.

"Shit." Anger flared again, this time at himself, at the bat, at Hazel, at the model for being in the wrong place. It was badly damaged. His first impulse was to obliterate it entirely, take out all the anger still pulsing in him. But the feeling waned, smothered by heavy regret. An ache pressed into his throat. He let the bat fall to the carpet.

ASH BLINKED UP FROM THE MODEL AT THE SOUND OF KNOCKING ON HIS door. He'd waffled on whether to repair the damage or shop for new gifts for his nieces at the last minute. All his usual tools and paints sat out of reach at his apartment, so he'd raided his mother's art supplies in the garage and was making them work, sort of. He'd just have to accept some imperfections.

June called impatiently through the door. "Are you clothed?"

"No."

She entered anyway, one hand plastered across her eyes, the other holding two mugs of coffee, one of which tilted and dripped onto the carpet. She parted her fingers and scoffed. "Liar."

"What do you want?"

She set one of the mugs on his dresser and cupped the other thoughtfully under her chin, openly surveying the wreckage around him. "So, what'd you do?" At his frown, she added, "Her car was here last night. Now it's not. We thought you had both gone, but Mom heard you hulking out up here earlier."

She sat on his bed, plucked an errant Popsicle stick from under her thigh, and tossed it into the trash bin. "There was a small chance she was still here, and you two were just into some weird, BDSM—"

"June," he warned tiredly.

"What? Like I wanted to come up here and see things I'd have to bleach from my brain later?"

"She's not here." Fuck, it hurt to say it out loud.

"And the parting was such sweet sorrow?" she said, morphing into a Shakespearean player. She was so irritatingly *June*, nosy, intrusive, perfectly capable of reading a room but always going for the joke anyway. "You missed breakfast. And now it's starting to feel like you're avoiding us. On Christmas Eve Eve."

Ash glued a new piece of trim to the model wall. He didn't have time to chat, nor did he want to address the accusation that he was avoiding everyone when they were the ones who had iced him out over the hospital visit.

"So, what happened? I mean, you're usually pretty uptight, but you actually seemed kind of normal around her," June said.

"I'm not uptight."

A hyena laugh burst out of her.

"Yeah, well, you don't know as much as you think you do. There are things on my plate that no one expects of you."

"Oh," June said, nodding. "You mean like you guys hiding shit from me? Yeah, it must have been tough to be trusted with what was going on with dad all these years."

"That—" he started. He'd never considered that they'd been *bad* at keeping the details hidden or that his sisters might resent the protection.

"So, what happened with Hazel?"

He sighed. "I told you. She left."

"Because . . ."

"Because . . . I don't know. Because she has a shitty relationship with her parents, and she had a shitty first boyfriend, and now she thinks every relationship can only be shitty."

"Okay. Were you guys in a relationship?"

"Barely." He ran a hand over his hair in frustration. "I mean, yeah, it was going somewhere. It was real. She just didn't think it could end up any other way. And I—I got too involved with her issues with her dad, and that didn't help."

June nodded, suddenly affecting some serene therapist. "So, you went with her story?"

"What?"

"That things couldn't end up another way."

"No. She didn't give me a choice. She left."

"Okay, so you're just sitting here feeling sorry for yourself? It's not like she's Liam Neeson's daughter in *Taken*. And you have this newfangled thing called a phone. *Call* her."

"June," he said, frustrated. "She's ignoring my texts. Even if I knew where she was, she made it pretty clear she wants space. She has this thing with *afters*." He waved off her confusion. "I'm sure this will shock you, but me trying to fix things is part of the fucking problem. She asked for space. If I go after her, I'll just push her away more."

June cast him an uncharacteristically sympathetic look. "That's quite an impasse."

"Did you come up here just to make me feel worse?"

"No. I'm really sorry. I like Hazel. I like you with Hazel." She nodded at the model. "Do you need help with that?"

The word *no* was right there on the tip of his tongue, but he took a breath. "Actually, yeah, I do."

AT LUNCH, HAZEL'S FATHER CALLED THE LANDLINE.

Ash took the wireless receiver down the hall to the bathroom and locked himself in, saying carefully, "Hi, Mr. Elliot. Hazel's not here."

There was a long pause. "Okay. I understand you feel protective of my daughter."

"I'm not covering for her. She's really not here," he said. His jaw and fists clenched with a surge of bitterness. If Dan hadn't pushed him to explain Hazel's outburst at the party, she would still be here.

But the fight left him as soon as Dan said, "I'm sorry if I put you in a tough position last night. I was—I *am*—" He cleared his throat. "Would you pass along that I'd like to talk when she's ready?"

"Wish I could." Ash rubbed his face. As much as he blamed Dan for last night and for all the mistakes he'd made with Hazel before, Ash heard the man's weariness and guilt and found a pocket of compassion amidst the anger. Ash wasn't blameless, either. "She's . . . not answering my messages right now."

"Oh."

"I guess she didn't go home?"

"No."

Ash sat on the edge of the tub. He'd tried not to imagine Hazel behind the wheel as upset as she'd been this morning.

"Do you have any idea where she might have gone?"

Ash squeezed his neck. "Back to her apartment? Maybe Houston to see her old roommate?"

"All right. I've got to make some more calls then."

"Sir? Could you . . ."

"I'll let you know when I find her."

Ash gave him his cell number, and they hung up.

When he brought the phone back to the kitchen, his mother had cleared the dishes. He could hear June's lilting voice belting out instructions to walk like an elephant, then a series of big and small thudding steps tromping through a back bedroom. He raised his eyebrows at his parents, Leanne, and Laurel, sitting in silence.

"June told us you and Hazel had a fight. I'm sorry," his mother said.

"I don't really want to talk right now."

She pulled out his chair. "Tough. Sit."

Reluctantly, he did.

His father slid a check across the table to him, nodded to the twins, who fidgeted in their seats.

"What is this?"

"The money you gave us," Leanne said.

"We've been earning it back," Laurel added. "And we're sorry we lied to you."

"And we won't ever do it again."

"Okay. Thanks," he said, eyeing the check and then his sisters' contrite faces, "but I don't need this."

His mom nudged the check closer. "Put it toward a new car."

"No, Mom," he said, pushing it back. "I really don't need it. I have savings. I have plenty."

"So do we."

"It's time to do things differently," his father said. "Girls, you can go."

Laurel's and Leanne's chair legs scraped with the urgency of their departure. His sisters offered identical sheepish smiles, and even though physical contact of any kind felt like it might crack him open right now, he pulled them each in for a quick hug before they retreated to their room.

"Do what differently?" he said on a sigh, sitting back down.

"It's come to my attention that I'm not the easiest patient." His father popped his knuckles, and Ash realized he was doing the same thing under the table. "Well, I already knew that, I guess. What I've really come to see is that my frustration with my . . . uh, limitations, puts other people—your mother, you—in the position of having to manage more than what's fair."

Ash's mother cut in. "For the record, supporting you isn't a burden. We've both needed each other at different times, and that's as it's supposed to be. No one's keeping count."

He nodded. "The burden I mean is my pride about it, my *occasional* desire to reject all the support. Feels like people telling me what to do, fretting over me, managing me, even though I know it's only you all wanting me to stay healthy. You," he said, meeting Ash's eyes, "don't know if you can trust me to take care of myself. I hate that you've taken that on. I hate that you've planned your whole life around that. So, here's the deal, son. I'm taking responsibility for myself. And your mom has my back. And beyond that, there are doctors, health insurance, home care if or when it comes to that, all the safety nets that mean our kids don't have to limit their lives just in case things go south."

Ash's mother leaned across the table toward him, her expression pleading, a little watery even, which put Ash on high alert. She shook her head at his sudden straightening but doubled down on her imploring expression. "The only person we need you to take care of is yourself."

"I do take care of myself."

"You're living like you expect the sky to fall. And like you're the only one who could hold it up. I know you don't want to accept it, but you can't stop the inevitable. Not the people you love having infuriating minds of their own, and not the MS."

Ash swallowed. His throat felt thick and tight.

"And because you can't stop it, you should choose what makes you happy *now*, and trust that you'll rise to the occasion when you need to. Don't deny yourself the comforts you can afford. Don't put off having what you want. Because, who knows, a meteor could wipe us all out tomorrow anyway."

"Jesus, Mom."

"Well?" She shrugged.

The irony of her telling him this *today* burned. *Hazel* made him happy. She was the first thing in a long time that did. Her laugh, the big, loud version of it when amusement snuck up on her and she couldn't filter it. That was all he wanted. Her, laughing like that. But the way she'd left, the finality of it—he couldn't see how to fix it. He'd overstepped with his parents in the hospital, and even though he'd tried to avoid the same mistake with Hazel—had heard what she was saying, knew how scared she was—he'd pushed too hard with her, too. And now he didn't even know where she was, or if she'd ever hear him out.

"I cannot emphasize enough how badly we want that for you," his mom continued. "The freedom to live an ordinary, happy life, based on what *you* want, not what you imagine everyone else needs." She swiped a tear from her cheek, and Ash had to blink away the sting in his own eyes.

"Okay," he said, partly to stop her from crying over him and partly because . . . he did want that. An ordinary, happy life.

"You'll try?"

He hardly knew what that would even look like. His life felt like a game of Whac-A-Mole, and he got so caught up in the urgency of bashing down every new problem that it never occurred to him to set down the mallet and let the game play itself out. That was essentially what they were asking him to do, wasn't it? Not attempt to stem the tide of his dad's illness. Not to write the ending of a story before he was even through the twisting, turning middle. Let it play out.

If he didn't follow his usual instincts with Hazel, if he gave her the space she'd asked for, she might just run and never look back. That was a real possibility.

But a lot of things that he'd never thought possible had also happened this week. And they'd happened because he *hadn't* been the only one in the driver's seat. Hell, from the start of this, Hazel had literally taken the wheel. He could give up control, as scary as that was.

Ash nodded toward his father and said, "If he can try, I can try."

Twenty-Four

For hours, Hazel drove. At first, she drove through big, deep, wracking sobs that burned her throat and blurred her vision. She drove through every new chime on her phone. She drove until the rising sun made her squint and realize she was headed southeast, back toward school. She hadn't decided this, but it made sense. Turning her phone off to quiet the notifications left only the radio for a distraction. Every thirty minutes or so, she had to find another station that wasn't punched through with static.

The flat West Texas prairie gave way to gradual rises and falls. Two days before Christmas, and yet Hazel didn't see another car or house or any sign of civilization, only empty crop fields. She'd said she needed space. This was certainly space. A forever road through endless, rough landscape and limitless gray sky. Where waist-high crops might have waved in summer, there was mostly just empty dirt, everything brown and dead. She'd driven herself into the literal middle of nowhere, and she had never felt so achingly, brutally alone.

When Paul McCartney's "Wonderful Christmastime" started up on the radio, she laughed bitterly.

But a billboard stopped the sound in her throat. It featured a pale blue Victorian house beneath the bold claim that the Roadrunner Inn was the "Crown Jewel of Garrettsville." She

wasn't on the freeway, had taken a back road without a destination in mind—one of those two-lane farm-to-market ones
she'd given Ash shit for a week ago—and somehow, she'd ended
up right back here, two miles from where she'd gotten stuck
with him.

Was it a sign?

Well, it was a literal sign. But Hazel's blood sang with something magnetic, some visceral frequency only her body could
understand. She took the turn the billboard indicated, and
soon, the inn was there in front of her.

It was shabbier in the bright daylight than it had looked
when they'd taken refuge inside, far from magical with no snow
left on the ground, only muddy puddles where it had melted. But
still, the sight of its chipped paint and crooked shingles pulled
at her heart. It was proof. Of life. Of something new. A tiny spark
of a thing just last week, which had since quietly engulfed her
whole life. Ash had already taken on the role of her buffer the
night they stayed here, tucking her under his arm against the
biting wind. He'd let her lean on him while they watched *The Office* in bed. Warmed her icy hands in the dark. Murmured in his
low, sleepy voice until she'd drifted to sleep.

It hit her all at once. Her infuriating pattern. Her running.
She was never running *to* anything, never running *with* anyone.
Except last night, when Ash had helped her ransack her room at
her father's house, when he'd taken her keys and driven her to
his home.

Be with me, she'd said.

I am.

All this running had gotten her what? Not safety. Not happiness. She was as alone and untethered as she'd ever been. As she
drew boundaries around every new source of hurt, her world
only got smaller. Even if she could stomach resuming her ban on

Lockett Prairie, there was still school, still the café. Still this ramshackle, overpriced, weird fucking place in the middle of nowhere, where she'd unknowingly started something that it already hurt to breathe without. And she knew if she ever came back here, it would no longer bring her joy, only regret. That was the whole point of the running. To not have to feel this.

Except she would always know this place was here. And she'd feel the deep ache she felt now, even if she didn't look at it.

Continuing another mile away from Ash and her father and Lockett Prairie would only keep her trapped in the same terrible pattern. She knew that now. But going back? She couldn't quite do that, either. And she couldn't bear to set one foot inside the Roadrunner Inn.

Instead, she paid for a room at the Motel 6. She would go nowhere until she figured out her next step. Whatever that was.

When she turned her phone back on, the answer was right there among the sea of messages and ignored calls from her dad and Ash.

SYLVIA: Proof of life, please! How was the fancy party?

Yesterday, she'd wanted to finally tell Sylvia everything about Ash. Now . . . just thinking of their fight this morning triggered a wave of nausea and cold sweat. But Sylvia was her last person left. She couldn't bear to lose anyone else.

HAZEL: I'm alive.

SYLVIA: Proof?

Hazel chose a nondescript corner of the room and framed the shot to cut off her puffy nose and eyes.

SYLVIA: What is that wallpaper? Why is the lighting so bad? IS THIS A HOSTAGE SITUATION?

HAZEL: You've watched too many true crime shows.

SYLVIA: HAS THERE BEEN A CRIME??

HAZEL: Not that I'm aware of.

SYLVIA: HAZEL

Before she could respond, her phone was ringing. No, not just ringing. Sylvia was trying to video call her.

"You've been crying," Sylvia said as soon as they connected. "Don't you dare try to tell me it's allergies."

"Someone was smoking in here," Hazel argued half-heartedly.

"Where is *here*? You're not at your dad's."

Hazel slumped into a surprisingly hard, upholstered chair. "It's a motel."

"What are you doing crying in a motel?"

"Is Dave with you?" Hazel asked, stalling. She squinted at the bit of background she could see behind Sylvia. It hit her that she hadn't yet seen Sylvia's new place, not even in proofs of life. Sylvia was always the person demanding evidence of Hazel's continued existence, not the other way around.

"Dave's out picking a kitten for my Christmas gift. He thinks it's a secret."

Hazel laughed despite the heavy gloom pressing in on her. "How do you—"

"When is everybody going to realize that I know and see all? You can't get anything past me. Speaking of which, I've been extremely patient with you sending me crumbs of details, but now I have to know what the hell is going on out there."

"I don't even know where to start, Syl."

"I'd get excited about you being in a motel right now if I thought you and some hottie hooked up, but since you're alone and you've been crying, I'm guessing things went a different way."

"Something like that," Hazel squawked, her throat tight.

Sylvia let silence pulse between them, her face on the screen somehow both patient and unyielding. Of course Sylvia knew the secret to getting around Hazel's evasions and deflections— even Hazel couldn't dodge from nothing.

But that was the point. She didn't want to dodge anymore.

"I yelled at my dad, flipped a table, snuck out a bathroom window, slept with Ash Campbell, broke up with Ash Campbell, left town, and now I'm here at this Motel 6 in Garrettsville because I can't bring myself go back, but I can't go to my place, either. I'll have to spend Christmas here. And maybe live here forever."

Sylvia's eyebrows rose slowly, eyes round. "Wait." She opened her mouth, struggled to find words. "Wait."

"I'm waiting. I literally have nowhere else to go."

Sylvia's face filled the screen as she scrutinized Hazel. "Asher, the asshole chair thief from the café? I thought we hated him."

"It's just Ash, actually." Hazel smiled sadly. "And he's not just from the café. We went to high school together. I gave him a ride home. You actually met him once, that first party freshman year."

"And you slept together? Wait. Oh my God. *Hazel.*" Sylvia's screen bounced as she changed positions on her couch. A million late-night conversations rushed back to Hazel. Sylvia, tucking her legs under her, buzzing with whatever juicy gossip she had to share. She would slap the back of the couch or Hazel's thigh with each new detail.

"Okay," Sylvia said. "God, I have missed *a lot.* This is why you have to stop going AWOL."

Hazel rolled her eyes, but the gesture was half-assed since tears brimmed behind her lower lashes.

"Was the sex good?"

"Does it matter? We broke up."

Sylvia's eyebrows shot up.

Hazel backtracked. "If you could even call it a breakup. We were barely..." She swallowed thickly. She didn't want to downplay this week with Ash any more than she wanted to admit it was already over.

"I'm having to do a lot of guesswork here. You can at least tell me if the sex was good."

"Even at the expense of my feelings?"

"The fact that you *have* feelings about him is why I need all the details."

Hazel groaned and tipped her face up to the ceiling, resting her head against the chairback. "The sex was . . ."

Unbelievable? So good it had maybe broken something in her and put it back together all at once? *How is it like this?* Ash had asked, the very same sentiment on the tip of her own tongue.

"It was good, Syl. But I think it was a mistake. And even if it wasn't, I fucked it all up." She hoped to sound distanced from the pain of this morning, but instead, her voice shook, and her ever-present tears ran from the outer corners of her eyes into her hair.

"Oh, babe."

Hazel set her phone on the dresser, screen pointing up to the ceiling. Sylvia didn't demand to be turned back at her while Hazel covered her face and sobbed.

When she calmed down to sniffles and lifted the phone again, Sylvia said, "You're not spending Christmas at a Motel 6. You *do* have somewhere else to go. Here with me."

"I can't crash your first Adult Christmas with Dave." Instead of staying with her parents, like she and Hazel had always done, Sylvia's plan was to stay at her apartment with Dave for "sexy time" tomorrow night before they went over to see her family Christmas morning.

"Oh, shut up. That's the flimsiest excuse I've ever heard."

Hazel started to protest, but Sylvia cut her off.

"Seriously, Hazel. I know you think it's been some huge favor for me to share my family with you these last few years, but don't you get that we're sisters? I never had one, and now I do, and it's amazing. But you get in the way of it sometimes with this inability to let yourself be loved and accepted the way you are. Which is awesome. The way you are, that is, not the way you sabotage relationships."

"I don't sab—"

"You do. If you didn't, you would have called me before you panicked and left or . . . flipped a table?" She frowned but shook her head like they would have to come back to that detail later. "Or you would have just come here for Christmas like always."

"My dad is getting married. I had to come."

"Why?"

Hazel rubbed her forehead where a deep ache pulsed. She was tired of explaining the concept of familial obligation to people who didn't need a reason or an invitation to see their families. "It would have been a bigger issue if I hadn't."

"So, you came for the wedding. But now you're in a motel in some other town two days before Christmas, and the wedding is . . ."

"Tomorrow."

"And you're going to go back, or . . ."

Hazel groaned. This was the exact problem. "I don't know."

"Seems like avoiding making an issue has made it a bigger issue."

"Thanks. I see that." Hazel snapped, then winced. "Sorry. I'm sorry."

Sylvia gave her a pitying look. "Are you upset he's getting married?"

Sure, she'd been surprised to see how involved her father was with Val and her kids. His proud presence at Lucy's choir performance had struck a nerve. Not comparing him now to him five or ten years ago was impossible, as much as the comparison was also pointless. But Val was warm and kind, not the Stepford wife she'd originally pictured. And when Hazel managed not to think too hard about her parents' relationship, it was kind of nice to see her father with Val. She didn't want him to be unhappy. She didn't want him to never change or grow, even if she might have benefited from him doing it sooner.

"I accepted the way things were before, that I just didn't have deep relationships with my parents. I figured it would never change, so why get worked up about it? Why wish for something else just to be disappointed? But as it turns out . . ."

"He changed for them," Sylvia concluded.

Hazel shrugged, not wanting to admit her best friend was right on the money.

"Both your parents should have tried harder, you know. You made everything easier on them because they were going through their own shit. Your mom *deserved* her fancy job, the life she waited for all those years. Your dad *deserved* to be a lead reporter after putting in so much work. That's how you explained it to me—what *they* deserved, why it was all okay that you didn't get what *you* deserved: their presence, the kind of love that leaves no room to question it. They should have known better than to let you make things easier on them. You're still doing it." She put on a bright smile. "'Don't worry about me. I'm fine with whatever.'"

"I don't sound like that."

"Please. Do you know the moment I realized we were actual friends and not just decent roommates? It was when the north-side dining hall started making those rocky road cookies. Remember? I was obsessed with them. I had been bringing extras of the chocolate chip ones back to our room for you, but I switched, and you stopped eating them, and I was like, 'Why aren't you eating the cookies? Are you sick? Are you on a diet? Are you mad at me?'"

Hazel snorted, remembering.

"And you told me you preferred chocolate chip."

"Wait, that was, like, sophomore year."

Sylvia nodded slowly, eyes wide, like this proved her point. "It took you living with me almost two years to tell me you had a cookie preference."

"That doesn't mean we weren't friends before."

Sylvia shrugged. "You're a tough nut to crack, Hazel. But you're one of my favorites."

"Don't make me cry again."

"This is actually another special moment for me—you crying. It means I'm your person, too."

"Well." Hazel exhaled. "You might be my only person at this point."

"Nope. We're going to fix this. But you're going to have to tell me everything."

So, Hazel did. She recounted the initial deal and every obstacle that followed, from the storm that stranded her and Ash to the security gate, her father's Christmas tree allergy, the cranberry dress, Winter Fest. By the time she got to the dinner, all the toasts, every slight that had incensed Ash and which she'd tried to ignore, her father inviting Justin, and finally her outburst over the family photo, she was worked up all over again. She'd blown everything, undermined all her efforts since she'd arrived.

"Ash tried to tell me it was all going to be fine somehow, some *opportunity*. It was so infuriating. He just couldn't fathom things not working out. But things don't work out all the time."

"But sometimes they do," Sylvia offered gently.

"Not this time."

"With your dad or with Ash?"

Hazel shrugged, wiping at fresh tears.

"So, you took off?"

"And turned off my phone."

Sylvia was quiet.

Finally, Hazel prompted her. "Why aren't you saying anything?"

"How do you think that made them feel?"

"I don't know. Probably annoyed. What?"

"You think your dad feels annoyed right now? Or do you think, maybe, he's worried out of his mind?"

For the first time since she'd run from the party last night, Hazel imagined her father in his new house, at the dining table where everyone had a specific seat, even her. She saw him typing out those text messages, one every hour, waiting for the clock to okay the next one.

"Worried," she admitted. "I should probably tell him I'm not dead in a ditch somewhere, huh?" It was a sign of just how truly dysfunctional she was as a person that such a message, proof of life for her own father, felt like it would dangerously overexpose her.

"Probably," Sylvia said. "Now the other thing."

"What thing?"

"Could you be in love with Ash?"

Hazel closed her eyes. Ash, holding her fruitcake. Offering his old Christmas ornaments. Scribbling her height on his laundry room door. Cradling her face, his touch soft despite the desire in his taut muscles and dark eyes. *Pretty sure I'm falling for you. Don't panic, okay?* He always found the softest way to say hard things.

"I can't even deal with that. It's enough that my dad thinks—"

"A, you don't know what your dad thinks because you haven't talked to him. And B, wouldn't it maybe be a relief if he knew?"

"Knew what?"

"Everything. That you miss him. That you wish he knew you—the actual you, not the perfect, polite daughter who never needs anything."

"How—"

"I know and see all," Sylvia reminded her. Then, softly, "I'm sorry, but Ash wasn't wrong. You want a relationship with your dad. Maybe this *is* an opportunity. But you won't know if you don't try."

Hazel didn't know what to say. Even if she could fix any of it—and that was a big if—it all felt too huge at the moment.

Sylvia seemed to sense her exhaustion and said, "Okay, enough tough stuff. I'm going to send you pictures of the kittens Dave is choosing between."

And for the rest of the afternoon and into the evening, they kept talking, even through dinner—Sylvia and Dave at their dining table with a meal he'd cooked, Hazel on the motel bed with a spread of vending machine chips and peanut M&Ms. Her phone nearly died, and she had to scramble to find her charger, Sylvia yelling dramatically, "Do not die on us! Not at Christmas!"

When her exhaustion from the day finally made it impossible to stay awake, Hazel said, "You can watch me sleep like a weirdo, but I'm closing my eyes now."

"Wait," Sylvia said on a yawn. "Don't forget. Call your dad."

Hazel opted for a text: I'm in Garrettsville. I'm okay. Sorry if I made you worry.

The dots indicating his reply looped several times before a message finally came: Thank you.

Twenty-Five

Hazel checked that she had everything before she pulled the motel room door closed. She'd jolted awake just before five a.m. with the crystal-clear realization that a text had not been enough. She was only about thirty percent on board with her new plan to drive back to Lockett Prairie but didn't have time to second-guess it. Her father's wedding was at noon. She didn't know what would happen when she turned up for it, if anything could possibly be fixed, but missing it felt like the exact worst thing.

From around the corner, down another block of rooms, a stringent male voice pleaded, "Sir, you must stop, or I will have to call security."

There was a quick, harsh knock, a door opening.

"Ma'am, I'm so sorry for this. Sir. Sir, please," the man said.

Then footsteps, one pair long and purposeful, the other scuffing and quick, came down the cement walk toward Hazel's side of the building.

"You are waking all the guests."

"If you'd give me her room number—" a familiar voice bit back.

Hazel was groggy, but there was no mistaking that voice. Her heart lurched. He was here.

"Hazel?" he called, knocking on another door.

"That's it. I'm calling security."

Hazel flew around the corner. "Dad?"

A young motel employee with dark eye circles and days-old scruff was pacing a few feet away, tapping into his phone and offering a weak, apologetic smile down the length of the building at the confused guests poking their heads out of their rooms.

"Don't call security," Hazel said. "He'll stop now."

The man eyed her father, uncertain.

"What are you—" She was cut short by arms pulling her in, her face crushed to her father's blue windbreaker. The embroidered Channel 2 emblem pressed against her cheek. He held her so tightly her lungs ached.

"Hazel," he murmured into her hair. "Thank God."

She turned her face to catch her breath. The motel employee sobered at the sight of their embrace and backed away.

When her father finally let her go, her teeth chattered, giving her an excuse to go back into her room, rummage around in her bag for a sweater, turn on a lamp without having to make eye contact again just yet. He stood inside the closed door, jiggling his keys in his jacket pocket.

"Did you drive all night?"

Stupid question. She'd texted him after midnight. He'd had just enough time to look up lodging in Garrettsville, drive here, negotiate with the motel attendant for her room number, give up, and knock on a half dozen doors, which she guessed was exactly what he'd done.

He rubbed his face, the adrenaline that had been there moments ago fading right before her eyes. He was exhausted. He looked around the room before finding the chair and dropping heavily into it. "Got a speeding ticket two miles from home," he admitted with a sheepish smile.

She wanted to tell him she'd been on her way back, but he

looked so haggard, she was a little afraid to speak. She perched on the corner of the nightstand, realized that was horribly uncomfortable and awkward, and moved to the bed. "I didn't mean to make you drive all this way."

He frowned, and the thick silence that followed made her squirm. "You didn't think I would?"

"I sent the text so you wouldn't worry."

He dropped his face into his hands, shaking his head slowly back and forth, and she wasn't sure if he was about to laugh or cry, both unnerving options. "Of course—" he said sharply. He drew in a long breath, controlled his voice. "Of course I was worried. Ever since you left the party. We went home as soon as we realized you'd taken off, and all your stuff was gone. No note. You didn't answer any of my calls. By the time I tracked down your friend's number, you'd left there, too."

Ash. Her insides twisted. That he'd had to explain her absence, or cover for her, or just deal with her baggage, yet again . . .

"First word I hear from you, you're five hours away in the middle of nowhere. Worried is a goddamned understatement, kiddo."

Hazel swallowed loudly. "Sorry. I didn't realize."

"Yeah, I'm starting to see there's a lot you don't realize. That's my fault." He wiped his palms down his thighs and patted his knees absently. Her father could stand completely still on camera and look natural, had trained away his nervous tics for his job, but he was miles away from his TV personality now, fidgeting in joggers and mud-caked tennis shoes, hair uncombed. He looked ten years older.

"I don't know how to . . ." He shook his head, set his jaw, and looked her in the eye. "I should have been calling you more. I should have come to those parents' weekends."

Hazel picked at the seam of the comforter under her.

"I don't want to excuse anything. I should have pushed my way in. You just never seemed to—"

He looked up to the ceiling, tried again. "When you were little, your mom was the one who knew what you liked to eat, your favorite books, which stuffed animal you needed to sleep. When she left, I didn't know the simplest things about taking care of you. I was a wreck, Hazel. But not you. You handled it all so well. That counselor at your school told me you were adjusting great, better than expected. I couldn't even cook a decent meal. What I wanted seemed . . ."

Emotion surged in her chest. "What did you want?"

He lifted a shoulder, a painfully helpless gesture. "I had a lot to process that first year. I wish I'd handled it better. By the time I started to come out of that place, I realized things were different between you and me—distant. I didn't know how to get back in. I didn't want to disrupt your life more than I already had— my job, my failure with your mom."

That wording, *my failure with your mom*, didn't sit right. Her mother had made plenty of mistakes, too.

But it was another part of his speech that she latched on to. He didn't know how to get into what? Her life? She was right there, through a single, unlocked door in his own home. He was the one who hadn't come in.

"I thought I'd have more time to figure it out. It was years, I know. But they passed so quickly. Then, when you went to college, it really was too late. You were all the way across the state, this totally independent person. Not like you needed me for much by then. I didn't blame you for never wanting to come back. And now . . ." He scratched his neck, his face full of regret.

Hazel studied the muted, gray wallpaper behind him, sinuses burning, hands clenching the comforter so tightly her knuckles hurt.

"Go ahead," he said.

She shook her head, barely unclenched her teeth to say, "Go ahead and what?"

He gave her a sad smile. "I can take it, kiddo."

"You sure about that?"

"Yep."

"Okay." She pushed up and paced across the dingy, thread-bare carpet. "Okay, fine. You should have tried sooner, or harder. I couldn't change that Mom was gone. I accepted it. But you were *there*. Only, really, you weren't." Her heartbeat galloped in her ears. Her hands shook, palms sticky with sweat. Getting the words out made her feel sick. "So, I went to college, and you figured that was it, huh? Then they came along, and you got a do-over? I'm not really sure why you asked me to come home. Aren't I just a reminder of everything you did wrong? Don't I ruin the perfect picture of your life now?"

She whirled around to face him, tears spilling hot down her cheeks. She drew in a big breath to keep going, but the sight of him stopped her. He was looking right at her, not hiding from her criticism or fidgeting in discomfort, just taking it, even though his eyes were red and glassy and full of raw anguish. His lips trembled, and he pressed them closed. She had never seen him look so fragile.

"I'm sorry," he said gruffly, not bothering to wipe his eyes. He opened his palms on his knees. "You don't ruin anything. *I* messed up. I'm so damn sorry, honey."

Hazel sank back down onto the edge of the bed. She wiped her sweater sleeve across her face and blew out a shaky breath. She felt heavy and tired and, despite everything he'd said, confused. "Why was it so hard to love me?"

"No," he croaked. "Look at me. That was never the case."

"Then, what?"

Her father pulled two tissues from the box on the nightstand and finally blotted his face with one, passing her the other. "It wasn't your fault. When your mom left, I was ashamed. I couldn't give her what she needed. I failed with her. And worse, my failure didn't only devastate me. It was my fault *you* lost her, too. I knew by the time I came around and tried to fix my mistakes, you might have some resentments. I understood why you were harder to reach. My therapist insisted it was just preteen moodiness and I should keep trying, but I didn't want to upset you just to get what I needed."

Hazel frowned. "I was moody?"

"Now I know a little better what's normal." He didn't mention Lucy, but Hazel read the omission. "I should have encouraged you to decorate your room. Didn't realize how important a bedroom is to a girl that age. You spent every minute in there. I thought—"

"I didn't want to be with you?"

He sat beside her on the bed. "It must sound crazy that I could not know so much. I was so afraid I'd only be bad for you, just like I was for your mom."

Hazel frowned. That wasn't fair. For all that Hazel thought she understood her mother and had accepted her choices, she'd still *left*. And not just a husband who worked too much and a stifling life in a small town. She'd left her *daughter*. It wasn't right that Hazel's father blamed himself for that choice, nor that his shame had apparently made him doubt how much she'd needed him.

"And there you were," he went on, "my beautiful, smart, compassionate, perfect daughter, behind a door with your music and your books, and I didn't know what you needed. Wasn't sure I had it, whatever it was. Which is my shortfall, not yours."

"Dad." She didn't know what else to say. He was right that

she'd spent hours in her room, whether he was home or not. He'd taken ages to unpack at the new house, to make it feel anything like a home. Though it was plenty large for two, unopened boxes encroached in all the shared living spaces. Those boxes and his silence when he was around made every room feel too tight, like she was taking up too much air. She couldn't remember if, after that initial hard year, she'd ever ventured out to find him, to watch TV or talk, or if she'd expected him to be the one to knock on her door from the very start.

As for the moodiness, she remembered blaring music—*sad girl acoustic*—and escaping into her schoolwork, not necessarily to send a message or put up a wall, but because those things distracted her from her terrible loneliness.

"I didn't know," she said simply. "I didn't know any of that."

He put one arm around her shoulders and squeezed her into his side, saying into her hair, "That's the awful long and short of it, isn't it? Wish I could go back and do it all differently. You always belonged with me. Always. I'll never forgive my—"

Hazel snaked her arm around his back and pressed her face into his shoulder. "I've missed you, too." The admission came with a sob, the words held in for too long.

She hoped forgiveness was in the cards for them, too. And as strongly as he insisted the blame in this was his, she realized she'd have to reconcile her small part in it, all the years they could have had if she had simply spoken up, made the first move.

Her stomach growled. She pulled away as he asked, "They got a diner around here? I could sure go for some pancakes."

She laughed, started to tell him about the absurd place down the block, but stopped, slapping a hand to her forehead. "No. Dad, your wedding. We have to go now."

She hefted her bag back onto her shoulder, snatched her

keys, but her father was still sitting on the bed. "What are you doing? Come on."

"There's no hurry."

"But—your wedding."

He shrugged. "I'd like to take my daughter to breakfast."

"Dad. I'm going to need a shower once we get there, and I'll have to do my hair, fix my face."

"We've got time. And if we have to start a little late, Val will understand." At her raised eyebrow, he waved his phone then thumbed the screen. "I'm telling her we're going to eat."

His phone buzzed, and he read the message to her, "'Take your time. No more speeding tickets.'"

"Oh."

"Plus . . ." He dropped his gaze to his knees. "I didn't want to assume you were ready for all that. We haven't discussed how you feel about it."

"What, your wedding? Yes. Dad. I'm ready. I was leaving to get there in time when I heard you waking up the entire motel. I never had a problem with you getting married."

Was that true? Her old *everything's fine* reflex would take some time to kick, her true feelings harder to dial in on quickly, but she thought about Val and her kids, how hard they'd worked on her bedroom, her designated seat at their dining table, the custom stocking and all those Christmas packages under their tree. She hadn't given them much of a chance, but that had nothing to do with them.

"They're all great. You seem really happy together," she said, and she meant it.

"I want you to be part of it. A real part."

Hazel let the familiar knee-jerk resistance, the impulse to cling to an exit strategy, roll through. On the other side of that feeling, a little spark of excitement surprised her. A house full of people where she wasn't just a visitor. How that would come to be, exactly, she wasn't sure, but it wasn't a terrible thought.

WHEN THEY ENTERED THE HOUSE JUST AFTER ELEVEN, VAL, LUCY, AND Raf were eating popcorn in pajamas in front of the TV. No one looked ready for a wedding. They swarmed Hazel and her father, glad she was back, glad she was safe, as if she had been taken from them rather than having left of her own free will.

She turned to her father. "Didn't you tell them we'd make it?"

Val waved a hand. "I told the minister to come back this afternoon."

"I'm so sorry," Hazel said. She hoped Val understood that she meant the apology for so much more than the delay, for all the stress her leaving had caused them, for however personally Val must have taken her behavior this week. "Is there anything that needs to be done before the ceremony?"

"Nope. We're just watching an old movie. *Casablanca.*"

"I love *Casablanca,*" Hazel said.

Some silent understanding passed between Hazel's father and Val, then Lucy. He squeezed Lucy's shoulder. "Ah. Your dad's favorite."

There was something palpably tender between all of them. The sudden, thick emotion enveloping them made her wonder, for the first time, about the history of this family before her father came into the picture. She'd assumed Val had gotten divorced, that Lucy and Raf split their time between her home and their dad's, wherever that was. But the silence held too much gravity.

Then, Hazel remembered a photo in the curio cabinet among all of Val's Peruvian art and alpaca figurines. Now, with a sinking feeling, she was pretty sure she understood. And right there on the mantle over the fireplace was another photo of him, with a toddler in a white dress on his shoulders and one hand on a little boy's back. She'd missed it every time she walked through here this week, caught up in her own little world.

Lucy said, "We're only a few minutes in. We can start it over."

THE WEDDING TOOK PLACE IN THE BACKYARD. HER FATHER AND VAL stood under a plain wooden arch. Val held a modest bouquet of red roses, no larger than the white ones given to Hazel and Lucy. Tall heaters kept them from shivering through the short ceremony. Hazel, Lucy, and Rafael stood not in the traditional places, flanking the couple, but in a semicircle directly in front of them, so that altogether with the minister, who was a family friend, they made a closed ring. Afterward, the minister snapped the family photos Val had wanted.

It was all so understated, aside from the semiformal wear. Within a half hour, they were all back inside the house, cutting into a small, round cake. It didn't have a topper on it, just a single evergreen sprig and each of their names piped in Val's careful hand.

In the evening, they ate Christmas Eve enchiladas. Her father nearly fell asleep over his meal. Hazel was exhausted, too, and followed suit when he went to bed early. In the hall, he paused to pull her into another long hug and murmured, "Love you, kiddo," before they parted ways. It was enough for now.

Finally, back in her bedroom, Hazel picked up her phone. She expected a sea of messages like yesterday, braced and hoped for something from Ash. But the only message was from her mother wishing her a *"Joyeux Noel"* from Paris. She echoed the same message back, then switched to her text history with Ash.

Before the string of his messages she'd ignored was the photo of the two of them curled up together in his bed from the night following Winter Fest. He'd asked for it right after she'd taken it. Then, with her right there watching him thumb the message in, he'd texted, You're so pretty. "You're a dork," she'd said.

She started and deleted several messages—apologies, explanations. Then smaller missives—I'm back. I'm okay. I'm ready to talk. But typing them out made her breath come in short pants, her fingers go cold and tremble. If he didn't respond, she'd be devastated.

Tomorrow. She'd find the right words tomorrow.

Twenty-Six

On Christmas morning, it took less than ten minutes for Ash's nieces to tear through their mountain of presents. When Cosette unwrapped her own house in miniature, she shrieked, "A dollhouse!" and immediately dug out from the mess of wrapping paper her new bounty of Barbies and My Little Ponies to put in it. Ash's smile faltered only a bit at the word *dollhouse*—Hazel would have loved that no one else besides him would call it a model.

It ached that she wasn't here. Though they hadn't specifically made plans to see each other on Christmas, when he'd helped her leave her dad's house, it felt like she'd spend the morning with his family. And all of that aside, she was just *supposed* to be here. He felt it in his bones.

But she wasn't. And she still hadn't reached out, though her father had passed along that she was safe. No other details. That drove him pretty fucking crazy. But if she was safe and she was in contact with her dad, of all people, what did it say that she still hadn't tried to contact *him*?

It was creeping up on noon, and across the living room, Maggie checked her phone for the hundredth time, just like Ash had been doing, then pulled out knitting needles and green yarn.

"Any news?" Ash asked, joining her on the brick hearth. Nick's flight had been delayed again. He had officially missed Christmas.

"He was on standby for a flight to Midland, but I don't know if he got on it."

"Since when do you knit?"

"Since I needed to feel like I was doing something when there's nothing I can do."

Ash nudged his knee against hers. Her hands paused as she dipped her head to his shoulder. She breathed in deeply then righted herself and resumed knitting.

His father pushed up from his recliner then, catching Ash's eye. "We still doing this?"

Ash checked his watch. "Yeah."

After their conversation yesterday, he'd skimmed some used car listings. He'd intended just to prepare himself for the eventual expense a few weeks or even months from now. But he'd promised he'd *try*. And a local dealership was having a holiday sale. And suddenly he had his eye on an Altima with a bit of mileage, a moonroof, and a decent stereo. Most importantly, it wouldn't be a constant source of worry.

He stepped into his boots and followed his father into the chilly, gray morning.

As Ash began to back his father's truck down the driveway, another car pulled in beside them. It was white, like Hazel's car, and absolute euphoria surged in his chest, only to crash a second later. It was an entirely different make and model than hers.

Then, Maggie ran out onto the driveway, feet shoved into June's fuzzy boots, a throw blanket falling from one shoulder. Nick emerged from his rental car, and she threw her arms around her husband.

Ash and his father got out of the truck as everyone else poured from the house. Maggie cried, and then his mom burst into tears at the sight of the girls in Nick's arms, and hell, Ash got misty-eyed too at the happy reunion.

After welcoming Nick, Ash and his dad headed to the dealership once more. They rode in silence for several minutes until his dad said, "Any word from Hazel?"

"Nope."

"What's your plan, then?"

Ash shook his head. "I don't actually have a plan. I'm waiting. I'm buying a car. Beyond that . . ." He shrugged.

The light ahead turned red, and he slowed to a stop. His dad shifted in his seat. Ash wondered if he was uncomfortable, but if his dad needed something, he could ask. They both looked around the empty intersection. No one was out today.

After a minute, his dad said, "You think she'll come around?"

The light finally turned green, and Ash pulled forward. "I'm kind of counting on it."

Twenty-Seven

By Christmas evening, Hazel knew what she had to do: drive to Ash's house and, once she was there in front of him, . . . magically figure out what to say. She was unlocking her car when her phone buzzed. *JUST ASH.* The happy surprise of his name on her phone sent her heart into her throat. She had to swipe twice to open the message.

JUST ASH: Hey, just wanted to let you know I've got a ride home. Merry Christmas, Hazel.

She waited, but nothing more came. It felt abrupt and final. No opening for questions, for persuading him otherwise. Even that *Merry Christmas* stung—like he'd done her a favor, freeing her from her obligation to him. *Merry Christmas! You never have to face me again!*

Yes, she'd said horrible things. Yes, she'd cut him off. But only for two days. She was back. She was ready—or at least *willing*—to face the mess she'd made, to figure out how to fix it with him, even if that meant trapping them in her car for eight hours until they talked everything out.

But the longer she mulled over his message, the more her stomach twisted and her hopes withered. He'd gone to the trouble of finding another way home so he wouldn't have to ride with her. This, from the guy who'd worked so hard to fix his last relationship, the girl had to cheat to get rid of him. The guy who, at his essential core, *kept trying*. He was just . . . giving up. Just like that.

So, she sent the only response that wouldn't expose how crushed she felt: a cheery, totally fine Okay. Merry Christmas!

Then she immediately texted Sylvia, asking if she could come see her for a few days, and retreated to the comfort of her bed.

Not five minutes later, a knock sounded on her door, and then it cracked open, and Val and Lucy were standing at the threshold. Val held up a basket of nail polishes. "We were just about to do our nails. Want to join?"

Hazel eyed their coordinating Christmas-red hair and wondered if their nails would match, too. But where she'd once found their matching a bit cringey, she saw it differently now—a mother who was willing to look a little silly in the name of bonding with her daughter. Hazel saw the love in the gesture, and she surprised herself by saying, "Okay."

To her further surprise, they both moved in and flanked her on the bed. Hazel flipped over a few bottles half-heartedly, trying not to let her focus drift to her phone and thoughts of Ash, and read the polish names: Teal It Like It Is, Burn It Down, Reclaiming My Thyme, Blood of My Enemies. "These are . . . intense," she said with a laugh. "They're, like, weirdly aggressive feminist affirmations."

Val waved a bottle of bright purple. "I'm doing Nobody's Girlfriend."

"Is there one for getting over a—" *Break up,* she almost said.

It didn't matter that she cut herself off. Something about Val's soft-eyed head tilt told Hazel she knew. Maybe her sudden lack of plans with Ash after running off with him all week hadn't slipped Val's notice. Hazel took a deep breath and said instead, "Getting over academic imposter syndrome?"

Lucy selected a light brown. "How about Taupe of the Class?"

Hazel took it.

Val started filing her nails. "So, what's this imposter syndrome about?"

Hazel shrugged.

"You know, this is kind of my wheelhouse. My foundation helps shape smart, driven, sociologically disadvantaged women for leadership roles in business, media, local politics . . . Nine times out of ten, these amazing women, like you, already have the goods a million times over. They just don't believe in themselves yet."

Hazel considered brushing off her admission but decided instead, as they filed and then began to paint their nails, to tell them about her struggle to handle all her grad assistant responsibilities, Sheffield's endless errands, the hostile upper-year student making her lab hell, and her hesitation to request the transfer to Dr. Tate.

"So, wait. You're actually thinking of staying in the lab with the jerk," Lucy piped up, "just so you don't have to disappoint your professor, who doesn't even let you do the work you want and takes total advantage of you?"

It wasn't far from what Ash had said that night at the Country Kitschin'.

Val raised an eyebrow at Hazel. "I don't want to tell you what to do, but . . ."

"But I should submit my transfer request?"

"Right now."

With her non-polished hand, Hazel opened her laptop and did just that.

NOW THAT SHE AND HER FATHER WERE SPEAKING MORE OPENLY, HAZEL wasn't quite ready to leave. He seemed to feel the same, circling her car for the third time, checking every inch of it for some sign of impending threat, some excuse, she thought, to make her stay longer. Finally, he said, "Well, kiddo, guess you're good to go." He hugged her, one hand securing her head to his chest. "Friday. Don't forget."

They'd agreed to a weekly phone call to keep their respective doors more open to each other. "Five o'clock," she confirmed. "I won't forget."

It felt like she was locked in a time loop, retracing her route out of town again so soon. She half expected to end up stuck in Garrettsville a third time.

She did *not* expect a detour that sent her through her old neighborhood.

Though she didn't have to, Hazel took a few extra turns and eased to a stop in front of her old house. An inflatable snowman lay airless in the lawn, like it had melted. A basketball hoop had been mounted over the garage. She wondered if the same boy she'd assumed put *Star Wars* posters on her old walls returned to this home from college on holidays, or if a new family lived here now.

Once, every little change had felt like she was losing a piece of herself. She'd thought if she didn't see it, she wouldn't feel it. But now, Hazel didn't feel heartbroken, only curious.

In the side yard, a tree stretched its branches into the clear sky, and she realized it was the pecan sapling her father had planted, which had never produced nuts before they moved. Now mature and tall, it cast shade over a good portion of the yard—more in summer probably, when its leaves were full. And dangling from its branches and littering the ground below was an absolute bounty of pecans.

Twenty-Eight

For three days Ash gave himself whiplash, jerking his head every time the Living Room door jangled with a new customer. It was never Hazel. Each day she didn't show chipped away at his commitment not to reach out to her.

But he knew her well enough to stay the course. Hazel might not believe in afters, but she did believe in fresh starts.

This time, the source of his whiplash was Cami's entrance. The café was closing at three p.m. for New Year's Eve, and no customers were coming in, but still, he snapped around with the same wild hope. Cami frowned sympathetically. "Still no sign of her?"

"Who?" piped up Jade, a new employee he'd been training.

Cami raised a teasing eyebrow, which Jade didn't miss.

"Someone who's had you checking over your shoulder every two minutes since I got here?" Jade guessed.

Ash shook his head at Cami and dug two sets of keys out of his pocket, slid them across the counter. "Thanks for letting me borrow your truck," he said, then pointed upstairs, indicating the loft space. "And for the last two years."

"You can always come back if you need to," she said.

"Thanks." He followed both of them to the door, where he pinned an envelope to the community board, just in case.

Outside, Jade invited him once more to a New Year's Eve party, but he wasn't in the mood for a party. He'd fantasized all day about tracking down Hazel's address, showing up at her place tonight, laying his heart out for her. A grand gesture. The old Ash, breaking through the surface.

But the only gesture left for him was the most modest. Trusting and waiting. He still believed she'd come, when she was ready. And he wasn't going anywhere.

« CHAPTER »
Twenty-Nine

A few days in Houston turned into a week. Hazel spent it catching up with Sylvia, sleeping in way too late, and playing with the little orange kitten, which to her boyfriend's horror, Sylvia had named Baby Dave. Being with her best friend replenished something vital Hazel had been missing, though she still checked her phone obsessively, hoping Ash would text and anticipating Dr. Sheffield's response to her transfer request.

The latter came on New Year's Eve, just as she, Sylvia, and Dave were finishing dinner.

Ms. Elliot,

I've reviewed your request to transfer your assistantship to Dr. Tate. As she has indicated a willingness to take on the extra load, I see no reason to block the transfer, though I will admit I had higher hopes for our illustrious Benning Scholar to rise to the standards of my lab. I've removed you from the listserv and revoked your access to our digital spaces. A final word in my role as your advisor: The PhD isn't for everyone. If you are, in fact, questioning this path, do yourself, your colleagues, and Dr. Tate the courtesy of honest reflection before you return and waste anyone else's time.

—R.S.

Hazel let go of the breath she'd sucked in at the sight of his name in her inbox, and out with it came a laugh. His response was exactly as harsh as she'd expected it to be, but instead of falling into a spiral of doubt and worry, Hazel felt pure relief. Sure, she would still see him on campus. She'd know he thought of her as someone who couldn't hack it, who had taken the easy way out. But what did that matter when she'd gotten what she wanted—research she cared about and an advisor who was eager to hear her ideas? For the first time since school had started in the fall, Hazel felt *excited*.

And the person she most wanted to tell was Ash.

But Sylvia was more than up to the task of celebrating her good news since it bolstered her argument for ringing in the New Year dancing in Midtown. She dragged Hazel from the table all the way into her closet. "Shave your legs and put this on," she said, thrusting a shimmery red number at Hazel. "Chop chop."

Hazel did her best to enjoy the evening, but when the clock struck midnight, and Sylvia smacked a kiss on her cheek before pulling Dave in for the real thing, it hit Hazel like a gut punch. No matter the distance or passage of time, she would always have a place with Sylvia, but right now, this wasn't where she was supposed to be.

She pulled out her phone, desperate for a missed call, a text, anything from Ash, but her screen was blank. She felt like one big blank herself, empty through and through.

"Okay. We did the thing," Sylvia announced over partygoers drunkenly singing "Auld Lang Syne." She tossed her party glasses and cardboard top hat onto a table. "Let's go and cry over street tacos."

"I'm not going to cry," Hazel said right as the first tear fell.

Two blocks away, under a gas-powered outdoor heater, with tacos in their laps and their shoes discarded, Dave asked, "So, that's it, right? He didn't text on New Year's, and now we're moving on?"

Sylvia slugged his arm. "What's wrong with you?"

"Hey! I'm just saying, if he was thinking of her, he would have texted." He squeezed Hazel's ankle in an awkward consoling gesture. "Sorry."

"No." Sylvia fixed Hazel with a stern eyebrow. "No. We asked for space, so we're not reading into him not texting."

"He didn't want to ride home with me," Hazel pointed out. Every time she mustered the courage to reach out to him, this was what stopped her.

"We asked for space," Sylvia repeated. "We don't get to hold it against him when he understands the assignment."

"When did this become a 'we' situation?" Hazel asked.

Dave clutched his chest. "I'm deeply invested, personally."

"And you know I'm staying on you like white on rice after the last few months." Sylvia scooped up Hazel's unwanted jalapeños and popped them into her mouth. "So, what are we going to do now?"

Hazel could text him. If he'd truly missed her the way she'd missed him but was giving her space, as she'd requested, then the only person who could break their silence was *her*. She could send a simple *Happy New Year* and see what he said back.

Except a text wasn't good enough. She'd left him, gone dark, despite him begging her to stay and work things out.

She stood abruptly. "Shit. I have to go home."

Sylvia jumped up, too, and they both stumbled, still tipsy. "We're ready? We love him?"

"This 'we' thing is getting weird. But yes," she said on a laugh-sob. "We love him."

SYLVIA MADE HER WAIT TO LEAVE UNTIL THE FOLLOWING MORNING when she was sober and somewhat rested. But now, at mid-morning on January first—another fresh start, she hoped—Hazel pulled into the café parking lot. She was a little hungover, her back hurt from driving, but she was here. She was here for him.

Her spirits deflated at the glaring absence of Ash's car in the lot. But it had been in the shop. Maybe it still was.

The bell chimed above her head. There was movement in the kitchen. She waited. Finally, a college-aged woman Hazel didn't recognize emerged, stuttered her step when she saw Hazel, and said breathlessly, "Oh, sorry. I didn't hear you. I'm a little—" She looked over her shoulder like she was expecting someone else to come out and rescue her. "I'm new. The other girl is on her break. I'm not usually the only one." She tugged at her name tag nervously. It said *JADE*. "What can I get you? Oh, but the espresso machine is down, so . . ."

Hazel would have smiled if she weren't recalculating her carefully rehearsed steps. She hadn't accounted for Ash not being here. He was always here.

"Did you want coffee? Or tea?"

"I'm looking for Ash." At the girl's blank stare, Hazel prompted, "Tall guy who works here?"

"Oh, right. I don't think he works here anymore, though."

"He doesn't work here anymore?"

"I think?"

"He quit?"

"I'm not sure. But he's not on the schedule."

"Like, in the last week, he just stopped working here?"

Jade pressed her lips together and nodded as if she thought ceasing verbal replies might break this unproductive loop.

Hazel fumbled an abrupt goodbye and speed-walked around

the corner of the building to the other entrance, taking the staircase two steps at a time. She knocked on Ash's closed door and called his name. Her voice echoed in the tight space. She knocked again then tried the knob. Locked. But when she jostled it, the door cracked open.

And inside, she saw . . . nothing. The entire apartment was empty. No bed. No coffee table. The models that had once lined the living room wall were gone.

She deflated against the doorjamb, stomach churning. If his Christmas Day text message felt abrupt and final, then this was an atom bomb. He'd moved out. He'd quit his job. He'd left the building altogether in one week. *Just like we agreed*, she realized. He'd given her exactly what she'd said she wanted.

She walked back to the café, unsure what to do. She sat in the green chair, everything just as it had always been, except nothing felt right. Ash was supposed to be smirking at her from the counter or dropping into the wobbly chair across from her and messing with her stacks of papers. Even the chair itself, which used to inspire feelings of greatness, of being exactly where she should be, doing exactly what she was meant to do, felt wrong.

When the tears threatened to spill, she gathered herself up and headed for the door.

And that was when she saw it: an envelope with her name on it in familiar, assertive black pen. She ripped it open to find an address written on the inside and a single line: *Whenever you're ready*.

HER HEART WAS A HUMMINGBIRD IN HER CHEST WHEN SHE ARRIVED AT a small apartment complex near the edge of town and willed her shaky legs up a metal staircase. She knocked before she could chicken out. And when she heard the slide of a lock, she mentally reached for her speech, only to realize she'd lost it entirely.

Ash filled the doorway in a navy T-shirt and gray sweats, his hair mussed on one side, stubble almost thick enough to call it a beard. His eyebrows arched in surprise, but otherwise he was cautious, guarded, his grip tight on the edge of the door. "Haze."

"Hi." She was panting from running up the steps, and the tightness in her chest only ratcheted up her panic at forgetting what she'd meant to say. There'd been a checklist, one point setting up the next. But at the sight of him, all she could think was, *Please.*

"You moved," she blurted. "And you quit the café."

Ash looked at his hand on the door, the other rising to scratch his neck. She couldn't read him.

"Because of me? Because of our deal?"

"Yes and no. That's hard to answer." His eyebrows drew together in debate as he started to say more but stopped. He fought a smile, and her heart flipped at that tiny, lifted corner. "Um, what does this mean? Why'd you come?"

She blinked. Even though she held his message in her hand—his handwriting, her name—she feared she'd somehow misunderstood or made the whole thing up in desperation. "Sorry," gusted out of her.

"No. Just—"

A rush of cold wind blew her hair off her neck, and her teeth chattered. She hugged herself, turned from the wind, from him.

He stepped out onto the landing in his socks, halving their distance, and warmth enveloped her wrist as he circled it with his hand. His inhale made a scraping sound like the wind through the leafless trees around the parking lot below. "It's cold. Come inside?"

His apartment was sparsely furnished with stuff from his

old place. He gestured for her to sit on the futon, but he remained standing by the door. If she'd known he wasn't going to sit with her, she would have stayed on her feet. "I came to—"

Something red underneath the coffee table caught her eye. Distracted, she bent to grab it, assuming it was a throw blanket that had fallen to the floor. But loose yarn trailed from one end. It wasn't a blanket. It was much narrower and still in progress. Knitting needles fell to her feet with a faint clicking sound. "What is this?"

He held her questioning gaze for so long, she wondered if he'd even heard her. But finally, he dragged a hand down his face. "Something I've been doing to pass the time."

"You've been . . . knitting?"

"Not well," he said with a grunt.

She surveyed his work in her hands. Some of the lines were wobbly at one end, but by the middle, he'd gotten the hang of it.

"You've been knitting," she repeated.

"Maggie said . . ." He shook his head, color tingeing his ears. "When she can't do anything, she knits. You said you needed space. I'm not that great at just sitting around. So, every time I wanted to call you, I just . . . did that instead."

"You wanted to call?"

He laughed, and it was tight, a bit incredulous. "Hazel. You came here with something to say, right? Can you please just say it?"

She set his knitting on the coffee table and searched mentally for the loose threads of her speech. "I'm sorry," she said. "For leaving the way I did and turning off my phone."

He nodded, face carefully neutral. She recognized the cautious restraint. It was in her, too, insisting she get a peek at his cards before she showed all her own.

But restraint had made them stop talking for a week. Restraint had allowed him to pack up his life and quit his job without her even knowing. If she kept clinging so tightly to caution, what else would she lose?

"I should have stayed. I would have been scared—I don't know how not to be scared by all of this yet—but I should have been scared there, *with* you. I should have slowed down and talked it through like you wanted. I was going to. On the drive back here. But then you made other arrangements, so I assumed . . ."

"Wait, you thought— No, I just bought a car."

"What?"

He jutted a thumb over his shoulder, gesturing outside. "I didn't need a ride because I bought a car." At her stunned expression, he quickly clarified, "Not because I didn't want to ride home with you. There was a sale. It happened kind of fast. And when you said you needed space, I wanted to take you seriously. Unless needing space is just something you say when you don't want to say it's over."

"Oh." This was the problem with gauging someone else's level of self-disclosure and making sure she didn't go any deeper herself. It was a game of reverse chicken where instead of sailing headfirst into danger, both parties eased off the gas, slowed to a crawl, fiddled with the radio and their mirrors, and waved the other on. *No, you go.*

But safety *was* the danger. One of them had to put everything on the table. And this time, it had to be her.

She stood because she felt ridiculous having this conversation eight feet across the room from him and seated when he clearly had no intention of leaving his perch by the door.

"I'm a coward," she said, letting her hands fall with a slap to her thighs. "But I'm working on it. I talked to my dad. Really talked, like you said. It's still weird, but I think one day it won't be. Turns out, weird and uncomfortable is still better than nothing."

His eyes softened, and he looked like he was going to say something gentle and encouraging despite the limbo they were in with each other, like this was what she'd come here to tell him. It wasn't.

"Which brings me to you."

"Weird and uncomfortable brings you to me? Not *loving* that segue."

She huffed a laugh, grateful for the small mercy of his humor. Rounding the coffee table toward him, she ripped off the Band-Aid. "I was afraid to do this. But I'm more afraid not to. Because I already know not talking to you, not seeing you every day is *awful*. I want to remember the Lovebird Suite or that crazy telephone diner or getting pulled over for having the world's largest Christmas tree or hooking up in a *barn* or getting stuck in a dress, and I want to know it all *mattered*. When I made you promise to give me the café if things changed between us, I didn't want to lose my one easy, comfortable place in town. But life is unpredictable and weird and messy, and last week, *everything* changed, and now . . . it's not the *place* that I need. I need *you*."

His eyes were steady on her, mouth a firm line.

"At the risk of stating the obvious—" She took a deep breath. "Ash, I lo—"

"I love you."

She released a full chest of air. "You didn't let me say it."

He shuffled the last few steps forward so that their toes touched. He slipped one hand around to the small of her back, face finally released from its careful neutral mask. A smile played on his lips. "I knew where you were going with it. Didn't want to leave you hanging."

"I can't believe you interrupted my big declaration. I drove all the way over here. I had a whole speech."

"Sorry, was there more?"

"I mean . . . no, that was basically it. Unless you needed convincing."

He feigned consideration then tugged her closer, his arms sliding all the way around her. His forehead dropped to hers. "Hazel," he said, voice low and serious, "you had me at weird and uncomfortable."

A laugh burst from her throat.

He kissed her right then, catching her mid-smile. The press of his lips was confident, certain, casting the last vestiges of her fear away. Relieved, she deepened the kiss. She wanted to make up for the entire week of kissing they'd lost.

But something still niggled at her. "Hold on. Did you quit the café or not? I didn't mean for you to actually leave because of our agreement. I mean, at the time, I did. But when I showed up, and you weren't there . . ."

Ash smoothed her hair back from her face. "I didn't quit. I took some time off to take care of some stuff. Moving here, for one."

"And?"

"Remember that night we talked at the Country Kitschin', and I told you about the restoration I worked on last summer?"

She nodded.

"You made it seem so simple, that if I wanted to do restorations, I should go for it. And then my mom was on my case to make some changes—better apartment, reliable car, actual . . . happiness."

"Smart woman."

He smiled. "I agree. So, I reached out to a firm that works on historical sites in the area. They asked to see some of my work, said if I was serious about doing my professional hours with them after I graduate, I should consider a master's with a specialization in preservation. I looked into the program here, and the application for next year is due in a few weeks. I've done most of it, just need to get recommendation letters. Then, wait and see." He released a long, heavy sigh and raked his fingers through his hair.

"Wow."

"Yeah."

"So, you'll be a grad student next year."

"Hopefully."

"And you're not quitting the café?"

"Not yet. I can still pour your coffee."

"I'm only thinking of Frank. Poor guy would be lost if you left for good."

Ash bumped his shoulder into hers, sighing again. This time it sounded more relaxed, less like he'd been holding his breath. "I was only giving you space, not giving up. I thought if I came after you when you explicitly told me to back off, it would only hurt. I know I pushed you too hard with your dad."

She started to interrupt, but he raised his palm to halt her.

"I thought knitting that scarf would be, like, a calming distraction, but it's way fucking harder than Maggie made it look. I got a little impatient. But leaving that envelope was only halfway cheating. You still had to come to the café to see it. And you did."

She reached for the pile of yarn on the coffee table. "So, this is a scarf?"

"That's . . . generous."

"It's almost the same color as my old one."

Ash scratched his eyebrow and gave her a sheepish smile. "Yeah, the colors all looked identical after about ten minutes in the yarn aisle. I panicked and hoped for the best."

"Wait. Were you making this for me?"

"You loved that scarf," he said simply.

Hazel fought to tamp down her smile and finally hid it by wrapping the scarf around her neck and over her mouth. "I love this one more," she said into the yarn.

Ash tugged the material down and brushed his thumb across her lips. "It's not finished."

"Too bad. I'm never taking it off."

"Kind of warm in here," he pointed out.

She pushed up her sleeves. "You can take my sweater, but you'll never take this scarf from my neck."

His eyes lit up with mischief.

"What's that look?" she asked, wary.

"I have a fantasy like that. You in your scarf. Just your scarf."

She blushed. "Really . . ."

He nodded, trailing one exploring finger under the edge of the scarf, from one collarbone to the other.

She bit her lip, and a ragged breath ghosted out of him. "God, I missed you," he said, voice low and eyes dark. Then, his perfect, hot mouth found her neck around all that material, and she yanked him down on top of her.

Four Months Later

The sign on Hazel's office door was flipped to **CLOSED**. Beside it, a schedule clearly listed her available hours, which Ash knew was exactly the allotment she was required to offer and not a minute more. She didn't see students on Fridays at all because that was the day she conducted interviews at the women's prison for Dr. Tate's lab. "Boundaries" was a new mantra for them both these days.

He rapped one knuckle against the door, nudging it open so he could see her, face bent over a book, loose curls freed from her usual bun and tumbling down over one shoulder. She'd expanded her wardrobe to include this new gray vest she liked to wear over a white button-down. He wasn't sure why the more buttoned-up she was, the hotter he found it, but the effect was undeniable.

"My office hours are over," she murmured, head still bent.

"Please? It's important."

He'd caught the twist of her lips, an irritated tic at the interruption, before she recognized his voice. When she looked up, though, her face was deliberately impassive, playing along. "Is it, though? Let's hear it."

He bit his own smile back. Which way to play this? He wanted to know what she was wearing under that desk, but a quick scan of the book in her hands and the others stacked beside her sent him in a different direction. "Piaget," he said.

One eyebrow arched up. "You have a question about Jean Piaget?"

"More of a comment than a question."

He nearly got a laugh, but she schooled her face. "Go on."

"I find his work on developmental stages fascinating. The concept of schemas. Assimilation. Equilibration." He was just saying terms he'd seen on student papers she'd been grading this week, but he could tell from the tilt of her face she was mildly impressed he recalled them. "The Zone of Proximal Development."

She *tsked*. "So close. That one's Lev Vygotsky."

"Gesundheit."

This finally broke her, and she laughed, shaking her head at him. "What are you doing here, Asher?"

"Had to meet with my new advisor about summer classes. Thought I'd walk you out, steal you for a study date."

"I can't go to your apartment," she said reluctantly. "We don't get any work done there."

He couldn't help his wolfish grin, and she rolled her eyes.

This might have been a good time for the question he was intending to ask her tonight—if she had a plan for when the lease at her place ended soon, if she would officially move in with him. He would have asked her weeks ago, but it seemed too soon. Not that it *felt* too soon. It felt like he'd been waiting for Hazel for years, not mere months. But he had a plan. It was best to stick to the plan.

"Luckily for you, I meant the café, although we are going to my place after."

"You're very sure of yourself."

"Optimistic," he corrected.

"Haven't you been at the café all afternoon?"

"Yes. But I know you have work to finish today, and I'm going to require your undivided attention later."

"More optimism?" she teased.

"Always."

She packed up her books and papers. He let his eyes drift down to see she'd chosen the wraparound skirt today, the one that looked like it would unwind with a simple tug. A solid choice. She was saying something about her dad, and he forced his brain back online. "He's at the station this evening, so I need to call him early."

Ash checked his watch. "You can call while we walk."

"You sure?"

He motioned for her to go ahead and moved her bag from her shoulder to his own.

"Oh, and I sent you the hotel information for August," she said.

As they walked leisurely to the parking lot and Hazel gushed about her research to her dad, Ash found an email with their hotel reservation on his phone. They were going to her old friend Franny's wedding in August—another road trip, this one to Oklahoma City and hopefully less eventful, though if a hailstorm or tornado made them stop another night somewhere, he wouldn't complain.

Sorry, she mouthed a few minutes later, phone still pressed to her ear, when he opened the passenger door to his Altima for her. He waved her off. He was glad she was sticking to their weekly call, that she and Dan seemed to be making progress.

As Ash rounded the car to the driver's side, he passed by the custom sticker Hazel had snuck onto the back bumper that said **I VIBE TO PSYCHEDELIC SPACE TRANCE**. "For old times' sake," she'd reasoned.

It wasn't really like old times, though, and he was glad. Now, she rode in the front seat beside him. Now, he got to hold her hand, trace lazy designs on her thigh, lean over to kiss her at red lights. He got to hear all about her day.

Over the past four months, she'd gotten so comfortable in his car, he had her black hair ties in the cup holder, one of her reusable water bottles rolling around on the passenger floor-board, a sweatshirt—one of his own that she'd claimed—in his back seat, and a poster she'd made to cheer him on in the intra-mural softball league he'd joined. Though he usually kept his car pretty neat, even when his car had been such a clunker, her mess, the way she just sprawled through his space like she be-longed there, didn't bother him at all.

It'd be nice to have her belongings strewn about his place—their place—too.

She hung up as he pulled into the café parking lot.

Jade was on shift tonight. She was helping a customer, so they bypassed the counter and headed straight for Hazel's chair. He'd swapped the table with one of the larger ones, the rickety wooden chair with a sturdier one, and now they could both sit there comfortably. Sometimes he kicked himself for not making those changes sooner, sharing the space with her last semester, but he couldn't regret the way anything had worked out.

Per their deal, she still got the chair for the rest of the semes-ter, but they both knew it was hers forever at this point. In fact, he was just glad he'd managed to keep it under wraps that the chair was terrible for his back. His only real interest in it had ever been about flirting with her.

"Everything good with your dad?"

"Apparently, he's joined TikTok," Hazel said, pulling her lap-top from her bag. "He asked me what a thirst trap is, so honestly, I'm glad I can farm some things out to Lucy."

Cami meandered over with a carafe. "When did you two get here?"

"Just now," he said. He looked to the counter, where Jade's customer was leaving. He rose, but Cami pushed his shoulder back down.

"Stay. I'll get your drinks."

Ash drummed his fingers on the table. He was nervous. He shouldn't be. Hazel already basically lived with him. But it wasn't *nothing*, asking her. She was better about talking through what scared her, letting him be on the same side with her instead of shutting him out, but this was still big.

Hazel slid one palm over his tapping fingers. She squeezed his hand, glanced over her laptop with an amused grin, and went back to her work.

With a steadying breath, he pulled out his own laptop, doing his best to put the little wooden box inside his messenger bag out of his mind. He would wait until she didn't need to focus on her work, and then he'd ask her, and everything would be fine.

Two mugs clunked down on the table. They thanked Cami, each of them distracted, until Hazel drew hers up to her mouth and huffed in mock exasperation. The mugs were the sickeningly cutesy pair with the brushstroke lettering that said *Wifey* and *Hubby*. "Still hilarious," she called to Cami's retreating back.

Cami pulled this little joke every few weeks. To be honest, it didn't bother Ash. In fact, he probably liked it—the idea of marrying Hazel someday—a little too much.

Hazel set the mug down next to his and caught his eye for a long, loaded moment before pink washed over her cheeks. She glanced away.

"What?"

"Nothing." Her fingers tapped lightly across her keyboard,

not actually typing, though her eyes were laser focused on her screen. She did this when she was looking for the right words, this erratic non-typing. He assumed she'd leave it at that, but she closed her laptop and fixed him with an intense stare. "Actually, not nothing."

Ash's heart rate spiked. Did she know he was thinking of some way-distant, though maybe not *that* distant, future when he asked her to marry him? Christ, he was nervous enough as it was, carrying around a box containing an apartment key. He'd probably develop an ulcer with a ring in there.

She tucked her hair nervously behind her ear. Then, she lifted her chin confidently, looked him straight in the eyes, and said, "I want to move in with you when my lease is up."

His insides swooped. Was this what zero gravity felt like? What fucking *swooning* felt like? He needed a damn fainting couch. "Haze," he said with a slightly agonized groan. For all his nerves, he'd wanted to ask her. He'd planned it all out.

"Oh. Is that a no?" She shook her head quickly, waved a hand in the air as if to wipe away what she'd said. "Never mind. It's stupid. It's too soon. It's crazy."

"No," he said firmly, reaching for his bag and the box inside it. "Don't take it back. Just—"

She pressed her hands to her cheeks, embarrassed. "It's fine. It's fine."

He set the box on the table between them. "Why don't you just open that?"

She eyed him warily as she held the box close to her chest. "Why do you have a box?"

He laughed again. "Don't panic. It's not a ring."

It wasn't as small as a ring box, and if she'd given it the tiniest shake, she would have heard the key sliding around. She carefully lifted the top and peeked inside. A little frown. She was confused. Then, she turned it on its side and dumped the contents into her palm. The key was connected to a miniature green wingback chair, identical to the one she was sitting in.

"I wanted to wait until you were finished working, but you beat me to it."

"It's my chair."

"And a key," he said, turning it over in her palm. "Just in case you missed that part. I'm asking you to move in with me."

She blinked across the table, eyes shining. She gave a little shrug that turned into a vigorous nod. "You were right to be optimistic earlier."

"About what?"

She began packing up her things, pausing only to gesture impatiently for him to do the same.

"You barely got any work done," he pointed out.

She stood and pulled him up out of his chair, planted a firm kiss to his mouth. "I'm ready to give you my undivided attention. At home."

"At home," he repeated, a slow smile tugging at his lips. "So . . . that's a yes?"

"Technically, I asked you first."

"Technically, you didn't ask. You declared."

She rolled her eyes.

"It's a yes," he said, pulling her back for another kiss.

Hazel's mouth, soft and electric, dragged to the shell of his ear, and she whispered, "Then take me home."

« Acknowledgments »

First, I must thank my agent, Allison Hunter, who is the reason this book exists in the world and not just on my computer. Thank you for being an aggressive champion of this book and me since the beginning. You told me you knew just what to do with *Take Me Home*, and you did! Thanks also to Natalie Edwards and the rest of the team at Trellis Literary Management.

An enormous thank you to Kate Dresser, my editor, for your perfect blend of sharp editorial instincts and magical energy. I knew from our very first conversation that Hazel and Ash were in the right hands with you, and you have been an absolute dream to work with. I'm so grateful to have you on my team from the beginning for the next one. Thanks to the many people at G. P. Putnam's Sons who helped bring this book to life—Tarini Sipahimalani, Leah Marsh, Shannon Plunkett, Emily Mileham, Maija Baldauf, Shina Patel, Samantha Bryant, Nicole Biton, Ashley McClay, Alexis Welby, and Sally Kim.

Thanks to the team at Harper Fiction for bringing Ash and Hazel to the UK.

A huge thank you to my first readers. Erin Dillard, I love that in addition to reading for me, you have read just about every other romance novel I've ever wanted to talk about! Heather Frankland, thanks for workshopping this whole book in chapter-length installments from the very start—the slowest possible slow burn! I hope we keep up our Sunday chats forever. A special thank you to Adriana Wilson for reading this book, for talking about *all the romance things*, and for manifesting outrageous success for me. You are a force, and I'm so lucky you're in my corner.

Thanks to Nicole Lozano, who answered my questions about psychology. If I got anything wrong, that's my mistake!

A lot of people helped shape this book before my first vision of a fabulous, velvet green wingback chair in a coffee house. To my teachers and mentors—Rus Bradburd, Connie Voisine, Robert Boswell, Robin Romm, Scott Kaukonen—thank you for my writing foundation. Cat Jonet, your classes rewired my brain in the best way. Thanks to Laura Williams for your friendship, cat pictures, and art swaps. To my writer friends—Zach Vande Zande, Dana Barcellos-Allen, Anna Pattison, Camille Acker, Chris Schacht, Phillip Hurst, Annie Olson, Carrie Murphy, Christopher Rosenbluth—thanks for your friendship and for the time and care you've put into my work.

Jessica Sanchez, Joli Ammons, Heather Lang, Jessica James, Casey Eakes, Megan Freeman, and anyone who has ever swooned over a romance novel with me—thank you for loving what I love.

Thanks to Jen Prokop for early insight on this book, to Andrea Guevara for branding guidance, and to Ryanna Battiste for teaching me how to breathe.

Romance has such a vibrant community of writers, readers, reviewers, librarians, bookstores, artists, podcasters, and more. Thank you for making the space lovely. And if you've spent your time reading, listening to, sharing, or talking about my book—I'm so grateful!

I want to thank all my parents—Mike and Susan Sweeney, Carol Holguin and Gary Maxwell, Fran and Lloyd Bowen—for always believing this would happen and for helping *make* it happen with practical support, pep talks, prayers, and probably more that I don't know about. If you're reading this book, there's a good chance one of them told you about it.

Mom, thanks especially for reading everything I've ever written and enduring *hours* of me talking at you about fictional people. You are essential to all of this.

Extended family—grandmothers, aunts and uncles, cousins, in-laws—thank you for your support.

Kyle Sweeney, no one in the world has a better brother. You are my first home, my oldest friend, and my favorite person to get Christmas Eve milkshakes with.

To my kids—thanks for your patience all those times I worked instead of going to the pool. I love you so much.

And Joshua Bowen. You are the one who showed me that real partnership—real romance—isn't just a fantasy. In fact, you are such an ideal partner for me that if I ever wrote you, no one would believe it! Too kind, too self-aware, too funny, and not nearly flawed enough. Thank you for not only encouraging me to write this book back on New Year's Day 2020, but for all your support after that. You rearranged our home life to help me prioritize writing this book. You have always taken up slack without complaint or expectation. From your grandest gestures to your smallest, everyday actions, you are *my* real-life romance hero. I love you, I love you, I love you.

« Discussion Guide »

1. *Take Me Home* is set in author Melanie Sweeney's home state of Texas. What expectations of Hazel and Ash's romance did the location set up for you?

2. Since leaving home for college, Hazel has avoided returning to her hometown. What feelings and memories do you have about your hometown and how have they evolved over the years?

3. Both Hazel and Ash find comfort in the big green chair of their beloved coffee shop. Do you have a favorite study or work spot? What makes it special?

4. Discuss Hazel and Ash's first interaction in college. Do you think Hazel is justified in reacting the way she did? How would you have responded?

5. *Take Me Home* opens with an unexpected road trip back to Hazel and Ash's hometown. Thematically, what does the road trip represent? Narratively, how does the road trip bring the frenemies closer together?

6. Hazel is studying for a master's in psychology. How do you think this area of interest and growing expertise informs her reactions to her own conflicts? To what extent are we able to compartmentalize our intellectual interests with our emotional experiences?

7. Hazel has a knack for hiding her true feelings, whether from Ash, her father, Franny, or Sylvia. What do you think finally makes Hazel start to open up to the people in her life? In what ways does she do that differently with each of them?

8. *Take Me Home* is by turns heartwarming, sexy, and funny. At which point in Hazel and Ash's relationship were you rooting for them to "just get together already," or did you feel they rushed things romantically?

9. Throughout the novel, we are given a glimpse into who Hazel and Ash were during their high school years. Think about yourself in high school: How have you changed? How have you remained the same? Do you think if you met your current partner in high school, you'd have paired up?

10. As with any romance, Hazel and Ash have a few arguments. In these moments, who did you sympathize with more and why? Did you think one of them was more justified in their reactions than the other?

11. Throughout the novel, Ash worries about his family and how his family's challenges might impact his relationship with Hazel, but instead, they both gain insights into their familial conflicts through their developing romance. Which of those insights feels most significant?

12. *Take Me Home* is an ode to the people and places we call home. Discuss the various places in the novel and how they play the role of "home" to each of the characters.

13. Hazel prefers a clean break rather than working to fix relationships. Are there times in real life when a clean break might be the best or healthiest option?

14. Ash is the only male child in his family with four sisters. How might this dynamic have shaped his character? In what ways does his prominent role as a caretaker both uphold and work against traditional gender norms?

15. Having finished the book, where do you see Hazel and Asher now, and do you think they have what it takes to go the distance?

« ABOUT THE AUTHOR »

Image courtesy of Lenora Stein Photography

Melanie Sweeney holds an MFA in fiction from New Mexico State University. Her work has appeared at Babble.com, as well as in several literary magazines. *Take Me Home* is her debut novel.

VISIT MELANIE SWEENEY ONLINE

melaniesweeney.com

🐦 Mellie_Sweeney

📷 MelanieSweeneyWrites